BUZZ BOOKS 2015
YOUNG ADULT/SPRING

BUZZ BOOKS 2015
YOUNG ADULT/SPRING

EXCLUSIVE EXCERPTS FROM 26 NEW YOUNG ADULT TITLES

INGRAM.

CREDITS

Publishers Lunch has been the "daily essential read" for the book publishing business for over a decade, and is the largest-circulation news communication in the world for publishing professionals. Publishers Marketplace is the web site associated with Publishers Lunch, providing round-the-clock news and analysis, deal reports, job listings, and many unique databases and tools that help publishing professionals find critical information, connect with each other, and do business better electronically.

Bookateria is a giant online book discovery store driven by an "industry insider's" view. Our focus is books making news and building buzz, as we tap into our comprehensive coverage of the books and authors that booksellers, editors, agents, rights-buyers, reviewers and others are talking about. Our own staff catalogs "buzz books" that the industry is touting as new discoveries of note, and some of the other featured Bookateria lists draw on recommendations from a variety of booksellers and bellwether award nominations to connect avid readers everywhere to great reads.

Publishers Lunch
2 Park Place, #4
Bronxville, NY 10708
Information@publishersmarketplace.com
www.publishersmarketplace.com
www.buzz.publishersmarketplace.com

Michael Cader, Founder

Robin Dellabough, Projects Director

Michael Macrone, Chief Technology Officer

Sarah Weinman, Senior Editor

Kathy Smith, Editor

Cover design by Charles Kreloff

Distribution and printing by Ingram

Typesetting by Julie Ink

Ebook development by Brady Type

Buzz Books website design by ACW Concepts

Thanks to our publishing partner:

Ingram Content Group is the world's largest and most trusted distributor of physical and digital content. Our mission is helping content reach its destination. Thousands of publishers, retailers, libraries, and educators worldwide use our products and services to realize the full business potential of books, regardless of format. Ingram has earned its lead position and reputation by offering excellent service and building innovative, integrated print and digital distribution solutions. Our customers have access to best-of-class digital, audio, print, print on demand, inventory management, wholesale and full-service distribution programs.

CONTENTS

INTRODUCTION 9

BUZZ BOOKS AUTHORS APPEARING AT WINTER INSTITUTE 11

EXCERPTS BY PUBLISHER 13

ABOUT NETGALLEY 15

Renée Ahdieh
THE WRATH AND THE DAWN (Putnam Juvenile) 17

Kathleen Baldwin
A SCHOOL FOR UNUSUAL GIRLS (Tor Teen) 27

Michael Buckley
UNDERTOW (HMH Books for Young Readers) 33

Tina Connolly
SERIOUSLY WICKED (Tor Teen) 47

Katie Cotugno
99 DAYS (Balzer + Bray) 53

Sarah Dessen
SAINT ANYTHING (Viking) 65

Jacob Grey
FERALS (HarperCollins) 73

S. A. Harazin
PAINLESS (Albert Whitman Teen) 91

Maria Dahvana Headley
MAGONIA (HarperCollins) 99

Lisa Heathfield
SEED (Running Press Teens) 115

Alice Hoffman
NIGHTBIRD (Wendy Lamb Books) 127

David Levithan
ANOTHER DAY (Alfred A. Knopf Books for Young Readers) 141

Barry Lyga with Peter Facinelli and Robert DeFranco
AFTER THE RED RAIN (Little, Brown Books for Young Readers) 157

Katie McGarry
NOWHERE BUT HERE (Harlequin Teen) 179

Paige McKenzie
THE HAUNTING OF SUNSHINE GIRL: BOOK ONE
(Weinstein Books) 189

Margo Rabb
KISSING IN AMERICA (HarperCollins) 203

Geoff Rodkey
THE TAPPER TWINS GO TO WAR (WITH EACH OTHER)
(Little, Brown Books for Young Readers) 219

Monica Ropal
WHEN YOU LEAVE (Running Press Teens) 241

Carrie Ryan
DAUGHTER OF DEEP SILENCE (Dutton Juvenile) 251

Louis Sachar
FUZZY MUD (Delacorte Press) 267

Ted Sanders
THE KEEPERS: THE BOX AND THE DRAGONFLY (HarperCollins) 279

Amy Spalding
KISSING TED CALLAHAN (AND OTHER GUYS) (Poppy) 295

Rebecca Stead
GOODBYE STRANGER (Wendy Lamb Books) 307

Derek E. Sullivan
BIGGIE (Albert Whitman Teen) 323

Sabaa Tahir
AN EMBER IN THE ASHES (Razorbill) 333

Henry Turner
ASK THE DARK (Clarion Books) 355

Copyright 371

INTRODUCTION

Our first *Buzz Books* collection focused entirely on young adult literature was an unqualified hit and we are delighted to make *Buzz Books:
Young Adult* a standing part of our program. This new, expanded edition, with 26 exclusive pre-publication excerpts in all, previews both
young adult and middle-grade novels worth watching.

As fans and aficionados know, today's YA books are leading the entire publishing market (and spawning major film franchises), read by
a broad audience that spans younger readers and adult readers alike.
Our selection of spring/summer titles reflects the broad spectrum of
today's YA, including new work from a number of well-known bestselling authors including Sarah Dessen, David Levithan, Barry Lyga, Michael
Buckley and Carrie Ryan. We also feature nearly as many renowned
middle-grade authors including Newbery winner Rebecca Stead, adult
author Alice Hoffman, and Louis Sachar (*Hole,* a *NY Times* bestseller*)*.

You'll get the first glimpse of highly-touted debuts, from anticipated
books by Margo Rabb and Maria Dahvana Headley to You Tube star
Paige McKenzie and author Alyssa Sheinmel's *The Haunting of Sunshine
Girl* (adapted from the web series of the same name and already in development as a film from the Weinstein Company) and Sabaa Tahir's
debut *An Ember In the Ashes* (already sold to Paramount Pictures in
a major deal).

Sample *Buzz Books: Young Adult Spring* to find your next great reads
for the months ahead and be the first in your crowd to start sampling
these hot new titles before they are published! Then share the fun by
telling your friends and family to download this edition of *Buzz Books*
for themselves at buzz.publishersmarketplace.com.

For an even broader range of notable books on the way, check out our
regular edition of *Buzz Books 2015: Spring/Summer*, with previews
from nearly 40 adult works of fiction and nonfiction.

Michael Cader

January 2015

BUZZ BOOKS AUTHORS APPEARING AT WINTER INSTITUTE

Michael Buckley

Maria Dahvana Headley

Katie McGarry

Geoff Rodkey

Ted Sanders

Sabaa Tahir

EXCERPTS BY PUBLISHER

ALBERT WHITMAN

S. A. Harazin/*Painless* (Albert Whitman Teen)

Derek E. Sullivan/*Biggie* (Albert Whitman Teen)

HACHETTE

Barry Lyga/*After the Red Rain* (Little, Brown Books for Young Readers)

Geoff Rodkey/*The Tapper Twins Go to War (With Each Other)* (Little, Brown Books for Young Readers)

Amy Spalding/*Kissing Ted Callahan (and Other Guys)* (Poppy)

HARLEQUIN

Katie McGarry/*Nowhere but Here* (Harlequin Teen)

HARPERCOLLINS

Katie Cotugno/*99 Days* (Balzer + Bray)

Jacob Grey/*Ferals*

Maria Dahvana Headley/*Magonia*

Margo Rabb/*Kissing in America*

Ted Sanders/*The Keepers: The Box and the Dragonfly*

HOUGHTON MIFFLIN HARCOURT

Michael Buckley/*Undertow* (HMH Books for Young Readers)

Henry Turner/*Ask the Dark* (Clarion)

MACMILLAN

Kathleen Baldwin/*A School for Unusual Girls* (Tor Teen)

Tina Connolly/*Seriously Wicked* (Tor Teen)

PENGUIN RANDOM HOUSE

Renee Ahdieh/*The Wrath and the Dawn* (Putnam Juvenile)

Sarah Dessen/*Saint Anything* (Viking Childrens)

Alice Hoffman/*Nightbird* (Wendy Lamb Books)

David Levithan/*Another Day* (Alfred A. Knopf Books for Young Readers)

Carrie Ryan/*Daughter of Deep Silence* (Dutton Childrens)

Louis Sachar/*Fuzzy Mud* (Delacorte)

Rebecca Stead/*Goodbye Stranger* (Wendy Lamb Books)

Sabaa Tahir/*An Ember in the Ashes* (Razorbill)

PERSEUS

Lisa Heathfield/*Seed* (Running Press Teens)

Paige McKenzie/*The Haunting of Sunshine Girl* (Weinstein Books)

Monica Ropal/*When You Leave* (Running Press Teens)

ABOUT NETGALLEY

At the end of some excerpts, you may find a link to read or request the full galley from NetGalley. NetGalley is a website where professional readers (reviewers, media, booksellers, librarians, educators and bloggers) can access digital galleys from participating publishers. NetGalley is completely free for professional readers, and over 300 publishers list their titles on the site. There are over 210,000 professional readers already using the service, and digital galleys can be read on all major reading devices and tablets.

The galleys are protected files that cannot be shared, and you'll find specific instructions about how to access the files at the end of each excerpt.

Note: Publishers can choose how to provide access to the full galley, so you'll see two kinds of links here.

Questions? Email us at support@netgalley.com, or ask a question on Twitter @NetGalley. Happy reading!

"An intoxicating gem of a story."
—MARIE LU, New York Times
bestselling author of the Legend series

THE WRATH & THE DAWN

· RENÉE AHDIEH ·

SUMMARY

Every dawn brings horror to a different family in a land ruled by a killer. Khalid, the eighteen-year-old Caliph of Khorasan, takes a new bride each night only to have her executed at sunrise. So it is a suspicious surprise when sixteen-year-old Shahrzad volunteers to marry Khalid. But she does so with a clever plan to stay alive and exact revenge on the Caliph for the murder of her best friend and countless other girls. Shazi's wit and will, indeed, get her through to the dawn that no others have seen, but with a catch . . . she's falling in love with the very boy who killed her dearest friend. She discovers that the murderous boy-king is not all that he seems and neither are the deaths of so many girls. Shazi is determined to uncover the reason for the murders and to break the cycle once and for all. Inspired by *A Thousand and One Nights*, this sumptuous and epically told love story heralds the arrival of an exciting new voice in YA.

EXCERPT

Prologue

It would not be a welcome dawn.

Already the sky told this story with its sad halo of silver beckoning from beyond the horizon.

A young man stood alongside his father on the rooftop terrace of the marble palace. They watched the pale light of the early morning sun push back the darkness with slow careful deliberation.

"Where is he?" the young man asked.

His father did not look his way. "He has not left his chamber since he gave the order."

The young man ran a hand through his wavy hair exhaling all the while. "There will be riots in the city streets for this."

"And you will put them to rout, in short order." It was a terse response, still made to a somber stretch of light.

"In short order? Do you not think a mother and father regardless of birth or rank will fight to avenge their child?"

Finally the father faced his son. His eyes were drawn and sunken as though a weight tugged at them from within. "They will fight. They should fight. And you will ensure it amounts to nothing. You will do your duty to your king. Do you understand?"

The young man paused. "I understand."

"General al-Khoury?"

His father turned toward the soldier standing behind them. "Yes?"

"It is done."

His father nodded, and the soldier left.

Again, the two men stared up at the sky.

Waiting.

A drop of rain struck the arid surface beneath their feet, disappearing into the tan stone. Another plinked against the iron railing before it slid its way into nothingness.

Soon, rain was falling around them at a steady pace.

"There is your proof," the general said, his voice laden with quiet anguish.

The young man did not respond right away.

"He cannot withstand this, Father."

"He can. He is strong."

"You have never understood Khalid. It is not about strength. It is about substance. What follows will destroy all that remains of his, leaving behind a husk—a shadow of what he once was."

The general winced. "Do you think I wanted this for him? I would drown in my own blood to prevent this. But we have no choice."

The young man shook his head and wiped the rain from beneath his chin.

"I refuse to believe that."

"Jalal—"

"There must be another way." With that, the young man turned from the railing and vanished down the staircase.

Throughout the city, long-dry wells began to fill. Cracked, sunbaked cisterns shimmered with pools of hope, and the people of Rey awoke to a new joy. They raced into the streets, angling their smiling faces to the sky.

Not knowing the price.

And, deep within the palace of marble and stone, a boy of eighteen sat alone before a table of polished ebony . . .

Listening to the rain.

The only light in the room reflected back in his amber eyes.

A light beset by the dark.

He braced his elbows on his knees and made a crown of his hands about his brow. Then he shuttered his gaze, and the words echoed around him, filling his ears with the promise of a life rooted in the past.

Of a life atoning for his sins.

One hundred lives for the one you took. One life to one dawn. Should you fail but a single morn, I shall take from you your dreams. I shall take from you your city.

And I shall take from you these lives, a thousandfold.

Meditations On Gossamer And Gold

They were not gentle. And why should they be?

After all, they did not expect her to live past the next morning.

The hands that tugged ivory combs through Shahrzad's waist-length hair and scrubbed sandalwood paste on her bronze arms did so with a brutal kind of detachment.

Shahrzad watched one young servant girl dust her bare shoulders with flakes of gold that caught the light from the setting sun.

A breeze gusted along the gossamer curtains lining the walls of the chamber. The sweet scent of citrus blossoms wafted through the carved wooden screens leading to the terrace, whispering of a freedom now beyond reach.

This was my choice. Remember Shiva.

"I don't wear necklaces," Shahrzad said when another girl began to fasten a jewel-encrusted behemoth around her throat.

"It is a gift from the caliph. You must wear it, my lady."

Shahrzad stared down at the slight girl in amused disbelief. "And if I don't? Will he kill me?"

"Please, my lady, I—"

Shahrzad sighed. "I suppose now is not the time to make this point."

"Yes, my lady."

"My name is Shahrzad."

"I know, my lady." The girl glanced away in discomfort before turning to assist with Shahrzad's gilded mantle. As the two young women eased the weighty garment onto her glittering shoulders, Shahrzad studied the finished product in the mirror before her.

Her midnight tresses gleamed like polished obsidian, and her hazel eyes were edged in alternating strokes of black kohl and liquid gold. At the center of her brow hung a teardrop ruby the size of her thumb; its mate dangled from a thin chain around her bare waist, grazing the silk sash of her trowsers. The mantle itself was pale damask and threaded with silver and gold in an intricate pattern that grew ever chaotic as it flared by her feet.

I look like a gilded peacock.

"Do they all look this ridiculous?" Shahrzad asked.

Again, the two young women averted their gazes with unease.

I'm sure Shiva didn't look this ridiculous . . .

Shahrzad's expression hardened.

Shiva would have looked beautiful. Beautiful and strong.

Her fingernails dug into her palms; tiny crescents of steely resolve.

At the sound of a quiet knock at the door, three heads turned—their collective breaths bated.

In spite of her newfound mettle, Shahrzad's heart began to pound.

"May I come in?" The soft voice of her father broke through the silence, pleading and laced in tacit apology.

Shahrzad exhaled slowly . . . carefully.

"Baba, what are you doing here?" Her words were patient, yet wary.

Jahandar al-Khayzuran shuffled into the chamber. His beard and temples were streaked with grey, and the myriad colors in his hazel eyes shimmered and shifted like the sea in the midst of a storm.

In his hand was a single budding rose, its center leached of color, and the tips of its petals tinged a beautiful, blushing mauve.

"Where is Irsa?" Shahrzad asked, alarm seeping into her tone.

Her father smiled sadly. "She is at home. I did not allow her to come with me, though she fought and raged until the last possible moment."

At least in this he has not ignored my wishes.

"You should be with her. She needs you tonight. Please, do this for me, Baba? Do as we discussed?" She reached out and took his free hand, squeezing tightly, beseeching him in her grip to follow the plans she had laid out in the days before.

"I—I can't, my child." Jahandar lowered his head, a sob rising in his chest, his thin shoulders trembling with grief. "Shahrzad—"

"Be strong. For Irsa. I promise you, everything will be fine." Shahrzad raised her palm to his weathered face and brushed away the smattering of tears from his cheek.

"I cannot. The thought that this may be your last sunset—"

"It will not be the last. I will see tomorrow's sunset. This I swear to you."

Jahandar nodded, his misery nowhere close to mollified. He held out the rose in his hand. "The last from my garden; it has not yet bloomed fully, but I wanted to give you one remembrance of home."

She smiled as she reached for it, the love between them far past mere gratitude, but he stopped her. When she realized the reason, she began to protest.

"No. At least in this, I might do something for you," he muttered, almost to himself. He stared at the rose, his brow furrowed and his mouth drawn. One servant girl coughed in her fist while the other looked to the floor.

Shahrzad waited patiently. Knowingly.

The rose started to unfurl. Its petals twisted open, prodded to life by an invisible hand. As it expanded, a delicious perfume filled the space between them, sweet and perfect for an instant . . . but soon, it became overpowering. Cloying. The edges of the flower changed from a brilliant, deep pink to a shadowy rust in the blink of an eye.

And then the flower began to wither and die.

Dismayed, Jahandar watched its dried petals wilt to the white marble at their feet.

"I—I'm sorry, Shahrzad," he cried.

"It doesn't matter. I will never forget how beautiful it was for that moment, Baba." She wrapped her arms around his neck and pulled him close. By his ear, in a voice so low only he could hear, she said, "Go to Tariq, as you promised. Take Irsa and go."

He nodded, his eyes shimmering once more. "I love you, my child."

"And I love you. I will keep my promises. All of them."

Overcome, Jahandar blinked down at his elder daughter in silence.

This time, the knock at the door demanded attention rather than requested it.

Shahrzad's forehead whipped back in its direction, the blood red ruby swinging in tandem. She squared her shoulders and lifted her pointed chin.

Jahandar stood to the side, covering his face with his hands, as his daughter marched forward.

"I'm sorry—so very sorry," she whispered to him before striding across the threshold to follow the contingent of guards leading the processional. Jahandar slid to his knees and sobbed as Shahrzad turned the corner and disappeared.

With her father's grief resounding through the halls, Shahrzad's feet refused to carry her but a few steps down the cavernous corridors of the palace. She halted, her knees shaking beneath the thin silk of her voluminous *sirwal* trowsers.

"My lady?" one of the guards prompted in a bored tone.

"He can wait," Shahrzad gasped.

The guards exchanged glances.

Her own tears threatening to blaze a telltale trail down her cheeks, Shahrzad pressed a hand to her chest. Unwittingly, her fingertips brushed the edge of the thick gold necklace clasped around her throat, festooned with gems of outlandish size and untold variety. It felt heavy . . . stifling. Like a bejeweled fetter. She allowed her fingers to wrap around the offending instrument, thinking for a moment to rip it from her body.

The rage was comforting. A friendly reminder.

Shiva.

Her dearest friend. Her closest confidante.

She curled her toes within their sandals of braided bullion and threw back her shoulders once more. Without a word, she resumed her march.

Again, the guards looked to one another for an instant.

When they reached the massive double doors leading into the throne room, Shahrzad realized her heart was racing at twice its normal speed. The doors swung open with a distended groan, and she focused on her target, ignoring all else around her.

At the very end of the immense space stood Khalid Ibn al-Rashid, the Caliph of Khorasan.

The King of Kings.

The monster from my nightmares.

With every step she took, Shahrzad felt the hate rise in her blood, along with the clarity of purpose. She stared at him, her eyes never wavering. His proud carriage stood out amongst the men in his retinue, and details began to emerge the closer she drew to his side.

He was tall and trim, with the build of a young man proficient in warfare. His dark hair was straight and styled in a manner suggesting a desire for order in all things.

As she strode onto the dais, she looked up at him, refusing to balk, even in the face of her king.

His thick eyebrows raised a fraction. They framed eyes so pale a shade of brown they appeared amber in certain flashes of light, like those of a tiger. His profile was an artist's study in angles, and he remained motionless as he returned her watchful scrutiny.

A face that cut; a gaze that pierced.

He reached a hand out to her.

Just as she extended her palm to grasp it, she remembered to bow.

The wrath seethed below the surface, bringing a flush to her cheeks.

When she met his eyes again, he blinked once.

"Wife." He nodded.

"My king."

I will live to see tomorrow's sunset. Make no mistake. I swear I will live to see as many sunsets as it takes.

And I will kill you.

With my own hands.

You've just read an excerpt from The Wrath and the Dawn.

ABOUT THE AUTHOR

Renée Ahdieh lives in Charlotte, North Carolina with her husband and their tiny overlord of a dog. *The Wrath and the Dawn* is her debut.

Imprint: Putnam Juvenile
Print ISBN: 9780399171611
Print price: $17.99
eBook ISBN: 9780698185890
eBook price: $10.99
Publication date: 5/12/15
Publicity contact:
Marisa Russell, mrussell@penguinrandomhouse.com
Editor: Stacey Barney
Agent: Barbara Poelle
Agency: Irene Goodman

Promotional information:
- *The Wrath and the Dawn* sampler box
- Author blog tour
- Consumer advertising campaign including print and online
- National media campaign
- Promotion at C2E2 (April 2015), Romantic Times (May 2015), Comic Con International (July 2015), and Fall consumer book festivals
- Online promotion and social media outreach
- Promotion and galley distribution at all national school and library conferences

A School for Unusual Girls

A STRANJE HOUSE NOVEL

Kathleen BALDWIN

SUMMARY

It's 1814. Napoleon is exiled on Elba. Europe is in shambles. Britain is at war on four fronts. And Stranje House, a School for Unusual Girls, has become one of Regency England's dark little secrets. The daughters of the beau monde who don't fit high society's constrictive mold are banished to Stranje House to be reformed into marriageable young ladies. Or so their parents think. In truth, Headmistress Emma Stranje, the original unusual girl, has plans for the young ladies—plans that entangle the girls in the dangerous world of spies, diplomacy, and war.

EXCERPT

The headmistress, Miss Emma Stranje, sat behind her desk, mute, assessing me with unsettling hawk eyes. In the flickering light of the oil lamp, I couldn't tell her age. She looked youthful one minute, and ancient the next. She might've been pretty once, if it weren't for her shrewd measuring expression. She'd pulled her wavy brown hair back into a severe chignon knot, but stray wisps escaped their moorings giving her a feral cat-like appearance.

I tried not to cower under her predatory gaze. If this woman intended to be my jailer, I needed to stand my ground now or I would never fight my way out from under her thumb.

My mother cleared her throat and started in, "You know why we are here. As we explained in our letters—"

"It was an accident!" I blurted and immediately regretted it. The words sounded defensive, not strong and reasoned as I had intended.

Mother pinched her lips and sat perfectly straight, primly picking lint off her gloves as if my outburst caused the bothersome flecks to appear. She sighed. I could almost hear her oft repeated complaint, '*why is Georgiana not the meek biddable daughter I deserve.*'

Miss Stranje arched one imperious eyebrow, silently demanding the rest of the explanation, waiting, unnerving me with every tick of the clock. My mind turned to mush. How much explanation should I give? If I told her the plain truth she'd know too much about my unacceptable pursuits. If I said too little I'd sound like an arsonist. In the ensuing silence, she tapped one slender finger against the dark walnut of her desk. The sound echoed through the room—a magistrate's gavel, consigning me to life in her prison. "You *accidentally* set fire to your father's stables?"

My father growled low in his throat and shifted angrily on the delicate Hepplewhite chair.

"Yes," I mumbled, knowing the fire wasn't the whole reason I was here, merely the final straw, a razor sharp spear-like straw. Unfortunately, there were several dozen pointy spears in my parents' quiver of *what's-wrong-with-Georgiana*.

If only they understood. If only the world cared about something beyond my ability to pour tea and walk with a mincing step. I decided to tell Miss Stranje at least part of the truth. "It was a scientific experiment gone awry. Had I been successful—"

"Successful?" roared my father. He twisted on the flimsy chair putting considerable stress on the rear legs as he leaned in my direction, numbering my sins on his fingers. "You nearly roasted my prize hunters alive! Every last horse — scared senseless. Burned the bleedin' stables to the ground. *To the ground!* Nothing left but a heap of charred stone. Our house and fields would've gone up next if the tenants and neighbors hadn't come running to help. That ruddy blaze would've taken their homes and crops, too. *Successful?* You almost reduced half of High Cross Greene to ash."

Every word a lashing, I nodded and kept my face to the floor, knowing he wasn't done.

"As it was, you scorched more than half of Squire Thurgood's apple orchard. I'll be paying dearly for those lost apples over the next three years, I can tell you that. And what about my hounds!" He paused for breath and clamped his teeth together so tight that veins bulged at his temples and his whole head trembled with repressed rage.

In that short fitful silence, I could not help but remember the sound of those dogs baying and whimpering, and the faces of our servants and neighbors smeared with ash as we all struggled to contain the fire, their expressions—grim, angry, wishing me to perdition.

"My kennels are ruined. Blacker and smokier than Satan's chimney..."

He lowered his voice, no longer clarifying for Miss Stranje's sake, and spit one final damning indictment into my face. "You almost killed my hounds!" He dismissed me with an angry wave of his hand. "Successful. Bah!"

My stomach churned and twisted with regret. *Accident*. It *was* an accident. I wished he had slapped me. It would've stung less than his disgust.

I wanted to point out the merits of inventing a new kind of undetectable invisible ink. If such an ink had been available, my brother might still be alive. As it was, the French intercepted a British courier and Robert's company found themselves caught in an ambush. It wouldn't help to say it. I tried the day after the fire and Father only got angrier. He'd shouted obscenities, called me a foolish girl, "It's done. Over. He's gone."

Nor would it help to remind him that I'd nearly died leading the horses out of the mews. His mind was made up. Unlike my father's precious livestock, my goose was well and truly cooked. He intended to banish me, imprison me here at Stranje House just as Napoleon was banished to Elba.

Miss Stranje glanced down at my mother letter. "It says here, that on another occasion Georgiana jumped out of an attic window?"

"I didn't jump. Not exactly."

"She did." Father crossed his arms.

It had happened two and a half years ago. One would've thought they'd have forgotten it by now. "Another experiment," I admitted. "I'd read a treatise about DaVinci and his—"

"*Wings*." My mother cut me off and rolled her eyes upward to contemplate the ceiling. She employed the same mocking tone she always used when referring to that particular incident.

"Not wings," I defended, my voice a bit too high pitched. "A glider. A kite."

Mother ignored me and stated her case to Miss Stranje without any inflection whatsoever. "She's a menace. Dangerous to herself and others."

"I took precautions." I forced my voice into a calmer, less ear-bruising range, and tried to explain. "I had the stable lads position a wagon of hay beneath the window."

"Yes!" Father clapped his hands together as if he'd caught a fly in them. "But you missed the infernal wagon, didn't you?"

"Because the experiment worked."

"Hardly." With a scornful grunt he explained to Miss Stranje, "Crashed into a Sycamore tree. Wore her arm in a sling for months."

"Yes, but if I'd made the kite wider and taken off from the roof—"

"This is all your doing." My father shot a familiar barb at my mother. "You never should've allowed her to read all that scientific nonsense."

"I had nothing to do with it," she bristled. "That bluestocking governess is to blame."

Miss Grissmore. An excellent tutor. A woman of outstanding patience, the only governess in ten years able to endure my incessant questions, sent packing because of my foolhardy leap. I glared at my mother's back remembering how I'd begged and explained over and over that Miss Grissmore had nothing to do with it.

"I let the woman go as soon as I realized what she was." Mother ignored Father's grumbled commentary on bluestockings and demanded of Miss Stranje, "Well? Can you reform Georgiana or not?"

You've just read an excerpt from A School for Unusual Girls.

ABOUT THE AUTHOR

Kathleen Baldwin has written three award-winning traditional Regency romances for adults, including *Lady Fiasco,* winner of Cataromance's Best Traditional Regency, and *Mistaken Kiss,* a Holt Medallion Finalist. She lives in Plano, Texas, with her family.

Imprint: Tor Teen
Print ISBN: 0765376008
Print price: $17.99
eBook ISBN: 1466849274

eBook price: $9.99

Publication date: 5/19/15

Publicity contact: Alexis Saarela, alexis.saarela@tor.com

Rights contact: Laura Langlie

Editor: Susan Chang

Agent: Laura Langlie

Agency: Laura Langlie Agency

Promotional information

- National advertising targeting science fiction/fantasy and YA readers
- National advertising in trade media
- Promotion at San Diego and New York Comic Con
- Select appearances
- Online publicity campaign
- Educational marketing including extensive galley distribution, Booklist Webinar and Book Buzz title, major conferences, outreach to librarians/educators, and Booklist email blasts
- Digital promotion on social networking sites, the Tor/Forge blog and newsletter, and Goodreads

UNDERTOW

COVER
NOT
FINAL

NEW YORK TIMES BEST-SELLING AUTHOR

MICHAEL
BUCKLEY

SUMMARY

Sixteen-year-old Lyric Walker's life is forever changed when she witnesses the arrival of 30,000 Alpha, a five-nation race of ocean-dwelling warriors, on her beach in Coney Island. The world's initial wonder and awe over the Alpha quickly turns ugly and paranoid and violent, and Lyric's small town transforms into a military zone with humans on one side and Alpha on the other. When Lyric is recruited to help the crown prince, a boy named Fathom, assimilate, she begins to fall for him. But their love is a dangerous one, and there are forces on both sides working to keep them apart. Only, what if the Alpha are not actually the enemy? What if they are in fact humanity's best chance for survival? Because the real enemy is coming. And it's more terrifying than anything the world has ever seen.

EXCERPT

Chapter Four

People talk about Coney Island's pre-Alpha days like they were magical, like we all lived in the Disneyland of Brooklyn. They forget our "Disneyland" was really a garishly painted slum in a crumbling neighborhood with rampant crime, a busy sex trade, a methadone clinic, and a school system in the toilet. Sure, the Alpha didn't help. They turned the place into a police state. But it's not like we were all out in the streets singing "Kumbuya" the day before.

There's also this idea that the Alpha caused all the weird racism and xenophobia, too, but whatever. This part of town was always a hotbed of racial sludge, and the various groups never played nice. The Chinese hated the Japanese, and the Jamaicans hated the Koreans, and the Mexicans hated the African Americans, and the Russians hated the Orthodox Jews, and the white people hated all of them. And sometimes, on very hot days, someone got stabbed because of the flag on his car. If America is a melting pot Coney Island is the overcooked crusty stuff on the bottom of the pan.

It shouldn't come as a surprise to anyone that our memories of the place are a little distorted. Back when I had time for books, I read a poem that described memories like clay—malleable and squishy and easily molded into whatever you needed. Over time, people sculpt their miserable experiences into something more esthetically pleasing, stretching the interesting moments, and kneading the uncomfortable facts. What they end up with is no longer a memory but a story, and the two rarely resemble one another. The story of the Alpha's arrival is just as sculpted. Some still call it an invasion, an act of war, even a sign of the end of days. I can't say that my story is any less convoluted, but I was there when it happened. I saw it first hand, not on television and not on some Internet site. And I think my version has more merit than most because I know something that most people do not: the Alpha actually arrived the night before the world went crazy.

It was the first night of the summer break between my eighth and ninth grade year, the night when the wild things ran loose. That's what Bex used to call us and that night was our Wild Rumpus. We drank. We hooked up. We launched bottle rockets into the sky, motored down streets assaulting the neighborhood with bone-rattling bass-lines. Anyone who disagreed with us could go to hell.

I ran with Bex and Shadow, the centers of my known universe even back then, and we had twenty kids following our every step. We crashed parties and chugged beers in parking lots, and I flirted with boy after boy after boy. Anything we missed was reported to us in texts, tiny bite-sized dispatches from the front lines of stupidity. Someone threw-up on a cop, so-and-so made out with so-and-so, and this person got into a fight with that person. By midnight we had hundreds of texts, each a blossoming legend of teenage debauchery we knew we'd talk about for years to come. I remember that a sophomore named Jessie Combs woke up under the boardwalk spooning a hobo.

I drank up the hot June heat, endless spectacle, and noise until my brain rebelled and a migraine showed up around midnight to spoil my fun.

"Bad head?" Bex asked when I sat down on a vacant stoop.

"Bad head." The steady pounding had started hours earlier but I shoved it down and hoped it would die from lack of attention. Unfortunately this headache had a tenacious rhythm that grew and grew.

"C'mon, we'll take you home," Shadow said.

The hangers-on groaned with complaints. Bex and Shadow should have been pissed at me, too; after all I had ruined lots of good times with my "condition," but Bex turned on the others, firing off insults and demanding their allegiance to me. Bex = besty.

"Drop me at the beach," I said.

"Will she be there?" Bex asked.

I nodded. She was always there.

Bex grabbed my hand, Shadow the other, and we ran toward Surf Avenue, dodging the livery cabs that sped past at all hours of the night and zigzagging through the pervy drunks who milled in and out of the seedy bars. At the old wooden boardwalk ramp near the Wonder Wheel we ignored the "park closed" sign, and rushed to greet the Atlantic Ocean. I took in a greedy breath of salty air and anticipated the relief. The beach would fix everything.

As I predicted, we found my mother sitting cross-legged on the sand, her flip-flops tossed nearby, and her hair tied back with a band. She was a beautiful Buddha, hypnotically gorgeous with olive skin, full-lips, and eyes both blue and smoky. Her body, like mine, was tall, long-legged, and hippy like a belly dancer's, but she didn't have an ounce of the insecurity that plagued me. She loved her body and it showed. Another's perceived flaw was her dazzling asset, and thus she was the cause of much rubber necking in our neighborhood. People fell in love with her at first sight. Even her walk, a danceable jig that made small children giggle, transcended goofy into oddly seductive.

"Can you sign for this package?" Shadow asked.

My mother frowned. "Your father would have a contraption fit if he knew you were out this late," she said.

"It's a conniption fit, mom," I said.

The group chuckled.

"I'm always messing up words," she apologized. "Migraine?"

I nodded. "Probably an F3."

the longest time there was no sign of her at all and in my growing panic I charged in after her until I was waist-deep. I shouted her name until my throat was raw, but when I still could not find her I went into hysterics. I was sure she had drowned. I ran back to the beach for my cell phone to call my father but quickly realized I had burned out the battery with all the texting. I was helpless and alone.

After several excruciating minutes she finally surfaced a few yards away but everything that was Summer Walker had changed. What came out of that water looked like my mother but seemed more like a cornered animal.

"What's out there? What did you see?"

"We should get back to the apartment," she said, and without another word she turned and led us home. I begged for answers the whole way, but she refused to speak of what had just happened and as soon as we were home she locked herself inside her bedroom.

"Mom?" I called out through the door.

"Go to bed, Lyric," she whispered back. "You'll wake your father."

My dreams were brutal that night. In them my mother fought against a hungry sea with waves like greedy hands pulling her down into its dark, insatiable maw. I dove in to rescue her but only found myself pulled in as well. In the morning I woke shivering, my sheets soaked with sweat. I changed and charged into the living room, ready to demand answers but my mother was gone. Instead, I found my father leaning on the kitchen counter, his face buried in a letter in my mother's handwriting. He didn't notice me at first, but when he caught me sneaking a peek he crunched it into a ball and shoved it into his pocket.

"Is that about the whale?" I asked.

"Huh?"

"The noise from last night. It was crazy loud. It could have been a whale. Maybe it's still there. Maybe we should go down and see."

"NO!" he commanded. "I want you off the beach today."

"Okay, you don't have to yell!"

"What did your mother do when she heard it?"

"She jumped into the water."

His face went pale, and I felt I had somehow betrayed her, though I couldn't tell why.

"Dad? What's wrong?"

He ignored me. He reached into his pocket, pulled out his phone, and dialed a number.

"Mike, it's me. I'm not coming in today. Yeah, I've got this thing in my chest," he said, not even bothering to fake a cough or the sniffles. I was stunned. My father never took a day off from work. He always said we couldn't afford it, and our collection of "as-is" IKEA furniture was proof. Being one of New York's Finest also made him one of New York's Brokest, and he dragged himself into the precinct when most men would be planning their funerals.

"Stay here," he said when he hung up. "Keep the door locked and your phone near you, and stay off of it. If anything happens, I'll come home right away. Wait for me."

"What could happen?"

"If your mother comes back, keep her here and call me. Do not let her leave this apartment."

He raced into the bathroom and I heard him take the lid off the toilet tank. Curious, I followed him and saw that he was pulling a storage bag from inside. It was filled with money. He reached into it, grabbed a handful, and stuffed it all into my hands. It was more cash than I had ever seen - fifties and hundreds - easily a thousand dollars. The rest he put back where he found it.

"What is this?" I cried.

"For emergencies," he said as he darted to his bedroom.

"What emergencies?" I shouted but was again ignored. Through the open door I could see him pulling on his work shirt and strapping on his gun belt. A moment later he was taking his pistol out of its lock box under the bed and shoving it into its holster.

"Dad, why do you need your gun if you aren't going to work?" I asked, but he didn't answer. He blasted through the front door and was gone.

I had my shoes in my hand before the door closed. I had heard what he said but I wasn't having any of it. The way I saw it he was only in charge as long as he was sane, and something crazy was clearly taking place. I skipped the elevator and flew down four flights, hoping I could stop him the second he hit the lobby, but when I got there he was gone. I dashed into the street, craning my neck in both directions, but he was nowhere in sight.

I stood in the middle of the road concocting horrible scenarios. My mother had left my father. The note was a "Dear John" letter. It had sent him over the edge. He was going to stop her, maybe even kill her. I was going to be an orphan.

Yes, a little dramatic, especially in light of the fact that my parents were desperately, disgustingly, embarrassingly in love. They were so into one another, it was gross. I couldn't count how many times I had walked in on them and their baby-making practice. No way my mom would leave him, and no way my dad would hurt her, right?

But then my brain reached into its hard drive and found about a hundred stories my father had shared about arresting some husband or wife who had snapped and killed their spouse.

"No one saw it coming," was how he ended every one.

So, yeah, I was flung back into freak-out mode. I ran up and down the beach looking for them. I snooped around the minor league baseball stadium and explored the end of the pier where the Mexican kids used raw chicken legs as bait for crabs. I searched the streets and alleys like a lost kid in the supermarket fighting back hysterics. Eventually I was too tired and overheated to keep looking, so I made my way to a bench outside of Rudy's Bar and pulled out my phone. With nothing else to do, I resorted to a strategy that had always worked for me in the past - passive-aggressive texting. The first text went to my mother.

GOOD MORNING. IT'S UR DAUGHTER. REMEMBER ME?

When I didn't hear anything, I cut back on the passive and amped up the aggressive.

WHERE THE HELL R U?

Cursing had always been the right bait for a quick callback, but ten minutes passed without a reply so I turned my frustrations onto my father.

IS EVERYONE ON DRUGS?

Nothing. It was time for something more drastic.

I'M PREGNANT AND I'M KEEPING IT.

After ten minutes without a peep, I just couldn't hold back the tears.

BOTH OF U R GROUNDED.

I pulled myself together and decided the best thing I could do was go home, after all. Maybe Mom would show up. When she did, she could tell me this was all a big nothing. We'd have a good laugh. It would be a story they'd tell when I was an adult: *The time Lyric thought her father was going to kill me. Ha, ha, ha!* I was all set to go when I noticed a group of people on the beach. I counted nineteen of them, all walking hand in hand toward the surf. When they got to the water's edge, they knelt down as if to pray. At first I didn't think much of them. It wasn't unusual to see congregations on the beach back then. People got married there, baptized themselves and their squalling babies, and even launched little canoes full of flowers and candles, meant to sail to the dearly departed in the afterworld. But this group was different because my mother was with them.

I hopped the tiny fence that lined the beach and ran to her side. When I reached her, I bent down and saw the same worried gaze from the night before. She was transfixed on the ocean, and it took me several seconds to pull her out of her trance.

"Lyric, go home," she begged, suddenly frightened. Her eyes were wild, her pupils dilated. She took my hands in her own and I could feel she was trembling.

"Why? What is this? Who are these people?"

"Don't question me. Just go!"

I took a step back. My mother had never raised her voice to me before, even when I deserved it. I had no frame of reference for her fury. It confused me, froze me where I stood. We caught the attention of a woman kneeling beside her, a tall beauty with platinum hair. She turned toward us and shot us a wrathful glare, then barked threateningly -- yes, barked, like a dog, or rather like the deep-throated sea lions at the aquarium. It was loud and ridiculous and shocking, so I laughed, because that's what you do when a crazy person does something crazy and you're feeling a little crazy yourself. It only made the woman howl at me louder.

"Lyric, please," my mother pleaded. "Just go!"

"But –"

We were interrupted by the loud, vibrating sound that I'd heard the night before. In response, a man in the group cried out in excitement. He leaped to his feet and pointed toward the waves, but I couldn't look. I was too astonished. The man was Mr. Lir, a guy who had babysat me, had put bandages on my bloody knees, and had taken me and his son Samuel to the Bronx Zoo every summer until I was ten.

"Lyric, go, now!" my mother said, as she and her friends got to their feet. They linked their hands together and raised them over their head, facing out at the horizon.

"They are her!" Mr. Lir shouted.

I turned my eyes to the water and my throat was seized by dread. There were people rising out of the surf, about fifty of them. Yet they were not people. They were something else. Each was easily over six feet tall, with skin like a copper penny and dressed in bizarre armor made from bones and shells. Each held a weapon—tridents or spears or huge, heavy hammers—and they waved them around aggressively. Behind them was a second wave of people who were not as hulking as the first group, but just as intimidating. They held no weapons because theirs were in their bodies, vicious blades that came right out of their arms. Two men from this group were at the center and stood out amongst the rest. One had a shaved head and wore a goatee sculpted into a point beneath his chin. The other had long, golden hair like a lion and wore sea glass around his neck and hands. With them was a woman whose breathtaking beauty seemed to multiply with every step she took toward me, yet there was something unsettling about her as well, something predatory and vicious, like a Great White shark hiding in the body of a woman. To her right was an elderly woman wearing what would best be described as a nun's habit, only made from the skin of some dark-furred animal. It covered her entire body exposing only her face and hands, and "the habit" formed a strange hammerlike shape on either side of her head.

And then there was the boy. He was about my age with hair cut short and eyes both blue and bright, eyes that burned a glowing echo I could see when I closed my own. He looked lost and confused, troubled by what he was seeing around him, like he was seeing the world for the first time.

Behind him came others who were far more strange and whose names I would learn later: the Nix with their teeth and claws, the quietly confident Ceto, and the Sirena whose every emotion was revealed with colorful scales. There were some I haven't seen since that day—translucent-skinned ones and people with tentacles for limbs. All of them were in a state of metamorphosis. Tails became legs. Fins sank into flesh. Gills vanished, causing their owners to choke on their first breaths of air. There were elderly creatures and babies, teenagers, and families, all climbing onto the beach, eyeing us with wide-eyed wonder. At first they numbered in the hundreds, then thousands, until eventually I could no longer see the sand for all the bodies.

Panic broke out all around me. Sunbathers abandoned towels, coolers, and chairs. They trampled one another to get away, and children became separated from parents. Yet in the chaos I heard someone calling my name. I searched the crowd, careful not to get knocked over in the rush, and spotted my father sprinting toward us with his gun in hand.

"Summer! You promised Lyric would not be part of this!" he shouted.

"It's not my fault. She found me, Leonard!" my mother cried. "Please take her home."

"We're all going!" he demanded.

My mother pulled away from him. "You know I have to do this. I have a responsibility to them."

"What about your responsibility to us?" my father said.

"Will someone please tell me what's happening?" I screamed.

Mr. Lir pushed his way through people to join us. "Summer, send your family away. It is not safe for them to be here."

My father waved him off. "It's not safe for any of us, Terrance. People will take pictures of this—they're taking pictures right now—and if we stay on this beach any longer, we are all going to be in them. They'll figure out what you are, what Samuel and Lyric are, and they'll come for them. They'll come for all of us."

"What did you say?" I cried. "What am I?"

"I'm sorry, Lyric. We didn't know how to tell you," my mother said, and as she took my face in her hands I saw faint pink- and rose-colored patches appear on her neck and forearms. They were scales, like those on a fish or a snake, both beautiful and terribly wrong.

I shrieked and fell backward. "What are you?" I cried.

"We can explain later, Lyric," my father cried. "Right now we have to get out of here. Summer, come with us."

My mother stared at him for a long moment, perhaps weighing every day of their life together against the responsibility she felt to the strange visitors, and then she turned to the ocean and her scales turned fire-engine red and blistering white.

"Tell them I'm sorry, Terrance," she said without even looking at him. "Try to make them understand."

"Summer, you cannot turn your back on your people," Mr. Lir shouted. "They'll call you a traitor. You'll be an untouchable!"

"We have to run," she said as she took my hand.

You've just read an excerpt from Undertow.

ABOUT THE AUTHOR

Michael Buckley's two middle grade series, the *Sisters Grimm* and *NERDS*, have sold more than 2.5 million copies. Before starting to write children's books, he worked as a stand-up comic, television writer, advertising copywriter, and a singer in a punk rock band. He lives in Brooklyn, New York. Visit his website at www.michaelbuckleywrites.com.

Imprint: HMH Books for Young Readers
Print ISBN: 9780544348257
Print price: $18.99
eBook ISBN: 9780544348622
eBook price: $18.99
Publication date: 5/5/15
Publicity contact: Rachel Wasdyke rachel.wasdyke@hmhco.com
Rights contact: Candace Finn Candace.finn@hmhco.com
Editor: Sarah Landis
Agent: Alison Fargis
Agency: Stonesong

Promotional information:
- Major prepublication buzz campaign targeting key media
- National print and online advertising and media campaign
- 7-10 city national author tour
- Fall 2014 Regional appearances and bookseller events
- Extensive social media promotion
- Dedicated bookseller, librarian, industry bigmouth mailings
- Major promotions at school, library and bookseller
- Discussion guide with Common Core connections

THE ONLY THING WORSE
THAN BEING A WITCH
IS LIVING WITH ONE.

SERIOUSLY WICKED

Magic
For
Beginners

TINA
CONNOLLY

A NOVEL

SUMMARY

Camellia's adopted mother wants Cam to grow up to be just like her. Problem is, Mom's a seriously wicked witch.

Cam's used to stopping the witch's crazy schemes for world domination. But when the witch summons a demon, he gets loose—and into Devon, the cute new boy at school.

Suddenly Cam's got bigger problems than passing Algebra. Her friends are getting zombiefied. Their dragon is tired of hiding in the RV garage. For being a shy boy-band boy, Devon is sure kissing a bunch of girls. And a phoenix hidden in the school is going to explode on the night of the Halloween Dance.

To stop the demon before he destroys Devon's soul, Cam might have to try a spell of her own. But if she's willing to work spells like the witch... will that mean she's wicked too?

EXCERPT

True Witchery

I was mucking out the dragon's garage when the witch's text popped up on my phone.

BRING ME A BIRD

"Ugh," I said to Moonfire. "What is—I can't even... Ugh!" I shoved the phone in my jeans and went back to my broom. The witch's ring tone cackled in my pocket as I swept.

Moonfire looked longingly at the scrub brush as I finished. "Just a few skritches," I told her. "You know what the witch is like." I grabbed the old yellow bristle brush and rubbed her scaly blue back. My phone cackled insistently and I pulled it out again.

HANG SNAKESKINS OUT TO DRY

FEED AND WALK WEREWOLF PUP

MUCK OUT DRAGON'S QUARTERS

DEFROST SHEEP

Done all those, I texted back. *Been up since 5AM.* Out loud I added, "Get with the program," but I did not text that.

The phone cackled back immediately.

DONT BE SNARKY

THESE ARE CHORES BY WHICH ONE MUST UNDERSTAND TRUE WITCHERY

NOW BRING ME A BIRD

"Sorry, Moonfire," I said. "The witch is in a mood." At least she hadn't asked me about the spell I was supposed to be learning. I stowed the brush on a shelf and hurried out the detached RV garage and back into the house. Thirteen minutes to get to the bus stop, to get to school on time. I threw my backpack on as I crossed to the witch's old wire bird-cage sitting in the living room window. Our newly acquired goldfinch was hopping around inside. The witch had lured him in with thistle seeds. "C'mon, little guy," I said, and carried the cage up the steps of the split-level to the witch's bedroom.

The witch was sitting up in bed as I knocked and entered. Sarmine Scarabouche is sour and pointed and old. Nothing ever lives up to her expectations. She is always immaculate, with a perfect silver bob that doesn't dare get out of place. Right then she was all in white. The bed is white, too, and the sheets, and the walls—everything. She spritzes her whole room with unicorn hair sanitizer every morning so it stays spotless. It's deranged.

"Put the bird on the table, Camellia," she said. "Did you finish this morning's worksheet?"

I plopped down on a white wicker stool, fished out three sheets of folded paper from my back pocket, and passed the top one to her. "The Dietary Habits of Baby Rocs—regurgitation, mostly."

Her sharp eyes scanned the page. "Passable. And the Spell for Self-Defense? Have you made *any* progress?"

The question I had been dreading. I unfolded the second sheet from my pocket while the witch studied me.

Because here's the thing: trying to learn spells is The Worst.

In the first place, spells look like the most insane math problems you've ever seen. Witches are notoriously paranoid, so every spell starts with a list of ingredients (some of which aren't even used) and then has directions like this:

Step 1: Combine the 3rd and 4th ingredients at a 2:3 ratio so the amount is double the size of the ingredient that contains a human sensory organ.

In this case, the ingredient that contained a human sensory organ was pear. P-*ear*.

Har de har har.

That was the only part I'd managed to figure out, and I've been carrying around this study sheet for four months now.

The witch looks at these horrible things and just understands them, but then again, she's a witch. Which brings me to reason two why I hate this.

I'm *not* a witch.

Maybe I have to live with her, but I'm never going to be like her. There was no way I could actually work this spell, so Sarmine's trying to make me solve it was basically a new way to drive me nuts.

"Well, it's going," I said finally. "Say, what are you going to do with that bird? You aren't going to hurt him, are you?"

The witch looked contemptuously down her sharp nose at me. "Of course not. This is merely another anti-arthritis spell, which will probably work just as well as the last forty-seven I've tried." She drew out a tiny down feather from the white leather fanny pack she wore even in bed, clipped a paperclip on the end, and held it out to me. "Please place this feather in the cage." She picked up her brushed-aluminum wand from the bedside table.

"Isn't this a phoenix feather?" I asked as I obeyed. "I thought you couldn't work magic on those."

"But I can on a paperclip," she said. She touched her wand to a pinch of cayenne pepper from her fanny pack, flicked it at the cage, and the paperclipped feather rose in the air. It stayed there, hovering.

I tried to remember what some long-ago study sheet had said about phoenix feathers. Very potent, I thought. Had a habit of doing something unexpected, like—

The feather burst into flame.

The goldfinch shot to the ceiling of the cage, startled.

"Watch out!" I said.

The paperclipped feather levitated and began chasing the finch. The finch cheeped and darted. The flaming feather maneuvered until it was chasing the bird in tight clockwise circles.

"You said you weren't going to hurt it," I shouted, moving toward the cage.

"Back away," said the witch, leveling her wand at me. "I need sixty-three rotations of finch flight to work my spell."

I knew what damage the wand could do. The witch was fond of casting punishments on me whenever I didn't live up to her bizarre standards of True Witchery. Like once I refused to hold the neighbor's cat so she could permanently mute its meow, and she turned me into fifteen hundred worms and made me compost the garden.

But the finch was frightened. A fluff of feather fell and was ashed by the fire. Another step toward the cage . . .

The witch pulled a pinch of something from her pack and dipped her wand in it. "Pins and needles," she said.

"Pardon?"

"If at any time you start to disobey me today, random body parts will fall asleep."

"Oh, really?" I said politely. "How will the spell know?" One foot sneaked closer to the cage, down where the witch couldn't see.

"Trust me, it'll know," Sarmine said, and she flicked the wand at me, just as I took another step.

My foot went completely numb and I stumbled. "Gah!" I said, shaking it to get the blood flowing again. "Why are you so awf—?" I started to say, but then I saw her reach for her pouch and I instead finished, "er, so *awesome* at True Witchery? It's really amazing. It's taken me all this time to figure out just one ingredient in the self-defense spell."

The wand lowered. Sarmine eyed me. "Which one did you figure out?"

"Pear." I didn't say it very confidently, but I said it.

She considered me. I thought a smile flickered over her angular face. But the next moment it was gone.

You've just read an excerpt from Seriously Wicked.

ABOUT THE AUTHOR

Tina Connolly lives with her family in Portland, Oregon, in a house that came with a dragon in the basement and blackberry vines in the attic. Her stories have appeared all over, including in *Strange Horizons, Lightspeed*, and *Beneath Ceaseless Skies*. She is a frequent reader for Podcastle, and narrates the Parsec-winning flash fiction podcast Toasted Cake. In the summer she works as a face painter, which means a glitter-filled house is an occupational hazard.

Imprint: Tor Teen
Print ISBN: 0765375168
Print price: $17.99
eBook ISBN: 1466880740
eBook price: $9.99
Publication date: 5/5/15
Publicity contact: Desirae Friesen, Desirae.friesen@tor.com
Rights contact: Ginger Clark, gc@cbltd.com
Editor: Melissa Frain
Agent: Ginger Clark
Agency: Curtis Brown Ltd

Promotional information:
- National advertising targeting science fiction/fantasy and young adult audiences, librarians and educators
- Promotion at consumer fan conventions
- Select author appearances
- Online publicity campaign
- Educational marketing to include extensive galley distribution, YA Galley Outreach, Book Buzz title, submissions to major awards
- Digital promotion on Fac
- EBOOK, Tumblr,Twitter, and the Tor/Forge blog and in the newsletter; sweepstakes

99 Days

KATIE COTUGNO

SUMMARY

From the author of *How to Love* comes another stunning contemporary novel, about a girl who returns to her hometown for 99 Days—to face the two brothers she loved and left. Day 1: Julia Donnelly eggs my house my first night back in Star Lake, and that's how I know everyone still remembers everything. She has every right to hate me, of course: I broke Patrick Donnelly's heart the night everything happened with his brother, Gabe. Now I'm serving out my summer like a jail sentence: Just ninety-nine days till I can leave for college, and be done. Day 4: A nasty note on my windshield makes it clear Julia isn't finished. I'm expecting a fight when someone taps me on the shoulder, but it's just Gabe, home from college and actually happy to see me. "For what it's worth, Molly Barlow," he says, "I'm really glad you're back." Day 12: Gabe wouldn't quit till he got me to come to this party, and I'm surprised to find I'm actually having fun. I think he's about to kiss me—and that's when I see Patrick. My Patrick, who's supposed to be clear across the country. My Patrick, who's never going to forgive me. Eighty-seven days of summer to go, and history is repeating itself. The last thing I want is to come between the Donnelly brothers again . . . but the truth is, the Donnellys stole my heart a long time ago.

EXCERPT

Day One

Julia Donnelly eggs my house the first night I'm back in Star Lake, and that's how I know everyone still remembers everything.

"Quite the welcome wagon," my mom says, coming outside to stand on the lawn beside me and survey the runny yellow damage to her lopsided lilac Victorian. There are yolks smeared down all the windows. There are eggshells in the shrubs. Just past ten in the morning and it's already starting to smell rotten, sulfurous and baking in the early summer sun. "They must have gone to Costco to get all those eggs."

"Can you not?" My heart is pounding. I'd forgotten this, or tried to, what it was like before I ran away from here a year ago: Julia's reign of holy terror, designed with ruthless precision to bring me to justice for all my various capital crimes. The bottoms of my feet are clammy inside my lace-up boots. I glance over my shoulder at the sleepy street beyond the long, windy driveway, half-expecting to see her cruising by in her family's ancient Bronco, admiring her handiwork. "Where's the hose?"

"Oh, leave it." My mom, of course, is completely unbothered, the toss of her curly blonde head designed to let me know I'm overreacting. Nothing is a big deal when it comes to my mother: The President of the United States could egg her house, her house itself could *burn down*, and it would turn into not a big deal. *It's a good story,* she used to say whenever I'd come to her with some little-kid unfairness to report, no recess or getting picked last for basketball. *Remember this for later, Molly. It'll make a good story someday.* It never occurred to me to ask which one of us would be doing the telling. "I'll call Alex to come clean it up this afternoon."

"Are you kidding?" I say shrilly. My face feels red and blotchy and all I want to do is make myself as small as humanly possible--the size of a dust mote, the size of a speck--but there's no way I'm letting my mom's handyman spray a half-cooked omelet off the front of the house just because everyone in this town thinks I'm a slut and wants to remind me. "I said where's the *hose*, Mom?"

"Watch the tone, please, Molly." My mom shakes her head resolutely. Somewhere under the egg and the garden I can smell her, the lavender-sandalwood perfume she's worn since I was a baby. She hasn't changed at all since I left here: the silver rings on every one of her fingers, her tissue-thin black cardigan and her ripped jeans. When I was little I thought my mom was the most beautiful woman in the world. Whenever she'd go on tour, reading from her fat novels in bookstores in New York City and Chicago and LA, I used to lie on my stomach in the Donnellys' living room and look at the author photos on the backs of all her books. "Don't you blame me. I'm not the one who did this to you."

I turn on her then, standing on the grass in this place I never wanted to come back to, not in a hundred million years. "Who would you like me to *blame*, then?" I demand. For a second I let myself remember it, the cold sick feeling of seeing the article in *People* for the first time in April of junior year, along with the grossest, juiciest scenes from the novel and a glossy picture of my mom leaning against her desk: *Diana Barlow's latest novel,* Driftwood, *was based on her daughter's complicated relationship with two local boys.* The knowing in my ribs and stomach and spine that now everyone else would know, too. "Who?"

For a second my mom looks completely exhausted, older than I ever think of her as being--glamorous or not, she was almost forty when she adopted me, is close to sixty now. Then she blinks and it's gone. "Molly—"

"Look, don't." I hold up a hand to stop her, wanting so, so badly not to talk about it. To be anywhere other than here. Ninety-nine days between now and the first day of freshman orientation in Boston, I remind myself, trying to take a deep breath and not give in to the overwhelming urge to bolt for the nearest bus station as fast as my two legs can carry me—not as fast, admittedly, as they might have a year ago. Ninety-nine days, and I can leave for college and be done.

My mom stands in the yard and looks at me: She's barefoot like always, dark nails and a tattoo of a rose on her ankle like a cross between Carole King and the first lady of a motorcycle gang. *It'll make a great story some-day.* She *said* that, she *told* me what was going to happen, so really there's no earthly reason to still be so baffled after all this time that I told her the worst, most secret, most important thing in my life—and she wrote a bestselling book about it.

"The hose is in the shed," she finally says.

"Thank you." I swallow down the phlegmy thickness in my throat and head for the backyard, squirming against the sour, panicky sweat I can feel gathered at the base of my backbone. I wait until I'm hidden in the blue-gray shade of the house before I let myself cry.

Day Two

I spend the next day holed up in my bedroom with the blinds closed, eating Red Vines and watching weird Netflix documentaries on my laptop, hiding out like a wounded fugitive in the last third of a Clint Eastwood movie. Vita, my mom's ornery old tabby, wanders in and out as she likes. Everything up here is the same as I left it: blue and white striped wallpaper, the cheerful yellow rug, the fluffy gray duvet on the bed. The *Golly, Molly* artwork a designer friend of my mom's did when I was a baby hanging above the desk, right next to a bulletin board holding my track meet schedule from junior year and a photo of me at the Donnellys' farmhouse with Julia and Patrick and Gabe, my mouth wide open mid-laugh. Even my hairbrush is still sitting on the dresser, the one I forgot to take with me in my mad dash out of Star Lake after the *People* article, like it was just waiting for me to come crawling all the way back here with a head full of knots.

It's the photo I keep catching myself looking at, though, like there's some kind of karmic magnet attached to the back of it drawing my attention from clear across the room. Finally I haul myself out of bed and pull it down to examine more closely: it's from their family party the summer after freshman year, when Patrick and I had only been dating for a couple of months. The four of us are sitting sprawled on the ratty old couch in the barn behind the farmhouse, me and all three Donnellys, Julia in the middle of saying something snarky and Patrick with his arm hooked tight around my waist. Gabe's looking right at me, although I never actually noticed that until after everything happened. Just holding the stupid picture feels like pressing on a bruise.

Patrick's not even home this summer, I know from creeping him on Facebook. He's doing some volunteer program in Colorado, clearing brush and learning to fight forest fires just like he always dreamed of doing when we were little and running around in the woods behind his parents' house. There's no chance of even bumping into him around town.

Probably there's no good reason to feel disappointed about that.

I slap the photo facedown on the desktop and climb back under the covers, pushing Vita onto the carpet— this room has been hers and the dog's in my absence, the sticky layer of pet hair has made that much abundantly clear. When I was a kid, living up here made me feel like a princess, tucked in the third-floor turret of my mom's old haunted house. Now, barely a week after high school graduation, it makes me feel like one again--trapped in a magical tower, with no place in the whole world to go.

I dig the last Red Vine out of the cellophane package just as Vita hops right back up onto the pillow beside me. "Get out, Vita," I order, pushing her gently off again and rolling my eyes at the haughty flick of her feline tail as she stalks out the door, fully expecting her to turn up again almost immediately.

Day Three

Vita doesn't.

Day Four

Imogen doesn't, either. When I was staring down my summer-long sentence in Star Lake, the idea of seeing her again was the only thing that made it feel at all bearable, but so far my *hey I'm back* and *let's hang out* texts have gone resolutely unanswered. Could be she hates me, too. Imogen and I have been friends since first grade and she stuck by me pretty hard at the end of junior year, sitting beside me in the cafeteria at school even as everyone else at our lunch table mysteriously disappeared and the whispers turned into something way, way worse. Still, the truth is I didn't exactly give her a heads up before I left Star Lake to do my senior year at Bristol—an all-girls boarding school plunked like a missile silo in the middle of the desert outside Tempe, Arizona.

Absconded under the cover of darkness, more like.

By Tuesday it's been a full ninety-six hours of minimal human contact, though, so when my mom knocks hard on the bedroom door to let me know her cleaning lady is coming, I pull some clean shorts out of the pile of detritus already accumulated on my floor. My t-shirts and underwear are still in my giant duffel--I'll have to unpack at some point, probably, although the truth is I'd almost rather live out of a suitcase for three months. My sneakers are tucked underneath the desk chair, I notice while I'm crouched down there, the laces still tied from the last time I slipped them off—the day the article came out, I remember suddenly, like I thought I could somehow outrun a national publication. I sprinted as hard and as fast as I could manage.

I threw up on the dusty side of the road.

Woof. I do my best to shake off the memory, grabbing the photo of me and the Donnellys--still facedown on the desk where I left it the other night--and shoving it into the back of the drawer in my nightstand. Then I lace my boots up and take my neglected old Passat into Star Lake proper.

It's cool enough to open the windows, and even through the pine trees lining the sides of Route 4 I can smell the slightly mildewy scent of the lake as I head for the short stretch of civilization that makes up downtown: Main Street is small and rumpled, all diners and dingy grocery stores, a roller rink that hasn't been open since roughly 1982. That's about the last time this place was a destination, as far as I've ever been able to tell--the lakefront plus the endless green stretch of the Catskill mountains was a big vacation spot in the sixties and seventies, but ever since I can remember Star Lake has had the air of something that used to be but isn't anymore, like you fell into your grandparents' honeymoon by mistake.

I speed up as I bypass the Donnellys' pizza shop, slouching low in my seat like a gangbanger until I pull up in front of French Roast, the coffee shop where Imogen's worked since we were freshmen. I open the door to the smell of freshly-ground beans and the sound of some moody girl singer on the radio. The shop is mostly empty, a late morning lull. Imogen's standing behind the counter, midnight dark hair hanging in her eyes, and when she looks up at the jangle of the bells a look of guilty, awkward panic flashes across her pretty face in the moment before she can quell it.

"Oh my God," she says once she's recovered, coming around the counter and hugging me fast and antiseptic, then holding me back at arm's length like a great-aunt having a look at how much I've grown. Literally, in my case—I've put on fifteen pounds easy since I left for Arizona--and even though she'd never say anything about it, I can feel her taking it in. "You're here!"

"I am," I agree, my voice sounding weird and false. She's wearing a gauzy sundress under her French Roast apron, a splotch of deep blue on the side of her hand like she was up late sketching one of the pen-and-ink portraits she's been doing since we were little kids. Every year on her birthday I buy her a fresh set of markers, the fancy kind from the art supply store. When I was in Tempe I went online and had them shipped. "Did you get my texts?"

Imogen does something between a nod and a head-shake, non-committal. "Yeah, my phone's been really weird lately?" she says, voice coming up at the end like she's unsure. She shrugs then, always oddly graceful even though she's been five-eleven since we were in middle school. Somehow she never got teased. "It eats things, I need a new one. Come on, let me get you coffee." She heads back around the counter, past the rack of mugs they give people who plan to hang out on one of the sagging couches, and hands me a paper to-go cup. I'm not sure if it's a message or not. She waves me off when I try to pay.

"Thanks," I tell her, smiling a little bit helplessly. I'm not used to making small talk with her. "So hey, RISD, huh?" I try—I saw on Instagram that that's where she's headed in the fall, a selfie of her smiling hugely in a Rhode Island School of Design sweatshirt. As the words come out of my mouth I realize how totally bizarre it is that *that's* how I found out. We told each other everything—well, *almost* everything—once upon a time. "We'll be neighbors in the fall, Providence and Boston."

"Oh, yeah," Imogen says, sounding distracted. "I think it's like an hour though, right?"

"Yeah, but an hour's not that long," I reply uncertainly. It feels like there's a river between us, and I don't know how to build a bridge. "Look, Imogen--" I start, then break off awkwardly. I want to apologize for falling off the face of the earth the way I did--want to tell her about my mom and about Julia, that I'm here for ninety-five more days and I'm terrified and I need all the allies I can get. I want to tell Imogen everything, but before I can get another word out I'm interrupted by the telltale chime of a text message dinging out from inside the pocket of her apron.

So much for a phone that eats things. Imogen blushes a deep sunburned red.

I take a deep breath. "Okay," I say again, pushing my wild, wavy brown hair behind my ears just as the front door opens and a whole gaggle of women in yoga gear come crowding into the shop, jabbering eagerly for their half-caf non-fat whatevers.

"I'll see you around, okay?" I ask, shrugging a little. Imogen nods and waves goodbye.

I head back out to where my car's parked at the curb, pointedly ignoring the huge *Local Author!* display in the window of Star Lake's one tiny bookstore across the street--a million paperback copies of *Driftwood* available for the low low price of $6.99 plus my dignity. I'm devoting so much attention to ignoring it, in fact, that I don't notice the note tucked under my wipers until the very last second, Julia's pink-marker scrawl across the back of a Chinese takeout menu:

dirty slut

The panic is cold and wet and skittering in the second before it's replaced by the hot rush of shame; my stomach lurches. I reach out and snatch the menu off the windshield, the paper going limp and clammy inside my damp, embarrassed fist.

Sure enough, there it is, idling at the stoplight at the end of the block: the Donnellys' late-nineties Bronco, big and olive and dented where Patrick backed it into a mailbox in the fall of our sophomore year. It's the same one all three of them learned to drive on, the one we all used to pile into so that Gabe could ferry us to school when we were freshman. Julia's raven hair glints in the sun as the light turns green and she speeds away.

I force myself to take three deep breaths before I ball up the menu and toss it onto the passenger seat of my car, then two more before I pull out into traffic. I grip the wheel tight so my hands will stop shaking. Julia was my friend first, before I ever met either one of her brothers. Maybe it makes sense that she's the one who hates me most. I remember running into her here not long after the article came out, how she turned and saw me standing there with my latte, the unadulterated loathing painted all over her face.

"Why the fuck do I see you everywhere, Molly?" she demanded, and she sounded so incredibly frustrated--like she really wanted to know so we could solve this, so it wouldn't keep happening over and over again. "For the love of God, why won't you just go away?"

I went home and called Bristol that same afternoon.

There's nowhere for me to go now, though, not really: all I want is to floor it home and bury myself under the covers with a documentary about the deep ocean or something, but I make myself stop at the gas station to fill my empty tank and pick up more Red Vines, just like I'd planned to.

I can't spend my whole summer like this.

Can I?

I'm just fitting my credit card into the pump when a big hand lands square on my shoulder. "Get the fuck out of here," a deep voice says. I whirl around, heart thrumming and ready for a fight, before I realize it's an exclamation and not an order.

Before I realize it's coming from *Gabe*.

"You're *home*?" he asks incredulously, his tan face breaking into a wide, easy grin. He's wearing frayed khaki shorts and aviators and a t-shirt from Notre Dame, and he looks happier to see me than anyone has since I got here.

I can't help it: I burst into tears.

Gabe doesn't blink. "Hey, hey," he says easily, getting his arms around me and squeezing. He smells like farmer's market bar soap and clothes dried on the line. "Molly Barlow, why you crying?"

"I'm not," I protest, even as I blatantly get snot all over the front of his t-shirt. I pull back and wipe my eyes, shaking my head. "Oh my God, I'm not, I'm sorry. That's embarrassing. Hi."

Gabe keeps smiling, even if he does look a little surprised. "Hey," he says, reaching out and swiping at my cheek with the heel of his hand. "So, you know, welcome back, how have you been, I see you're enjoying your return to the warm bosom of Star Lake."

"Uh-huh." I sniffle once and pull it together, mostly--God, I didn't realize I was so hard up for a friendly face, it's ridiculous. Or, okay, I *did*, but I didn't think I'd lose it quite so hard at the sight of one. "It's been awesome." I reach into the open window of the Passat and hand him the crumpled up takeout menu. "For example, here is my homecoming card from your sister."

Gabe smoothes it out and looks at it, then nods. "Weird," he says, calm as the surface of the lake in the middle of the night. "She put the same one on my car this morning."

My eyes widen. "Really?"

"No," Gabe says, grinning when I make a face. Then his eyes go dark.

"Seriously though, are you okay? That's, like. Pretty fucked up and horrifying of her, actually."

I sigh and roll my eyes—at myself or at the situation, at the gut-wrenching absurdity of the mess I made. "It's—whatever," I tell him, trying to sound cool or above it or something. "I'm fine. It is what it is."

"It feels unfair though, right?" Gabe says. "I mean, if you're a dirty slut, then I'm a dirty slut."

I laugh, I can't help it, even though it feels colossally weird to hear him say it out loud. We never talked about it once after it happened, not even when the book—and the article--came out and the world came crashing down around my ears. Could be enough time has passed that it doesn't feel like a big deal to him anymore, although apparently he's the only one. God knows it still feels like a big deal to me. "You definitely are," I agree, then watch as he balls up the menu and tosses it over his shoulder, missing the trashcan next to the pump by a distance of roughly seven feet. "That's littering," I tell him, smirking a little.

"Add it to the list," Gabe says, apparently unconcerned about this or any other lapses in good citizenship. He was student council president, when he was a senior. Patrick and Julia and I hung all his campaign posters at school. "Look, people are assholes. My sister is an asshole. And my brother--" he breaks off, shrugging. His shaggy brown hair curls down over his ears, a lighter honey-molasses color than his brother and sister's. Patrick's hair is almost black. "Well, my brother is my brother, but anyway he's not here. What are *you* doing, are you working, what?"

"I—nothing, yet," I confess, feeling suddenly embarrassed at how reclusive I've been, humiliated that there's virtually nobody here who wants to see me. Gabe's had a million friends as long as I've known him. "Hiding, mostly."

Gabe nods at that. But then: "Think you'll be hiding tomorrow, too?"

I remember once, when I was ten or eleven, that I stepped on a piece of glass down by the lake and Gabe carried me all the way home piggyback. I remember that we lied to Patrick for an entire year. My whole face has that clogged, bloated post-cry feeling, like there's something made of cotton shoved up into my brain. "I don't know," I say eventually, cautious, intrigued in spite of myself—maybe it's just the constant ache of loneliness but running into Gabe makes me feel like something's about to happen, a bend in a dusty road. "Probably. Why?"

Gabe grins down at me like a master of ceremonies, like someone who suspects I need a little anticipation in my life and wants to deliver. "Pick you up at eight," is all he says.

You've just read an excerpt from 99 Days.

ABOUT THE AUTHOR

Katie Cotugno went to Catholic school for thirteen years which makes her, as an adult, both extremely superstitious and prone to crushes on boys wearing blazers. She is a 2011 Pushcart Prize nominee whose work has appeared in *The Mississippi Review, The Apalachee Review, The Iowa Review* and *Argestes*, among other literary magazines, as well as on Nerve.com. She lives in Boston with her husband, Tom. She is also the author of *How to Love*. You can visit Katie online at www.katiecotugno.com.

Imprint: Balzer + Bray
Print ISBN: 9780062216380
Print price: $17.99
eBook ISBN: 9780062216403
eBook price: $13.99
Publication date: 4/1/15
Publicity contact: Caroline Sun caroline.sun@harpercollins.com
Rights contact: Allison Hellegers AllisonH@rightspeople.com
Editor: Alessandra Balzer
Agent: Sara Shandler and Joelle Hobeika
Agency: Alloy Entertainment
Promotional information:
- Online Goodreads consumer advertising campaign and galley give-away promotion
- RT Book Reviews Magazine group print ad
- Alloy cover reveal
- Summer 2015 Epic Reads teen group promotion, advertising, and tour
- "Epic Reads Shames Shaming" week-long promotion
- Epic Reads consumer sweepstakes to win themed prize pack
- Epic Reads author video content

SARAH

DESSEN

SAINT
ANYTHING

SUMMARY

Peyton, Sydney's charismatic older brother, has always been the star of the family, receiving the lion's share of their parents' attention and—lately—concern. When Peyton's increasingly reckless behavior culminates in an accident, a drunk driving conviction, and a jail sentence, Sydney is cast adrift, searching for her place in the family and the world. When everyone else is so worried about Peyton, is she the only one concerned about the victim of the accident? Enter the Chathams, a warm, chaotic family who run a pizza parlor, play bluegrass on weekends, and pitch in to care for their mother, who has multiple sclerosis. Here Sydney experiences unquestioning acceptance. And here she meets Mac, gentle, watchful, and protective, who makes Sydney feel seen, really seen, for the first time.

EXCERPT

Chapter One

When I walked in my house, the first thing I saw were the candles. They were the ones my mom only pulled out for special occasions, like Christmas and Thanksgiving, kept stored in the sideboard behind the liquor. If you didn't know this, you'd have to search for them. They sat on the table, not yet lit.

"Hey there," Ames said, appearing in the kitchen doorway. He was wearing a button-down shirt, jeans, and sneakers, and holding one of our wooden spoons. "How was school?"

It was all just so *weird*, the juxtaposition of this question, which my mom asked me every day, and the candles, which indicated something almost romantic.

"Where's Marla?" I asked. It wasn't like she had a presence that filled a room or anything, but I could just feel there were only two of us there.

"Sick," he replied. "Stomach flu. Poor kid. Sucks, right?"

By the way he turned, walking back into the kitchen, I could tell he expected me to follow him. But I stayed where I was, feeling my face grow flushed. Marla wasn't coming? At all?

"You didn't have to cook," I said.

"I know. But you haven't lived until you've had my spaghetti with meat sauce. I'd be doing you a disservice not letting you experience it."

"I'm actually not that hungry," I said.

At this, he turned, a flicker of irritation on his face. As quickly as it appeared, though, it was gone. "Just have a taste, then. You won't regret it, I promise."

Everywhere I turned, I was stuck. I wasn't prone to panicking, but suddenly I could feel my heart beating. "I'm, um, going to go put my stuff away."

"Okay," he said. "Don't be too long. I want to catch up. It's been a while."

I took the stairs two at a time, like someone was chasing me, then ducked into my room, shutting the door behind me. I sat down on my bed, pulling out my phone, and tried to think. A moment later, I heard music drifting upstairs, and somehow, I knew he'd now lit the candles. That was when I looked up a number and dialed it.

A man answered. "Seaside Pizza. Can you hold?"

I'd been expecting Layla. Now I didn't know what to do. "Yes."

A click, and then silence. I thought about hanging up, but before I could, he was back. "Thanks for holding. Can I help you?"

Shit. "Um . . . I want to place a delivery order?"

I could hear talking in the background, but none were a girl's voice. "Go ahead."

"Large half pepperoni, half deluxe," I said.

"Anything else?"

"No."

"Address?"

I took a breath. "It's 4102 Incline—"

There was a clanging noise in the background. "Sorry, can you hold another minute?"

"Sure," I said. Downstairs, the song had changed, and I could smell garlic, wafting up under my closed door.

"Sorry about that," a voice said on the other end of the line. It was a girl. Oh, my God. "So that's a half pepperoni, half deluxe, large? What's the name?"

"Layla?"

A pause. "Yeah?"

"It's Sydney."

"Oh, hey!" She sounded so pleased to hear my voice that I almost burst into tears. "What's up? Regretting you only had one slice this afternoon?"

"Do you want to spend the night tonight?"

I literally blurted this; I doubted she'd even made it out. But again, she surprised me. "Sure. Let me just ask."

There was a clank as she put the phone down. As I sat there, listening to the register beep and some other muffled conversation, I realized I was holding my breath. When she came back, I still didn't exhale.

"I'm in," she said cheerfully. "Mac can bring me with the pizza. In, like, twenty minutes or so?"

"Great," I said, entirely too enthusiastically. "Thank you."

"Sure. Just give me your address and a phone number, okay?"

I did, and then we hung up. I went into the bathroom and washed my face, telling myself I could handle anything for twenty minutes. Then I went downstairs.

Ames was at the stove when I walked in, his back to me. "Ready to eat? I've got the table set."

I glanced into the dining room: sure enough, the candles were lit, two plates laid out with silverware and folded paper napkins. "I actually, um, have a friend coming over. She's bringing a pizza."

He didn't say anything for a moment. Then he turned around to face me. "I told you I was cooking."

"I know, but—"

"Your mom didn't mention anything to me about a friend visiting," he told me.

She also thought Marla was going to be here, I thought.

"It's not very polite, Sydney, to make other plans when a person has gone out of their way to do something for you."

I didn't ask you to do anything. "I'm sorry . . . I guess signals got crossed."

He looked at me for a long moment, not even trying to hide his irritation. Then, slowly, he turned back around. "You can at least have a taste. Since I've gone to all this trouble."

"Okay," I said. It was weird to see an adult pout. "Sure."

At the table, he served us both, then picked up his glass of cola, holding it up. "To good friends," he said.

I clinked my drink against his, then took an obligatory sip as he watched me over the rim of his glass. I glanced at my watch. It had been ten minutes.

"So I rented a couple of movies," he said, twirling some noodles around his fork. "Thought we'd settle in on the couch, have some popcorn. Hope you're a fan of heavy butter. Or else we can't be buds anymore."

If only it were that easy. "Yeah. Sure."

He smiled at me then, in a forgiving way. Like I'd earned another chance or something. Everything was wrong here.

Twelve minutes.

"This is good," I said, forcing myself to try the pasta. "Thanks for cooking."

"Of course." He smiled, clearly pleased. "It's the least I can do, since you're stuck with me all weekend. Speaking of which, what are you up to to-morrow? I'm heading to see Peyton in the morning, but I'll be free all afternoon. I was thinking we could hit a movie or go bowling, then have dinner out somewhere."

"I actually have a school thing," I said. "It's, um, kind of mandatory."

A pause. "On the weekend?"

I nodded. "Community service project. I'll be gone most of the day."

"Huh." One word, so many connotations. "Well, we'll see."

My stomach tightened, and for a beat or two, I was sure the few bites I'd managed to get down were going to rejoin us. But then, thank God— thank everything in the world—the doorbell rang.

"I'll get it," I said, leaping up and tossing my napkin onto my seat. Starting for the door, I hit the edge of the table with my hip, causing something to clank loudly. I didn't slow down to see what it was.

In the foyer, I flipped the dead bolt, then yanked the door open hard, clearly startling Layla, who was standing right in front of it, holding a pizza box. I could see Mac in the truck, parked in the driveway.

"Hi," I said, breathless. "I'm so glad you're here."

"Well, it's nice to get such an enthusiastic welcome." She looked up at the tall windows on either side of the door, eyes widening. "Your house is gorgeous."

"Thanks. Come in. I'll, um, get the money for the pizza."

"Oh, don't worry about it," she said. "It's on the—"

She stopped talking suddenly, staring over my shoulder. Instantly, her expression went from open and friendly to guarded. Before I even glanced behind me, I knew Ames had appeared.

"This is the friend?" he said when I did look his way.

"Layla," I told him. To her, I added, "Come on in."

She didn't move. Instead, she turned her head toward Mac. I couldn't make out her expression, but a second later, he was getting out of the truck. When he joined her on the steps, she finally stepped inside.

"Ames Bentley," Ames said to them, extending a hand. "Close friend of the family."

"This is Mac," I said. They shook. I took the pizza from Layla. "Come on in the kitchen."

We went, with me leading, Ames right behind, and the Chathams bringing up the rear. Right away, I saw Layla surveying the scene in the dining room. When she saw the candles, she looked right at me.

"Pretty fancy," she said. "What's going on?"

"Just showing off my cooking skills for Sydney," Ames said. "Thought I'd wow her with my sauce, but she went and ordered a pizza. She's a heartbreaker, this one."

"Where's your mom, again?" Layla asked me, ignoring this.

"She and my dad are at a conference."

"All weekend?"

"Now, don't get any ideas about parties," Ames said, holding up his hands. "That's what I'm here to prevent."

"I wasn't going to have a party," I said quietly.

"Sure." He grinned, then looked at Mac. "You guys want some dinner? Or a drink? Nonalcoholic only. House rules."

"No, thanks," Mac said, just as his phone beeped. He pulled it out, glancing at the screen, then said to Layla, "Another order. I should get going."

"Lucky me," Ames said. "Spending the evening with two lovely ladies."

In response, Mac just looked at him, his expression flat and unsmiling. After a beat, he said to Layla, "You left your stuff in the truck."

"Oh," she said. "Right. I'll come out with you."

He turned to walk to the door. As she fell in behind him, she looked at me, clearly wanting me to follow. Before I could, I felt Ames put his hand on my shoulder. "Little help cleaning up, Sydney?"

I followed him back into the dining room, where he gathered up his plate. Lowering his voice, he said, "When your mom calls, you know I have to tell her about this."

"I'm not doing anything wrong," I said.

"She didn't expect you to have company, though." I looked at him, his head bent as he picked up his napkin, and felt a surge of anger bolt through me. Like my mom *was* anticipating what he'd intended for that evening. Turning toward the kitchen, he added, "Don't worry, I'll spin it the best I can. You just owe me."

To this, I said nothing, instead just standing there as, slowly, Mac's truck began backing down my driveway. When he reached the road, his headlights swept across the window, catching me in their sudden glow. He sat there for a beat. Another. Then, slowly, he drove away.

You've just read an excerpt from Saint Anything.

ABOUT THE AUTHOR

Sarah Dessen is one of the most popular writers for young adults. She is the #1 *New York Times* bestselling author of many novels, which have received numerous awards and rave reviews, and have sold more than seven million copies. She lives in Chapel Hill, North Carolina, with her husband, Jay, and their daughter, Sasha Clementine. Visit her online at www.sarahdessen.com.

Imprint: Viking

Print ISBN: 9780451474704

Print price: $19.99

eBook ISBN: 9780698191419

eBook price: $10.99

Publication date: 5/5/15

Editor: Regina Hayes

Agent: Leigh Feldman

Agency: Writers House

Promotional information:
- 9-copy floor display with SIGNED copies
- Pre-order easel (ships in April)
- National author tour
- Extensive blogger outreach
- National consumer advertising campaign including print, radio, subway, and online
- Promotion at Romantic Times (May 2015) and Fall consumer book festivals
- National media campaign
- Extensive online promotion and social media outreach
- Promotion and galley distribution at all national school and library conferences

CAST OUT BY HIS PARENTS.

RAISED BY CROWS.

HUNTED BY DARKNESS.

FERALS

Jacob Grey

SUMMARY

For years, Caw has lived on the streets of Blackstone City with only three crows for company. Caw has never known why he can understand the crows. But when he rescues a girl named Lydia from a vicious attack, he discovers others like him: ferals who can speak to certain animals. And some of them are dangerous. Now, the most sinister feral of all—the Spinning Man—is on the move again. To save his city, Caw must quickly master abilities he never knew he had... and prepare to defeat a darkness he never could have imagined.

EXCERPT

Chapter One

The night belonged to him. He wore its shadows, tasted its scents. He savored its sounds and silences. Caw leaped from roof to roof, a boy witnessed only by the white eye of the moon and the three crows that soared in the dark sky above him.

Blackstone sprawled like a bacterial growth on all sides. Caw took in flashes of the city—skyscrapers rising to the east, and to the west, the endless slanting roofs of the poorer districts and the smoking chimneys of the industrial quarter. In the north loomed abandoned tenements. The river Blackwater was somewhere to the south, a roiling sludge carrying filth away from the city but never making it any cleaner. Caw could smell its fetid stench.

He skidded up against the dirty glass panel of a skylight. Laying his hands softly on the glass, Caw peered into its soft glow. A hunched janitor wheeled a mop and bucket through the hallway below, lost in his own world. He didn't look up. They never did.

Caw took off again, startling a fat pigeon and skipping around an ancient billboard, trusting his crows to follow. Two of the birds were barely visible—flitting shadows black as tar. The third was white, his pale feathers making him glow like a ghost in the darkness.

I'm starving, muttered Screech, the smallest of the crows. His voice was a reedy squawk.

You're always starving, said Glum, his wing beats slow and steady. *The young are so greedy.*

Caw smiled. To anyone else, the crows' voices would merely sound like the cries of regular birds. But Caw heard more. Much more.

I'm still growing! said Screech, flapping indignantly.

Shame your brain isn't, Glum cackled.

Milky, the blind old white crow, drifted above them. As usual, he said nothing at all.

Caw slowed to gather his breath, letting the cool air fill his lungs. He took in the sounds of night—the swish of a car across slick tarmac, the thump of distant music. Farther away, a siren and a man shouting, his words unclear. Whether his voice was raised in anger or happiness, Caw didn't care. Down there was for the regular people of Blackstone. Up here, among the skyline silhouettes . . . it was for him and his crows.

He passed through the warm blast of an air-conditioning vent, then paused, nostrils flaring.

Food. Something salty.

Caw jogged to the edge of the rooftop and peered over. Down below, a door opened onto an alley filled with Dumpsters. It was the back of a twenty-four-hour restaurant. Caw knew they often threw out perfect-ly good food—leftovers, probably, but he wasn't fussy. He let his glance flick into every dark corner. He saw nothing that worried him, but it was always risky, at ground level. Their place, not his.

Glum landed next to Caw and cocked his head. His stubby beak glinted gold, reflecting a streetlight. *You think it's safe?* he asked.

A sudden motion drew Caw's gaze; a rat, rooting in garbage bags below. It lifted its head and eyed him without fear. "I think so," Caw said. "Stay sharp."

He knew they didn't need the warning. After years of scavenging togeth-er, he could trust them better than he could himself.

Caw swung a leg over the lip of the roof and landed softly on the platform of the fire escape. Screech swooped down and perched on the side of a bin, while Glum glided to the corner of the roof, overlooking the main street. Milky dropped onto the fire-escape railing, his talons scratching the metal. All keeping watch.

Caw crept down the steps. He crouched for a moment, eyes on the back door of the restaurant. The smell of food made his stomach rumble violently. *Pizza,* he thought. *Burgers too.*

He fished inside the nearest Dumpster and found a yellow polystyrene box, still warm. He cracked it open. Fries! He shoveled them into his mouth. Greasy, salty, a little burned at the edges. They were good. The acid vinegar caught in his throat, but he didn't care. He hadn't eaten for two days. He swallowed without chewing and almost choked. Then he crammed more down. One fell from his hand and Screech was there in a second, attacking the scrap with his beak.

A hoarse cry from Glum.

Caw flinched and cowered beside the bin, eyes searching the darkness. His heart jolted as four figures filled the end of the alley.

"Hey!" said the tallest. "Get away from our stash!"

Caw scrambled back, holding the box to his chest. Screech took flight, his wings slapping the air.

The figures stepped closer, and an arc of streetlight caught their faces. Boys, perhaps a couple of years older than him. Homeless by the looks of their tattered clothes.

"There's enough," said Caw, nodding toward the Dumpster. He felt awkward, talking to other people. It happened so rarely. "Enough for all of us," he repeated.

"No, there's not," said a boy with two rings in his upper lip. He walked ahead of the others with a shoulder-rolling swagger. "There's only enough for *us*. You've been stealing."

Shall we get them? said Screech.

Caw shook his head. It wasn't worth getting injured over a few fries.

"Don't shake your head at me, you filthy little thief!" said the tall one. "You're a liar!"

"Gross—he stinks, too," said a smaller boy, sneering.

Caw felt his face getting hot. He took a step backward.

"Where do you think you're going?" asked the boy with the lip rings. "Why don't you stay awhile?" He stepped up to Caw and shoved him roughly in the chest.

The sudden attack took Caw by surprise and he fell, landing on his back. The box flew from his hands, and fries spilled over the ground. The boys closed in.

"Now he's throwing them on the ground!"

"You gonna pick them up?"

Caw scrambled to his feet. They had him trapped. "You can have them."

"Too late for that," said the leader. He ran his tongue over his lip rings. "Now you gotta pay. How much money you got?"

Caw turned out his pockets, his heart thumping. "None."

The glint of a blade, emerging from the boy's pocket. "In that case, we'll take your thieving fingers instead."

The boy lunged forward. Caw grabbed the edge of the Dumpster and vaulted up on top of it.

"He's quick, isn't he?" said the boy. "Get him."

The other three surrounded the bin. One swiped at Caw's ankle. Another started to shake the Dumpster. Caw staggered for balance. They were all laughing.

Caw saw a drainpipe ten feet to his left and jumped. But as his fingers caught the metal, the piping broke from the wall with a burst of brick dust. He fell and hit the tarmac on his side, the air exploding from his lungs. Four grinning faces closed in.

"Hold him down!" said the leader.

"Please . . . no . . ." Caw struggled, but the boys sat on his legs and pulled at his arms. He was spread-eagled as the one with the knife loomed over him. "Which will it be, boys?" He pointed the tip of the blade at Caw's hands in turn. "Left or right?"

Caw couldn't see his crows. Fear pumped through his veins.

The boy crouched down, resting his knee on Caw's chest. "Eenie, meenie, miney, mo." The knife's tip danced from side to side.

Watch out, Caw! called Glum. The boys all looked up at the crow's piercing cry. Then a hand reached down from above and gripped the knife wielder by the back of his collar. The boy yelped as he was jerked away from Caw.

There was a cracking sound—skin against skin—and the knife clattered to the ground.

Where'd he come from? said Screech.

Caw sat up. A tall, thin man was holding the boy with the lip rings by the back of his neck. Brown, wiry hair protruded from beneath the man's stained hat. He was wearing several layers of dirty clothing, including an old brown trench coat fastened around his waist with a belt of frayed blue cord. A tufty beard coated his jawline in uneven patches. Caw guessed he was in his midtwenties, and homeless.

"Leave him be," said the man, his voice rasping. In the semidarkness, his mouth was a black hole.

"What's it to you?" said the boy holding Caw's left arm.

The man shoved the boy with the lip rings hard at the Dumpster.

"This guy's crazy!" said the boy holding Caw's legs. "Let's go."

Their leader picked up his knife and brandished it at the homeless man.

"Lucky you're so filthy," he snarled. "Don't want to get my knife dirty. Come on, fellas." The four attackers turned and tore out of the alley.

Caw scrambled to his feet, his breath coming hard. Looking up, he saw his crows perched together on the fire-escape railing, watching silently.

After the gang had rounded the corner, another smaller shape slipped from the alley's darkness to stand close beside the man. It was a boy of about seven or eight, Caw guessed. His narrow face was pale, and his dirty-blond hair stood on end. "Yeah, and don't come back!" he shouted, shaking a fist.

Caw darted toward the fries scattered on the ground. He started dropping them back into the box. No need to waste a good meal. All the while, he felt the gaze of his rescuer and the boy on his back.

When he'd finished, he stuffed the box inside the deep pocket of his coat and hurried to the fire escape.

"Wait," said the man. "Who are you?"

Caw turned to face him but kept his eyes on the ground. "I'm no one."

The man snorted. "Really? So where are your parents, No One?"

Caw shook his head again. He didn't know what else to say.

"You should be careful," said the man.

"I can take care of myself."

"Doesn't look like that to us," said the boy, tilting his chin upward.

Caw heard the crows' claws shifting on the railing above him. The man's eyes flicked up to them and narrowed. His lips turned in the ghost of a smile. "Friends of yours?" he asked.

Time to go home, said Glum.

Caw started up the steel ladder without looking back. He climbed quickly, hand over hand, his nimble feet barely making a sound on the fire escape. When he reached the roof, he took one last glance and saw the man watching him as the young boy rooted in the Dumpster.

"Something bad's coming," called the man. "Something really bad. You get into trouble, talk to the pigeons."

Talk to the pigeons? Caw only talked to crows.

Pigeons! Screech said, as if he'd heard Caw's thought. *You'd get more sense out of a rock!*

Probably off his rocker, said Glum. *A lot of humans are.*

Caw heaved himself onto the roof and set off at a jog. But as he ran, he couldn't shake the man's parting words. He hadn't seemed crazy at all. His face was fierce, his eyes clear. Not like the old drunks who stumbled around the streets or squatted in doorways begging for money.

And, more than that, he had helped Caw. He'd put himself at risk, for no reason.

Caw's crows flew above him, wheeling around buildings and circling back as they made their way to the safety of the nest. Home.

His heart began to slow as the night took him into its dark embrace.

Chapter Two

It's the same dream. The same as always.

He's back at his old house. The bed is so soft he feels like he's lying on a cloud. It's warm too, and he longs to turn over, pull the duvet tight to his chin, and fall back asleep. But he never can. Because the dream isn't just a dream. It's a memory.

Hurried footsteps on the stairs outside his room. They're coming for him.

He swings his legs out, and his toes sink into the thick carpet. His bedroom is in shadow, but he can just make out his toys lining the top of a chest of drawers and a shelf stacked with picture books.

A crack of light appears under his door and he hears his parents' voices, urgent and hushed.

The door handle turns, and they enter. His mother is wearing a black dress, and her cheeks are silver with tears. His father is dressed in brown corduroy trousers and a shirt open at the neck. His forehead is sweaty.

"Please, no . . . ," Caw says.

His mother takes his hand in hers, her palms clammy, and pulls him toward the window.

Caw tries to tug back, but he's young in the dream, and she's too strong for him.

"Don't fight," she says. "Please. It's for the best. I promise."

Caw kicks her in the shins and scratches at her with his nails, but she gathers him close to her body in a grip of iron and bundles him to the window ledge. Terrified, Caw fastens his teeth over her forearm. She doesn't let go, even when his teeth break her skin. His father draws back the curtains, and for a second Caw catches sight of his own face in the black shine of the window—pudgy, wide-eyed, afraid.

The window is flung open, and the cold night air rushes in.

Now his father holds him as well—his parents have an arm and a leg each. Caw bucks and writhes, screaming.

"Hush! Hush!" says his mother. "It's all right."

The end of the nightmare is coming, but knowing that doesn't make it any less terrible. They push and pull him over the ledge, so his legs are dangling, and he sees the ground far below. His father's jaw is taut, brutal. He won't look Caw in the eye. But Caw can see that he's crying too.

"Do it!" says his father, releasing his grip. "Just do it!"

Why? Caw wants to shout. But all that comes out is a child's wailing cry.

"I'm sorry," says his mother. That's when she shoves him out of the window.

For a split second, his stomach turns. But then the crows have him.

They cover his arms and legs, talons digging into his skin and pajamas. A dark cloud that appears out of nowhere, carrying him upward.

His face is filled with feathers and their earthy smell.

He's floating, up and up, carried beneath their black eyes and brittle legs and snapping wings.

He gives his body to the birds and the rhythm of their flight, prepares to wake. . . .

But tonight, he does not.

The crows descend and set him down lightly on the pavement, looping back toward his house along a pale driveway running between tall trees. He sees his parents at his window, now closed. They're hugging, holding each other.

How could they?

Still, he does not wake.

Then Caw sees a figure, a thing, materializing from the darkness of the front garden, taking slow, deliberate strides to the door of the house. It's tall, almost as tall as the doorway itself, and very thin, with spindly limbs too long for its body.

The dream has never continued like this before. This is no longer part of his memory—somehow Caw knows that, deep in his bones.

By some trick, he can see the thing's face, close up. It's a man—but the likes of which he's never seen. He wants to look away, but his eyes are drawn to the pale features, made paler still by the blackness of the man's hair, which sits in jagged spikes over his forehead and one eye. He would be handsome if it weren't for his eyes. They're completely black—all iris, no white.

Caw has no idea who the man is, but he knows that he is more than just bad. The man's slender body draws the darkness to him. He has come here to do harm. Evil. The word comes unbidden. Caw wants to shout, but he is voiceless with fear.

He is desperate to wake, but he does not.

The visitor's lips twist into a smile as he lifts a hand, the fingers like drooping arachnid legs. Caw sees that he's wearing a large golden ring as his fingers enfold the door knocker, like a flower's petals closing. And now the ring is all he sees, and the picture inscribed on its oval surface. A spider carved in sharp lines, eight legs bristling. Its body is a looping single line, with a small curve for the head and a larger one for the body. On its back, a shape that looks like the letter M.

The stranger knocks a single time, then turns his head. He's looking right at Caw. For a moment the crows are gone, and there is nothing in the world but Caw and the stranger. The man's voice whispers softly, his lips barely moving.

"I'm coming for you."

Caw woke up screaming.

Sweat was drying on his forehead, and goose pimples covered his arms. He could see his breath, even under the cover of the tarpaulin that stretched between the branches overhead. As he sat up, the tree creaked and the nest rocked slightly. A spider scuttled away from his hand.

A coincidence. Just a coincidence.

What's up? said Screech, flapping across from the nest's edge to land beside him.

Caw closed his eyes, and the image of the spider ring burned behind his lids.

"Just the dream," he said. "The usual one. Go back to sleep."

Except tonight it *hadn't* been. The stranger—the man at the door—that hadn't really happened. Had it?

We were trying to sleep, said Glum. *But you woke us twitching like a half-eaten worm. Even poor old Milky's up.* Caw could hear the grumpy ruffle of Glum's feathers.

"Sorry," he said. He lay back down, but sleep wouldn't come, not with the dream throwing its fading echoes through his mind. After years of the same nightmare, why had tonight been different?

Caw threw off his blanket and let his eyes adjust to the gloom. The nest was a platform high up in a tree, ten feet across, made of scrap timber and woven branches, with a hatch in the floor he'd made using a sheet of corrugated semitransparent plastic. More branches were knitted together around the nest's edge, with pieces of boarding he'd scavenged from a building site, making a bowl shape with steep sides about three feet tall. His few possessions lay in a battered suitcase he'd found on the banks of the Blackwater several months ago. An old curtain could be pinned across the middle if he wanted privacy from the crows, though Glum never quite got the hint. At the far end, a small hole in the tarpaulin roof offered an entrance and exit for the crows.

It was cold up here, especially in winter, but it was dry.

When the crows had first brought him to the old park eight years ago, they'd settled in an abandoned tree house in a lower fork of the tree. But as soon as he was old enough to climb, Caw had built his own nest up here, hidden away from the world. He was proud of it. It was home.

Caw unhooked the edge of the tarpaulin and pulled it aside. A drop of rainwater splashed onto the back of his neck, and he shuddered.

The moon over the park was a small sliver short of full in a cloudless sky. Milky perched on the branch outside, motionless, his white feathers silver in the moonlight. His head swiveled and a pale, sightless eye seemed to pick Caw out.

So much for sleep, grumbled Glum, shaking his beak disapprovingly.

Screech hopped onto Caw's arm and blinked twice. *Don't mind Glum,* he said. *Old-timers like him need their beauty sleep.*

Glum gave a harsh squawk. *Keep your beak shut, Screech.*

Caw breathed in the smells of the city. Car fumes. Mold. Something dying in a gutter. It had been raining, but no amount of rain could make Blackstone smell clean.

His stomach growled, but he was glad of his hunger. It sharpened his senses, pushed back the terror into the shadows of his mind. He needed air. He needed to clear his head. "I'm going to find something to eat."

Now? said Glum. *You ate yesterday.*

Caw spotted last night's fries container on the far side of the nest, along with the other rubbish the crows liked to collect. Glittering stuff. Bottle tops, cans, ring pulls, foil. The remains of Glum's dinner were scattered about too—a few mouse bones, picked clean. A tiny broken skull.

I could eat too, said Screech, stretching his wings.

Like I always say, said Glum with a shake of his beak. *Greedy.*

"Don't worry," Caw told them. "I'll be back soon."

He opened the hatch, swung out from the platform and into the upper branches, then picked his way down by handholds he could have found with his eyes shut. As he dropped to the ground, three shapes—two black, one white—swooped onto the grass.

Caw felt a little stab of annoyance. "I don't need you to come," he said, for what seemed like the thousandth time. *I'm not a little kid anymore,* he almost added, but he knew that would make him sound even more like one.

Humor us, said Glum.

Caw shrugged.

The park gates hadn't been opened for years, so the place was empty as always. Quiet too, but for the whisper of wind in the leaves. Still, Caw stuck to the shadows. The sole of his left shoe flapped open. He'd need to steal a new pair soon.

He passed the rusty climbing frame where children never played, crossed the flower beds that had long ago given way to weeds. The surface of the fishpond was thick with scum. Screech had sworn he saw a fish in there a month ago, but Glum said he was making it up. Blackstone Prison loomed beyond the park walls on the left, its four towers piercing the sky. On some nights Caw heard sounds from inside, muted by the thick, windowless walls.

As Caw paused by the empty bandstand, covered in graffiti scrawls, Screech landed on the step, talons tip-tapping on the concrete.

Something's wrong, isn't it? he asked.

Caw rolled his eyes. "You don't give up, do you?"

Screech cocked his head.

"It was my dream," Caw admitted. "It wasn't quite the same. I don't understand."

The nightmare forced its way into his mind again. The man with the black eyes. His shadow falling across the ground like a shard of midnight. The hand reaching out, and the spider ring . . .

Your parents belong in the past, said Screech. *Forget them.*

Caw nodded, feeling the familiar ache in his chest. Every time he thought of them, the pain was like a bruise, freshly touched. He would never forget. Each night he relived it. The empty air beneath his wheeling feet; the crack and flap of the crows' wings above.

Since then many crows had come and gone. Sharpy. Pluck. One-legged Dover. Inkspot, with her taste for coffee. Only one crow had remained at his side since that night eight years ago—mute, blind, white-feathered Milky. Glum had been a nest-mate for five years, Screech for three. One with nothing useful to say, one with nothing cheerful, and one with nothing to say at all.

Caw scaled the wrought-iron gates, gripped the looping *B* of *Blackstone Park*, and hauled himself up onto the wall. He balanced easily, his hands stuffed casually in his pockets as he walked along the top of it. For Caw, it was almost as easy as walking down the street. He could see Milky and Glum circling high overhead.

I thought we were getting food, said Screech.

"Soon," Caw told him.

He stopped opposite the prison. An ancient beech tree overhung the wall, and he was almost hidden by its thick leaves.

Not here again! squawked Glum, making a branch quiver as he landed.

"Humor me," said Caw pointedly.

He stared at the grand house across the road, built in the shadow of the prison.

Caw often came to look at the house. He couldn't really explain why. Perhaps it was seeing a normal family doing normal things. Caw liked to watch them eating dinner together, or playing board games or just sitting in front of their TV.

The crows had never understood.

A shadow in the garden snatched him suddenly back to his nightmare. The stranger's cruel smile. The spider hand. The weird ring. Caw focused intently on the house, trying to drive the terrifying images away.

He wasn't sure what time it was, but the windows of the house were dark, the curtains drawn. Caw rarely saw the mother, but he knew that the father worked at the prison. Caw had seen him leaving the prison gates and returning home. He always wore a suit, so Caw guessed he was more than just a guard. His black car squatted in the driveway like a sleeping animal. The girl with the red hair, she'd be in bed, her little dog lying at her feet. She was about his age, Caw guessed.

AWOOOOOOOOO!

A wailing sound cut through the night, making Caw jerk up. He dropped into a crouch on the wall, gripping the stone as the siren rose and fell, shockingly loud in the moonlit silence.

From the four towers of the prison, floodlights flashed on, throwing arcs of white light into the prison and on the road outside. Caw shrank back, sheltering under the branches, away from the glare.

Let's scram, said Screech, twitching his feathers nervously. *There'll be humans here soon.*

"Wait," said Caw, holding up a hand.

A light blinked on in the upstairs room where the girl's parents slept.

For once I agree with Screech, said Glum.

"Not yet."

More lights came on behind closed curtains, and a minute or two later, the front door opened. Caw trusted the darkness to shield him. He watched as the girl's father stepped out. He was a slender but tough-looking man, with fair hair receding a little at the front. He was straightening a tie and speaking into a phone clamped against his shoulder.

It's the one who walks that horrible dog! Glum said, hissing with disgust. Caw strained his ears to hear the man's voice over the siren.

"I'll be there in three minutes," shouted the man. "I want complete lock-down, a timeline, and a map of the sewers." A pause. "I don't care whose fault it was. Meet me out front with everyone you can spare." Another pause. "Yes, of *course* you should call the police commissioner! She needs to know about this, and fast. Get on it now!"

He slipped the phone away and strode fast toward the prison.

"What's going on?" Caw muttered.

Who cares? said Screech. *Human stuff. Let's go.*

As Caw watched, the girl appeared in the doorway of the house with the dog at her heels. She was wearing a green dressing gown. Her face was delicate, almost a perfect inverted triangle, with wide-set eyes and a small, pointed chin. Her red hair, the same color as her mother's, hung loose and messy to her shoulders. "Dad?" she said.

"Stay inside, Lydia," snapped the man, barely looking back.

Caw gripped the wall tighter.

Her father broke into a trot down the pavement.

The spider this way crawls, said a voice, close to Caw's ear.

Caw flinched. He glanced up and saw Milky perched in a branch. Glum snapped his head around.

Did you just . . . speak? he said.

Milky blinked, and Caw stared into the pale film of the old crow's eyes. "Milky?" he said.

The spider this way crawls, said the white crow, again. His voice was like the rasp of wind over dried leaves. *And we are but prey in his web.*

I told you the old snowball's bonkers, cackled Screech.

Caw's throat had gone dry. "What do you mean, *the spider*?" he asked.

Milky stared back at him. Lydia was still at the door, watching.

"What spider, Milky?" Caw said again.

But the white crow was silent.

Something was happening. Something big. And whatever it was, Caw wasn't going to miss it.

"Come on," he said, at last. "We're following that man."

You've just read an excerpt from Ferals.

ABOUT THE AUTHOR

Little is known of the mysterious Jacob Grey. He is said to live in a big city in the USA, where he wanders the streets at night dreaming up his dark and twisted tales. He has a deep love of animals and even talks to crows himself...although no one knows if he understands their replies.

Imprint: HarperCollins
Print ISBN: 9780062321039
Print price: $16.99
eBook ISBN: 9780062321053
eBook price: $9.99
Publication date: 4/28/15
Publicity contact: Olivia Russo Olivia.russo@harpercollins.com
Editor: Erica Sussman
Agent: Working Partners, Ltd.
Agency: Working Partners, Ltd.
Territories sold:
Rights sold in 32 territories

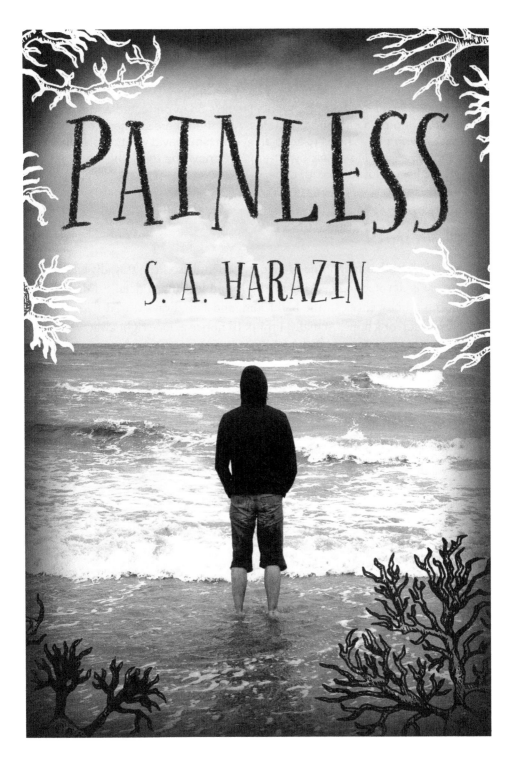

SUMMARY

David Hart shouldn't be alive now. He can't feel pain. He has scars for wounds he's never felt. Kids who have the kind of rare condition he has don't usually survive childhood, but at seventeen, David's beaten the odds. So far, at least. For his whole life he's been protected and monitored, living by a careful set of rules. And then there's Luna, the nurse trainee who's been hired to keep an eye on him. David wants more than anything to live life on his own terms. But now the things he wants to live for have a lot to do with Luna.

EXCERPT

Chapter Three

My grandmother taught me to follow a schedule so I can stay alive. Half my life is devoted to checking my body and looking at details. I do the morning body check in the bathroom, and I'm always scared I'll see a burn, a cut, or a bone. Actually, I think I'd notice a bone right away. Then I shower and apply special lotion because my skin dries out from not ever sweating.

I dress and go back into my room.

"Happy New Year," Nana says. "Are you doing okay today?"

This is why I always dress in the bathroom. I never know when Nana will be waiting for me in my room.

"I'm fine," I say with a smile. "Happy New Year."

Last night we watched the apple drop.

"Did you do your body check?" she asks.

I sit on the bed. "Yes. You know you don't have to ask me that all the time."

She ignores my whining. "What's your temperature?"

"Ninety-seven." I could make up anything.

"Did you go to the bathroom?"

I cringe. "Don't ever ask me that again," I say.

It isn't the first time I've told her that.

With shaky hands, Nana checks my blood pressure and my pulse. She peers down my throat using a penlight. Then she looks into my eyes and ears. I don't know what I have inside me that's so interesting. Last of all, I pull up my shirt, and she takes a look at my back.

Spencer does this when he's around, but nobody sees me naked. I have my pride.

I smooth out my shirt, look at her, and see how pale and out of breath she is. "You okay?" I ask.

"I'm all right for now," she says. "But I can't even find my shoes. I'm old and tired and dying, and you need to be prepared."

I just sit staring. I can't move. Can't breathe. It's like the world is really flat, and I've sailed over the end.

Once in the hospital I had a pneumothorax—a collapsed lung—and I was fighting to breathe, and there was no way I could keep breathing without help. All I could do was gasp hungrily for air, and then I stopped gasping. I think I died for a moment. Everything turned black.

Later when I awoke, I had a big, fat tube in my chest, and I was breathing.

Nana's probably just saying stuff because of the dementia. Sure, she's old, but she doesn't drink, smoke, or eat unhealthy food.

In the kitchen, my vitamins and minerals are lined up on the counter. They're to make me smarter and stronger. They do not work, and I don't like them. I usually throw them away when Nana isn't looking.

She's sitting at the table. "What's the date?" I ask.

She looks up from her coffee. "January first." She smiles at me, shaking her head.

I didn't think she'd know. I take the vitamins. She's fine.

***

"Happy New Year," Spencer says. He's carrying an old TV. "The VCR is built into the TV. Sorry I couldn't bring it over sooner. I got home yesterday. Aspen was great. You should've come with me."

"I wish."

"No you don't," he says.

I can see it now. I'm sitting in the ski lodge in front of the fireplace reading a book. People laugh and head out to go skiing. I stay where I am.

Here's what I know about skiing. It's fun to watch on TV, but when you have a messed-up leg, it's not a good idea to go skiing unless you like hanging out alone in a lodge with only your brain to talk to you.

"I'd probably hit a tree," I tell Spencer.

"Look on the positive side," he says. "You wouldn't feel a thing."

"You wouldn't either," I say. "Because you'd be dead."

Spencer laughs and connects the TV. "What's on the tape?"

"Nana said it was a surprise."

He rolls his eyes and slides the tape into the TV.

The picture's fuzzy, but I can see a man sitting in a room and the white wall behind him. "We're Off to See the Wizard" plays.

Spencer adjusts the controls, and the picture clears. He increases the volume and sits on the bed.

I sit in front of the TV. Nana would say I'd go blind sitting too close. She's also said I'd go deaf from loud music. Wonder what I did to destroy my nerve endings.

I see a man and he starts talking.

Dear David, I've collected pictures from some of your birthday parties and made this video for you so you don't forget.

I think he's somebody I'm supposed to know.

Dear David, you turned two today. I am sorry I don't have a recording of your very first birthday, but you had two parties for your second birthday.

I see me. I'm wearing gloves, long sleeves, a mouth guard, and a pinkish helmet. I look like I'm from outer space.

Hi, son. Today you are three. We had your party in the hospital, and all the nurses sang happy birthday to you. I hung a stuffed elephant from your IV pole.

"HE'S MY DAD!" I turn my head toward Spencer. "MY DAD. DID YOU HEAR ME?"

"Yeah," he says in a depressing voice.

I look like I'm sleeping. I'm getting oxygen through a mask.

"I wonder what happened to the elephant," I say to Spencer.

"He probably dumped him somewhere," Spencer says.

I almost wish I was watching this alone. Spencer doesn't understand. The video continues.

Dear David, here we are, celebrating your fourth birthday. I can't believe how fast time flies. You are amazing. Don't ever forget that.

He quits talking. I'm sitting in front of a piano, banging on the keys, and singing "Happy Birthday to Me."

There aren't any kids in the picture, and I have a toothless smile on my face. If I was so amazing, why did he dump me at Nana's and never come back?

"If I Only Had a Brain" starts playing, and my dad speaks.

I thought if you could make it until you were a teenager, you wouldn't have as much to deal with because you would have learned so much about your condition. But things happened. Do you remember when we watched The Wizard of Oz? *The Lion wanted courage, the Scarecrow wanted a brain, and the Tin Man wanted a heart. But it didn't matter because they already had what they sought, only they didn't know it.*

There's a collage of everything with "Over the Rainbow" playing. Suddenly my dad starts talking and crying.

Dear David, well, it isn't your birthday, but today is a big day for you. I'm taking you to Nana's house for a while. You'll be safe and happy with her.

I can't believe this. He leaves me a lousy tape when he could've visited me. It's been eleven years, and he's never sent me a card or anything. He's pathetic.

Spencer turns off the TV and ejects the tape. When he hands it to me, he doesn't look at me.

It's the look-away that happens when somebody feels embarrassed for the other person.

"Anybody ever say you look like your father?" he asks.

I smile. "Only Nana. Nobody else knew him."

"If you don't mind me asking, what happened to your mother? She isn't in any of the pictures."

Maybe she didn't like me. Maybe she went shopping. Maybe she was taking a nap. Maybe she was filming the video. There are too many maybes. "I don't know," I finally say.

"They don't call or come to see you?"

I shake my head.

"It doesn't matter," Spencer says. "You know what your grandmother said about you? She said the Creator sent you to your grandfather and her. She said you saved them."

I probably did save them. I kept them from doing much of anything.

Spencer unplugs the TV.

I ask him if he wants to hang out a while.

"I can't," he says. "We have company, and Cassandra is coming over. My mom's fixing a huge dinner."

Cassandra plays the keyboard in Spencer's band. I don't know her very well, but she has an argument with Spencer about once a week. I over-heard her talking to Spencer about me. "Aren't you embarrassed?" she asked. "Poor little rich kid has you to make up his bed for him."

She doesn't know about me. It's not like I advertise I can't feel pain.

He sits back down on the bed. "Remember a few weeks ago when I told you I made it into Vanderbilt and how I'm going to be really busy this semester?"

"Yes."

"I'm quitting, but I've found somebody to replace me. I'll be here early tomorrow morning to show Ms. Smith what to do," Spencer says. "You wouldn't believe how many people I talked to before I found the right person. You need somebody new anyway. We're around each other all the time."

I'm getting a sick feeling, kind of like I ate too much pizza and exploded.

"Not as much lately," I say.

"We do the same thing day in and day out. Trust me. It's time for both of us to move on. This way I can come over whenever I want to and not feel like I have to."

"Is it because Cassandra says it's demeaning for you to work for me?"

"No."

"I understand," I say. I really do. He knows it's his time to move on.

***

"James gave me the tape the day he left you here," Nana says from her recliner. "I watched it back when we had a VCR and then forgot about it."

"But I don't understand why he didn't come back."

"I don't think we'll ever understand. Your parents divorced, and James brought you here. Then they disappeared," Nana says. "I've told you before. We searched. We filed missing persons' reports. We hired detectives."

"How can anybody disappear like that?"

"When they don't want to be found," she says, trying to catch her breath. "You were constantly covered with bruises. You'd jump out of a tree. You'd bang your head. You'd chew your mouth or your hands. They were accused of child abuse every time you were taken to the emergency room."

She's paler than I've ever seen. "It was like that for us when you first came to live here. Your grandfather was arrested once, but then Dr. Goodman explained to the authorities about CIPA. Even then, they did not believe him at first. Joe managed to make the authorities understand your condition."

"It's all right," I say. I can't ask her any more questions. Not now. Maybe not ever.

"Joe's trying to locate James," she says.

"He'll find him," I say, but Joe needs to hurry. Time's running out.

***

My body-check routine is repeated in the evenings. Sometimes I turn on the song "Staying Alive" and listen to the music for inspiration. I'm so good at being careful that I hardly ever see blood anymore.

You've just read an excerpt from Painless.

ABOUT THE AUTHOR

S. A. Harazin has been both writing and working in hospitals since she was in her teens. She is a registered nurse and her first novel, *Blood Brothers*, was an Edgar Allan Poe award nominee. She lives in north Georgia.

Imprint: Albert Whitman Teen

Print ISBN: 9780807562888

Print price: $16.99

eBook ISBN: 9781504002219

eBook price: $9.99

Publication date: 3/1/15

Publicity contact: Annette Hobbs Magier: annette @albertwhitman.com

Rights contact: John Quattrocchi: JohnQ@albertwhitman.com

Editor: Wendy McClure

Agent: Steven Chudney

Agency: The Chudney Agency

Promotional information:
- Trade, library, and consumer print and online advertising
- Prepublication buzz campaign, including ARC distribution to industry big mouths, media, booksellers, and bloggers
- ARC distribution at ALA Midwinter
- Social media campaign across Albert Whitman and Company profiles
- Giveaway via Albert Whitman and Company Twitter
- Select author appearances.

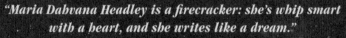

M A G O N I A

MARIA DAHVANA HEADLEY

SUMMARY

An epic fantasy following one girl from the familiar confines of her high school life on Earth to the heights of a fantastical sky world where she discovers she possesses immense power and must choose between destroying or saving the world she left behind.

EXCERPT

Prologue

I breathe in. I breathe out. The sky's full of clouds. A rope is looping down from above, out of the sky and down to earth. There is a woman's face, looking at me, and all around us, hundreds upon hundreds of birds. The flock flows like water, surging up and into the air, black and gold and red, and everything is safe and cold, bright with stars and moon.

I'm tiny in comparison, and I'm not on the ground.

I know everyone has dreams of flying, but this isn't a dream of flying. It's a dream of floating, and the ocean is not water but wind.

I call it a dream, but it feels realer than my life.

Chapter One

AZA

My history is hospitals.

This is what I tell people when I'm in a mood to be combination funny and stressful, which is a lot of the time.

It's easier to have a line ready than to be forced into a conversation with someone whose face is showing "fake nice," "fake worry," or "fake interest." My preferred method is as follows: make a joke, make a half-apologetic/half-freaky face, and be out of the discussion in five seconds flat.

Aza: "Nothing really majorly wrong with me. Don't worry. I just have a history of hospitals."

Person in Question: "Er. Um. Oh. I'm so sorry to hear that. Or, wait, *glad*. You just said that nothing's really wrong with you! Glad!"

Aza (freaky face intensifying): "It's *incredibly* nice of you to ask."

Subtext: It isn't. Leave it.

People don't usually ask anything after that. Most are polite. My parents, my family, not so much, but the randoms? The substitute teacher who wonders why I'm coughing and having to leave the room—then having to go to the nurse's office—then having to have a nice 911 call to summon an ambulance to spirit me back to my white linoleum homeland?

People like that don't want to remind me of things I no doubt already know. Which I very much do. Don't be stupid. Also, don't think *I'm* stupid.

This is not, like, *Little Women*. Beth and her nice, invalid Beth-ness have always made me puke. The way people imagined she wasn't dying. The way she blatantly was. In stories like that, the moment someone decides to wrap you in blankets and you accidentally smile weakly, you're dead.

Hence, I try not to smile weakly, even if I feel weak, which I sometimes secretly or unsecretly do. I don't want to make myself into a catastrophic blanket-y invalid.

Bang, bang, you're dead. Close your eyes and go to bed.

Side note: *invalid*. Whoever invented that word, and made it the same word as not-valid? That person sucked.

So, right, the question of death comes up in my presence on a regular basis. Adults don't like to talk about it. Seriously, it's not like *I* like talking about it either. But other people my age do.

They're like, DEATH DEATH DEATH, like we're all in cars, driving slowly past accidents on the highway all day long. They're grossly fascinated.

Some of us, the ones actually dying, are maybe less fascinated than others. Some of us, maybe, would rather not get stuck in rooms where people are regularly talking about celebrity death-y things, whichever kind you want, the OD, the car crash, the mystery fall-apart . . .

People my age like to cry and speculate dramatically over how people our age could die. Take it from one who knows. Take it from one whose role has been, for years, *The Girl I Knew Really Well, Who Tragically Died One Day.*

Not that I've died yet. I am still totally here. Which is why all the artistic, goth morbidity is a bummer.

Adults like talking about death way less than people my age do. Death is the Santa Claus of the adult world. Except Santa Claus in reverse. The guy who takes all the presents away. Big bag over the shoulder, climbing up the chimney carrying everything in a person's life, and taking off, eight-reindeered, from the roof. Sleigh loaded down with memories and wineglasses and pots and pans and sweaters and grilled cheese sandwiches and Kleenexes and text messages and ugly houseplants and calico cat fur and half-used lipstick and laundry that never got done and letters you went to the trouble of handwriting but never sent and birth certificates and broken necklaces and disposable socks with scuffs on the bottom from hospital visits.

And notes you kept on the fridge.

And pictures of boys you had crushes on.

And a dress that got worn to a dance at which you danced by yourself, before you got too skinny and too breathless to dance.

Along with, probably, though this isn't worthy of huge thinking, a soul or something.

Anyway, adults don't believe in Santa Claus. They try hard not to believe in Reverse Santa Claus either.

At school, the whole rare-disease-impending-doom situation makes me freakishly intriguing. In the real world, it makes me a problem. Worried look, bang, nervous face, bang: "Maybe you should talk to someone about your feelings, Aza," along with a nasty side dish of what-about-God-what-about-therapy-what-about-antidepressants?

Sometimes also what-about-faith-healers-what-about-herbs-what-about-crystals-what-about-yoga? *Have you tried yoga, Aza, I mean have you, because it helped this friend of a friend who was supposedly dying but didn't, due to downward dog?*

No. I haven't tried yoga to cure my thing, because yoga isn't going to cure my thing. My thing is a Mystery and not just a Mystery, but Bermuda—no sun, only Triangle.

Unknowable. Unsolvable.

I take handfuls of drugs every morning, even though no one is entirely sure what the thing that's wrong with me actually is. I'm rare like that. (Rare like, *what?*)

Rare like bloodwork and tests and things reaching down my throat. Rare like MRIs and X-rays and sonograms and swabs and never any clear diagnosis.

Rare, like my disease is standing onstage in a tuxedo belting out a torch song that has a chorus along the lines of *"Baby, you're the only one for me."* And then the disease just stands there, waiting for me to walk into its arms and give up resisting.

Rare, as in: so far, I'm the only person on earth who's been diagnosed with this particular precision awesomeness.

Maybe I sound like I'm exaggerating. No. My disease is so rare it's named *Azaray Syndrome.*

After me, Aza Ray Boyle.

Which is perverse. I don't want a doppelgänger in disease form, some weird medical case immortality, which means medical students'll be saying my name for the next hundred years. No one asked ME when the lab published a paper in *Nature* and gave this disease my name. I would've said no. I'd like to have named my disease myself: the Jackass, or maybe something ugly like Elmer or Clive.

None of the above topics, the death and dying topics, are things I actually feel like talking about. I'm not depressed. I'm just fucked up. I have been since I remember anything. There's not a version of my life that *isn't* fucked up.

Yes. I'm allowed to say that word if I feel like it, and I do. I feel like swearing about this. It's me in this body, thank you, snarled and screwed up and not going to make it, let's not go on about things we can't revise. I'm an edited version of a real live girl, or at least, that's what I say when I want to tell you something and I would rather not talk about it but have to get out of the way so we can move on to better topics.

Yeah, I totally know I don't look well. No, you don't need to look concerned. I know you wish you could help. You can't. I know you're probably a nice person, but seriously? All I really want to talk to strangers about is anything other than this thing.

The facts of it, though? Basic, daily of Elmer /Clive/the Jackass/Azaray Syndrome? I have to live in rooms kept free of dust. This has been true almost since forever. When I was born, I was healthy and theoretically perfect. Almost exactly a year later, out of nowhere, my lungs stopped being unable to understand air.

My mom came into the room one morning and found me having a seizure. Because my mom is my mom, she had the presence of mind to give me mouth-to-mouth and breathe for me. She kept me alive until they could get me to the hospital. Where they also—barely—kept me going, by making a machine do the breathing. They gave me drugs and did things to make the oxygen density of the air less, rather than more. It got a little better.

I mean, a lot better, given that here I still am. Just not better enough. Early on, I slept for what felt like centuries inside a shell of clear plastic and tubing. My history is made of opening my eyes in rooms where I didn't fall asleep, the petting of paramedics, the red and white spinning shriek of sirens. That's a thing that just *is*, if you're the lucky girl who lives with Clive.

I look weird and my inner workings are weird, and everyone's always like, huh, never seen *that* shit before. Mutations all over my body, inside, outside, everywhere but my brain, which, as far as anyone can tell, is normal.

All the brain chemical-imbalance misery that some people have? I don't. I don't wake up riddled with apocalypse panic, and I don't feel like doing anything like biting my own fingers off, or drinking myself into a coma. In the scheme of things, having a brain that mostly obeys your instructions is not nothing.

Otherwise, I'm Aza-the-Exhibition. I'm like the World's Fair. (All I want,

ALL I WANT, is for there to be a *World's Unfair Exposition*, preferably in a city near where I live. Booths full of disappointments, huge exhibits of structures built to fail. No Oh-My-God-the-Future-Will-Be-Amazing Exhibits, but the reverse. No flying cars. Cars that squinch along like inchworms.)

I try not to get involved with my disease, but it's persuasive. When it gets ahold of me, the gasping can put me on the floor, flopping and whistling like something hauled up from a lake bottom. Sometimes I wish I could go back to that bottom and start over somewhere else. As some*thing* else.

Secretly, as in only semi-secretly, as in this is a thing I say loudly sometimes—I think I wasn't meant to be human. I don't work right.

And now I'm almost sixteen. One week to go.

SCHOOL NURSE: You're a miracle! You're *our* miracle!

AZA RAY BOYLE: (retching noises)

Because I'm still alive I'm thinking about having a party. There's that thing about sixteen. That big-deal factor. Everything changes and suddenly you're right in the world, like wearing a pink dress and kissing a cute boy or doing a dancey-prancy musical number.

I clarify, that's what happens in movies. In this life? I don't know what happens from here. Nothing I majorly want to think about.

Who would I invite? EVERYONE. Except the people I don't like. I *know* enough people to categorize the group of people I know as everyone, but I like maybe five or six of them, total. I *could* invite doctors, in which case the group would radically grow. I said this to my parents a couple days ago, and now they hover, considering my questionable attitude. Which they've been considering since forever.

But I ask you, wouldn't it be worse if I were perfect? My imperfections make me less mournable.

Nobody likes birthdays. Everyone in the house is nervous. Even the plants look nervous. We have one that curls up. It isn't allowed to share a room with me, but sometimes I visit it and touch its leaves and it cringes. It's curled up now into a tight little ball of Leaves Me the Hell Alone.

Get it?

Leaves? (Oh, haha. Oh very haha.)

High school. First bell. Walking down the middle hall. Past a billion lockers. Late for class. No excuse, except for the one I always have.

I raise my fist to bump with Jason Kerwin, also late, who doesn't acknowledge me with his face, just as I don't acknowledge him with mine. Only fists. We've known each other since we were five. He's my best friend.

Jason is an exception to all rules of parental worry re: Hanging With Humans Other Than Parents, because he knows every possible drill of emergency protocol.

He's allowed to accompany me places my parents don't want to go. Or *do* want to go, but do not want to spend hours at. Aquariums, natural history museum bug collections and taxidermy dioramas, rare bookstores where we have to wear masks and gloves if we want to touch, back rooms full of strange butterfly, bone and life-size surgical model collections discovered on the internet.

Et cetera.

Jason never talks about death, unless it's in the context of morbid cool things we might want to hunt the internet for. Aza Ray and the Great Failure of Her Physical Everything? Jason leaves that nasty alone.

Second bell, still in the hall, and I raise one casual relevant finger at Jenny Green. Pink streak in her hair, elbows sharper than daggers, tight jeans costing roughly the equivalent of a not un-nice used car. Jenny has pissed me off lately by being. I mean, not by basic being. Mean being. We have a silent war. She doesn't deserve words at this point, though she called me some a couple days ago, in a frenzy of not-allowed. Calling the sick girl names? Please. We all know it's not okay.

I kind of, semi, have to respect her for the transgression. It's a little bit badass, to do the thing no one else has ever dared do. Lately, there's been this contagious idea that I look like a hungry, murdery ghost girl from a Japanese horror movie, so Jenny came to school in blue lipstick and white powder. To mock me.

Jenny smiles and blows me a kiss full of poison. I catch it and blow it back through my today very indigo lips, thoroughly creeping her. I give her a little shudder gasp. If ghost girl is going to be my deal, I might as well use it to my advantage. She looks at me like I've somehow played unfair, and takes off at a repulsed run for homeroom.

Insert meaningless pause at locker. Slow walk. Look into classroom windows, through the wire mesh they put in there to discourage people like me from spying on people like them.

My little sister, Eli, senses me staring, and looks up from her already deep-in-lecture algebra. I rock out briefly in the hallway, free, fists up, at liberty like no one else is this time of morning. Sick-girl privilege. Eli rolls her eyes at me, and I walk on, coughing only a little bit, manageable.

Seven minutes late to homeroom and it's Mr. Grimm, eyebrow up. *The Perpetually Tardy Mizz Aza Ray*, his name for me, and yeah, his name is Grimm, really. Blind bat eyes, thick-frame glasses, skinny tie like a hipster, but that look's not working for him.

Mr. Grimm's muscle-bound, though he never rolls up his sleeves. He has the kind of arms that strain against fabric, which fact tells me he has no actual life, and just veers between being a teacher and drinking protein shakes.

He looks like he belongs in the PE end of the building, except that when he opens his mouth he's nerdtastic. I also think he has tattoos, which he's tried to cover up in various ways. Pancake makeup. Long sleeves. Not too smart to get a skull/ship/naked girl (?) permanently marked on you. You have to button your cuffs all the time.

Mr. Grimm's new this year. Youngish, if you can call thirty young. But the tattoo is interesting. I can't tell exactly what it is because I've never seen the full extent of it.

It makes me want tattoos. I want one that's worse than whatever his is.

He's got a constant complaint going that I could work up to my potential if I'd only pay attention instead of burying my face in a book while he lectures. He can't lament too successfully, considering that I am one of, oh, what, four people in this school who read.

And I know that's trite. Yes, I'm a reader. Kill me. I could tell you I was raised in the library and the books were my only friends, but I didn't do that, did I? Because I have mercy. I'm neither a genius nor a kid destined to become a wizard. I'm just me. I read stuff. Books are not my only friends, but we're friendly. So there.

I don't need to pay attention to Mr. Grimm's lecture. I read it already, whatever it is, in this case, Ye Olde Man vs. Ye Olde Sea.

Obsessed guy. Big fish. Variety of epic fails. I have to wonder how many generations of sophomores have been oppressed by stories about this same damn thing.

Why? Which of us is or will one day be engaged in a death struggle with a big fish? What is the rationale?

I've read *Moby Dick*, another version of Obsessed Dude, Big Fish, and taxonomies of sorrow and lost dreams.

I know, whale = not fish. Mammalian cetacean. Still, whales have always been the prototype for Big Fish Stories, which makes all kinds of sense given how wrong humanity always is about things.

I even read the *Moby Dick* chapters that no one reads. I could tell you anything you ever needed to know about flensing. Trust me on this, though, you don't want that information.

Ask me about *Moby Dick*, Mr. Grimm. Go on. Do it.

He did do that once, about a month ago, thinking I was lying about reading it. I gave a filibuster-quality speech about suck and allegories and oceans and uncatchable dreams that I then merged into a discussion of pirate-themed movies, plank-walking, and female astronauts. Mr. Grimm was both impressed and aggravated. I got extra credit, which I don't need, and then detention for interrupting, for which punishment, in truth, I respect him.

I glance over at Jason Kerwin, who is ensconced in his own book. I eye the title. *Kepler's Dream: With the Full Text and Notes of Somnium, Sive Astronomia Lunaris.* It looks old and semi-nasty, recycled hardcover library copy. Big picture of the surface of the moon on the front.

No clue: me.

I slink my hand over to his desk and snatch it to read the flaps. The first science-fiction novel, it says, written in the 1620s. An astronomer tells a story of a journey to the moon, but also he attempts to encode in the novel a defense of Copernican theory, because he's looking for a way to talk about it without getting executed for heresy. Only later did people realize all the fantasy bits are pretty much Kepler's code for astronomy and equations.

I thumb. There's a flying alien witch.

Awesome. Kind of my kind of book. Except that I'd like it better if I could write one of my own. This is always the problem with things containing imaginary languages and mysteries. I want to be the cryptographer. I'm not even close to being a cryptographer, though. I'm just what used to be called "an enthusiast." Or maybe a hobbyist. I learn as much as I can learn in like fifteen minutes of internet search, and then I fake, fast and furious.

People therefore think I'm smarter than they are. It gives me room to do whatever I want, without people surrounding me and asking questions about things. It keeps people from inquiring about the whole dying situation. I invoke factoid privilege.

"Give," Jason whispers. Mr. Grimm shoots us a *shut-up* look.

I consider how to pacify my parents about the birthday party. I think they have visions of roller-skating and clown and cake and balloons—like the party they had for me when I was five.

That time, no one showed up beyond two girls forced by their mothers, and Jason, who crashed the party. Not only did he walk a mile uninvited to my birthday party, he did it in formal dress: a full alligator costume leftover from Halloween. Jason didn't bother to tell his moms where he was going, and so they called the police, convinced he'd been kidnapped.

When the squad cars showed up outside the roller rink, and the cops came in, it became immediately clear that Jason and I were destined to be friends. He was roller-skating in the alligator suit, spinning elegantly, long green tail dragging behind when they demanded that he show himself.

That party was not all bad.

For birthday sixteen, though, I'm drawing a better vision in my notebook: a dead clown, a gigantic layer cake from which I burst, a hot air balloon that arrives in the sky above me. From the hot air balloon's basket dangles a rope. I climb. I fly away. Forever.

How much pain would this solve? So much. Except for the pain of the dead clown, who died not according to his own plan, but mine.

Apparently, Mr. Grimm hears me snort.

"Care to enlighten us, Miss Ray?"

Why do they always use this phrase? Rest of the class is taking a quiz. They look up, relieved to be legitimately distracted. Jason smirks. There's nothing like trouble to make a day pass faster.

"Do you really want enlightening?" I ask, because I'm working it today. "I was thinking about dying."

He gives me an exasperated look. I've used this line before in Mr. Grimm's classroom. It's a beautiful dealbreaker. Teachers melt like wet witches when I bring it up. I kind of like Mr. Grimm, though, because he sees through me. Which means he's actually looking. Which is, in itself, weird. No one looks at me too closely. They're afraid my unsustainability is going to mess them up. That plastic bubble I lived in when I was little? It's still there, but invisible now. And made out of something harder than plastic.

"Dying, in the context of which literary work, Aza?" he asks. No mercy.

"How about *The Tempest*?" I say, because there it is, on the syllabus, looming. Everything is ocean this semester. "Drowned twins."

"Nope, because they don't really drown," he says. "Try it again, Ray."

I'm at a loss, unfortunately.

"Play it again, Sam?" I say, illegally using Mr. Grimm's first name. Then I embark on my traditional method: one-fact-that-makes-them-think-you-have-all-the-facts. You can learn the oddest little items from a wiki page.

"Except that that's a misquote. 'Play it, Sam,' it should be, but people want it more romantic and less order-givey."

Grimm sighs. "Have you even seen *Casablanca*? Ten more minutes till pencils up. I'd do the quiz if I were you, Aza. And don't call me Sam. It's Samuel. Only people who don't know me call me Sam."

He's won, because he's right. I so haven't seen *Casablanca*. That fact was all I had. I cede the field and pick up my pencil to navigate old man and marlin.

Samuel. Who names their kid Samuel these days? I consider making a remark about pen names: Samuel Clemens, Mark Twain, and *Life on the Mississippi*, recently read, but I don't. Last time we did this it became a duel, and there's something about my chest right now that makes me uncertain whether I can properly duel without coughing.

There's a storm kicking up outside, and trees are whacking against the windows. The blinds are rattling like crazy, because this building is a leaky, ancient thing.

Jason flips a note onto my desk. Mr. Grimm is vigilant about phones buzzing, so we go low-tech. *Giant squid*, it says. *Tomorrow, five o'clock. Your house.*

We were supposed to watch the footage a couple nights ago, but I was coughing so hard I had to go to the hospital. Which sucked.

I had to have a scope and when I revived all the way from the anesthetic, the surgeon was looking at me with the usual *whoa, never seen that before* look.

Mutant, I scribbled on the notepad they'd given me in case of complaint.

The surgeon looked at me, and then laughed. "No," he said. "You're a special young lady. I've never seen vocal cords like yours before. You could be a singer."

If I could breathe, I wrote, and he had the grace to look mortified.

In solidarity, Jason didn't watch the squid footage without me, though he attempted to convince them to put it on in the ER. He couldn't get permission from the nurses. They're hard core in there.

Speaking of ocean and big fish in it. This is the first footage of a giant squid ever taken in which the squid is swimming around in its own environment. Imagine this sea-monstery unbelievable thing with eyeballs the size of a person's head, and a body and tentacles twenty-five feet long. Double school bus. Now, realize that no one's ever seen one moving around down there before. It's a pretty huge miracle, and if this exists, maybe there are things in Loch Ness too. Maybe there are things everywhere, all over the place. Maybe there is . . . hope?

Because every time someone finds a new animal, or a new amazing thing on earth, it means we haven't broken everything yet.

Up till now there's only been video of really dead or really sick giant squid, but a scientist went down in a submersible and found one and filmed it.

Someone Jason knows has a hack on Woods Hole, the oceanographers in Massachusetts, and he caught wind of expedition communications. He snatched the video from a server four days ago, and hasn't stopped crowing since.

I look over at Jason to smile at him, but he's deep in his book. I lower my head to get down to the quiz, when out the classroom window, over the top of the iguana terrarium, I see something in the sky.

It's only for a second but it's weirdly familiar, like I dreamed it, or saw it in a picture, maybe.

A mast. And a sail.

More than one sail—two, three. Tall-ship style. Big, white, flapping. And out of the storm comes the prow of a ship.

Which . . .

I've hallucinated before, but nothing like this. I read something recently about mirages in the sky, *fata morgana*, that's what they're called.

Someone once saw Edinburgh hanging in the sky over Liverpool for half an hour. But what's this—this *boat* reflecting from? We're inland. Deep inland.

I reach out and tug Mr. Grimm's sleeve. He looks at me, irritated. I point.

He looks, and for a moment, he doesn't move, staring hard out the window. Then he takes off his glasses and glances again.

"Shit," he says.

"What?" I say. "You see it? Do you see it?"

He shakes his head.

"Storm," he says, and yanks at the blinds.

As the blinds clang to the bottom of the sill and the room goes back to just being a room, I hear a whistle, long and high. Not exactly a whistle. More than a whistle.

Let me correct that. *Much* more than a whistle.

Aza, it says, the whistle. *Aza, are you out there?*

You've just read an excerpt from Magonia.

ABOUT THE AUTHOR

Maria Dahvana Headley is a memoirist, novelist, and editor, recently of the novel *Queen of Kings* and the *New York Times* bestselling anthology *Unnatural Creatures* (coeditor with Neil Gaiman). As the author of the work of short fiction "The Traditional" she has been nominated for a Shirley Jackson award. She lives in Brooklyn with a seven-foot stuffed crocodile and a collection of star charts from the 1700s. You can find her at www.mariadahvanaheadley.com.

Imprint: HarperCollins
Print ISBN: 9780062320520
Print price: $17.99
eBook ISBN: 9780062320544
eBook price: $10.99
Publication date: 4/28/15
Publicity contact: Gina Rizzo gina.rizzo@harpercollins.com

Editor: Kristen Pettit
Agent: Stephanie Cabot
Agency: The Gernert Agency

SEED

Lisa
Heathfield

SUMMARY

At fifteen years old, all that Pearl knows can be encapsulated in one word: Seed. It is the isolated community that she was born into. It is the land that she sows and reaps. It is the center of her family and everything that means home. And it is all kept under the watchful eye of Papa S. Now she is finally old enough to be chosen as Papa S.'s companion. She feels excitement . . . and surprising trepidation that she cannot explain. The arrival of a new family into the Seed community—particularly the teenage son, Ellis—only complicates the life and lifestyle that Pearl has depended upon as safe and constant. Ellis is compelling, charming, and worldly, and he seems to have a lot of answers to questions Pearl has never thought to ask. But as Pearl digs to the roots of the truth, only she can decide what she will allow to come to the surface.

EXCERPT

Chapter One

Here, crouched beside the toilet, I'm terrified I'm dying. My stomach must be bleeding, or my liver, or my kidneys. Something inside me has somehow got cut. Spots of blood smear my underwear. I wipe myself with toilet paper and there's more blood. Am I being punished for something I have said or done?

"Elizabeth!" I shout, running from the coffin-small room. "Elizabeth!"

I run from room to room. Kindred Smith is mending a bed in one. Rachel sweeps in another. The children play in the day room.

"Elizabeth!"

I wonder if the bleeding is worse. I look behind, but there are no drops of red following me along the wooden floorboards. I rattle the doors of the rooms that are locked. Elizabeth is not in the dining room, but in the kitchen she is coming through the back door, her rain-drenched dress clinging to her pregnant belly.

"What is it, Pearl?" she asks, putting down a bag of muddied potatoes. "Is someone hurt?"

I don't want to tell her. I don't want to tell her that I'm dying. Will the shock damage the tiny baby in her tummy?

"Pearl?" She stands, looking at me, and I see the worry in her eyes.

"My stomach is bleeding," I whisper.

"Where? How?" Elizabeth steps back, looks at my top. "Did you cut yourself in the field?"

"Inside. It's bleeding inside me."

"What do you mean?" she asks. I've never seen someone turn so pale in the time it takes for me to take a breath.

"I'm sorry, Elizabeth," I say. And I can't stop the tears. Because I don't want to die. I want to meet her baby. I want more days swimming in the lake. I want more days dancing in the rain.

Then Elizabeth's face changes and she starts to smile. "Why do you think your stomach is bleeding?"

Why is she happy that I might soon die?

"Is there blood in your underwear?"

As I nod my head, she laughs and wraps her arms around me. I feel the bump of her baby under her skin. It presses against me. Against my stomach, which is bleeding inside.

Elizabeth steps back and I see that she's crying. So I'm right—I am dying.

She kisses her thumb, presses it to her belly, and then puts it onto my forehead, onto my chest and then onto my own stomach.

"Are you trying to heal me?" I whisper. And she smiles.

"You don't need healing. You're not dying, Pearl. You are fifteen years old and you're changing from a child to a woman."

Then she's hugging me again, and her words slowly sink in. So this is what I've been waiting for? A bleeding stomach?

I look at Elizabeth, but she doesn't seem like she's mocking me.

"Come on," she says, and she takes my hand.

In the bedroom, she changes my underwear, takes away my old ones, which are now heavily lined with a muddy red. I concentrate on the faded yellow wallpaper as she fills my new underwear with a thick, woven slab that makes me waddle like a duck.

"You'll get used to it." She smiles at me so warmly. "Now, not a word," she says and I follow her out onto the landing. I focus on her long blonde hair as we go down the stairs to the kitchen. In silence, she reaches for the lantern and matches on the shelf, and then we walk out the back door.

I'd forgotten it was raining and it hits down on us hard, soaking us within seconds. I hear nothing but its drumming on the ground as Elizabeth takes my hand again. She leads me through the herb garden with its high brick walls, where the smells have almost been washed away. She opens the rickety door at the other end and we're walking through the strawberry field. The plants are heavy with red fruit.

I feel the slab of linen rubbing my legs as I walk. I imagine the blood dripping onto it. Will I bleed forever now? Will I never be able to walk or run freely again?

I stumble after Elizabeth, confused about wanting to cry when I have waited so long to be a woman. In the distance, I see the figures in the vegetable patch, where I was less than an hour ago, when I was still a child. I see the shape of Heather, her long brown hair stuck with rain down her back. Then I remember. I'll be able to grow my hair. Finally, after all these years of waiting, I'll be able to let my blonde hair grow. I'll look like Elizabeth, with it flowing over my shoulders and down to my waist.

I'm filled with happiness. Suddenly the bleeding and the strange, uncomfortable way of walking are absolutely fine, because now I am a woman.

"Elizabeth," I say. But the water is falling too loudly for her to hear.

The sound changes as we head into the woods and the rain hits the leaves far above us.

"Where are we going?" I ask, but Elizabeth just smiles.

Finally, we get to the clearing where Papa S.'s Worship Chair sits in the middle. It has fresh ivy woven around its frame. Elizabeth walks toward it, and then she's going too close—she's walking into the forbidden circle.

I look around, but no one is here to see. I look up into the branches, but no Kindreds are hidden there.

I hold my breath as she reaches for the chair. "No, Elizabeth," I whisper.

"It is bidden," she says quietly as she starts to lift the chair. I can see that it is heavy, but I can't help. Papa S. sees everything and Elizabeth is in the forbidden circle, touching his Worship Chair.

She drags it to the side and begins to kick at the thick leaves underneath. Then she's on her hands and knees, moving the leaves away until underneath I see a large metal hoop. She pulls it, and it opens a small wooden door flat on the ground.

"What are you doing?" I ask.

She is not smiling now. "I promise you will be okay," she says. She takes the matches from her apron, strikes one and lights the lantern.

And then I understand. I look down into the hole. There are steps that end in blackness. She wants me to go down.

"I want to go back to the house," I say. But I don't move. I don't run away.

"You must trust me, Pearl." Her wet hair still shines so blonde. She holds the lantern in one hand, the other hand resting on her pregnant belly.

And I know I love her, so I know I must trust her. I step forward, *into* the forbidden circle, and start to go cautiously down the steps. Elizabeth follows me and the light from the lantern shows us the way. At the bottom is a tiny room dug into the earth.

I look at Elizabeth. In the candlelight her cheeks look sunken, her eyes hollow. Is there fear hidden within her?

"I've seen it now," I say quietly. My voice sounds flat as it catches in the earth. "Can I go?"

"We have all done this, Pearl. Every woman at Seed. I promise you will be all right."

"What do you mean?"

"When you get your first Blessing, when you first start to bleed, you must stay with Nature so that she may give you the gift of a healthy womb," she says.

I don't understand. I just stare at her in the flickering light.

"You must stay deep in her womb, so your own womb may become fertile."

"What do you mean, fertile?"

"So that when it is your time, you will be able to have children."

"I don't want to be here, Elizabeth." My voice cracks as I start to cry. I look at the earth circling me and I'm suddenly filled with terror. Does she want me to stay here?

She puts the lamp down and wraps her arms around me, her face hidden in the shadows. "You know that you must not cry. Your life spirit will leave you and without it, you are nothing."

I can smell the sweetness of her vanilla scent. It masks the smell of the blood and the damp earth that is blocking the air.

"It won't be for long."

"So you'll shut the trapdoor?" The words fall from my mouth.

Elizabeth steps back and nods. She's trying to smile.

"But how will I breathe?"

Elizabeth picks up the lantern and shines it on the bottom of the curved earth walls. Tiny black pipes stick out all around. "I have been here, Pearl. It's all right."

"It's not," I say, and I start to cry again. "I don't want to stay." My voice is getting louder and Elizabeth looks up the steps toward the light above.

"Shh, now. Papa S. must not hear you cry. And Nature is hearing every word." Then she puts down the lantern once again and turns to go up the steps.

I can't move. Something holds me to the ground. I want to run after Elizabeth, pull her back, to escape, but I just watch as she goes up toward the air. The last thing I see is her blonde hair as she quickly lowers the trapdoor. It shuts with a muffled thud.

Faintly, I can hear Elizabeth scrabbling about with the leaves. Then I hear a dragging of something heavy. She must be pushing the wooden Worship Chair back over the top.

Every part of me wants to scream. Every nerve, every cell, wants to run up the steps and bang on that wooden door and scream until my lungs burn. But I don't. I know that Nature is watching me. And Papa S. will know.

So I stand and stare at the flickering earth walls, with their overwhelming dank smell. I stand and stare at the mud above me and around me and under me. I stand and listen to the sound of my own breathing.

Surely she will be back soon?

Chapter Two

The candle is burning down so slowly. I don't want to move. The ground is cold through my trousers. I try to imagine that I'm dreaming, but I know I'm not.

Elizabeth does not come. The melting wax makes slippery shapes on the earth wall. The flame bulges and straightens, dancing in the silence.

I must have been here an hour, if not more. There's no one above me. No one is coming. When the candle burns down, I will disappear into the darkness.

"Elizabeth?" I call out softly. Of course she can't hear me. No one can hear me. There's no one there.

My stomach is starting to hurt with hunger, a rumbling pain. It's something I've barely felt before. At Seed, no one is hungry. There is always food, there is always drink.

"Thank you, Nature," I whisper. I kiss my palm, press it flat into the earth. It's bumpy against my skin. I imagine how deep the earth goes beneath me.

Kate and Jack will notice I'm gone. They will ask about me.

I close my eyes. It can't be long now.

But I'm finding it difficult to breath. What if those pipes don't work? What if they're blocked and I slowly run out of air? My breath is sticking in my throat. It's got nowhere to go. Am I going to suffocate? Is this how I am going to die?

"Help me, Nature," I say. She must hear me, because there's a rustling of leaves above my head, a heavy scraping of the Worship Chair. And as the door is lifted, the sunlight floods in so sharply that I have to cover my eyes.

I am free. So I start to move toward the steps, just as Elizabeth comes down to get me. She is carrying something. When she reaches the bottom, she takes off the cloth covering it. It is a bowl of soup. A spoon and a chunk of bread sink into it.

"I must be quick," Elizabeth says, her voice hushed as she puts the bowl on the floor.

"But I'm coming with you," I reply.

"I'll be back in the morning. Just after sunrise." She tries to hug me, but I grab at her hands.

"No, Elizabeth, you can't leave me here." I'm crying, sudden and startling in the quiet circle of earth.

"Think of the rewards, Pearl. You will have a healthy womb. And when Papa S. says it is the right time, you will have children."

"No." I'm trying to stay calm. "No, I can't stay here."

"You must." She's trying to peel my hands away.

"I'll die if you leave me. I can't breathe in here, Elizabeth." I want her to look at me. I want her to understand, but she's looking back up the stairs. She's trying to get away.

"Pearl, you must let me go," she says quietly. Then she looks at me with those eyes of clover green. "Nature will protect you. There's no harm that can come to you here. You are privileged." Elizabeth finally frees her hands and kisses me on the head. "You are safe, Pearl, you are loved."

Then she rushes up the steps. I reach for the material of her skirt, but she's gone.

The trapdoor has closed out the sunlight. There's just the silence and me. Somewhere, there are beetles burrowing, but I can't hear them. All I can hear is the sound of my short breathing and my heart thudding in the cramped air.

I kneel down and reach for the bowl of soup. The smell of it should make my mouth water, but as I bring the spoon to my lips, I feel sick. Still, I force it into my mouth, feel its warmth in my chest. It helps the ache in my stomach and so I gently scrape until every last drop has gone.

The smell of the ancient mud finds me once more. It creeps into my nose and slides down inside me.

I close my eyes and start to count. One, two, three. On and on. But the panic is rising again. *Breathe, Pearl, breathe. Trust in Elizabeth.* I focus on her smile, on the baby growing in her. Will I have a brother or a sister? I hope for a brother. If it's a girl, she will be forced into this hole. And I couldn't sit by, knowing that she is here.

I will think of the baby. Each little finger. Each little toe. Think about Papa S. and all that he gives us. Now I am a woman, maybe I can be his Companion. I imagine his hand in mine. I'm getting cold, but he will keep me warm.

I must sleep.

Somewhere there is music. And someone is singing, quietly. I open my eyes to blackness and silence. I am in the earth and the candle has burnt itself out. I move onto my knees as I sweep around with my hands. There's nothing but the rough, damp mud. Then my fingers hit the bottom of what must be the steps and I stumble up them. At the top I feel the closed trapdoor. If I'm desperate enough, I'll be able to open it. I push it with all my strength. I push it until I feel like my wrists will snap in two. But it doesn't move.

I bang it, feeble now. And I'm crying again as I curl myself onto the step. It's so dark that I can't even see my fingers. Darker than the silence in our sleeping room. Darker by far than the night. Nothing exists now, except the sound of my crying, getting soaked up by the earth. My life force dripping away.

Slowly I feel my way down the steps. I lie at the bottom. My bones ache from the cold and the hard floor.

"Please come, Elizabeth," I whisper. I kiss my palm and hold it above me, into the hollow blackness.

I'm woken by the sound of the trapdoor opening. There is light, muffled yet sharp enough to hurt my eyes.

"I'm here, Pearl."

It's Elizabeth. She lights a lamp and I can see again. "It's all right," she says. "It is over." And she smiles at me. "You can change into this."

She hands me a flowing green skirt. It's beautiful. I reach out to touch its material in the flickering candlelight. It feels so soft.

"It's silk," she says. "I made it for you when you were born."

I take off my trousers. As I put the skirt on, it feels like water on my bare legs. Elizabeth passes me a new slab of linen.

"Change this for the one in your underwear. We must leave the old one here for seven days."

"Will I have to come back to get it?" I ask, the panic rising like bile in my throat.

"You will not have to come back here," she says gently.

Elizabeth takes the old slab from me. It's heavy with my blood. When she has laid it face down in the earth, she turns to me. "You must never speak of this to anyone," she says.

She blows out the candle and starts to go back up the steps. I hurry after her.

When we're outside, she lowers the trapdoor, covers it with leaves, and pushes the heavy Worship Chair back into its place.

As we walk away in the early morning air, the birds are singing. The rain has stopped. My emerald-green skirt will tell everyone that now I am a woman.

You've just read an excerpt from Seed.

ABOUT THE AUTHOR

Lisa Heathfield is a former secondary school English teacher, specializing in working with hearing-impaired children. *Seed* is her debut novel. She lives in Brighton, England, with her husband and three children.

Imprint: Running Press Teens
Print ISBN: 9780762456345
Print price: $16.95
eBook ISBN: 9780762456369
eBook price: $16.95
Publication date: 3/10/15
Publicity contact: Valerie Howlett,
valerie.howlett@perseusbooks.com
Rights contact: Sarah Sheppard,
sarah.sheppard@perseusbooks.com
Editor: Lisa Cheng
Agent: Veronique Baxter
Agency: David Higham Associates

Territories sold:
Egmont UK – UK
Egmont – German
Albatros Publishing – Czech and Slovak

Promotional information:
- National print and online reviews
- Author blog tour
- Library outreach
- Social media marketing campaign targeting teen readers

NIGHTBIRD

A bewitching tale from the bestselling author

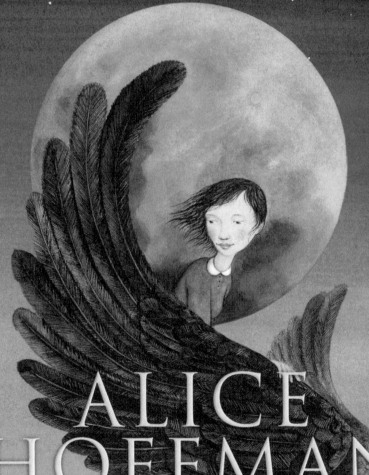

ALICE
HOFFMAN

SUMMARY

Twelve-year-old Twig's town in the Berkshires is said to hide a winged beast, the Monster of Sidwell, and the rumors draw as many tourists as the town's famed pink apple orchards. Twig lives in the orchard with her mysterious brother James and her reclusive mother, a baker of irresistible apple pies. Because of a family secret, an ancient curse, Twig has had to isolate herself from other kids. Then a family with two girls, Julia and Agate, moves into the cottage next door. They are descendants of the witch who put the spell on Twig's family. But Julia turns out to be Twig's first true friend, and her ally in trying to undo the curse and smooth the path to true love for Agate and James.

EXCERPT

You can't believe everything you hear, not even in Sidwell, Massachusetts, where every person is said to tell the truth and the apples are so sweet people come from as far as New York City during the apple festival. There are rumors that a mysterious creature lives in our town. Some people insist it's a bird bigger than an eagle; others say it's a dragon, or an oversized bat that resembles a person. Certainly this being, human or animal or something in between, exists nowhere else in this world. Children whisper that we have a monster in our midst, half man, half myth, and that fairy tales are real in Berkshire County. At the Sidwell General Store and at the gas station tourists can buy T-shirts decorated with a red-eyed winged beast with VISIT SIDWELL printed underneath.

Every time I see one of these shirts in a shop, I casually drop it into the garbage bin.

In my opinion, people should be careful about the stories they tell.

All the same, whenever things go missing the monster is blamed. Weekends are the worst times for these odd thefts. Bread deliveries to the Starline Diner are several loaves short of the regular order. Clothes hanging on the line vanish. I know there's no such thing as a monster, but the thief has struck my family, as a matter of fact. One minute there were four pies sitting out on the kitchen counter to cool, and the next minute the back door was left open and one of the pies was missing. An old quilt left out on our porch disappeared one Saturday. There were no footprints on our lawn, but I did have a prickle of fear when I stood at the back door that morning, gazing into the woods. I thought I spied a solitary figure running through a thicket of trees, but it might have only been mist, rising from the ground.

No one knows who takes these things, whether pranks are being played, or someone—or something—is truly in need, or if it is the creature that everyone assumes lives within the borders of our town. People in Sidwell argue as much as people do anywhere, but everyone agrees on one thing: Our monster can only be seen at night, and then only if you are standing at your window, or walking on a lane near the orchards, or if you happen to be passing our house.

We live on Old Mountain Road, in a farmhouse that is over two hundred years old, with nooks and crannies and three brick fireplaces, all big enough for me to stand in, even though I am tall for twelve. From our front door there's a sweeping view of the woods that contain some of the oldest trees in Massachusetts. Behind us are twenty acres of apple orchards. We grow a special variety called Pink. One of my ancestors planted the first Pink apple tree in Sidwell. Some people say Johnny Appleseed himself, who introduced apple trees all over our country, presented our family with a one-of-a-kind seedling when he wandered through town on his way out west. We make Pink applesauce, Pink apple cake, and two shades of Pink apple pie, light and dark. In the summer, before we have apples, we have Pink peach berry pie, and in the late spring there is Hot-Pink strawberry rhubarb pie, made from fruit grown in the garden behind our house. Rhubarb looks like red celery; it's bitter, but when combined with strawberries it's delicious. I like the idea of something bitter and something sweet mixed together to create something incredible. Maybe that's because I come from a family in which we don't expect each other to be like anyone else. Being unusual is not unusual for the Fowlers.

My mother's piecrust is said to be the finest in New England and our Pink cider is famous all over Massachusetts. People come from as far away as Cambridge and Lowell just to try them. We bring most of our pies and cupcakes to be sold at the General Store that's run by Mr. Stern, who can sell as many as my mother can bake. I've always wished that I was more like her instead of my awkward, gawky self. As a girl my mother attended ballet lessons at Miss Ellery's Dance School in town, and she's still graceful, even when she's picking apples or hauling baskets of fruit across the lawn. But my arms and legs are too long, and I tend to stumble over my own feet. The only thing I'm good at is running. And keeping secrets. I'm excellent at that. I've had a lot of practice.

My mother has honey-colored hair that she pins up with a silver clip whenever she bakes. My hair is dark; sometimes I don't even know what color it is, a sort of blackish brown, the color of tree bark, or a night that has no stars. It gets so tangled while I'm out in the woods that this year I cut it out of frustration, just hacked at it with a pair of nail scissors, and now it is worse than ever, even though my mother says I look like a pixie. Looking like a pixie was not what I was after. I wanted to look like my mother, who everyone says was the prettiest girl in town when she was my age, and now is the most beautiful woman in the entire county.

But she's also terribly sad. If my mother smiles it's something of a miracle, that's how rare it is. People in town are always kind to her, but they whisper about her, and refer to her as "poor Sophie Fowler." We aren't poor, though my mother has worked hard since her parents passed away and she came back to take over the orchard. All the same, I know why people feel sorry for her. I feel sorry for her, too. Despite the fact that my mother grew up in this town, she's always alone. In the evenings, she sits out on the porch, reading until the sun sinks in the sky and the light begins to fade. She reminds me of the owls in the woods that fly away whenever they see anyone. When we head down Main Street, she hurries with a walk that is more of a run, waving if one of her old high school friends calls hello but never stopping to chat.

She avoids the Starline Diner. Too sociable. Too many people she might know from the past. The last time we went in together it was my birthday and I begged for a special treat. Maybe because I've always had piles of cakes and pies and cupcakes, the dessert I yearn for is ice cream. It is perhaps my favorite food in the world, what I imagine real pixies would eat, if they ate anything at all. I love the shivery feeling eating ice cream gives you, as if you were surrounded by a cold cloud.

My mother and I sat in a corner booth and ordered ice cream sodas to celebrate my turning twelve. Twelve is a mysterious number and I'd always thought something exceptional would happen to me after that birthday, so I was feeling cheerful about the future, which is not usually my nature. I ordered chocolate, and my mother asked for strawberry. The waitress was a friendly woman named Sally Ann who'd known my mother growing up. She came over to our table, and when I blurted out that it was my birthday she told me that she and my mother had been best friends when they were twelve. She gazed sadly at my mother. "And now all these years have passed right by and I never hear a word from you, Sophie." Sally Ann seemed genuinely hurt that the friendship had ended. "Why are you hiding up there on Old Mountain Road when all your friends miss you?"

"You know me," my mother said. "I always kept to myself."

"That is not one bit true," Sally Ann insisted. She turned to me. "Don't believe her. Your mother was the most popular girl in Sidwell, but then she went off to New York City and when she came back she wasn't the same. Now she doesn't talk to anyone. Not even me!"

As soon as Sally Ann was called back to the counter, my mother whispered, "Let's go." We sneaked out the door before our ice cream sodas appeared. I don't know if my mother had tears in her eyes, but she looked sad as could be. Even sadder when Sally Ann ran after us and handed us our sodas to go in paper cups.

"I didn't mean to chase you away," Sally Ann apologized. "I was just saying I missed you. Remember when we were in ballet class together and we always went to the dance studio early so we could have the whole place to ourselves and dance ourselves silly?"

My mother smiled at the memory. I could see who she once was in the expression that crossed her face.

"I always liked Sally Ann," she said as we drove away. "But I could never be honest with her now, and how can you have a friend if you can't tell her the truth?"

I understood why my mother couldn't have friends, and why my fate was the same. I couldn't tell the truth either, though sometimes I wanted to shout it out so much my mouth burned. I could feel the words I longed to say stinging me, as if I'd swallowed bees that were desperate to be free.

This is who I am. That's what I'd shout. *I may not have a life like you do, but I'm Twig Fowler, and I have things to say!*

On most evenings and weekends we stayed at home and didn't venture out. That was our life and our fate and it wouldn't do any good to complain. I suppose you could call it the Fowler destiny. But I knew Sally Ann was right. It hadn't always been this way. I'd seen the photographs and the scrapbooks in a closet up in the attic. My mother used to be different. In high school she was on the track team and in the theater club. She always seemed to be surrounded by friends, ice-skating or having hot chocolate at the Starline Diner. She raised money for Sidwell Hospital's children's center by organizing a Bake-a-thon, baking one hundred pies in a single week that were sold to the highest bidders.

When she finished high school she decided she wanted to see the world. She was brave back then, and independent. She kissed her parents goodbye and left town on a Greyhound bus. She was young and headstrong and she'd dreamed of being a chef. Not someone who cooked in the Starline Diner, which she did on weekends all through high school. A real chef in a world-class restaurant. Pastries were always her specialty. She ran off to London and then to Paris, where she lived in tiny apartments and took cooking classes with the best chefs. She walked along foggy riverbanks to farmers' markets where she bought pears that tasted like candy. At last she wound up in New York City. That was where she met my father. The most she would tell me was that a mutual acquaintance had thought they'd be perfect for each other, and as it turned out, they were. My father was waiting for her when her plane touched down, there to help her find her way in Manhattan. Before the taxi reached her new apartment, they'd fallen in love.

But they split up before my mother came back home for her parents' funeral—my grandmother and grandfather had been in a car crash in the mountains during mudslide season. It happened in the Montgomery Woods, where the trees are so old and tall it seems dark even at noontime and there are several hairpin turns that make your stomach lurch when you drive around them. It was terribly sad to lose my grandparents, even though I was just a little girl. I can remember them in bits and pieces: a hug, a song, laughter, someone reading me a fairy tale about a girl who gets lost and finds her way home through the forest by leaving bread crumbs or following the blue-black feathers of crows.

When we came to Sidwell I was in the backseat of the old station wagon, which barely made it to Massachusetts. I was only a small child, but I remember looking out the window and seeing Sidwell for the first time. My mother changed our names back to Fowler from whatever my father's name was and she took over the farm. Every year she hires people traveling through town who need work. They pick apples and make the cider, but she does all the baking herself. If she's ever invited to a party or a town event, she writes a note politely declining. Some people say we're snobs because we once lived in New York and we expect life to race by with thrills like it does in Manhattan, and others say we think we're too good for a little town where not much ever changes. Still others wonder what happened to the husband my mother found and lost in New York.

People in Sidwell can talk all they want. They don't know the whole story. And if we're smart, they never will.

When we came home from New York I wasn't the only one in the backseat of the car.

That's why we arrived after dark.

Though I'm shy, I know most people in Sidwell, at least by name, except for the new neighbors who were just moving into the house at the edge of our property. I'd heard about them, of course, at the General Store. I'd biked over to the store to deliver two boxes of strawberry cupcakes that were so sweet I had what seemed like an entire hive of bees trailing after me. There's a group of men who have their coffee at the General Store before they head out to work. I secretly think of them as the Gossip Group. They're carpenters and plumbers, and even the postman and the sheriff sometimes join in. They have opinions on everything and comments about everyone and they tell jokes about the monster they seem to think are funny: *What do you do with a green monster? Wait for it to ripen. How does a monster play football? He crosses the ghoul line.*

When the talk turns serious, some of the men vow that one of these days there's going to be a monster hunt and that will be the end of things disappearing in town. That sort of conversation always gives me the chills. Thankfully, most of the recent talk has been about whether the woods will be turned into a housing development—over a hundred acres owned by Hugh Montgomery. People see even less of him than they do of us. The Montgomerys live in Boston and only come to Sidwell on holidays and weekends. They used to spend summers here, but now people say they're more likely to go to Nantucket or France. Lately, there have been trucks up in the forest, early in the morning, when the hollows are misty. Soon enough folks figured out that the water and soil were being tested. That's when people in town became suspicious about Montgomery's intentions.

I had other things to think about, so I didn't pay too much attention. The woods had always been there and I figured they always would be. I was more focused on the fact that new neighbors were moving into the property next to our orchard. That was big news to us. We'd never had neighbors before. Mourning Dove Cottage, deserted for ages, always had doves nesting nearby. You could hear them cooing when you walked up to the overgrown yard that was filled with brambles and thistles. The cottage had broken windows and a caving-in roof that was covered with moss. It was a grim and desolate place, and most folks avoided the area. It's not just the Gossip Group fellows who say a witch lived there long ago. Everyone agrees that the Witch of Sidwell was a resident until she had her heart broken. When she disappeared from our village, she left a curse behind.

Kids may stand at the edge of the lawn and listen to the doves, they may dare one another to go up to the porch, but they run away when one of those rare black Sidwell owls flies across the distance, and they never go inside. I made it onto the porch one time. I opened the front door, but I didn't step over the threshold, and afterward I had nightmares for weeks.

Every August a play about the Witch of Sidwell is performed at Town Hall by the youngest group in the summer camp. When I was little, the drama teacher, Helen Meyers, wanted me to be the witch.

"I have a feeling you'll be the best Agnes Early we've ever had," she told me. "You have natural talent, and that doesn't come along often."

It was an honor to be given the starring role and I was proud to have been chosen. From the time I was tiny I longed to be an actress, and maybe even write plays when I got older. But my mother came down to rehearsals before I'd said my last line—*Do not pry into my business if you know what's best for you and yours!*

Upset, she took Mrs. Meyers aside. "My daughter is the witch?"

"She's a natural," Mrs. Meyers cheerfully announced.

"A natural witch?" My mother seemed confused and insulted.

"Not at all, my dear. A natural actress. Not many have true talent, but when they do, it's usually the shy ones. They just bloom onstage."

"I'm afraid my daughter won't be able to continue on," my mother told Mrs. Meyers.

I was so shocked I couldn't say a word. All I could do was watch, speechless, as my mother informed the drama teacher that I would not be in the play, not even as a member of the chorus. I had a friend back then, my first and only one, a boy I shared my lunch with every day. We were both shy, I suppose, and we were both fast runners. What I remember is that he came to stand beside me on the day I left camp, and he held my hand, because I had already started to cry. I was only five, but I was so disappointed that when we got home, I sobbed until my eyes were rimmed red. My mother sat beside me and tried her best to console me but I turned away from her. I didn't understand how she could be so mean. At that moment I thought of myself as a rose cut down before I could bloom.

That night my mother brought dinner to my room, homemade tomato soup and toast. There was a Pink peach berry pie, but I didn't touch my dessert. I could tell that my mother had been crying, too. She said there was an unfortunate reason I couldn't be in the play. We were not like other people in town. We knew well enough not to mock a witch. Then my mother whispered what a witch could do if you crossed her. She could enchant you, which is what she did to our family more than two hundred years ago. Because of this curse we were still paying the price. I could write my own plays and perform them up in the attic, making up stories, dressing in old clothes I'd found in a metal trunk. But I could not ridicule the Witch of Sidwell.

My mother had a look in her eye I'd come to know. When she made a decision, there was no going back. I could beg and plead, but once her mind was made up that was that.

We baked the Pink apple cupcakes to be served at the party after the play, but we did not attend the performance. Instead we sat on a park bench in the center of Sidwell as the dark fell across the sky. We could hear the bell above Town Hall as it chimed six. We could hear an echo as the audience applauded for the new witch once the play had begun.

I think that evening was the beginning of my feeling lonely, a feeling I carried folded up, a secret I could never tell. From then on, I didn't cry when I was disappointed. I just stored up my hurts, as if they were a tower made of fallen stars, invisible to most people, but brightly burning inside of me.

It was late spring when the new people moved into Mourning Dove Cottage, the time of year when the orchard was abloom with a pink haze. For months there had been carpenters hammering and sawing as they worked away on the cottage, fixing shingles onto the roof, removing broken glass, and restoring the tumbledown porch. Some of the Gossip Group had been employed by the new owners of Mourning Dove, and they loved to tell people at the General Store how much they were charging the newcomers for their renovations. They were city people, outsiders, and so they paid top dollar for their rebuilt roof and a non-sagging porch. I thought this wasn't very neighborly, and I could tell that Mr. Stern felt the same way.

"If you're honest with someone he'll be honest with you," he told the men who gathered near his checkout counter, but I think I was the only one paying attention.

In this season I always collect flowering branches, enough to fill every one of our vases so the scent of apple blossoms will filter through our house, from the kitchen all the way to the attic. I spend hours curled up in my favorite tree, an old, twisted one that is thought to be the original apple tree planted in Sidwell. It's knobby, with velvety black bark, but I think the branches are like arms. I read books and do my homework up here. I take naps under a bower of leaves. In my dreams men and women can fly and birds live in houses and sleep in beds. Sometimes the doves nest above me and I can hear the cooing of their fledglings as I doze peacefully.

I was up in my favorite tree the day I heard the moving van rumbling down the dirt road beyond our orchard, with a car following behind as our new neighbors headed toward their new home. Dust rose in little whirlwinds as the truck came closer, and from the car's open window there was the sound of girls singing.

I sat still and squinted. It must be like this to be a bird looking down at the strange things people do. The newcomers had rooms full of oak furniture and silky rugs that shimmered with color. There were two parents who looked friendly as they bustled in and out of the house, and a shaggy collie dog they called Beau. The older of the two sisters was named Agate. She appeared to be about sixteen, with blond hair that reached to her shoulders and a laugh I could hear all the way across the orchard. The other one, Julia, was my age. She raced about collecting boxes that had her name scrawled across them from where the movers had placed them on the grass. "Mine," she'd call out as she lugged each newly discovered box up to the porch. At one point, she kicked off her shoes and did a little dance in the grass. She looked like someone who knew how to have fun, a lesson I needed to learn. I couldn't help but think that if I were a different person, I would want her as a friend. But a friend might want to come to our house, and when I said that wasn't possible, she might want to know why, and then I'd have to lie and I'd feel the stinging in my mouth that I always had when I didn't tell the whole truth.

I couldn't tell anyone about my brother, so there was no point to it really.

No one even knew I had a brother, not my teachers or classmates, not even the mayor, who vowed he knew every single person in Sidwell and had shaken every hand. I'd seen the mayor not long ago at the General Store, where he was discussing the weather and the future of the Montgomery Woods. He hadn't come out for or against the plan to develop the woods and put in houses and stores and maybe even a mall, although there probably weren't enough people in Sidwell to shop there. Being wishy-washy seemed to keep the mayor in office. The last time I'd seen him in town, he'd shaken my hand and looked into my eyes in a piercing way, then insisted I tell him my name and age, even though I had met him half a dozen times before. "Twig. Twelve years old, and tall at that! I'll remember your face and your name and your age because that's what a mayor does!" But every time I saw him after that he'd narrow his eyes as if trying to think of who I might be. I didn't blame him. I considered myself to be a shadow, a footstep in the woods that disappeared, a twig no one noticed. It was better that way. My mother always said the only way for us to stay in Sidwell was to live in the corners of everyday life.

I was tucked so far into a corner I was just about invisible.

I probably would have never met the Hall sisters and we might have remained strangers forever, if I hadn't fallen out of the tree and broken my arm. I leaned forward on a branch that was split through. Ordinarily, I would have been more careful, but I was concentrating on my new neighbors, and the wavering branch broke the rest of the way with me on it. I went down hard and fast. I cried out before I could stop myself. The collie came running over, followed by the Hall sisters. There I was, sprawled out on the ground, so embarrassed I could only stutter a hello.

My full name is Teresa Jane Fowler but everyone calls me Twig because of how much time I spend climbing apple trees, although now it seemed climbing was over for me, at least for a while.

"Don't move! Our father is a doctor," the older sister, Agate, announced. She raced back to the cottage, leaving me there with the collie and the girl my own age.

Julia introduced herself, and when I told her I was Twig from next door she nodded thoughtfully and said, "I wished there would be someone living right near us who was my age and it happened!"

She was dark, like me, only not as tall. I felt even worse about cutting my hair so short. Hers was long and straight, almost to her waist. We looked like opposite versions of each other.

"Does your arm hurt?" she asked.

"I'm fine." I wasn't one to let my feelings show. "Perfect, as a matter of fact."

Julia's face furrowed with concern. "I once broke my toe. I screamed so much I lost my voice."

"I'm really okay. I think I'll just walk home now." I was trying to be nonchalant, but my arm was throbbing. When I tried to move I gasped. The pain shot through me.

"Are you sure you're all right?"

"I am so not all right," I admitted.

"Scream. You'll feel better. I'll do it with you."

We let loose and screamed and all the doves floated up into the sky. They looked so beautiful up above us, like clouds.

Julia was right. I did feel better.

You've just read an excerpt from Nightbird.

ABOUT THE AUTHOR

Alice Hoffman is the author of more than thirty bestselling works of fiction, including *Practical Magic,* which was made into a major motion picture starring Sandra Bullock and Nicole Kidman; *Here on Earth,* an Oprah Book club selection; the highly praised historical novel *The Dovekeepers*; and, most recently, *The Museum of Extraordinary Things.* Her books for teens include *Green Angel, Green Witch, Incantation, The Foretelling,* and *Aquamarine,* also a major motion picture starring Emma Roberts. Visit her online at alicehoffman.com.

Imprint: Wendy Lamb Books
Print ISBN: 9780385389587
Print price: $16.99
eBook ISBN: 9780385389600

eBook price: $10.99

Publication date: 3/10/15

Publicity contact: Casey Lloyd, clloyd@penguinrandomhouse.com

Editor: Beverly Horowitz

Agent: Tina Wexler

Agency: ICM Partners

Promotional information:

- Major Pre-Publication Media, Consumer, Trade, and Educator Buzz Campaign
- Pre-Pub Author Buzz Tour and National Author Events at On-Sale
- National Media Campaign
- National Consumer and Library Print and Online Advertising
- 9-Copy Floor Display
- Dedicated Pre-Pub Landing Page: WelcomeToSidwell.com
- Social Media Campaign Across All Platforms with Dedicated Hashtags #nightbirdbook and #welcometosidwell
- Major Promotions at All National School and Library Conferences and Regional Trade Shows
- Educational Kit, Including Guide with Common Core Correlations

ANOTHER DAY

DAVID LEVITHAN

SUMMARY

In David Levithan's *New York Times* bestseller *Every Day*, readers met A, a teen who wakes up every morning in a different body. A has made peace with that, even established guidelines by which to live: Never get too attached. Avoid being noticed. Do not interfere. It's all fine until the morning that A wakes up in the body of Justin and meets Justin's girlfriend, Rhiannon, and discovers what it means to want to be with someone—day in, day out, day after day. In *Another Day*, readers experience the same story from Rhiannon's perspective, as she seeks to understand A's life and discover if you can truly love someone who is destined to change every day.

EXCERPT

Chapter One

I watch his car as it pulls into the parking lot. I watch him get out of it. I am in the corner of his eye, moving toward its center . . . but he isn't looking for me. He's heading into school without noticing I'm right here. I could call out for him, but he doesn't like that. He says it's something needy girls do, always calling out to their boyfriends.

I wonder how I can be so full of him while he's so empty of me. The school door opens and the school door closes, and he doesn't realize I am on the other side of it.

I love him and I hate him because I know that I'm his.

I wonder if last night is the reason he isn't looking for me. I wonder if our fight is still happening. Like most of our fights, it's about something stupid, with other non-stupid things right underneath. All I did was ask him if he wanted to go to Steve's party on Saturday. That was it. And he asked me why, on Sunday night, I was already asking him about Saturday. He said I'm always doing this, trying to pin him down, as if he won't want to be with me if I don't ask him about it months ahead of time. I told him it wasn't my fault he's always afraid of plans, afraid of figuring out what's next.

Mistake. Calling him afraid was a big mistake. That's probably the only word he heard.

"You have no idea what you're talking about," he said.

"I was talking about a party at Steve's house on Saturday," I told him, my voice way too upset for either of us. "That's all."

But that's not all. Justin loves me and hates me as much as I love him and hate him. I know that. We each have our triggers, and we should never reach in to pull them. But sometimes we can't help ourselves. We know each other too well, but never well enough.

I am in love with someone who's afraid of the future. And, like a fool, I keep bringing it up.

I follow him. Of course I do. Only a needy girl would be mad at her boyfriend because he didn't notice her in a parking lot.

As I'm walking to his locker, I wonder which Justin I'll find there. It probably won't be Sweet Justin, because it's rare for Sweet Justin to show up at school. And hopefully it won't be Angry Justin, because I haven't done anything that wrong, I don't think. I'm hoping for Chill Justin, because I like Chill Justin. When he's around, we can all calm down.

I stand there as he takes his books out of his locker. I look at the back of his neck because I am in love with the back of his neck. There is something so physical about it, something that makes me want to lean over and kiss it.

Finally he looks at me. I can't read his expression, not right away. It's like he's trying to figure me out at the same time I'm trying to figure him out. I think maybe this is a good sign, because maybe it means he's worried about me. Or it's a bad sign, because he doesn't understand why I'm here.

"Hey," he says.

"Hey," I say back.

There's something really intense about the way he's looking at me. I'm sure he's finding something wrong, and the next words are going to be harsh. There's always something wrong for him to find.

But he doesn't say anything. Which is weird. Then, even weirder, he asks me, "Are you okay?"

I must look really pathetic if he's asking me that.

"Sure," I tell him. Because I don't know what the answer is supposed to be. I am not okay—that's actually the right answer. But it's not the right answer to say to him. I know that much.

Danger. If this is some kind of trap, I don't appreciate it. If this is payback for what I said last night, I want it over with, so we can move on.

"Are you mad at me?" I ask, not sure I want to know the answer.

And he goes, "No. I'm not mad at you at all."

I don't believe him.

When we have problems, I'm usually the one who sees them. I'm the one who's concerned. I do the worrying for both of us. I just can't tell him about it too often, because then it's almost like I'm bragging that I understand what's going on while he doesn't.

Uncertainty. Do I ask about last night? Or do I pretend it never happened—that it never happens?

"Do you still want to get lunch today?" I ask. It's only after I ask that I realize I'm trying to make plans again. I should learn, but I never do.

Maybe I am a needy girl, after all.

"Absolutely," Justin says. "Lunch would be great."

Bullshit. He's playing with me. He has to be.

"It'll be cool," he adds.

I look at him, and it seems genuine. Maybe I'm wrong to assume the worst. And maybe I've managed to make him feel stupid by being so surprised.

I take his hand and hold it. If he's willing to step back from last night, I am, too. This is what we do. When the stupid fights are over, we're good.

"I'm glad you're not mad at me," I tell him. "I just want everything to be okay."

He knows I love him. I know he loves me. That is never the question. The question is always how we'll deal with it.

Time. The bell rings. I have to remind myself that school is not a thing that exists solely to give us a place to be together.

"I'll see you later," he says.

I hold on to that. It's the only thing that will get me through the empty space that follows.

I was watching one of my shows, and one of the housewives was like, "He's a fuckup, but he's my fuckup," and I thought, Oh, shit, I really shouldn't be relating to this, but I am, and so what? That has to be what love is—seeing what a mess he is and loving him anyway, because you know you're a mess, too, maybe even worse.

We weren't an hour into our first date before Justin was setting off the alarms.

"I'm warning you—I'm trouble," he said over dinner at TGI Fridays. "Total trouble."

"And do you warn all the other girls?" I replied, flirting.

But what I got back wasn't flirtation. It was real.

"No," he said. "I don't."

This was his way of letting me know that I was someone he cared about. Even at the very beginning.

He hadn't meant to tell me. But there it was.

And even though he's forgotten a lot of other details about that first date, he's never forgotten what he said.

I warned you! he'll yell at me on nights when it's really bad, really hard. You can't say I didn't warn you!

Sometimes this only makes me hold him tighter.

Sometimes I've already let go, feeling awful that there's nothing I can do.

The only time our paths intersect in the morning is between first and second periods, so I look for him then. We only have a minute to share, sometimes less, but I'm always thankful. It's like I'm taking attendance. Love? Here! Even if we're tired (which is pretty much always) and even if we don't have much to say, I know he won't just pass me by.

Today I smile, because, all things considered, the morning went pretty well. And he smiles back at me.

Good signs. I am always looking for good signs.

I head to Justin's class as soon as fourth period is over, but he hasn't waited for me. So I go to the cafeteria, to where we usually sit. He's not there, either. I ask Rebecca if she's seen him. She says she hasn't, and doesn't seem too surprised that I'm looking. I decide to ignore that. I check my locker and he's not there. I'm starting to think he's forgotten, or maybe was playing with me all along. I'm starting to feel played. I decide to check his locker, even though it's about as far from the cafeteria as you can get. He never stops there before lunch. But I guess today he has, because there he is.

I'm happy to see him, but also exhausted. It's just so much work. He looks worse than I feel, staring into his locker like there's a window in there. In some people, this would mean daydreams. But Justin doesn't daydream. When he's gone, he's really gone.

Now he's back. Right when I get to him.

"Hey," he says.

"Hey," I say back.

I'm hungry, but not that hungry. The most important thing is for us to be in the same place. I can do that anywhere.

He's putting all of his books in his locker now, as if he's done with the day. I hope nothing's wrong. I hope he's not giving up. If I'm going to be stuck here, I want him stuck here, too.

He stands up and puts his hand on my arm. Gentle. Way too gentle. It's something I'd do to him, not something he'd do to me. I like it, but I also don't like it.

"Let's go somewhere," he says. "Where do you want to go?"

Again, I think there has to be a right answer to this question, and that if I get it wrong, I will ruin everything. He wants something from me, but I'm not sure what.

"I don't know," I tell him.

He takes his hand off my arm and I think, okay, wrong answer. But then he takes my hand.

"Come on," he says.

There's an electricity in his eyes. Power. Light.

He closes the locker and pulls me forward. I don't understand. We're walking hand in hand through the almost-empty halls. We never do this. He gets this grin on his face and we go faster. It's like we're little kids at recess. Running, actually running, down the halls. People look at us like we're insane. It's so ridiculous. I'm laughing at how absurd this is. He swings us by my locker and tells me to leave my books here, too. I don't understand, but I go along with it—he's in a great mood, and I don't want to do anything that will break it.

Once my locker's closed, we keep going. Right out the door. Simple as that. Escape. We're always talking about how we want to leave, and this time we're doing it. I figure he'll take me to get pizza or something. Maybe be late to fifth period. We get to his car and I don't even want to ask him what we're doing. I just want to let him do it.

He turns and asks, "Where do you want to go? Tell me, truly, where you'd love to go."

Strange. He's asking me as if I'm the one who knows the right answer.

I really hope this isn't a trick. I really hope I won't regret this.

I say the first thing that comes to my mind.

"I want to go to the ocean. I want you to take me to the ocean."

I figure he'll laugh and say what he really meant was that we should go to his house while his parents are gone and spend the afternoon having sex and watching TV. Or that he's trying to prove a point about not making plans, to prove that I like being spontaneous better. Or he'll tell me to go have fun at the ocean while he goes to get lunch. All of these are possibilities, and they all play at the same time in my head.

The only thing I'm not expecting is for him to think it's a good idea.

"Okay," he says, pulling out of the parking lot. I still think he's joking, but then he's asking me the best way to get there. I tell him which highways we should take—there's a beach my family used to go to a lot in summer, and if we're going to the ocean, we might as well go there.

As he steers, I can tell he's enjoying himself. Which should put me at ease, but it's making me nervous. It would be just like Justin to take me somewhere really special in order to dump me. Make a big production of it. Maybe leave me stranded there. I don't actually think this is going to happen—but it's possible. As a way of proving to me that he's able to make plans. As a way of showing he's not as afraid of the future as I said he was.

You're being crazy, Rhiannon, I tell myself. It's something he says to me all the time. A lot of the time, he's right.

Just enjoy it, I think. Because we're not in school. We're together.

He turns on the radio and tells me to take over. What? My car, my radio— how many times have I heard him say that? But it seems like his offer is real, so I slip from station to station, trying to find something he'll be into. When I pause too long on a song I like, he says, "Why not that one?" And I'm thinking, Because you hate it. But I don't say that out loud. I let the song play. I wait for him to make a joke about it, say the singer sounds like she's having her period.

Instead, he starts to sing along.

Disbelief. Justin never sings along. He will yell at the radio. He will talk back to whatever the talk radio people are saying. Every now and then he might beat along on his steering wheel. But he does not sing.

I wonder if he's on drugs. But I've seen him on drugs before, and it's never been like this.

"What's gotten into you?" I ask.

"Music," he says.

"Ha."

"No, really."

He's not joking. He's not laughing at me somewhere inside. I am looking at him and I can see that. I don't know what's going on, but it's not that.

I decide to see how far I can push it. Because that's what a needy girl does.

"In that case . . . ," I say. I flip stations until I find the least Justin song possible.

And there it is. Kelly Clarkson. Singing how what doesn't kill you makes you stronger.

I turn it up. In my head, I dare him to sing along.

Surprise.

We are belting it out. I have no idea how he knows the words. But I don't question it. I am singing with everything I've got, never knowing I could love this song as much as I do right now, because it is making everything okay—it is making us okay. I refuse to think about anything other than that. I want us to stay inside the song. Because this is something we've never done before and it feels great.

When it's done, I roll down my window—I want to feel the wind in my hair. Without a word, Justin rolls down all the other windows, and it's like we're in a wind tunnel, like this is a ride in an amusement park when really it's just a car driving down the highway. He looks so happy. It makes me realize how rare it is for me to see him happy, the kind of happy where there isn't anything else on your mind besides the happiness. He's usually so afraid to show it, as if it might be stolen away at any moment.

He takes my hand and starts to ask me questions. Personal questions.

He starts with "How are your parents doing?"

"Um . . . I don't know," I say. He's never really cared about my parents before. I know he wants them to like him, but because he's not sure they will, he pretends it doesn't matter. "I mean, you know. Mom is trying to hold it all together without actually doing anything. My dad has his moments, but he's not exactly the most fun person to be around. The older he gets, the less he seems to give a damn about anything."

"And what's it like with Lisa at college?"

When he asks this question, it's as if he's proud that he's remembered my sister's name. That sounds more like Justin.

"I don't know," I tell him. "You know we were more like sisters living under a truce than best friends. I don't know if I miss her that much, although it was easier having her around, because then there were two of us, you know? She never calls home. Even when my mom calls her, she doesn't call back. I don't blame her for that—I'm sure she has better things to do than get the latest family drama. And really, I always knew that once she left, she'd be gone. So I'm not shocked or anything."

I realize as I'm talking that I'm getting close to the nerve, talking about what happens when high school is over. But Justin doesn't seem to be taking it personally. Instead, he asks me if I think school is much different this year than last year. Which is a weird question. Something my grandmother would ask. Not my boyfriend.

I tread carefully.

"I don't know. School sucks. That's not different. But, you know—while I really want it to be over, I'm also worried about everything that's going to come after. Not that I have it planned out. I don't. I know you think that I have all of these plans—but if you actually look at the things I've done to prepare myself for life after high school, all you'll see is a huge blank. I'm just as unprepared as anyone else."

Shut up, shut up, shut up, I'm telling myself. Why are you bringing this up?

But maybe I have a reason. Maybe I'm bringing it up to see what he'll do. He tests me all the time, but I'm not exactly innocent in that department, either.

"What do you think?" I ask him.

And he says, "Honestly, I'm just trying to live day to day."

I know. But I appreciate it more when it's said like this, in a voice that acknowledges we're on the same side. I wait for him to say more, to edge back into last night's fight. But he lets it go. I am grateful.

It's been over a year, and there've been at least a hundred times when I've told myself that this was it—this was the new start. Turning the page, as if that meant we weren't still in the same story. Sometimes I was right. But not as much as I wanted to be.

Realistic. I will not let myself think that things are suddenly better. I will not let myself think that we've somehow escaped the us we always end up being. But at the same time, I will not deny what's happening. I will not deny this happiness. Because if happiness feels real, it almost doesn't matter if it's real or not.

Instead of plugging the destination into his phone, he's asking me to keep giving him directions. I screw up and tell him to get off the highway one exit too soon, but when I realize this, he doesn't freak out at all—he just gets back on the highway and goes one more exit. Now I'm no longer wondering if he's on drugs—I'm wondering if he's on medication. If so, it's kicking in pretty quickly.

I do not say a word. I don't want to jinx it.

"I should be in English class," I say as we make the last turn before the beach.

"I should be in bio," Justin says back.

But this is more important. I can make up my homework, but I can't make up my life. This is my life. Here is my life.

"Let's just enjoy ourselves," he says.

"Okay," I tell him. "I like that. I spend so much time thinking about running away—it's nice to actually do it. For a day. Instead of staring outside the window, it's good to be on the other side of the window. I don't do this enough."

Maybe this is what we've needed all along. Distance from everything else, and closeness to each other. Something is working here—I can feel it working.

So I run with it.

Memory. This is the beach my family would come to, on days when the house was too hot or my parents were sick of staying in the same place. When we'd come here, we'd be surrounded by other families. I liked to imagine that each of our blankets was a house, and that a certain number of blankets made a town. I'm sure there were a few kids I saw all the time, whose parents always took them here, too, but I can't remember any of them now. I can only remember my own family—my mother always under an umbrella, either not wanting to burn or not wanting to be seen; my sister taking out a book and staying inside it the whole time; my father talking to the other fathers about sports or stocks. When it got too hot, he would race me down into the water and ask me what kind of fish I wanted to be. I knew that the right answer was flying fish, because if I told him that, he would gather me in his arms and throw me into the air.

I don't know why I've never brought Justin here before. Last summer, we stayed indoors, waiting for his parents to leave for work so we could have sex in every room of the house, including some of the closets. Then, when it was done, we'd watch TV or play video games. Sometimes we'd call around to see what everyone else was doing, and by the time his parents came home, we'd be off at someone else's house, drinking or watching TV or playing video games or some mix of the three. It was great, because it wasn't school, and we were with each other. But it didn't really get us anywhere.

I leave my shoes in the car, just like I did when I was a kid. There's the awkward couple of steps when you're still in the parking lot and the pavement hurts, but then there's the sand and everything's fine. The beach is completely empty today, and even though I didn't expect there to be a lot of people here, it's still surprising, like we've caught the beach napping.

I can't help myself. I run right down into it, spin around. Mine, I think. The beach is mine. The time is mine. Justin is mine. Nobody—nothing— is going to interfere with that. I call out his name, and it's like I'm still singing along to a song.

He looks at me for a moment, and I think, oh no, this is the part where he tells me I look like an idiot. But then he's running down to me, grabbing hold of me, swinging me around. He's heard the song, and now we're dancing. We're laughing and racing each other to the water. When we get there, we splash-war, feeling the tide against our legs. I reach down for some shells and Justin joins me, looking for colors that won't be the same when they're dry, looking for sea glass and spirals. The water feels so good, and standing still feels so good, because there's a whole ocean pulling at me and I have the strength to stay where I am.

Justin's face is completely unguarded. His body is entirely relaxed. I never see him like this. We are playing, but it's not the kind of playing that boyfriends and girlfriends usually do, where there's strategy and scorekeeping and secret moves. No, we have scissored ourselves away from all that.

I ask him to build a sand castle with me. I tell him how Lisa always had to have her own, next to mine. She would build a huge mountain with a deep moat around it, while I would make a small, detailed house with things like a front door and a garage. Basically, I was building the dollhouse I was never able to have, while Lisa was creating the fortress she felt she needed. She would never touch my castle—she wasn't the kind of older sister who needed to destroy the competition. But she wouldn't let me touch hers, either. We'd leave them when we were done, for the tide to take away. Sometimes our parents would come over. To me, they'd say, How pretty! To Lisa, it would be, How tall!

I want Justin to work on a sand castle with me. I want us to experience what it's like to build something together. We don't have any shovels or buckets. Everything has to be done with our hands. He takes the phrase sand castle literally—starting with the square foundation, drawing on a drawbridge with his finger. I work on the turrets and the towers—balconies are precarious, but spires are possible. At random moments, he compliments me—little words like nice and neat and sweet—and I feel like the beach is somehow unlocking this vocabulary from the dungeon where he's kept it all these months. I always felt—maybe hoped—that the words were in there somewhere. And now I know they are.

It isn't very warm out, but I can feel the sun on my cheeks and my neck. We could gather more shells and begin to decorate, but I am starting to tire of the building, and putting our focus there. When the last tower is completed, I suggest we wander for a little while.

"Are you pleased with our creation?" he asks.

And I say, "Very."

We head to the water to wash off our hands. Justin stares back at the beach, back at our castle, and seems lost for a moment. Lost, but in a good place.

"What is it?" I ask.

He looks at me, eyes so kind, and says, "Thank you."

I am sure he has said these two words to me before, but never like this, never in a way that would make me want to remember them.

"For what?" I ask. What I mean is: Why now? Why finally?

"For this," he says. "For all of it."

I want so much to trust it. I want so much to think that we've finally shifted to the place I always thought we could get to. But it's too simple. It feels too simple.

"It's okay," he tells me. "It's okay to be happy."

I have wanted this for so long. This is not how I pictured it, but nothing ever is. I am overwhelmed by how much I love him. I don't hate him at all. There's not a single part of me that hates him. There is only love. And it isn't terrifying. It is the opposite of terrifying.

I am crying because I'm happy and I'm crying because I don't think I ever realized how much I was expecting to be unhappy. I am crying because for the first time in a long time, life makes sense.

He sees me crying and doesn't make fun of it. He doesn't get defensive, asking what he did this time. He doesn't tell me he warned me. He doesn't tell me to stop. No, he wraps his arms around me and holds me and takes these things that are only words and makes them into something more than words. Comfort. He gives me something I can actually feel—his presence, his hold.

"I'm happy," I say, afraid he thinks I'm crying for a reason besides that. "Really, I am."

The wind, the beach, the sun—everything else wraps around us, but our embrace is the one that matters. I am holding on to him now as much as he is holding on to me. We have reached that perfect balance, where each of us is strong and each of us is weak, each taking, each giving.

"What's happening?" I ask.

"Shhh," he says. "Don't question it."

I don't feel any questions—only answers. I don't feel fear, only fullness. I kiss him and continue our perfect balance there, let our separate breaths become one breath. I close my eyes and feel the familiar press of his lips, the familiar taste of his mouth. But something is different now. We are not just kissing with our whole bodies, but with something that is bigger than our bodies, that is who we are and who we will be. We are kissing from a deeper part of our selves, and we are finding a deeper part of each other. It feels like electricity hitting water, fire reaching paper, the brightest light finding our eyes. I run my hands down his back, down his front, as if I need to know that he's really here, that this is really happening. I linger on the back of his neck. He lingers on the side of my hip. I slip below his belt, but he leads me back up. He kisses my neck. I kiss beneath his ear. I kiss his smile. He traces my laugh.

Enjoying this. We are enjoying this.

I have no idea what time it is, what day it is. I have nothing but now. Nothing but here. And it is more than enough.

You've just read an excerpt from Another Day.

ABOUT THE AUTHOR

David Levithan is a children's book editor in New York City, and the author of several books for young adults, including Lambda Literary Award winner *Two Boys Kissing*; *Nick & Norah's Infinite Playlist*, *Naomi and Ely's No Kiss List*, and *Dash & Lily's Book of Dares* (co-authored with Rachel Cohn); *Will Grayson, Will Grayson* (co-authored with John Green); and *Every You, Every Me* (with photographs from Jonathan Farmer). He lives in Hoboken, New Jersey.

Imprint: Alfred A. Knopf Books for Young Readers

Print ISBN: 9780385756204

Print price: $17.99

eBook ISBN: 9780385756228

eBook price: $10.99

Publication date: 8/25/15

Publicity contact: Dominique Cimina, dcimina@penguinrandomhouse.com

Editor: Nancy Hinkel

Agent: Bill Clegg

Agency: William Morris Endeavor

Promotional information:

- Extensive pre-publication consumer, trade, and educator buzz campaign featuring major repromotion of every day
- National media campaign
- National author tour (8—10 cities)
- Book festival author appearances
- National consumer and library print and online advertising
- Solid and mixed floor displays
- Book club discussion guide featuring *Every Day* and *Another Day*
- Feature at Book Expo America and Book Con
- Feature at Comic-Con (San Diego, New York)
- Major promotions at all national school and library conferences and regional trade shows
- Promotion at Twitter Fiction Festival
- Extensive social media campaign across all platforms
- Promotion on Figment.com featuring author Q&A, writing contest, and social media posts
- Outreach to teen advisory groups

AFTER THE RED RAIN

BY *NEW YORK TIMES* BESTSELLING AUTHOR

BARRY LYGA
WITH
PETER FACINELLI
AND
ROBERT DeFRANCO

SUMMARY

A post-apocalyptic novel with a cinematic twist from *New York Times* bestseller Barry Lyga, actor Peter Facinelli, and producer Robert DeFranco. On the ruined planet Earth, where 50 billion people are confined to mega-cities, and resources are scarce, Deedra has been handed a bleak and mundane existence by the Magistrate she works so hard for. But one day, she comes across a beautiful boy struggling to cross the river. A boy with a secretive past and special abilities, who is somehow able to find comfort and life from their dying planet. A boy with an unusual name...Rose. But just as the two form a bond, it is quickly torn apart by the murder of the Magistrate's son, and Rose becomes the prime suspect. Little do they know how much their relationship will affect the fate of everyone who lives on the planet.

EXCERPT

Prologue

The Last Days of the Red Rain

The clank and rattle of what he thought of as The System had long since faded into mere background noise to Gus. Or maybe he was just going deaf. He was certainly old enough—beyond old enough—for it. In any event, it didn't matter. He was the only one tending to The System, so he was the only one to talk to. And he'd gotten bored with himself a long, long time ago. Stooped and twisted with age—nearly fifty years, if he remembered correctly, an almost unheard-of longevity—he limped around the chamber with only himself for company.

The System was a series of belts, tubes, pulleys, and wheels arranged in a circuitous route through a large chamber. It began at an inclined chute at one end and wended its clacking, whirring way through the chamber to the opposite end.

The System was all about bodies.

Tall, short, thin, fat, young, old, frail, robust, every color and shade decreed by Nature or by God—take your pick. The bodies wound through The System day and night, hauled along as machines snapped and plucked at them, stripping them of clothing, jewelry, and all the other accoutrements of the living world. They entered The System as they'd died; they left it as they'd been born: naked and alone.

Gus monitored The System. He attended to its needs. Though he had his suspicions, he didn't know where the bodies came from or where they went. Long ago he'd decided that it was best simply to be grateful he wasn't one of them.

This day, a sound came to him, pitched high above the muted rumble of the machinery. At first, he thought it had to be his imagination. Then he thought it must be his ears finally giving up the ghost after so many years of abuse. He scrabbled at one ear, then the other, with his little finger, digging around.

The sound persisted. High-pitched and abjectly terrified and definitely alive, not mechanical.

He peered around the chamber, seeking the source of the sound. In the echoing confines of The System, it was difficult to pinpoint a specific noise. Especially with ears fading, as his were. Standing still, he listened intently. Rotated and took a few steps. Paused again to listen, willing the sound to become louder.

Miraculously, it did. It rose to a bloodcurdling howl.

Gus rushed to the tunnel that opened up into The System. The noise had come from there, he knew it.

He gaped at what he saw.

Gus had worked The System as long as he could remember. Most of his life, really. Decades. He'd never tried to count the bodies that came through, and even if he had, he would have given up on tallying them long ago.

But this, he knew, was the first time he'd ever seen a living one.

A baby.

A tiny, defenseless baby lay on a series of grinding cylinders that bore the bodies into The System. She—for she was naked—squawked and squalled, waving one pudgy fist in terrified indignation, kicking her chubby legs.

She was stuck. As she'd slid down the chute, her left shoulder had been caught in the gears of the machinery. It pinched there, purple-going-black, and she howled.

Sometimes bodies got stuck like this. Gus had tools to break them loose. But such tools were for dead bodies, not living ones, and he froze for an instant, unsure what to do.

She cried out again, her face going purple now.

There was no time to hit the emergency shutdown switch—she would be ripped to shreds before then. And besides, hitting the switch would mean questions, and Gus understood that it was best not to have questions when he had no answers.

Wincing in sympathetic pain, he tugged at her, gently at first and then, finally, with all his strength when gently didn't suffice. With a yowl of pain, she came free from the machine, leaving behind an inch-wide strip of flesh from high up on her neck to her shoulder. Bright red blood spilled, and Gus nearly lost his grip on her as it flowed down to his hands, making her slippery.

"Shush, shush," he cooed, almost by instinct. A baby. When was the last time he'd seen a baby?

A living baby, he amended.

"Hush-a, hush-a," he tried, and still she wailed. He couldn't blame her.

He knew what he should do. He knew his job. Bodies came into The System, and bodies went through The System, and bodies left The System. His job was to make sure everything ran smoothly. And while he'd always assumed the bodies would be dead and had always seen only dead bodies . . . no one had ever specified dead.

He should put her on the rolling cylinders and let her leave The System as everyone else did, to go wherever they went.

She screamed and whimpered, and her blood spilled. Gus chewed at his bottom lip.

It had been so long since he'd cried that he didn't even realize he was doing it until the first fat tears splashed onto her round, little belly.

"Hush-a, hush-a," he whispered, bouncing her lightly. "Hush-a, hush-a. That ain't gonna heal on its own. Sorry, no. But I think old Gus can do what he can do."

He carried her to his workbench and swept his tools aside. The bench was dirty and scarred with age, but better than whatever lay beyond The System. He set her down and began rummaging in his toolbox, muttering to himself.

"Fishing line, fishing line . . ." He hadn't fished since he was a boy, and even then the rivers had been dead. But the line came in handy for a number of tasks, so he always kept a supply. He dug it out now and then found a needle from the kit he used to repair his clothes.

"This ain't gonna feel so good right now," he warned her, threading the needle with the fine, light filament, "but it'll feel better later, I promise."

He took a deep breath. He held her down and began to sew.

PART 1

Sixteen Years Later

Deedra and the Blue Rat

Chapter One

Deedra wouldn't have seen the blue rat that morning if not for her best friend, Lissa.

"What are you thinking about?" Lissa asked, and Deedra realized she'd been staring up at the bridge that crossed the river on the edge of the Territory. The bridge that used to cross the river, actually. Halfway, the bridge had crumbled—when the river ran low, you could still see chunks of concrete, sprouted with spider legs of steel, resting in the water where they'd fallen. She and Lissa had hiked out from the center of the Territory toward the border, maneuvering past the Wreck. Now they stood on the shell of what had once been a train car, or a truck or some kind of vehicle, turned on its side and rusting into oblivion. From here, they could see the whole putrid shoreline of the river.

Deedra shrugged. "Nothing," she lied, and held up a hand to shield her eyes from the nonexistent sun. On a good day there would be maybe a half hour of direct sunlight, usually in the morning. The rest of the time, like now, the sky clouded over, steeping the Territory and the wider City in gray murk.

Along one edge of the bridge, some long-ago vandal had spray painted **waiting for the rain**. The words were black, except for the last one, which had been sprayed bloodred.

"You're thinking of climbing the bridge," Lissa said knowingly, and Deedra couldn't help but smirk. Her friend knew her too well. Deedra was the risk-taker, the climber.

One time, years ago, she'd found a bird's nest out by the bridge. Birds were rare, a nest a rarer wonder still. It was up high, built of bits of wire and cabling and trash, more a web than a nest, caught in the spot where a fallen beam crossed a jutting bit of concrete. She had to figure out how to climb all the way up there, using a bunch of broken packing crates and some discarded lengths of wire to fashion a sort of flexible ladder. It swayed and dipped when she so much as blinked, but she made it, coaching herself along the way under her breath: *You can do this, Deedra. You can make it. You can do it.*

In the nest were four perfect little eggs. They were delicious.

"You're thinking of the *eggs*," Lissa said even more confidently, and Deedra groaned.

"Okay, yeah, you got me. I was thinking of the eggs."

"Lucky day," Lissa said with a shrug. "You're not going to get that lucky again."

Probably not. The odds of finding anything alive and edible in the Territory were slim. The rations they earned from working at one of the Territory factories were synthesized in laboratories, using DNA spliced from extinct species like turkeys and asparagus. Such rations kept them alive, but scavenging for something to eat could make the difference between simple survival and quelling the rumble of a never-full belly. Plus, it tasted a whole lot better.

The bridge was Deedra's personal challenge to herself. She swore to one day climb its supports and reach the top. "Who knows what's up there?" she asked, focusing on it as if she could zoom in. "I've never heard of anyone going up there. There could be all kinds of—"

"No one's ever gone up there because there's nothing worth seeing," Lissa said drily. "If there was anything worthwhile up there, don't you think the Magistrate would have claimed it already?"

Deedra shrugged. "The Magistrate doesn't know everything. No one ever even comes out here."

"Who can blame 'em?" Lissa hooked her thumb over her shoulder at the Wreck: easily a mile—maybe two, who was counting?—of old automobiles and other such vehicles, jammed together at angles, piled atop one another, packing the route back into the heart of the Territory. Picking a path through the Wreck was dangerous—any of the precariously positioned cars could tilt and crash down at any minute. Pieces of them—weakened by rust—had been known to drop off without warning, crushing or slashing the unwary.

"I can't believe I let you talk me into coming back out here," Lissa grumbled. "We get one day a week out of L-Twelve, and I'm spending it out here. You're going to get me killed one of these days."

"Not going to happen."

"Give it time. Oh, look!"

Deedra followed Lissa's pointing finger, then watched as her friend carefully clambered down from their vantage point to the ground.

Lissa was smaller than Deedra, with a mountain of wild jet-black hair that would have added two or three more inches to her height had it not been tied back in a tight, efficient ponytail. Like Deedra, she wore a gray poncho that covered her torso and arms, with black pants and boots underneath. A breathing mask dangled around her neck—the air quality wasn't too bad today, so they were bare-facing it.

She reached down for something on the ground, cried out triumphantly, and held up her prize.

Squinting, Deedra couldn't tell what it was, so she joined Lissa on the ground. Lissa held up a small, perfectly round disc. It was just the right size to be held with one hand. It had a similarly perfect hole in its center, and its face was smudged and scratched, but when Lissa flipped it over, the opposite side was clean and shiny.

"What is it?" Deedra asked.

"I thought you might know. You're the one who scavenges every free minute."

Deedra examined the disc. On the smudged side, she could barely make out what appeared to be letters: Two *D*s, with a *V* between them.

"I don't know what it is."

Lissa suddenly exclaimed with excitement. "Wait! Let me try. . . ."

She snatched back the disc and poked her finger through the hole in the middle, then held it with the shiny side out. "See? It's a mirror! You put your finger through to hold it and look at yourself in the shiny side."

Deedra's lip curled at the sight of herself. It was something she usually tried to avoid. Her muddy brown hair was down around her shoulders, even though it was more practical to tie it up while out scavenging. Even around her best friend, though, she couldn't abide the idea of exposing her scar. It was a knotty, twisted cable of dead-white flesh that wended from under her left earlobe all the way down to her shoulder, standing out a good half inch from her body. She flinched at her reflection and turned away.

"Sorry," Lissa mumbled. "Sorry, wasn't thinking—"

Deedra immediately felt terrible. The scar wasn't Lissa's fault. "Don't. It's okay. And I think you're right." She took Lissa's wrist and turned the disc so that it reflected Lissa instead. "It's a mirror. Very cool. Check out the pretty girl."

Lissa chuckled. She tucked the disc into her pack, which she'd slung over one shoulder. Already, it bulged with junk she'd scavenged on their careful slog through the Wreck. Lissa was a good friend but a terrible scavenger. She kept *everything*. Deedra had tried to tell her: *Save your pack for the trip back. It's less to carry that way, and it means you can save your space for the very best stuff you come across.* But Lissa never learned. She wanted it all.

The wind shifted and they caught a whiff of the river, which made them gag. Lissa slipped on her breathing mask. "Disgusting. We're not getting any closer, are we?"

Deedra shrugged. She'd come out here for one reason. And, yes, getting closer was a part of it. The river formed part of the boundary with Sendar Territory. Deedra and Lissa lived in Ludo Territory, under the auspices of Magistrate Max Ludo. Ludo and Sendar were part of the City, which—as far as anyone knew—didn't have a name. It didn't need one. It was the City.

Ludo Territory was under terms of a peace treaty with Sendar . . . but even long-standing peace treaties had been known to change without warning. So being out by the river was at least a little bit dangerous, and not just for the risk of breathing in the toxic brew.

Still, she wanted to climb the bridge. And today would be the day.

"Check it out!" Lissa cried, pointing.

Deedra turned and saw—right out in the open—an enormous rat. It had to be at least a foot long, standing three or four inches tall, and it had paused to scratch at the loose gravel on the ground.

"I see dinner," Lissa singsonged, and rummaged for her slingshot.

"Uh-uh." Deedra held out a hand to stop her. "Not that one. Look closer."

The rat stood still, shivering. It bore blue tufts of mangy fur.

"Mutant," she told Lissa. "You eat him, he'll be your last meal."

For weeks now, drones had swooped low over the Territory, warning everyone about the danger of the hybrid rats that had begun edging into the Territory. *Citizens should not harvest and eat blue rats*, they'd boomed. *Hybrid rats are a dangerous food source.*

"Citizens should not eat anything I don't give them," Lissa said, aping the Magistrate's voice. "Citizens should not blah blah blah."

"You want to risk it?" Deedra asked.

"Not a chance."

"Didn't think so."

Deedra picked up a nearby rock and tossed it at the rat. It landed in front of the rat and off to one side. The rat stared for a second, totally unafraid, then loped off toward the river.

"I'm going to follow it," Deedra said casually.

Lissa wrinkled her nose. "Why?"

"Maybe it shares a nest with normal rats."

"And maybe you just want to get closer to the bridge."

Deedra shrugged with exaggerated innocence but didn't deny it.

"I was wrong before," Lissa said. "You're not going to get *me* killed—you're going to get yourself killed. Go have fun doing it. I'm going to check over there." She pointed off to an overturned truck in the near distance. "Meet back here in ten?"

"Make it twenty." She didn't want to climb the bridge and have to come right back down.

They separated. The smell from the river grew more intense as she got closer, following the blue rat as it scampered away. She slid on her own breathing mask. It got twisted up in her necklace, so she paused for a moment to disentangle the pendant before slipping the mask over her mouth and nose.

The rat stopped and looked back at her. Deedra picked up a crushed tin can and hurled it. The rat ran a little way, then turned around again.

Deedra stomped after it, scooped up the can, and threw it again. She chased the rat nearly to the water before it disappeared into a pile of scrap and garbage.

The chase had taken her around to the far side of the abutment. A collapsed chunk of pavement leaned against the column. The pavement was nearly vertical, but she thought she could use the cracks in it as handholds and scale her way up to the bridge itself.

She could hardly believe her good luck. She had thought she would have to climb one of the other abutments, which didn't have nearly so many handholds.

"You're my hero, ugly mutant blue rat," she called. The rat, if it heard her, didn't bother to answer.

She tied her hair back to keep it out of her eyes as she climbed. "You can do this," she muttered. "You can do this . . ."

It was hard going, but she fell into a rhythm soon enough, using her legs to push herself up rather than pulling with her arms. That was the trick— using the bigger, stronger leg muscles for movement and the smaller arm muscles for balance and direction. She'd gotten about twenty feet up and was pretty pleased with herself. Below and off to her left, the river glimmered, oily and sick. Sometimes, in the rare sunlight, it was almost beautiful. Not today.

She kept a tight grip with her right hand and wiped sweat from her brow.

Stop daydreaming, Deedra. Get moving. Lissa will be waiting.

With a heavy sigh, she reached for the next handhold, flexing her legs for distance.

And the pavement under her right foot crumbled and peeled away.

Deedra gasped as her whole right side listed, suddenly hanging out in open air. Her right hand hadn't reached the new handhold yet, and her entire left side was already protesting the strain of holding her up. She flailed for a handhold, for a foothold, for anything at all, but her motion made her position only more precarious.

She glanced down. The ground swam at her.

It was only twenty feet, but the ground was studded with chunks of concrete, sharp bits of steel, and heavy rocks. If she dropped, she could easily bash her head open or break her back.

Her right hand slapped against the pavement, seeking purchase. She lifted her head; looking at the ground was stupid when she needed to find a handhold instead.

Across the river, something caught her attention. It was so unexpected that she actually forgot her situation for an instant.

Something—some*one*—was across the river, in Sendar Territory.

Running toward the river.

It was another girl.

***

Deedra flattened herself against the pavement and reached straight up with her free hand. She had to twist into a contorted, painful position, but she found a grip. Planting the heel of her loose foot against the wall, she stabilized herself.

Deep breaths. Deep, deep breaths.

When she looked into Sendar again, the other girl had made it to the opposite shore. At that distance, she almost disappeared into the background clutter of crumbled concrete, twisted steel, and broken glass.

If not for the coat she wore. It was long, down to her ankles, and from Deedra's position, it looked like a very dark green. Deedra had never seen a coat like that.

Maybe you should worry less about the coat and more about not dying.

It was at least an additional forty or fifty feet to the bridge, but she figured she'd risked enough for one day. Time to retreat back to the ground. Live again to climb another day.

And besides . . . it would be a chance to scope out the stranger.

With some difficulty, she managed to retrace her steps, finding by feel and memory the handholds and footholds that had gotten her this far. She inched down the incline and then dropped the last three feet to the ground.

She came around the bridge abutment for an unobstructed view of the river. The other girl was standing on the shore. Very slim, but tall and broad-shouldered. The weirdest girl she'd ever seen, for sure.

The girl started to undress. Her body, so different from Deedra's, came into view—those broad shoulders, a surprisingly flat chest, then a concave belly tapering down to slender hips, and . . .

And this was no girl. Not at *all*.

It was the prettiest, most exquisite boy Deedra had ever seen.

She shook her head to clear it, blinked her eyes. The pollution had to be affecting her sight. No man could look like that. It *had* to be a girl.

She looked again.

No. Still a boy.

Like no boy she'd ever seen. He seemed more chiseled into existence than born. His skin was unblemished and smooth; clean, unlike everyone else's. Even her own. He was slender, but not emaciated like most people. Healthy. Vibrant. He didn't stoop or slouch—he stood straight and tall after slipping out of his pants.

She couldn't help herself—she stared at him as, naked, he carefully folded his clothes, wrapping them in the coat. Then he stepped into the water.

The river was only a couple of feet deep at this spot. He waded in up to his knees, then his waist. Fording the river with his clothes held well above the water, he began to struggle as the current grew stronger toward the center. He'd started out with a good, strong stride but was growing weaker as he waded farther and farther in.

Deedra started fidgeting with her necklace, running the pendant—a circle with a Greek cross jutting out from it—back and forth along the chain. *Stupid kid. If he would just ditch his clothes, he could swim across easily.*

But he wasn't going to do that. And with each step, it was clear that he was getting more and more exhausted.

He wasn't going to make it. He would be swept downriver. And if he managed not to drown, he would wash up on one of the piers down by the Territory of Grevan Dalcord.

The Mad Magistrate, they called him. Max Ludo could be unfair, corrupt, and pigheaded, but at least he didn't execute criminals by sewing rats to their faces and letting the rodent gnaw its way free. That was the sort of thing Dalcord was known to do. Ludo Territory was technically at peace with Dalcord, too, but everyone knew it was only a matter of time before the Mad Magistrate launched an attack. It was inevitable.

The boy in the river was about halfway across, but making no further progress. The current was too strong.

She found herself running to the water's edge. There was something in her hand, and she realized as she ran that she was dragging a long, old piece of rebar, still straight except for a little crook at the end.

The boy was looking around, not panicked, but concerned, as the water began relentlessly shoving him downriver. She shouted, "Hey!"— it was all she could get out as she ran—and waved her free arm to get his attention.

He noticed her just as she got to the water. She heaved the heavy rebar with all her strength. It flopped—*splash!*—into the river, throwing up a sheet of filthy, grimy water. For a moment colors sparkled and hung in the air, distracting her with unexpected beauty.

Him, too. He stared at the kaleidoscope as the water tugged him farther away.

"Stop staring and grab this!" she yelled.

That snapped him out of it. He tucked his clothes under an arm and reached out for the rebar, but he couldn't find the end of it no matter how much he flailed.

She took a deep breath and planted her feet and groaned, levering the far end of the rebar out of the water. She couldn't hold it very high—just right at the level of the water. Just close enough?

Yes! He managed to grab hold of it. She braced herself, expecting his weight to overcome her muscles and drag her in. But he didn't. He must have weighed next to nothing.

"Don't let go!" she shouted. She took a precious second to reposition and replant her feet. The shore was mostly wet gravel and trash. She gouged at it with her heel until she'd dug a little ramp to brace herself against.

"Hold on!" she called to him, and when she looked up, he'd begun pulling himself along the rebar. He still had his clothes tucked under one arm, so it was awkward going, but he was making progress.

She heaved, pulling the rebar hand over hand.

They were close enough now that she could make out his expression. He didn't look terrified. Just . . . uneasy. The strain of keeping his grip seemed to bother him more than the idea of what would happen if he let go.

It felt like hours to haul him in—her groaning, fiery shoulders would *swear* it was hours—but it had to have been only a few minutes. Just as she thought her muscles would give out, his body emerged from the water down to his knees. She tried not to stare anywhere in particular as she found a final burst of power that allowed her to pull him even closer.

Once his knees cleared the water, he let go of the rebar without warning, and she stumbled backward down a slight grade. She yelped in surprise, then swore loudly, collapsing on her back. The mask slipped away from her face, and the reek of the river stabbed at her nostrils. Stones bit into her; she lost her breath.

When she managed to struggle up to a sitting position, she saw him there, on his back on the rocky ground, gazing straight up. He wasn't even breathing hard.

He stared at the sky, and she stared at him. Even up close, he was still perfect. She'd thought that maybe he only seemed so flawless at a distance, but here he was in front of her, and his pale skin was just as unmarked. Which was unusual because everyone had brands identifying their Territory. They were usually burned in along the left shoulder/neck area, but since Deedra's scar made that impossible, her own brand—in the shape of some kind of water creature that was the symbol of Ludo Territory—was on her right shoulder.

The boy had no brand. Not on either shoulder. Still naked and utterly self-possessed, he simply sat up and stared at her, studying her.

She couldn't imagine why he would want to. Why anyone would. Only once, long ago, as a child, had anyone told her she was beautiful. One of the caretakers at the orphanage where she'd grown up. But that had been a cruel joke. The truth was as obvious as her own skin: The hideous, mottled scar commandeering the left side of her neck, trailing down to her collarbone, made her nothing more and nothing less than ugly.

It was time to go. She had helped him. Fine. But for all she knew, he could be crazy. Or even—and it just occurred to her, in a rush of terror—a spy, sent to infiltrate Max Ludo's territory. Magistrates were supposed to keep out of one another's Territories, but that rule only applied to what could be proved in a Citywide Magistrates Council. If the Mad Magistrate thought he could steal some of Ludo's rations or encroach on the area to alleviate his own overcrowding, well, why not do it?

Wary of the incline, she took a careful step back and would have turned to run, but at that moment—as if he knew she was leaving—the boy twisted on the ground, rising with a smooth, easy motion into a crouch. His eyes—a deep and almost succulent green—met hers and locked; she couldn't have moved if the entire river had suddenly risen up behind him and threatened to devour them both.

He froze her.

Not with fear or worry. No. It took a moment, but she soon recognized the kindness and curiosity in his eyes. No sudden flinch of realization, no moment of recoil and disgust.

Her hair. It was still in a ponytail and he could see. Could see the scar.

Even though there was nothing but gentleness in his eyes, she still found herself reaching back and fumbling to let loose her hair and drag it around her left side.

And still he said nothing. Just watched.

"Thank you," he said, "for helping me."

His voice . . . it was somehow deep and light all at once, pleasant and alive in a way she didn't know voices could be. It was like a piece of him, set loose to drift in the air. Without even realizing it, she took a step toward him.

"You're welcome." Her own voice was clumsy and raspy, a stupid, harsh thing, not effortless like his. "Are you all right?"

He nodded, still completely unself-conscious about his nudity. Her neck and cheeks warmed again as she forced herself not to stare. With no particular urgency, he began to pull on his clothes, finishing with that peculiar dark green coat.

"I've never seen someone cross the river," she said, lamely. "Why would you leave Sendar Territory?" Glorio Sendar wasn't a great Magistrate, but she wasn't bad, either. Journeying from Sendar's territory to Ludo's was like trading a weekday ration for half a weekend ration. Same difference.

"I'm not really from there," he said. "I've been traveling. For a long time."

"What about your family?"

He simply shrugged. His expression didn't change at all.

"I'm an orphan, too," she whispered. For no reason, her eyes began to water, and she wiped at them angrily. She'd been alone her entire life. Being parentless, familyless, was nothing new. Why did it suddenly feel so powerfully wrong and painful?

She took a step closer to him—within reach now—and the boy flinched, jumping back.

Deedra flushed and turned partly away.

"I'm sorry," he said immediately. "I didn't mean to . . . I wasn't . . ." He groaned, clearly upset with himself. "Look, it just might be safer if you keep a little ways back."

He took another step back, as if to prove his point.

She had no idea what he meant. Was he worried about something from the river infecting her?

"I'm not afraid," she told him. "As long as you don't drink it or soak in it for too long, the water won't make you sick."

He frowned as though he didn't quite believe her. They gazed at each other for a few moments. She sucked in a deep breath and risked it: She held out her hand.

"My name is Deedra."

With a reluctant little nod, he shook her hand, then immediately pulled back, as though he'd pushed luck as far as he was willing. "I'm Rose."

Deedra blinked. "Wait, isn't Rose a girl's name?"

Rose shrugged. "It's mine."

She smiled and had no idea what to say next, and then the world took the necessity of speech away from her.

A drone buzzed overhead, its speakers blaring, "*Citizen Alert! Citizen Alert! Seek shelter! Seek shelter!*"

***

The drone had come from nowhere, sweeping in, its blast of sound doubled in volume as it echoed off the surrounding sheets of steel and glass from the nearby Wreck. Deedra hissed in a breath and clapped her hands to her ears, shutting her eyes reflexively against the assault of sound. The drone whizzed closer by, blasting out its warning again, nearly driving her to her knees.

Shelter. She had to find shelter.

She opened her eyes and looked up just in time to see the drone banking by the nearest abutment, cutting a sharp left to avoid crossing the Territorial boundary. Bleating out its warning again, it zoomed north.

Deedra looked around for shelter and realized in the same instant that the boy—Rose—was gone.

His sudden disappearance stunned her into paralysis. She forgot about shelter and stood rooted to her spot. How in the world had he disappeared so quickly? Where had he gone? She spun around, thinking maybe he'd ducked behind her or run off in that direction, but no. Nothing.

Not even a path of disturbed gravel where he would have run.

"Deedra!"

It was Lissa, screaming to her from near the Wreck. Deedra was shocked to see how tiny Lissa looked—in the mad rush to pull Rose from the river, she'd run farther from the Wreck than ever before, closer to the river than she'd ever dared.

"Come on!" Lissa shouted, gesturing wildly. Overhead, the drone cried out its warning again, this time farther distant and not so painfully. Deedra unfroze her legs and ran at top speed toward Lissa, who kept motioning for her to hurry. As she got closer, she saw that Lissa was propping up an old sheet of corrugated metal against a block of concrete. A decent enough shelter, in a pinch.

Lissa crawled in as Deedra neared her, throwing herself under the metal sheet as the drone's alarm faded into the distance.

Under the impromptu shelter, it was dark and the air—even filtered through her mask—tasted of rust. Deedra panted, catching her breath, as she curled into the tight, unyielding space with Lissa.

"Just like home," Lissa joked.

"I would laugh, but I don't have enough room."

They giggled, then suddenly stopped at a sound in the distance.

"Was that an explosion?"

"Could have been a . . ." Deedra broke off. She didn't know *what* it could have been. She just didn't want to think it was an explosion. Especially not when she was stuck out here at the edge of nowhere with only a sheet of metal between her and who-knew-what.

They held their breath together. Deedra counted to thirty in her head, straining to hear.

Finally, she blew out her breath, an instant after Lissa did.

"I don't think it was a bomb. There would have been another one, right? It could have been something falling over. Back in the Wreck."

Lissa shrugged. Given their close quarters, Deedra felt it more than saw it.

They waited. It was impossible to tell for how long. Eventually a drone buzzed by calling out the all-clear. They struggled out from under the makeshift shelter, untangling themselves from each other.

"That was fun," Lissa said, pulling down her mask. She inhaled deeply, coughed, and grimaced. "Not worth it."

Deedra pulled down her mask, too. The air smelled and tasted awful, but it was—for the moment—better than the hot, humid air in her mask. She turned away from Lissa, looking back down toward the river. From this vantage point, she could see a whole stretch of the riverbank and the bridge abutments. Rose was nowhere to be seen. She couldn't even see a place where he might have sheltered.

"What are you looking for?"

"A boy."

Lissa snorted. "That's pretty ambitious scavenge, Dee."

"No, seriously. There was a boy. Down there, by the river. A boy named Rose."

"Rose? Like the . . . what do you call it? Like the flower?"

The flower . . . *Oh, right,* Deedra remembered now. Flowers. They grew out of the ground, like weeds. She'd seen images of them, but never one in person. No one had, as best she knew. At least since the Red Rain. In fact, some people weren't even sure they existed at all. They were just mutant weeds, really. Weird flukes of nature, like the blue rat.

Or like me, she thought, and stroked one finger along her scar without intending to, only half-realizing it.

Lissa slapped her hand away from the scar. "Cut that out. It's not like you can make it go away."

Easy for Lissa to say; she didn't have to live with it. Deedra shook her hair into place over the scar with a long-practiced jerk of her head. "He was down there. He . . ." She sighed. "Never mind. He's gone."

"We should be gone, too. Just in case they alert again."

She was right, and Deedra knew it, even though it rankled her. She'd really wanted to climb the bridge today. And now she also wanted to know what had happened to Rose. Where had he gone? And just as important: Where had he come from *before* Sendar Territory? Why cross the river?

Lissa tugged at her poncho. "Let's go. It'll take a while to get through the Wreck."

They began to make their way deeper into the Territory, carefully retracing the path they'd taken through the Wreck.

"What do you think it was this time?" Deedra asked, trying to take her mind off Rose. For some reason, she had difficulty not thinking about him, in a way she'd never experienced before. "Another gridhack?"

"Nah. Another false alarm, I bet."

Deedra shrugged. The wikinets—the Territory-wide public-information system—would report later on the cause of the alarm. Maybe. Sometimes a Citizen Alert would be sounded, then canceled, with no reason offered, leaving everyone to wonder if it was just a glitch, a test, or something classified.

In the end, it didn't matter, she realized. One way or the other, when the drones said shelter, you had to shelter. There was no other option.

Danger meant shelter. Somewhere out there, she knew, Rose had run. She hoped he'd found shelter. She hoped he would continue to.

She didn't know why she hoped these things. But as she picked her way through the Wreck with Lissa, she realized when she thought of Rose, she was smiling.

***

From his perch above the claustrophobic crush of ancient metal and glass, in a hidden nook high up on a ruined bridge support, Rose watches Deedra thread her way into the distance through the Wreck with the other girl.

"Deedra," he says quietly. Then, drawing it out, testing it, tasting the syllables: "Dee-dra. Deeeee-draaaaa."

He purses his lips and begins to whistle.

You've just read an excerpt from After the Red Rain.

ABOUT THE AUTHOR

Barry Lyga is the author of several acclaimed young adult novels, including the *I Hunt Killers* series, and his debut, *The Astonishing Adventures of Fanboy and Goth Girl*. Peter Facinelli has appeared in films such as *Riding in Cars with Boys* and *Can't Hardly Wait*, and more recently as Dr. Carlisle Cullen in the *Twilight Saga* films. Rob DeFranco partnered with Peter Facinelli to form A7SLE Films, and has produced *Loosies*, *The Last Word*, and the upcoming *Street Soldier* for FOX.

Imprint: Little, Brown Books for Young Readers
Print ISBN: 9780316406031
Print price: $18.00
eBook ISBN: 9780316406048
eBook price: $9.99
Publication date: 8/4/15
Publicity contact: Lisa Moraleda; lisa.moraleda@hbgusa.com
Rights contact: Kristin Dulaney; kristin.dulaney@hbgusa.com
Editor: Alvina Ling
Agent: Fisher, Steve, APA Talent & Literary, Anderson, Kathleen, Anderson Literary Agency, Inc.
Agency: Fisher, Steve, APA Talent & Literary, Anderson, Kathleen, Anderson Literary Agency, Inc.

Territories sold:
World

Promotional information:
- National print and online advertising
- National review coverage
- Select author appearances
- Extensive blogger outreach
- Social media campaign

NOWHERE BUT HERE

KATIE MCGARRY

SUMMARY

Seventeen-year-old Emily has always known that her biological father belongs to a motorcycle club—the Reign of Terror—but she has so little contact with him that it almost seems like a myth. But when news of a death brings the whole family to Kentucky, Emily finds herself in the middle of a feud between rival clubs—and drawn to a guy she should have nothing in common with. New graduate and aspiring club member Oz is consumed with a recent mistake and has one shot at redemption—keeping Emily safe while making sure she doesn't learn the truth about her father's past.

EXCERPT

Oz

It's three in the morning, and Mom and I continue to wait. The two of us deal with the heaviness of each passing second differently. She paces our tiny living room at the front of our doublewide while I polish my combat boots in my room. Regardless of what happens tonight, we have a wake to attend in the morning.

The scratching of the old scrub brush against my black boot is the lone sound that fills the blackened house. We both pretend that the other isn't awake. Neither of us has turned on a lamp. Instead, we rely on the rays of the full moon to see. It's easier this way. Neither of us wants to discuss the meaning of Dad's absence or his cell phone silence.

I sit on the edge of my twin mattress. If I stretched my leg, my toe would hit the faux-wooden-paneled wall. I'm tall like my dad, and the room is compact and narrow. Large enough to hold my bed and an old stack of milk crates that I use as shelves.

Mom's phone pings, and my hands freeze. Through the crack in my door, I spot her black form as she grabs her cell. The screen glows to life, and a bluish light illuminates Mom's face. I quit breathing and strain to listen to her reaction or at least hear the roar of motorcycle engines.

Nothing. More silence. Adrenaline begins to pump into my veins. Dad should have been home by now. They all should have been home. Especially with Olivia's wake in the morning.

Unable to stomach the quiet any longer, I set the boot on the floor and open my door. The squeak of the hinges screeches through the trailer. In two steps, I'm in the living room.

Mom continues to scroll through her phone. She's a small thing, under five four, and has long, straight hair. It's black. Just like mine and just like Dad's. Mom and Dad are only thirty-seven. I'm seventeen. Needless to say, my mom was young when she had me. But the way she slumps her shoulders, she appears ten years older.

"Any word?" I ask.

"It's Nina." My best friend Chevy's mom. "Wondering if we had heard anything." Which implies neither Eli nor Cyrus have returned home.

From behind her, I place a hand on Mom's shoulder, and she covers my fingers with hers.

"I'll be out there watching their backs soon." Now that I've graduated from high school, I'll finally be allowed to enter the family business.

A job with the security company and a patch-in to the club is all I've thought about since I was twelve. All I've craved since I turned sixteen and earned my motorcycle license. "They're fine. Like I'll be when I join them."

Mom pats my hand, walks into the space that serves as our kitchen and busies herself with a stack of mail.

I rest my shoulder against the wall near the window. The backs of my legs bump the only piece of furniture in the room besides the flat screen—a sectional bought last year before Olivia became ill.

Without trying to be obvious, I glance beyond the lace curtains and assess the road leading to our trailer. I'm also worried, but it's my job to alleviate her concern.

I force a tease into my voice. "I bet you can't wait until Chevy graduates next year. Then there will be two more of us protecting the old men."

Mom coughs out a laugh and takes a drink to control the choking. "I can't begin to imagine the two of you riding in the pack when the image in my mind is of both of you as toddlers, covered in mud from head to toe."

"Not hard to remember. That was last week's front yard football game," I joke.

She smiles. Long enough to chase away the gravity of tonight's situation, but then reality catches up. If humor won't work, I'll go for serious. "Chevy would like to GED out."

"Nina would skin him alive. Each of you promised Olivia you'd finish high school."

Because it broke Olivia's heart when Eli, her son, opted out of finishing high school and instead tested to gain his GED years ago. Eli's parents, Olivia and Cyrus, aren't blood to me, but they gave my mom and dad a safe place to lay low years ago when their own parents went self-destructive. Olivia and I aren't related, but she's the closest I have to a grandmother.

"Chevy wanting to take his GED." Mom tsks. "It's bad enough you won't consider college."

The muscles in my neck tighten, and I ignore her jab. She and Olivia are ticked I won't engage them in conversation about college. I know my future, and it's not four more years of books and rules. I want the club. As it is, a patch-in—membership into the club—isn't a guarantee. I still have to prove myself before they'll let me join.

My dad belongs to the Reign of Terror. They're a motorcycle club that formed a security business when I was eleven. Their main business comes from escorting semi loads of high-priced goods through highly pirated areas.

Imagine a couple thousand dollars of fine Kentucky bourbon in the back of a Mac truck and, at some point, the driver has to take a piss. My dad and the rest of the club—they make sure the driver can eat his Big Mac in peace and return to the parking lot to find his rig intact and his merchandise still safely inside.

What they do can be dangerous, but I'll be proud to stand alongside my father and the only other people I consider family.

Mom rubs her hands up and down her arms. She's edgy when the club is out on a protection run, but this time, Mom's dangling from a cliff, and she's not the only one. The entire club has been acting like they're preparing to jump without parachutes.

"You're acting as if they're the ones that could be caught doing something illegal."

Mom's eyes shoot straight to mine like my comment was serious. "You know better than that."

I do. It's what the club prides themselves on. All that TV bull about anyone who rides a bike is a felon—they don't understand what the club stands for. The club is a brotherhood, a family. It means belonging to something bigger than myself.

Still, Olivia has mounting medical bills and between me, Chevy, my parents, Eli, Cyrus and other guys from the club giving all we have, we still don't have enough to make a dent in what we owe. "I hear that 1% club a couple of hours north of here makes bank."

"Oz."

As if keeping watch will help Dad return faster, I move the curtain to get a better view of the road that leads away from our house and into the woods. "Yeah?"

"This club is legit."

And 1% clubs are not legit. They don't mind doing the illegal to make cash or get their way. "Okay."

"I'm serious. This club is legit."

I drop the curtain. "What? You don't want gangsta in the family?"

Mom slaps her hand on the counter. "I don't want to hear you talk like this!"

My head snaps in her direction. Mom's not a yeller. Even when she's stressed, she maintains her cool. "I was messing with you."

"This club is legit, and it will stay legit. You are legit. Do you understand?"

"I got it. I'm clean. The club's clean. We're so jacked up on suds that we squeak when we walk. I know this, so would you care to explain why you're freaking out?"

A motorcycle growls in the distance, cutting off our conversation. Mom releases a long breath, as if she's been given the news that a loved one survived surgery. "He's home."

She charges the front door and throws it open. The elation slips from her face, and my stomach cramps. "What is it?"

"Someone's riding double."

More rumbles of engines join the lead one, multiple headlights flash onto the trailer, and not one of those bikes belong to Dad. Fuck. I rush past Mom and jump off the steps as Mom brightens the yard with a flip of the porch light. Eli swings off his bike. "Oz! Get over here!"

I'm there before he can finish his statement, and I shoulder my father's weight to help him off the bike. He's able to stand, but leans into me, and that scares me more than any monster that hid under my bed as a child.

"What happened?" Mom's voice shakes, and Eli says nothing. He supports Dad's other side as Dad's knees buckle.

"What happened!" she demands, and the fear in her voice vibrates against my insides. I'm wondering the same damn thing, but I'm more concerned with the blood dripping from my father's head.

"Medical kit!" Eli bursts through the door and the two of us deposit Dad on the couch. Mom's less than a step behind us and runs into the kitchen. Glass shatters when Mom tosses stuff aside in search of her kit. Mom's a nurse, and I can't remember a time she hasn't been prepared.

More guys appear in the living room. Each man wearing a black leather biker cut. Not one of them would be the type to leave a brother behind.

"I'm fine, Izzy." Dad touches the skin above the three-inch-long cut on his forehead. "Just a scratch."

"Scratch, my ass." With kit in hand, Mom kneels in front of him, and I crouch beside her, popping open her supply box as she pours antiseptic onto a rag. She glares at Eli. "Why didn't you take him to the ER?"

Dad wraps his fingers around Mom's wrist. Her gaze shifts to his, and when he has Mom's attention for longer than a second, he slowly swipes his thumb against her skin. "I told him to bring me home. We didn't want it reported to the police."

Mom blinks away the tears pooling in her eyes. I fall back on my ass, realizing that Dad's not dying, but somehow cracked his head hard enough that Eli wouldn't allow him to ride home solo.

"You promised you'd wear your helmet," Mom whispers.

"I wasn't on my bike," he replies simply.

Mom pales out, and I focus solely on Eli. He holds my stare as I state the obvious. "The run went bad."

Jacking trucks for the cargo inside is a moneymaker for hustlers, and the security company is good at keeping hustlers on their toes. But sometimes the company comes up against the occasional asshole who thinks they can be badass by pulling a gun.

"Someone tried to hit us during a break at a truck stop, but we were smarter." Eli jerks his thumb in Dad's direction. "But some of us aren't as fast as others."

"Go to hell," Dad murmurs as Mom cleans the wound.

"You should have reported it," Mom says.

A weighted silence settles in the room, and Mom's lips thin out. The security business is as thick as the club. Business in both areas stays private. Everyone is on a need-to-know basis, me and Mom included…that is until I patch in. I'll likely learn more when I'm initiated as a prospect, and I'm counting down the days until I'm officially part of the larger whole.

"He okay?" Eli asks.

"You of all people should know how hardheaded he is," Mom responds. Eli's a few years younger than my parents, but the three of them have been a trio of trouble since elementary school. "I believe everyone has a wake to attend in the morning, so I suggest sleep."

That's as subtle as Mom will get before she'll stick a pointed steel-toed boot up their asses. Everyone says some sort of goodbye to Mom and Dad, but my parents are too lost in their own world to notice.

"Walk me out, Oz?" Eli inclines his head to the door, and we head onto the front porch. The muggy night air is thick with moisture, and a few bugs swarm around the porch light.

Eli digs into his leather jacket and pulls out a pack of cigarettes and a lighter. He cups his hand to his mouth as he lights one. "We need you out on the road."

"They told me they'll send my official diploma next week." I was supposed to walk at graduation tomorrow, but Olivia's wake is the priority. Not caps and gowns. "You tell me when to start, and I'm ready to go."

"Good." He cracks a rare grin. "Heard that we might be adding a new prospect this weekend."

The answering smile spreads on my face. Becoming a prospect is the initiation period before the club votes on my membership. I've been waiting for this moment my entire life.

Eli sucks in a long drag and the sleeve of his jacket hitches up, showing the trail of stars tattooed on his arm. "Keep an eye on your dad. He cracked the hell out of his head when he hit the pavement. Blacked out for a bit but then shot to his feet. When his bike began swerving, I made him pull over and double with me."

"He must have loved that," I say.

"Practically had to put a gun to his head." Eli breaths out smoke.

"Was it the RMC?" The Riot Motorcycle Club. They're an illegal club north of here. I've heard some of the guys talk when they think no one else is listening, saying that our peace treaty with them is fracturing.

Eli flicks ashes then focuses on the burning end of the cigarette. "As I said, we need you on the road."

Our club and the Riot have had an unsteady alliance from the start. We stay on our side of the state, they stay on theirs. The problem? A new client that the business has contracted with resides in the Riot's territory.

"This stays between us," says Eli. "This new client we signed is skittish and doesn't want the PR related to possible truck-jackings. We need this business, and I need people I can trust with those loads. I need you in."

"Got it." I throw out the question, not sure if Eli will answer. "You had his back, didn't you? You knew there was going to be trouble so you pushed Dad to the ground."

A hint of a smirk plays on his lips, and he hides it with another draw. He blows out the smoke and flicks the cigarette onto the ground. "Be out here at six in the morning. I'll pick you up in the truck and we'll go get your dad's bike before the wake. I want him to sleep in."

Hell, yeah. "You going to let me drive his bike home?"

"Fuck, no. I'm bringing you along to drive the truck back. No one touches a man's bike, and in desperate situations only another brother can. You know better than that." Eli pats my shoulder. "See you tomorrow, and be dressed for the wake when I pick you up."

Eli starts his bike and rocks kick up as he drives off. I watch until the red taillight fades into the darkness. Through the screen door, I spot my mother still tending to my father. She uses special care as she tapes gauze to his head.

Mom smoothes the last strip of medical tape to his skin and when she goes to close the kit, Dad tucks a lock of her hair behind her ear. They stare at each other, longer than most people can stand, then she lays her head on his lap. Dad bends over and kisses her temple.

They need a moment together and, having nothing but time, I sit on the top step and wonder if I'll find someone who will understand and accept this life like my mother. Mom loves Dad so much that she'll take on anything. His job, this life and even the club. Maybe I'll be that lucky someday.

You've just read an excerpt from Nowhere But Here.

ABOUT THE AUTHOR

Award-winning and critically-acclaimed author Katie McGarry was a teenager during the age of grunge and boy bands and remembers those years as the best and worst of her life. She is a lover of music, happy endings, and reality television, and is a secret University of Kentucky basketball fan.

Imprint: Harlequin Teen
Print ISBN: 9780373211425
Print price: $17.99
eBook ISBN: 9781460341506
eBook price: $12.99
Publication date: 5/26/15
Publicity contact: Jennifer Abbots jennifer_abbots@harlequin.ca
Rights contact: Reka Rubin reka_rubin@harlequin.ca
Editor: Margo Lipschultz
Agent: Kevan Lyon
Agency: Marsal Lyon Literary

A new paranormal series based on the wildly
popular YouTube sensation

The Haunting of Sunshine Girl

A Novel

PAIGE MCKENZIE

SUMMARY

A new paranormal Young Adult series based on the wildly popular YouTube channel of the same name, which has been optioned for film and television by The Weinstein Company. Described as *Gilmore Girls* meets *Paranormal Activity* for the new generation, *The Haunting of Sunshine Girl: Book One* is about an "adorkable" teenager living in a haunted house. Shortly after her sixteenth birthday, Sunshine Griffith and her mother Kat move to the rain-drenched town of Ridgemont, Washington. Sunshine and her mother have always shared a special bond, but from the moment they cross the Washington state line, Sunshine feels a mysteriousness she cannot place. And even if Kat doesn't recognize it, Sunshine knows something about their new house is just... creepy. In the days that follow, things only become stranger, as Sunshine is followed by an icy breeze, and eventually, the child's voice she hears on her first night evolves into sobs. She can hardly believe it, but as the spirits haunting her house become more frightening—and it becomes clear that Kat is in danger—Sunshine must accept what she is, pass the test before her, and save her mother from a fate worse than death.

EXCERPT

Seventeen Candles

*She turned sixteen today. I watched it happen. Katherine, the woman who adopted her, baked her a cake: carrot cake, a burnt sort of orange color with white frosting smothered over the top of it. A girl named Ashley came over to her house with candles, which they lit despite the sweltering Texas heat. Then they sang—*Happy Birthday to you, Happy Birthday to you. *Our kind don't celebrate birthdays. Except, of course, for when one of us turns sixteen. Just as* she *did today.*

At precisely the time of her birth: 7:12p.m., Central Standard Time, August fourteenth, I sensed the change in the girl named Sunshine. I felt the instant the spirit touched her. Katherine had just set the cake down on the table in front of her: sixteen—no seventeen, why seventeen?—candles. Sunshine grinned and pursed her lips, preparing to extinguish the flames. But then, an instant of hesitation; the smile disappearing from her eyes.

Of course, she hadn't a clue what she was feeling or why she was feeling it. The moment the spirit touched her, her temperature dropped from 98.6 degrees Fahrenheit to 92.3; her heart rate jumped from 80 beats per minute to 110. She pressed her palm to her forehead like a mother checking for a fever. Perhaps she thought she was coming down with something: a cold, the flu—whatever it is that people suffer from. I recognized the culprit immediately: a twenty-nine year old male who'd perished in a car accident less than a mile away several weeks earlier, the blood on his wounds still fresh, the glass from the windshield still embedded in his face. Later, I would help him move on myself: his wounds will heal, his skin will be smooth. But now, I keep my focus on Sunshine.

I counted the seconds until her heart rate returned to normal: eleven. Impressive.

She took a deep breath and blew out her candles. Katherine and Ashley applauded. Sunshine stood up from the table and curtsied elaborately, garnering more applause. Her smile was back, planted firmly on her face, her bright green eyes sparkling. Almost as though she never felt anything at all.

My last student's temperature took 24 hours to rebound. But Sunshine's was back to normal by the time her mother cut the cake.

Of course, this was just a passing spirit. Soon, she'd have to contend with so much more.

Chapter One

Defending Creepy

"Mom, the house is creepy." We're only halfway up the gravel driveway to our new home and I can already tell. Even the driveway is creepy: long and narrow, with tall bushes on either side so that I can't see our neighbors' front yards.

"I prefer creeptastic," Mom answers with a smile. I don't smile back. "Oh come on," she groans, "I don't even get a sympathy laugh?"

"Not this time," I say, shaking my head.

Mom rented the house off of Craigslist. She didn't have time to be picky, not once she got offered the job as the head nurse of the new neo-natal unit at Ridgemont hospital. She barely had time to ask her only daughter how she felt about being uprooted from the town she'd lived in her whole life to the northwest corner of the country, where it rains more often than not. Of course, I said that I'd support her no matter what. It was a great opportunity for her, and I didn't want to be the reason she didn't take it. I'm just not sure that moving from Texas to Washington state is all that great an opportunity for *me*. Mom parks the car and eyes the house through the windshield. Two stories high, a front porch with an ancient-looking porch swing that looks like it couldn't support a baby's weight. In the pictures online, the house looked white, but in real life, it's gray, except for the front door, which someone decided to paint bright red. Maybe they thought the contrast would look cheerful or something.

"You can't tell a house is creepy from the outside," Mom adds hopefully.

"Yes, I can."

"How?"

"The same way I can tell that those jeans you bought before we left Austin will end up hanging in my closet instead of yours. I'm very, very intuitive."

Mom laughs. Our little white dog, Oscar, whines from the backseat, begging to be let out so he can explore his new home. As soon as Mom undoes her seatbelt and opens the door, he bounds outside. I stay in the car a second longer, breathing in the wet air blowing in from outside.

It's not just the house. Ever since we crossed the state line, the world has been gray, shrouded in fog so thick that Mom had to turn the headlights on even though it was the middle of the day. I didn't picture our new life in Washington as quite so colorless. To be honest, I didn't picture it much at all. Instead, I kind of pretended that the move wasn't happening even as our house back in Austin filled with boxes, even when my best friend, Ashley, came over to help us pack. It wasn't until we were actually on the road that I really *believed* we were moving.

Our new house is on a dead-end street backed-up against an enormous, fog-drenched field. Each of the houses we passed before we turned into our driveway was about two sizes too small for the size of its yard; I guess these are the kind of neighbors who want nothing to do with one another. There wasn't a single kid playing in his front yard, not a single dad getting ready to barbeque tonight's dinner, and the street was littered with pine needles from the towering Douglas Firs that block out any semblance of daylight. And our new yard is ringed by an ugly rusted chain-link fence.

Judging from the little I've seen so far, I'm pretty sure the whole flippin' town of Ridgemont, Washington is creepy. I mean, what could be creepier than a place at the foot of a mountain where the sky is gray even in the dog days of summer? And if it seems like I'm over-using the word creepy, it's not because I don't have access to a thesaurus like everyone else with a smartphone, it's because there is simply no other word that will do.

I shake myself like Oscar does after his bath. It's not like me to be so negative and I'm determined to snap out of it. I take a deep breath and open the car door. The house is probably adorable on the inside. Mom wouldn't have rented a place that didn't have some redeeming qualities. I reach into the backseat and grab the crate that holds our cat, Lex Luthor. Then I take out my phone and turn it on myself, texting a picture of me, Lex, and the house in the background to Ashley. We promised each other that we wouldn't grow apart, even with me living up here in Washington and her back in Texas. I mean, we've been best friends since seventh grade. If our friendship could survive middle school cliquey-ness I'm pretty sure it can survive a few thousand miles.

My Chuck Taylors crunch over the gravel driveway as I make my way to the front door. Mom and Oscar are already inside. It might be August, but that doesn't stop Ridgemont from being cold, colder than Austin is at Christmastime, and unfortunately, I'm still wearing the ripped up denim shorts that I put on before we left our motel in Boise, Idaho this morning. The brightly colored mustang on Mom's old high school t-shirt—my favorite shirt these days—looks out of place in the fog, the opposite of camouflage.

I hover in the doorway. "Mom!" I shout. No answer. Just the squeak of the screen door on its hinges while I hold it open, then the whistle of a gust of wind from behind me like it's trying to push me inside.

"Mom!" I repeat. Finally, I shout her full name: "Katherine Marie Griffith!" She hates when I call her by her first name, though she claims it has nothing to do with the fact that I'm adopted. We've never made a big deal about it—never had some big talk where my mother, like, revealed the news to me. The truth is, I don't remember a time when I didn't know. There are moments when I wonder who my birth-parents are and why they gave me up, but even Mom doesn't know those details. She was a pediatric nurse at the hospital in Austin where I was found—left swaddled in the emergency room, no parents, no paperwork, no nothing—and once she got her hands on me, she says, she knew she was never going to let me go. We were meant for each other, she'd say, simple as that.

Mom and I giggle when strangers comment on how much we look alike, because we don't. We just *act* alike—sometimes too much alike. But unlike me, Mom is a redhead with light skin, almost-gray eyes, pale skin and freckles. I have long brown hair that's usually trapped somewhere in between wavy and frizzy. And my eyes are green, not gray like Mom's. Ashley says they look like cat's eyes. You know how some people's eyes change color depending on the light or what they're wearing? Not mine. They're always the same milky, light kind of green. And even in the dark, my pupils never get big. I've literally never seen anyone with eyes that look like mine. They're so unusual that I'm pretty sure anyone whose eyes matched mine would probably be related to me. Like for real related, by blood.

Anyway, adopted or not, I'm closer to my mom than any other sixteen-year-old I've ever met. Or at least, I'm pretty sure we're closer than any of the mother/daughter combos I saw walking around the mall in Austin. If they weren't fighting they were barely talking. Ashley used to pick her phone up and pretend to be deep in conversation every time her mother walked into the room rather than answer when she asked about her day. I mean, how many sixteen-year-olds do you know who could spend three days straight locked up in a car with their mother driving across the country? Though I've only been sixteen for a week now.

From somewhere inside the house comes the sound of a toilet flushing. "Where did you think I was, Sunshine?" Mom asks, returning to the front door.

"My name never sounded that ironic in Texas," I mumble, shivering as I step over the threshold. The door slams shut behind me and I jump.

"It's just the wind, sweetie." Mom's got a twinkle in her eye like she's trying not to laugh at me.

"I think it's actually colder inside the house than it is outside." I don't think I've ever felt a cold like this before, not even when I was nine-years-old and Mom took me skiing in Colorado where the temperature was literally below freezing. *This* cold is something else entirely. It's snaking underneath my clothes and covering my skin in goosebumps. It feels kind of like when you have a fever and you're shivering despite the fact that your temperature is rising and you're bundled up under layers of covers in bed. The kind of cold that's damp, as though the whole house needs to be run through the dryer. It's ... all right, fine, I'll admit it: it's *creepy.* I say it out loud and Mom laughs.

"Is that your new favorite word?" she asks.

"No," I say softly. I can't remember ever having said it much before. But then, I never felt like this before.

"No one has lived in the house in months. It's just been empty too long. Once we get all of our stuff in here, it'll feel more homey. It'll be *great,* I promise."

But our stuff—the moving truck full of our furniture and my books and knick-knacks and clothes—won't get here until tomorrow. I guess the movers who were driving it from Texas weren't in as much of a hurry to get here as we were. Mom and I ascend the creaky staircase and briefly explore the second floor—two bedrooms, two bathrooms—but it's hard to imagine how our stuff will look in our rooms when most of our belongings are still a hundred miles away. I go into the room that will be mine and shudder at the bright pink wallpaper and carpet. I am not a pink kind of girl. The room is almost perfectly square, and I decide that I will put my bed in the corner to the right of the door and my desk under the window across from it. I walk to the narrow window and look out, but my view of the street is almost entirely blocked by the branches of a pine-tree in our backyard. Even if the sun were shining, I doubt much light would get in. Mom's room faces the front yard, but her windows are mostly blocked by branches, too.

We blow up our queen-sized air-mattress on the hardwood floor of the

living room and spread blankets over it so that the cat doesn't accidentally pop it with his claws when he climbs all over it, which of course
he immediately does. We drive into town for pizza, the sound of pine
needles hitting our roof in the car chorusing right along with the sound
of raindrops. Main Street is mostly empty, nothing like the crowds in
downtown Austin.

"It's quaint," Mom says hopefully, pointing out the charming non-chain
pharmacy and diner, and I nod, forcing myself to smile. On our way
home, the pizza cooling in the backseat, we drive past the hospital, and
Mom pulls into the parking lot. She hasn't been here since they flew her
in for a job interview a couple months ago. The hospital is at least half the
size of the one where she worked back in Austin. She unclicks her seatbelt, but doesn't move to get out of the car, so neither do I.

"Guess they don't have as many sick people in Ridgemont as they did
back home," I say, gesturing at the nearly empty parking lot.

"It's a small town," Mom shrugs, but she looks wary. She's going to have
a lot more responsibility in her new job than she did in Texas, and even
though she hasn't said so, I know she's nervous.

"Don't worry. You're going to knock their socks off."

Mom looks at me and smiles. "That's my Sunshine." She reaches across
the car to squeeze my shoulder, then puts her seatbelt back on and re-
starts the engine. She's turning the car around when the sound of sirens
fills the air. An ambulance comes barreling into the parking lot, speeding
toward the emergency entrance.

I guess there are sick people in Ridgemont after all.

We eat our pizza in our pajamas, sitting on the air mattress like we're
having a slumber party.

"This pizza is better than anything they have in Austin," Mom says as we
argue over the last piece.

"Who knew?" I say, ripping the remaining crust from her hands and gig-
gling. "Ridgemont, Washington, pizza capital of the USA."

"See? I knew you'd like it here."

"I like the *pizza*. That's not the same thing as liking the *place*."

"Maybe loving the pizza is just a hop, skip, and jump away from loving the place," Mom counters hopefully. I sigh. The truth is, we've barely been here three hours and it's really too soon to have an opinion one way or the other.

"Smells funny in here," I say, wrinkling my nose.

"It smells like pizza in here," Mom says, gesturing to the crustfilled box between us.

I shake my head. It smells like something else, a musty, moldy sort of smell, like someone left the air conditioning on too long. Not that you need AC here.

"Anyway, once we have all our stuff moved in, this house is going to smell like us," Mom promises, but I'm not so sure that the damp mildew-smell will go away so easily.

We read before bed. Mom's tackling the latest thriller to grace the bestseller list—she's a sucker for those kind of books even though I make fun of her for it—and I'm reading *Pride & Prejudice* for what has to be the fifteenth time. It's impossible to feel homesick with the familiar weight of the book in my hands. I like all the words no one uses anymore: *flutter* and *perturbation* and *enquiries*. Sometimes I find myself talking like one of the Bennett sisters. Super dorky, I know.

"Do you think maybe I was Jane Austen in a former life?" I ask sleepily when we finally turn off the lights. It must be after midnight. Oscar has weaseled his way in between us on the bed, but I don't mind because even though he takes up half the square footage of the mattress, I'm a lot warmer with him curled up beside me.

"Of course not," Mom says. She doesn't believe in things like past lives. She believes in logic and medicine, in things that can be proven with organic chemistry.

"Okay, but I mean if you *did* believe in that kind of thing—"

"Which I don't—"

"Okay, but if you *did*—"

"If I did, *then* would I also believe that you'd been Jane Austen in a former life?"

"Exactly."

"Nope."

"Why not?" I scoff, feigning offense. I can feel Mom shrug on her side of the bed like the answer is obvious.

"Statistics. Mathematically, the chances are infinitesimal."

"You're applying statistics to my hypothetical past life?"

"Numbers don't lie, Sunshine State." Mom calls me that sometimes, even though we've never even been to Florida, the actual Sunshine State. I'm pretty sure Washington is as far as you can get from Florida without actually leaving the contiguous United States. But Mom's always said that as long as she's with me, she's in a state of perpetual sunshine. She says she felt that way from the instant she picked me up when I was a just a newborn baby. That's why she named me Sunshine in the first place.

"Good night, sweetie," she says into the darkness.

"Good night."

The sound wakes me up. I'm not sure what time it is when I hear it. Hear *them*. Footsteps. Coming from the floor above us. I wasn't sleeping all that soundly anyway. Usually when I fall asleep after reading *Pride & Prejudice* I dream about Mr. Darcy, but tonight, I was having really weird dreams. I saw a little girl crying in the corner of a bathroom, but no matter what I said or did, her tears kept flowing. I tried to put my arms around her, but she was always out of reach, even when I was right beside her.

"What the freak?" I whisper, rolling over and reaching for Oscar. Dogs' hearing is supposed to be really good, so if he doesn't hear anything, then this is definitely just my imagination, right? But Oscar isn't on the bed anymore, and it's pitch dark in here so I can't see where he is. He can't be that far away, though, because I can smell the wet-dog-smell of his fur, which hasn't fully dried since we got here. Suddenly, the footsteps stop.

"Mom," I whisper, gently shaking her shoulder. "Mom, did you hear that?"

"Hmmm?" she answers, her voice thick with sleep. She was really tired after having driven so far. I should let her sleep. But then the footsteps start again.

Oh gosh, maybe this house doesn't feel creepy because it's been empty for months. Maybe it feels creepy because a crazed murderer has been squatting on the floor above us, waiting for some unsuspecting family to move in so that he could strangle them in their sleep. My heart is pounding and I take deep breaths, trying to slow it. But it just gets faster.

The footsteps don't actually sound like a crazed murderer's, though. They sound light, kind of playful—kind of like a child is skipping through the rooms above us.

"Mom," I repeat, more urgently this time. Maybe there really is a kid up there. Maybe he or she got lost or ran away from home?

"What is it?" Mom says sleepily.

"Do you hear that?" I ask.

"Hear what?"

"Those footsteps."

"All I hear is your voice keeping me awake," she says, but I can tell she's smiling. "It's probably just the cat," she adds, rolling over and putting her arms around me. "Go back to sleep. I promise this place won't seem so creepy in the morning." She emphasizes the word *creepy* like it's some kind of joke.

"It's not funny," I protest, but Mom's breathing has resumed its steady rhythm; she's already fallen back to sleep. "It's not funny," I repeat, whispering the words into the darkness.

The last thing I expect is an answer, but almost immediately after I speak, I hear it, clearly and softly as though someone is whispering in my ear.

Not footsteps this time, but a child's laugh: a giggle, light and clear as crystal, traveling through the darkness. I squeeze my eyes shut, willing myself to think about anything else: Elizabeth Bennett and Fitzwilliam Darcy, Jane and Mr. Bingley, even Lydia and Mr. Wickham. I try to picture them dancing at the Netherfield ball (even though I know Mr. Wickham wasn't actually there that night), but instead, all I can see is the little girl from my dream, her dark dress tattered with age, playing hopscotch on the floor above me. And again, I hear laughter. A child's laugh has never sounded quite so scary.

Before I know what I'm doing, I crawl out of bed and head for the stairs. If there's a little girl up there, she's probably just as frightened as I am, right? Though she didn't sound frightened. I mean, she was laughing.

I place my foot on the bottom step and look up. There's nothing but darkness above me. Oscar appears at my side, leaning his warm body against my leg. "Good boy." My voice comes out breathless, as though I've been running.

I put my foot on the second step and it creaks. Then, there's nothing but quiet: no laughter, no footsteps, no skipping. My heart is pounding but I take a deep breath and it slows to a steady beat.

"Maybe it's over," I say. Oscar pants in agreement. Other than our breathing, the house is silent. "Let's go back to bed," I sigh finally, turning around.

Oscar curls up beside me on the air mattress, and I run my fingers up and down his warm fur. I expect to lie awake, staring at the ceiling, for hours. Instead, my eyelids grow heavy, my breathing slows until it keeps time with Mom's.

But I swear, just as I'm drifting out of consciousness, in that place where you're more asleep than awake anymore, I hear something else. A phrase uttered in a child's voice, no more than a whisper: *Night Night.*

You've just read an excerpt from The Haunting of Sunshine Girl: Book One.

ABOUT THE AUTHOR

Paige McKenzie, the irresistible face of *The Haunting of Sunshine Girl*, began playing Sunshine as a high school junior. Today, the YouTube series boasts over 100 million total views. McKenzie was recently named one of *Seventeen* magazine's "Pretty Amazing" finalists. She lives in Portland, Oregon.

Imprint: Weinstein Books
Print ISBN: 9781602862722
Print price: $16.00
eBook ISBN: 9781602862739
eBook price: $16.00
Publication date: 3/24/15
Publicity contact: Kathleen Schmidt
kathleen.schmidt@weinsteinco.com
Editor: Cindy Eagan
Agent: Mollie Glick
Agency: Foundry Literary + Media

Promotional information:
- Reviews and features in trade publications; culture and entertainment magazines; teen/women's magazines
- Interviews and reviews in major newspapers
- National radio giveaway packages and interviews
- Extensive digital media and book trailer campaign; interviews/reviews on entertainment websites and outreach to YA book bloggers
- Major social media promotion targeting existing fans and YA readers, utilizing Sunshine Girl's extensive social media network and all relevant platforms. Campaign to include contests, cover reveals, giveaways, and special promotions
- Book signings and in-store events
- Close collaboration with existing Sunshine Girl properties and The Weinstein Company
- Advance reader copies

"I LOVED IT." – ELIZABETH GILBERT

Kissing

IN AMERICA

MARGO
RABB

SUMMARY

In the years following her father's death, 16-year-old Eva has sought the comfort of poetry and romance novels to assuage her grief. Then she meets Will, and through their connection, Eva is able to escape the pain of her dad's death and her difficult relationship with her mom. But then Will suddenly picks up and moves to California—and just like that, Eva is right back where she started. With the help of her best friend, Annie, Eva concocts a plan to leave New York City for the first time in her life and travel across the country to see Will. From cowboys to kudzu, and the endless roads in between, Eva and Annie learn the truth about love and all of its complexities.

EXCERPT

Part One

Love and Grief

> *Will it come like a change in the weather?*
>
> *Will its greeting be courteous or rough?*
>
> *Will it alter my life altogether?*
>
> *O tell me the truth about love.*
>
> *—W. H. Auden*

I hope your first kiss went a little better than mine did

According to my mother, my first kiss happened on a Saturday in July. The weather: steamy, blacktop-melting, jungle-gym-scorching New York City sunshine. The setting: the 49th Street playground in Queens, good on the sand quotient, low on the rats. The kisser: Hector Driggs, cute but a little bit smelly, like wet blankets and aged cheese. The event: one sopping, clammy-lipped, deranged, lunging kiss, directly on my lips.

I bit him.

I was three.

A mark bloomed on his arm like two tiny purple smiles and he cried for half an hour, but my mother felt no pity for him. In fact, she swelled with pride. "Even at that young age I knew you understood the need for girls and women to fight for our freedom, equality, and personal space," she said when she retold the story. "Plus, he smelled weird. I would've bit him too."

My mom is a professor of women's studies at Queens College. While other newborns were happily drifting to sleep to *Goodnight Moon*, my mom read to me in my crib from Simone de Beauvoir, Virginia Woolf, and Audre Lorde. In our living room there's a picture of me in my stroller at a women's rights march in Washington, clutching a sign with my tiny green mittens: *Well-Behaved Women Seldom Make History!*

And so, two years ago, when I was fourteen and began what my mom termed "your ultimate rebellion," she said I chose the worst thing possible. She would've preferred odd piercings, full-body tattoos, or even shoplifting to what I did.

I fell in love with romance novels.

It wasn't even just regular book-love. I was crazy for them, head-over-heels, obsessed. I read them in grocery aisles, on subways, buses, between classes, and most often, curled up in bed. Over the next two years I read one hundred and eighteen of them. (Not counting those I read twice.)

I'd discovered my first romance novel on the shelves of my best friend Annie Kim's apartment—she has two older sisters. Jenny, her middle sister, saw me gazing at the array of colorful spines and handed me *Cowboys on Fire* (book 1), with bare-chested cowboy Destry and gold-belt-buckled cowboy Ewing on the cover. (I'd get to know Destry and Ewing with a passion that bordered on the scientific.) "Here," Jenny said. "You have to read this."

Slowly, my room became plastered with posters of Destry and Ewing on horseback, riding bulls one-handed, and roping calves; of Sir Richard from *Torrid Tomorrow*, who led a double life as the pirate Diablo; and Gurlag, who was raised by wolves and known as *The Wilderness Rogue*.

My mom would come into my room and gaze at the books on my night table, at Ewing on his bronco or Gurlag swinging from a tree, and she'd sigh. "I didn't raise you to worship imbecilic apes."

Other times she'd grow more serious, looking at my books. "I've failed you as a mother, as a woman, and as a citizen of this world," she'd say.

It wasn't true. I called myself a feminist (to her at least—to my friends it would be like calling myself a maiden or some other dusty crusty ancient word). At school I was quick to point out whenever boys dominated class discussions, or girls were excluded from handball games. When a flasher was spotted in our schoolyard three times in one month, I organized a Take Back the Yard march, with forty-five eighth graders parading around the Intermediate School 125 grounds chanting, "Girls on guard! Take back the yard! And dude, put some clothes on!" The flasher was undeterred, but eventually caught and prosecuted.

Still, my books kept bothering my mother. "That happiness only comes from romantic love is the biggest myth of our society," she told me once. "They're selling you a fantasy version of love. It's dishonest. Misleading. And untrue. Real love is a mess. Complicated. Not like *this*." She picked up *Torrid Tomorrow*.

"But you haven't even read it."

As if possessed by a magic maternal sixth sense, she turned to the worst sentences in the whole book.

Sir Richard's chest sparkled with man-dew as he whispered, "Lilith, it may hurt you when I burst thy womanhood."

"Hurt me," Lilith breathed. Her rosy domes undulated like the sea as he joined her in a love that vanquished every sorrow known on Earth.

"The rest of the book is filled with a historical portrait of late nineteenth century American society, and Lilith is treated as an equal in the relationship—she's on the forefront of the suffrage movement," I pointed out, but my mom ignored my explanations, and tried to get me to read *Girls Be Strong: A Guide for Growing Up Powerful* instead.

Girls Be Strong wasn't a bad book. It had some semi-interesting advice about how a boy stealing your scarf may mean that he likes you, but you're still entitled to tell him to get the hell out of your way. And it included a funny piece by Gloria Steinem called "If Men Could Menstruate," which said: "Guys would brag ('I'm a three-pad man') or answer praise from a buddy ('Man, you lookin' good!') by giving fives and saying, 'Yeah man, I'm on the rag!'"

But it wasn't exactly a romantic book, either.

To my mother, my real problem was that I believed in love, in great love. I had this trickle of hope, always, that the future would be filled with romance. I didn't expect to meet a Sir Richard or a Destry exactly, but it didn't seem entirely impossible.

My mom says that the events of last summer all started because of those one hundred and eighteen romance novels percolating in my brain. I don't think so, though. I think everything started when I met Will and told him about my father.

* * *

I sang in my chains like the sea

The first thing Will ever said to me was: "Tell me the truth." Then he plunked several pieces of crumpled notebook paper on my desk.

It was last September, in the tutoring center in our school's crumbling north tower. Our high school was a charter school in a city-owned former mansion in the Bronx; it featured a faded fresco in the auditorium, gilt moldings on the first floor, and entire wings of the building that were never renovated or used. The north tower overlooked Van Cortlandt Park. Iron bars covered the windows, as if someone was afraid we'd be tempted to hurl ourselves out.

When Will appeared at the door, Mrs. Peech, our faculty advisor, read his form and announced, "William Freeman," as if everyone didn't know who he was already—he was like a part of the school you learned your first week, along with your map and schedule. "You're with Eva."

Seventeen faces watched him sit down. He barely fit in the small chair.

I felt like I'd stepped onto a shaky subway train. I'd had a crush on him for over a year, since I saw him my first day of high school. Now I tried not to stare at him. He had dark, wavy, unkempt hair like Gurlag, Destry, and all the windblown men on my romance novel covers, but he was different. He always carried books around—James Baldwin, Joseph Heller,

Kurt Vonnegut—and while his friends were laughing and talking on the 1 train home, sometimes he'd just read. He managed to be weird and popular at the same time. The trophy case on our school's second floor displayed a shelf of his swim team awards (he was the captain), and his photo. I glanced at it every time I walked by: his brown eyes and his smile that always seemed partly sad and partly amused, as if he was thinking of some dark, mysterious joke.

I picked up his pages and the words swam before me. I glanced across the room at Annie; we both tutored at the drop-in center every Friday afternoon. She raised her eyebrows.

Focus. *Focus*. Do *not* think of man-dew.

I smoothed his rumpled pages and read. It was a college application essay about a swim meet, with descriptions of butterfly strokes and buzzers ringing, and it was achingly boring.

"This sucks," I said.

"Don't hold back now."

"You said to tell the truth."

"Because I thought you'd say it was *good*."

"There's no punctuation."

He pointed to a period.

"A period is the wallflower of punctuation. And you only have three."

"Three good ones," he said. He gazed right at me, practically through me.

Rosamunde Saunders, author of *Torrid Tomorrow*, would describe him as having *cheekbones as big as apricots* and *café mocha skin*. I glanced at the pale scar on his chin, like a tiny river. He sat so close to me that I could smell soap and something else—was I imagining it?—like sugar. His leg, in his dark jeans, brushed mine.

He picked up Dylan Thomas's *Selected Poems* from my desk. I'd been reading it before he got there; he'd arrived forty-five minutes after tutoring hour had started. "He looks startled," he said, staring at Dylan Thomas's face.

"It's startling to be reinventing the English language," I said. "I mean— dingle starry!" I blurted, quoting from the book. *The night above the dingle starry . . .* I took a breath and tried again. "I mean, in the book, um . . ." Why was I babbling? What was wrong with me? It was like an evil spirit had overtaken my body. I couldn't believe I was talking to Will and we were talking about Dylan Thomas, and the sheer magnitude of it all turned my brain to goo. All that was left was Rosamunde Saunders's voice. *He's looking at you with liquid velvet eyes. Eyes that know how to love a woman and—*

The bell rang. Someone called his name. A girl who stood in the door- way, a swim team girl. Vanessa Valari. She and her friends bought entire pages in the yearbook to fill with photos of themselves in their bikinis on Rockaway Beach, their hands on their hips, laughing at the camera.

Will stood up, still holding the book. "Can I borrow this? I'll bring it back next Friday."

I nodded and watched him leave with the bikini girl.

The door closed behind them. "What's a dingle starry?" Annie asked me.

I took her phone—it was faster than my own Crapphone—and Googled Dylan Thomas's "Fern Hill," and showed it to her. "Fern Hill" was my fa- ther's favorite poem. He'd bought the book of *Selected Poems* for me one summer day after he phoned in sick to work (playing hooky, he called it), and we took the train to the Strand and picked out a whole pile of books, then went uptown and bought so much food at Columbus Comfort Kitchen that we could barely carry it all—fried chicken and fluffy bis- cuits and fried apple pies, still warm in tinfoil, and chocolate malt shakes smothered in whipped cream. We walked through Central Park and sat by Turtle Pond, and all afternoon we ate and wrote and read. I'd never heard the words *dingle starry* before but I could see the stars dingling and sparkling, the sun dappling hidden lakes and magical trees, every- thing feeling easy and light, and though I wouldn't be able to say exactly what it meant to *sing in my chains like the sea*, I knew that I'd felt it, that I hadn't known that feeling existed until I saw the words on the page. After we read the poems we wrote in notebooks—small spiral-bound col-lege-ruled ones from the drugstore—he never saved his, but mine were stashed in the back of my closet. I hadn't looked at them since he died.

"You let Will take your dad's copy of the book?" Annie asked me, in shock.

My insides dropped—why had I done that? What if he spilled something on it or lost it? All week I watched him in the cafeteria and schoolyard, but I never had the guts to say, *Hey, by the way, please be careful with my book!*

On Friday at tutoring, he brought the book back to me, in perfect shape.

"Good book," he said.

I'd hoped we'd have time to talk, but he was late again, and we had only fifteen minutes. Mrs. Peech kept glancing at us; we got right to his essay. He'd rewritten it. I read it quickly. "The punctuation is great now, but I think the swim team topic has got to go," I told him.

"Why? That's what I *do*."

"Everyone does a sport. Maybe if your sport was, I don't know—calf-rop-ing—that might be interesting, but they're going to get a million essays about swim meets."

"I've got nothing else to write about."

"I don't believe you. Dig deep," I said.

"How do I know you're giving me good advice?"

"My mom has been coaching me on my college application since I was a fetus. Plus Mrs. Peech makes all the tutors read a book about college essays."

The bell rang. The bikini girl waited in the doorway again. "See you next Friday," he said.

The week crept by. Annie and I studied—sometimes I felt like all we did was study—we studied on the 7 and the 1 train (the 1, when it reached the Bronx, was quieter), at the Woodside Library, the Sunnyside Library, the 42nd Street New York Public Library, and at Athens Diner, which was halfway between our apartments, and where they let you sit with a hot chocolate for three hours and never kicked you out. At night, before we fell asleep, she texted me updates about *Dancing with the Stars* and all her favorite reality shows, and I texted her quotes about Gurlag's manroot.

I couldn't wait to see Will again. When the day arrived I kept watching the door, expecting him to appear, which he did, only ten minutes late this time.

His new essay was about his dog, Silas.

"The college essay guide said no dogs," I said.

"What's wrong with dogs?"

"They get so many pet essays they usually toss them right out. Instant reject."

"My dog isn't a normal dog. He has three legs."

"I know. Silas sounds like a great dog. Still. Four-legged dogs, three-legged dogs—the book said they get tired of reading about dogs." I tapped his essay. "Also, the voice here doesn't sound like you. I mean, it could've been written by anybody. You want something that could only have been written by you."

I scribbled in the margin of his essay: "More you." He took the pen from me and put it down, and then touched my finger.

"You have a callus from writing so much," he said.

No one in my books ever pointed out a callus. *"I love your callus,"* Sir Richard said. *"What a beautiful callus."*

He ran his finger up and down mine. My face warmed; a flicker traveled under my skin. He let go as the bell rang. The door opened and there stood the bikini girl, as always.

He left without a word. I stared after him. I told Annie what happened as we packed up our things and walked down the hall.

"He touched my finger. He told me—he actually told me, '*You have a callus from writing so much.*'" I said it in a husky tone.

Annie squinted. "What's wrong with your voice? You sound like you have a throat disease."

Annie was a romantic only up to a point. She liked watching *Anne of Green Gables*, *Pride and Prejudice*, and even the occasional Lifetime Original Movie with me, and she loved her reality shows, but she drew the line at reading romance novels, or having a real-life romance right now. "We've got plenty of time for all that crap in college," she'd say.

In college. That was Annie's mantra. She always knew she'd wait till college to fall in love. Her sisters, Jenny, who was a junior, and Lala, who was a senior, got straight Cs and wasted all their time thinking about who they hoped to hook up with, or regretted hooking up with. Annie said they were on a fast track to folding sweaters at American Eagle for the rest of their lives.

Our wait-till-college plan was easy since no boys were interested in us anyway. At our nerd-heavy school, the boys rarely had the guts to speak to us, except when asking to borrow math notes or to pass a beaker in lab. The only guy who'd ever asked me out was David Dweener, who had oily hair and liked to a wear a T-shirt from the musical *Cats*. Will belonged to the good-looking elite, a small, ultracool crowd. I never thought in a million years that he'd ever speak to me.

Annie and I walked toward the subway. "Maybe next week you'll get lucky and he'll ask to touch your bunion," she said.

"That would be wonderful. Except I don't have a bunion."

"*Sadly, it was a short-lived romance, since Lady Eva's dead skin was not yet thick nor copious enough to satisfy Sir Will,*" Annie said.

Laughing about it made me feel a little less nervous when I thought about him, but the next Friday, my heart banged away when he walked through the door of the tutoring center.

He had a completely new essay:

The last time I saw my brother he looked perfect. They made his skin pink. His lips were bright red. He wore a fuzzy blue sleeper that had been given to him as a gift, but he'd never worn it while he was alive. My mom wanted each of us to give him something to be buried with, to take wherever he was going. My dad gave him a tiny telescope so that he could always see us on Earth. I gave him one of my stuffed animals, an orange monkey. My mom gave him a gold necklace that said "Mother" on it, which she'd been wearing the day he was born.

I was seven.

When people ask my mom how many children she has, she says two. For a while, if someone asked me how many siblings I had I said none. She got mad when I said that. She likes talking about him. It gives her comfort. *I had another son, a baby who died in his crib. They don't know what caused it. I put him to bed on his back. I didn't have a blanket in the crib. I didn't do anything wrong but it happened and you have to learn to live with it. It never gets easier.*

It doesn't bother her that people cringe and look away when she talks about him. They don't want to hear about it. She talks about him anyway. She takes out the album and looks at his photos, and she remembers his birthday every year and thinks of how old he would've been. Eleven now. He'd be eleven. My mother tells me *He will always be your brother. He was born, he lived, he died. Don't erase his life from yours.*

My mom says that if my brother hadn't died she never would've known who my father really was, that he was the type of man who would leave when things got hard. After my brother died my dad started drinking, staying out all night, stopped coming home. Then one day he left for good. I didn't see him again for ten years.

So I guess this essay is supposed to be about what's influenced me the most, but I think sometimes the biggest influence isn't what's present in your life, but what's absent. Those missing pieces that shape you and change you, the silences that are louder than the noise.

I was quiet for a long time. "It's good," I said. "Really good." My voice was soft. "I'm sorry about your brother and your dad."

I couldn't stand how lame *sorry* sounded. "I hate *sorry*—I mean—my dad's dead—he died almost two years ago. I've never figured out what the right thing to say is. Or to hear."

I knew what the next question would be before he even said it.

"How did he die?" he asked.

Truth

When people ask how my dad died, I lie. I say he died of a heart attack, in his sleep.

When I used to say the truth, when I used to say plane crash, there was always this look. This flash as their mouths opened, this unbearable hungry eager excitement. They'd want to know what kind of plane, how big it was, where it was going, what went wrong. They wanted more of this freakish thing that didn't happen to real people, not in real life, not to anyone they'd ever met, it didn't.

I understand the curiosity. I mean, I do it too—who doesn't click on links to accidents and scary things, kids falling down wells, burn victims, serial killers? People always ask bits and facts about the plane but what they really want to know is how it would be to die like that, to fall from the sky, how it would feel.

The heart attack happened in his sleep so he never felt a thing, I tell them. Peacefully. *Rest in peace.* I can never stop thinking about those words *rest in peace.*

The airline officials asked my mom for items so he could be identified. Hairs from a comb. Toothbrush. She gathered these specks of my father, specks because there might be nothing of him left from the impact, nothing but other matching specks.

"You'll feel relief when they identify the remains," said the grief counselor lady assigned to us. Her chest was the size of a jumbo loaf of Wonder bread. I called her Wonderboob. Wonderboob liked to tell my mom and me things like "You need to make the time to do your grief work," as if it was something I could add to my homework list after algebra and English. She led group sessions for the families; she belonged to a team of therapists who'd donated their services. During these weekly sessions she'd yawn and periodically check her texts. She recommended vanilla scented candles and Be Relaxed herbal tea. The plane had crashed deep into the ocean, and only a small amount of remains and wreckage had been recovered from the surface. As the search and DNA analysis continued, Wonderboob ended all our sessions by saying, in a businesslike tone, "I'll keep you updated on the status of the remains."

Remains. She really liked the word *remains.* You'd think that adults—social workers, grief counselors, people whose job it is *to make you feel better*—you'd think they'd come up with a better word than *remains.*

My mother attended all the sessions with me, but she never said a word during them and never seemed to hear anything anybody else said, either. She'd gaze into the distance, emotionless.

I never said a word during the sessions either, but I listened to everything. Back then, during those first six weeks after the crash, I was certain my dad was still alive, that he'd never gotten on that plane. I saw him everywhere around the city. I followed a man in a suit into a subway car, thinking it was him. I saw him in a taxi whizzing over the 59th Street Bridge. In a booth at McDonald's. It was never him.

I tried not to think about it. I didn't think about it, I'd be okay not thinking about it, and then I'd see a girl my age with her father and it was like someone was pulling my intestines out with their teeth.

There's a KFC on my walk home from the 52nd Street subway station, and sometimes I glance in the window and see them. Girls and their dads doing the tiniest most boring thing like sharing chicken wings (and I don't even like chicken wings), and I watch them through the window, wanting to soak up all this fatherness, this luxurious fatherness they don't even appreciate. Usually they're not even talking to their dads, they're texting or playing a video game in their laps. Don't they know? I want to shake them. Don't they know how lucky they are to sit in the KFC with their fathers?

Six weeks after the crash, they confirmed my dad's remains. They'd found a small part of his body.

Three months after that, my mom got rid of his stuff. His clothes, his shoes, his papers all went in the trash or in a Queens Thrifty-Thrift truck. The only things that she approved of me keeping were our photo albums, his books, and presents he'd given me—a horseshoe necklace, a silver bracelet for my birthday, three turquoise rings, pens, and notebooks.

I snuck some other things away before she could throw them out, though. I hid them in a large purple shoebox in my closet.

Things I kept:

spare glasses with brown plastic frames and scratched lenses

Brooklyn Bridge paperweight

eight postcards he sent from business trips

soft white Hanes T-shirt

collar he bought for our cat, Lucky

two blue handkerchiefs

striped silk tie

a receipt from Popeyes for 5 TENDER, 1 BISCUIT, SM PEPSI with his signature

six Toffee Crisp wrappers I found in the pockets of his coats

I take these things out sometimes; I touch the paperweight and T-shirt and candy wrappers and I lie on my bed, holding them.

A year after he died, my mom said our apartment was too big and expensive, so we moved to a smaller place nine blocks away. That's when I began saying *heart attack* to our new neighbors and the owner of the corner grocery store and any stranger who asked.

A heart attack. In his sleep. At the hospital. He went into the hospital with chest pains and had the heart attack there, in a comfortable hospital room with yellow walls and a striped curtain separating the beds. (I've only been to a hospital once, when my aunt Janet had fibroids removed, and that's what I pictured.) It was a quiet room with a flower painting and a window with an East River view. The caring nurses comforted my mom and me, and we held his hand and said good-bye and I kissed his forehead. I knew the whole scenario. I almost believed it myself. I called it *his passing*. I heard someone say this one time, *his passing*, about their father who had a heart attack in his sleep, and I envied it. I was actually jealous of how someone else's father died. The *passing*, the peaceful transition between life and death. Rest in peace. That's how I wanted it to be.

You've just read an excerpt from Kissing in America.

ABOUT THE AUTHOR

Margo Rabb is an acclaimed novelist whose debut, *Cures for Heartbreak*, was hailed by critics and young readers alike. Her essays and short stories have appeared in *The New York Times, The Atlantic, The Rumpus, Zoetrope: All-Story, Seventeen, Best New American Voices, New Stories from the South*, and *One Story*, and have been broadcast on NPR. She received the grand prize in the *Zoetrope* short story contest, first prize in the Atlantic fiction contest, and a PEN Syndicated Fiction Project Award. Margo grew up in Queens, New York, and currently lives in Austin, Texas with her husband and two children. You can visit her online at www.margorabb.com.

Imprint: HarperCollins
Print ISBN: 9780062322371
Print price: $17.99
eBook ISBN: 9780062322395
eBook price: $13.99
Publication date: 5/26/15
Publicity contact: Olivia Russo (Olivia.russo@harpercollins.com)
Rights contact: Molly Jaffa at Folio Literary (molly@foliolit.com) for translation; Emily Van Beek at Folio Literary (emily@foliolit.com) for everything else
Editor: Alexandra Cooper
Agent: Emily Van Beek
Agency: Folio Literary

Territories sold:
ANZ pending

Promotional information:
*   Epic Reads teen group tour and promotion

- Extensive blogger outreach
- National print and online consumer advertising campaign
- Epic Reads exclusive author content
- Extensive social media outreach
- Major librarian and educator outreach

BOOKSELLER BLURBS:

"Wonderful . . . Margo Rabb has created nothing less than a women's map of American mythologies, navigating from Emily Dickinson to Barbara Cartland, from the cowboys of the rodeos to the makeup studios of Hollywood, and from the bottom of the Atlantic to the spacious skies of the USA." — E. Lockhart, New York Times bestselling author of *We Were Liars*

"*Kissing in America* is a wonderful novel about friendship, love, travel, life, hope, poetry, intelligence and the inner lives of girls—all the things, to put it simply, that I like best in a book. Margo Rabb writes with compassion and clarity about lives that are worth telling, journeys that need to be taken, peace that needs to be reached. I loved it." — Elizabeth Gilbert, *New York Times* bestselling author of *Eat, Pray, Love*

THE TAPPER TWINS

GO TO WAR

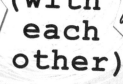

(with each other)

GEOFF RODKEY

SUMMARY

This brand-new series by a popular screenwriter is a pitch-perfect, contemporary comedy featuring twelve-year-old fraternal twins, Claudia and Reese, who couldn't be more different...except in their determination to come out on top in a vicious prank war.

EXCERPT

PROLOGUE

CLAUDIA

Wars are terrible things. I know this because I've read about a lot of them on Wikipedia.

And also because I was just in one. It was me against my brother, Reese.

That might not sound like a war to you. Trust me. It was. In fact, it was a lot like other famous wars I've read about on Wikipedia.

Just like World War II, it involved a sneak attack on a peaceful people who never saw it coming (me).

It was sort of like this:

Just like World War I, it lasted a lot longer and caused a LOT more problems than anybody expected, especially people who were totally innocent and didn't deserve it (me).

...and kind of like this:

And like all wars, when it was over, somebody had to write a book about it (me), so that historians of the future would know exactly what happened and whose fault it was (Reese's).

This is especially true of the part where the police got involved.

REESE

Calling it a war is kind of stupid. But Claudia always has to make a big deal out of everything.

I mean, yeah, it got out of hand for a while there. But it's not like anybody died.

Except on my MetaWorld account. THAT was a horrible, bloody massacre.

It wasn't actual blood or anything. It was pixels. But it was still pretty bad. There was, like, little red pixel blood splooshed all over the screen.

MetaWorld blood
(should be red, but Dad
won't buy color printer)

And that was all Claudia's fault, *{Editor note: NOT my fault (see above)}* and totally NOT COOL.

I would never, EVER do something that mean to my sister. I'm nice to her almost all the time!

Except when she's mean to me first. And then it doesn't count.

Also, I had nothing to do with the cops. That was all Claudia. I have a totally clean record. *{Editor note: wait a few years—this will change}* Seriously! Call the cops if you don't believe me.

MOM AND DAD (Text messages copied from Mom's phone)

(MOM) Claudia says she's writing a book
about the incident

(DAD) Like a novel?

No. Oral history. Interviews. Like that
zombie book. But real

Great! If published, will look good
on college apps

I'm worried it'll make us look like bad
parents

How?

She wants us to participate

By interviewing us? I might have
time after Entek deal closes. Getting
crushed at work right now

No interview. Says she just wants to
quote from our text messages

I don't like that

Me neither. But she already has all
of them

How?

I left my phone on the kitchen counter

last night

                                      Tell her no

I tried. She got upset. Now I feel guilty

                       Ugh. Fine. Let her use them

Really?

                Yes. If we don't like the book, we can always sue her to stop publication

Are you kidding? I can't tell

                         I can't either
             {Editor note: Dad has not sued me. (Yet.)}

CHAPTER 1

THE GATHERING STORM

CLAUDIA

Here is some background information about The War:

My name is Claudia Tapper. I live in New York City, and I have two goals in life: I either want to be a famous singer-songwriter like Miranda Fleet, or the President of the United States.

Or both, if I have time.

My brother's name is Reese. He has no goals in life. Unless you count being a professional soccer player, which is totally unrealistic.

We are, unfortunately, twins. I am twelve years old. Reese is six.

I know what you're thinking. "Really? Is that possible?"

No. It's not. Reese is twelve, too.

He just has the brain of a six-year-old. A six-year-old that ate too much sugar and did not get its nap, so it has to run around our apartment and kick soccer balls against the wall and make noises like "GRONK!" and "SKADOOSH!"

Honestly, living with him is the most annoying thing ever. It's a pretty small apartment.

We live on the Upper West Side. But we go to school at Culvert Prep, which is across Central Park on the Upper EAST Side. My parents like to say the Upper West Side is more "down to earth." As far as I can tell, this basically means our neighborhood has more burger places, and not as many stores that sell $800 shoes. (Which, BTW, is insane. The shoes aren't even that cute.)

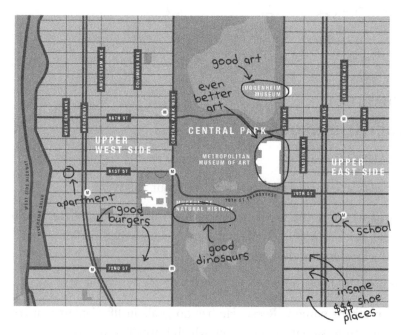

Culvert Prep is academically excellent, so there's no way Reese could have gotten in if he hadn't started going there in kindergarten. At that age, it's very hard for the admissions office to tell if a kid will turn out to be a total meathead.

Mom and Dad think Reese is perfectly smart, and he just needs to apply himself. They're wrong, but it's not worth arguing with them. If they had to admit the truth about their meathead son, it would make them incredibly sad.

And Dad is sad enough already, because he is a lawyer.

Anyway, back to Culvert Prep, which is where The War started.

Culvert Prep (mostly not meatheads) (except my brother) (and his friends)

To be totally specific, it started in the Culvert Prep cafeteria on Monday, September 8th, at approximately 8:27am. That's when Reese—in front of basically the whole sixth grade—launched a cruel and senseless sneak attack on me.

REESE

It didn't start at school. It started in our kitchen that morning, when Claudia ate my toaster pastry.

our kitchen (site of toaster pastry argument)

(me)

(Reese)

I paid $5 for these flowers at deli

CLAUDIA

That is SO not true. It wasn't even yours.

REESE

Yes, it was! There's six in a package. We each get three. And I only had two!

CLAUDIA

I only had two, too.

REESE

Liar!

CLAUDIA

It's true! I think Dad eats them when he gets home at night.

REESE

All I know is, brown sugar cinnamon's my favorite. And there was ONE left, and it was MINE.

And I was lying in bed, thinking, "Oh, man, I can't wait to narf that toaster pastry!"

Then I go into the kitchen, and you're, like, stuffing your face with it! And when I got mad, you laughed at me!

CLAUDIA

A) "Narf" is not even a word. And B) this is completely irrelevant.

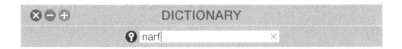

no results for **narf**.
did you mean **barf?**

REESE

It's totally revelant!

CLAUDIA

Relevant.

REESE

Whatever! It's important! I NEVER would've made fun of you in the cafeteria if you hadn't eaten my toaster pastry! And then laughed at me about it!

The whole thing was your fault!

CLAUDIA

That is ridiculous. I'm not putting it in the book.

REESE

You HAVE to! It's the whole reason the war started!

CLAUDIA

No way. Not going in. It's MY book.

REESE

Then I quit. Do your own stupid interviews. I'm going to go play MetaWorld. *{Editor note: site of major battle (like Gettysburg or Waterloo)}*

CLAUDIA

Reese!

Augh! Fine. I'll put it at the end. Like a footnote or something.

REESE

No way. It goes in the actual book. Right at the beginning! This exact argument.

CLAUDIA

That'll ruin the whole thing! Have you ever SEEN an oral history?

REESE

I don't even know what one is.

CLAUDIA

It's like, different people telling a story in their own words. But nobody, like, stops to argue with each other in the middle of it. ESPECIALLY not at the beginning.

REESE

This is supposed to be the true story of what happened, right? And you're recording it. So you have to put in EVERY WORD I'm saying. Or your book is a big skronking lie *{Editor note: also not a real word}* and I quit.

CLAUDIA

I hate you.

REESE

Duh.

CHAPTER 1½

THE STORM IS STILL GATHERING

CLAUDIA

I apologize for that last chapter.

But I had to leave it in because Reese talked to a lawyer. And the lawyer told him he could refuse to participate in the oral history if I didn't print our entire argument exactly how I recorded it on my iPad.

Which is ridiculous.

And I'm pretty sure the lawyer just told Reese that to make him shut up, because the lawyer was very tired from a long week of being a lawyer and just wanted to lie on the couch and fall asleep watching football.

lawyer
(asleep on couch)

(lawyer's popcorn)

But when I went to complain, he was already snoring even though it was only the first quarter. And I didn't want to wake him up, because I am a kind and considerate person.

And I couldn't appeal to a higher court, because Mom was at yoga.

Just to be clear, though, this says Chapter 1½, but really it's Chapter 1, and you should just ignore that other Chapter 1.

Back to The War.

Historians disagree about where exactly it began. Some claim it started not at 8:27am in the Culvert Prep cafeteria, but an hour earlier, in the kitchen of Apartment 6D at 437 West End Avenue.

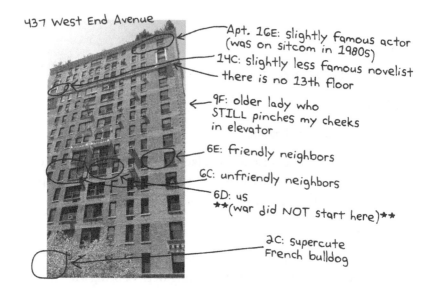

437 West End Avenue

Apt. 16E: slightly famous actor (was on sitcom in 1980s)

14C: slightly less famous novelist

there is no 13th floor

9F: older lady who STILL pinches my cheeks in elevator

6E: friendly neighbors

6C: unfriendly neighbors

6D: us
(war did NOT start here)

2C: supercute French bulldog

These historians are idiots. And they can't even count to three.

Which, BTW, is the maximum number of toaster pastries I have EVER eaten out of a box of six.

But whatever.

Here's exactly what happened:

First of all, it's important to know that on a normal weekday at 8:27am, pretty much the whole sixth grade is hanging out in the cafeteria. So if you're going to launch a vicious sneak attack on an innocent person and want to make sure everybody hears it for the greatest possible humiliating damage, the cafeteria is the place to do it.

Second, it's even MORE important to know this: I was not the one who farted.

REESE

I still think it was you.

CLAUDIA

It wasn't! And we are NOT discussing this.

REESE

Because you had Thai food the night before, which totally makes you fart the next day.

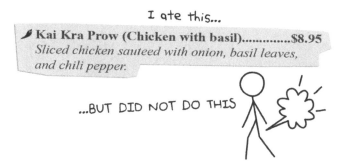

I ate this...

🍃 **Kai Kra Prow (Chicken with basil)**..............$8.95
*Sliced chicken sauteed with onion, basil leaves,
and chili pepper.*

...BUT DID NOT DO THIS

And it smelled exactly like it did when we got off the bus that morning—

CLAUDIA

WE ARE NOT DISCUSSING THIS! NO, NO, ABSOLUTELY NOT—

REESE

—and I KNOW you farted on the bus, because I didn't just smell it, I HEARD—

CLAUDIA

INTERVIEW OVER! I'M TURNING OFF THE VOICE MEMO APP!

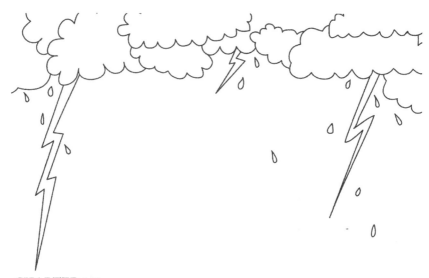

CHAPTER 1¾

THE STORM STOPS GATHERING AND STARTS STORMING

CLAUDIA

Sorry again.

I have decided not to even try to interview Reese about anything else until I can at least get to Chapter 2, because so far he is totally ruining my oral history.

Back to the cafeteria.

I was sitting with Sophie Koh, who is awesome and has been my one and only best friend since my original best friend, Meredith Timms, turned into a total Fembot and I had to take a vacation from not only being her best friend, but from even being her friend at all. Which is very sad and tragic, but is a whole other story.

Sophie and I were at the middle table by the window. I was telling her what happened in the latest episode of Thrones of Death, because Sophie's parents think she's too young to watch it. And they actually still have parental controls on their DVR.

Which is insane. But whatever.

MATURE AUDIENCES ONLY.
CONTENT WARNINGS
M L V T Q Z P B O G D

The Fembots were in their usual spot at the next table over, talking about shoes, or stabbing each other in the back, or whatever it is they do. Sophie and I call them "Fembots" because they all dress and act exactly the same way and have no idea how to think for themselves. And once when we were telling Sophie's mom about them, her dad overheard and said they sounded like Fembots, which are supposedly these girl robots from some movie I can never remember the name of.

Anyway, "Fembots" is kind of perfect for them. Athena Cohen is their leader, and she is a total nightmare.

So the Fembots were on one side of us, and on the other side were Reese and his stupid soccer friends. Including Jens Kuypers, who is from the Netherlands and had just started going to Culvert the week before.

It's a little sad that Jens immediately started hanging out with Reese and the other soccer idiots. Because Jens does not seem like a soccer idiot at all. For one thing, he doesn't just wear FC Barcelona jerseys and warm-up pants all the time—he actually wears normal clothes, too.

For example, on the first day of school, he wore these really cool dark green pants with a button-down shirt and a brown vest that looked like it might be suede or something, and brown leather shoes that kind of matched the vest, but not quite. (Which was even better, because if they'd matched perfectly, it would have looked dorky.)

Also, Jens has high cheekbones and a very nice smile, which I know be-cause he smiled at me on the first day when we were in line for trays at lunch and he let me go ahead of him. (This also shows that he has excellent manners, which is totally not true of any of the other soccer idiots.)

And because Jens is from the Netherlands—which means he is officially Dutch—he has this REALLY cool accent.

But even though Jens is not like the soccer idiots at all, I guess he started hanging out with them anyway because he is awesome at soccer. I wouldn't know, but that's what Reese says. And it makes sense, because Jens looks like he is very athletic.

So, Sophie and I were at the middle table in between the Fembots and the soccer idiots. There were also some other kids at the far end of our table, like Kalisha and Charlotte and Max, but they are not important to The War.

Except that one of them may have been the person who actually farted.

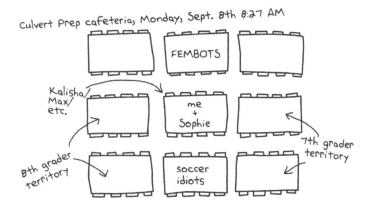

Sophie and I smelled the fart at almost exactly the same time. Her face scrunched up, and she put her hand to her nose, and I did the same thing, and we both went "Eeeew!" But not too loudly, because Sophie and I are mature enough to know that when somebody beefs, the polite thing is to not mention it and just try to avoid breathing for a while until it goes away.

Unfortunately, nobody else in the sixth grade is mature enough to know this.

And it was a very bad fart, so everybody smelled it.

Right away, Athena Cohen jumped up from her seat like a total drama queen and yelled, "Oh, that is DISGUSTING! Who DID that?"

The soccer idiots all started jumping up and making faces, and then Reese pointed at me and yelled, "IT WAS YOU!"

This was not only immature, but also totally unfair. Because, again, it was definitely NOT me.

So I said—in a very calm and mature voice considering the situation—"No, it wasn't."

But Reese wouldn't stop. He had one hand over his nose, and he was pointing at me with the other hand, and then he yelled, in a really loud and obnoxious voice, "JUST ADMIT IT, PRINCESS FARTS-A-LOT!"

And this is how totally immature the rest of the sixth grade is: everybody laughed.

The soccer idiots, the Fembots, even Charlotte and Max at the far end of the table.

It didn't matter at all that I was totally innocent, or that "Princess Farts-A-Lot" is not even funny. The whole world, or at least the whole sixth grade, was laughing at me for something I DIDN'T EVEN DO.

All because of Reese.

This, in case you couldn't tell, was the beginning of The War.

It was exactly like the sneak attack on Pearl Harbor that got America into World War II.

Well, not EXACTLY exactly, because there were no bombs, or ships, or planes, or actual death involved. But even so, it was horrible, and cruel, and totally unfair. And because I was so shocked and hurt, all I could do was say, "As if! Grow up, Reese!"

Or something like that. I can't remember exactly, because it was so stressful that my memory is kind of fuzzy. (I think this is what historians mean when they talk about "the fog of war.")

What I DO remember is that I had to grab my backpack and pretend to just casually walk away when really I was trying to get to the girls' bathroom ASAP so I wouldn't cry in front of everybody.

That is how cruel and horrible it was. It actually made me cry.

And because she is a true friend, Sophie went to the bathroom with me.

SOPHIE KOH, best friend of innocent victim

You were really upset. Because Jens was right there when Reese said it, and—

CLAUDIA

Not because of Jens. Because of everybody. EVERYBODY laughed at me.

SOPHIE

Well, eventually you were worried about everybody. But at first, you were all, "What if Jens thinks I—" Why are you making that hand gesture? What does that mean?

Ooooh! {*Editor note: I have NO IDEA what Sophie is talking about here*}

Okay! Sorry.

So, um… yeah, it wasn't about Jens. At all. It was… like… uh…

CLAUDIA

It was EVERYBODY.

SOPHIE

Totally. Like, I remember you were crying, and—wait, can I say that? That you were crying?

CLAUDIA

Yes.

SOPHIE

Good. So, yeah. You were crying, and you were, like, worried it was going to stick, and everybody was going to call you "Princess Farts-A-Lot" for the rest of your life.

CLAUDIA

Which totally could have happened! Remember that thing with Hunter {*Editor note: don't ask—it's disgusting*} in fourth grade?

SOPHIE

Oh, yeah. People STILL call him "Booger Hunter" sometimes. So, yeah, I could see how you'd be worried about that.

CLAUDIA

And it DID happen! James Mantolini called me "Princess Farts-A-Lot" until practically Halloween.

SOPHIE

Yeah, but James is an idiot. Even the boys don't like him.

CLAUDIA

And remember Athena and Clarissa at lunch? When they shortened "Princess Farts-A-Lot" into just the initials—"P-FAL"—and then tried to get everybody to call me that?

SOPHIE

Ugh. They're the worst. But they only called you "P-FAL" for like a day.

CLAUDIA

It was longer than that. It was practically the whole week. And that first day was AWFUL. I literally thought it was going to scar me for life.

SOPHIE

I know. I'm so sorry! I remember in the bathroom you were really upset. Like, we were almost late to homeroom because it took you so long to stop crying.

CLAUDIA

You were SUCH a good friend. Like, I would still be in that bathroom crying if it weren't for you. Do you remember what you said to get me to stop?

SOPHIE

Yeah. I said, "Don't worry. We are going to take SERIOUS revenge on your stupid brother."

That really helped. Like, the second you started thinking about getting revenge on Reese, you stopped crying.

And then you started to get kind of psyched about it.

You've just read an excerpt from The Tapper Twins Go to War (With Each Other).

ABOUT THE AUTHOR

Geoff Rodkey has written the hit films *Daddy Daycare* (starring Eddie Murphy), *RV* (starring Robin Williams), *The Shaggy Dog* (starring Tim Allen), and the Disney Channel original TV movie *Good Luck Charlie, It's Christmas*. He is also the author of the middle grade trilogy *The Chronicles of Egg*. He lives in New York City.

Imprint: Little, Brown Books for Young Readers
Print ISBN: 9780316297790
Print price: $13.99
eBook ISBN: 9780316297820
eBook price: $9.99
Publication date: 4/7/15
Publicity contact: Lisa Moraleda lisa.moraleda@hbgusa.com
Rights contact: Kristin Delaney kristin.delaney@hbgusa.com
Editor: Andrea Spooner
Agent: Josh Getzler
Agency: Hannigan Salky Getzler Agency

Territories sold:
Translation BULGARIAN Egmont Bulgaria Translation
DANISH Alvilda
Translation DUTCH The House of Books Kids/Moon (imprints of Dutch Media Books bv)
Translation FINNISH WSOY/Werner Soderstrom Oy
Translation FRENCH Editions Ada Inc.
Translation FRENCH Editions Nathan
Translation GERMAN Verlagsgruppe Random House Gmbh
Translation GREEK, MODERN (1453-) S. Patakis Publications S.A.
Translation HEBREW Keter Publishing House
Translation HUNGARIAN Maxim Konyvkiado
Translation ITALIAN RCS Libri SpA / Fabbri
Translation NORWEGIAN BOKM?L Gyldendal Norsk
Translation PORTUGUESE 20|20 Editora
Translation PORTUGUESE Editora Intrinseca Ltda.
Translation ROMANIAN NEMIRA Publishing House
Translation SPANISH Rba Libros S.A.
Translation SWEDISH B. Wahlströms Bokförlag
ENGLISH Orion Publishers

Promotional information:
- National print and online advertising
- National author tour [8-10 cities]
- National review coverage

WHEN YOU LEAVE

MONICA ROPAL

SUMMARY

When Cass begins her year at a wealthy new private school due to a paid scholarship, her plan is to blend in and not bring attention to her working class roots. However, when her cute locker neighbor, Cooper, shows an undeniable attraction toward Cass, keeping him at a safe distance isn't easy. Even though her Frogtown skater world and his do-gooder preppy one are so different, Cass and Cooper somehow mesh. But once Cass lets her guard down, the unthinkable happens: Cooper is mysteriously murdered. One of Cass's close friends from her skater world is suspected as the killer, and she isn't sure who she can trust anymore. Between investigating Cooper's murder and trying to understand what they really meant to each other, can Cass sift through the lies to discover the truth?

EXCERPT

Chapter One

I fought the tickle, my nose to the blackboard, stifling the urge to sneeze.

Old school detention was medieval. It would be a slow cruel death of boredom. Under my uniform skirt my knees bobbed. I glanced down to where my bag was flopped open on the floor next to me. I could see the inside pocket that held my phone. It would take me twenty seconds tops to text Mattie, my best friend. He'd give me a thumb lashing in return for getting in bad with the Sister again, but any communication would help dash away the quiet in the empty room and calm the noise in my brain.

I let my forehead roll against the cool slate.

Only three weeks into my three-year sentence at St. Bernadette's and already I was on the brink of a rep with Sister Rita for my attitude. The plan was to have no rep at all, to suffer through in anonymity in my long blonde hair and just-like-everyone-else uniform. I'd even gone as far as to practice straightening my slouch, and sitting pretty with my knees close together to appear like a girl who belongs at a private school, and not a skater girl who didn't.

I thought of Mattie again. Even with his ten minute skate ride from Kellogg Senior High he'd be out there waiting. And waiting. I'd barely flexed my fingers when the door clicked open causing me to snap to attention.

Footsteps moved behind me. Those tapping footsteps didn't belong to Sister Rita's clod hoppers, and neither did the musky cologne that overpowered the smell of chalk.

Drawers slid open and closed. Nothing like the controlled movements of Sister Rita.

I braved a full turn around. There, with his back to me, was Cooper McCay standing at Sister's desk. Cooper had his locker two down from mine, but our social statuses were on entirely different planes. He was part of a loud, obnoxious, in-love-with-themselves trio of guys that had girls wetting themselves at every smile tossed their way.

Typical pretty-boy. Except some things about him weren't. Like how he'd get easily distracted away from the fawning cheerleaders or emit the occasional irritated sigh in the wake of his buddies' foolishness. I'll admit to finding him more . . . interesting than the average St. B pretty-boy.

I took the opportunity to admire the strong line where his neck met the width of his shoulder. Not to mention other pleasing attributes that this view allowed. There was something about a good pair of khakis on a nice—

"Getting an eyeful, newbie?" he asked, pausing in his search to glance back at me. In the space of my pause, he returned to his searching, unruffled by me staring at him without anything to say. Cool cucumber, this one.

"It's Cass," I blurted out. Not even sure why. I usually wasn't one for blurting. Or sharing. "Does Sister Rita know you're going through her desk?"

He shrugged. "Maybe I'm the new cleaning staff?"

"And maybe you're trying to steal her rosary."

"Well, Cass, maybe—"

There were voices in the hall and I swung around toward the door, realizing we were about to be found out. I heard Cooper bump the edge of

Sister Rita's desk. In three long strides his arm was around me, pulling me against him. Before I could blink his lips were on mine. It could only have been sudden insanity that had me going along and not kneeing him in the balls.

"Mister McCay!" Sister Rita drew out the 'S,' hissing her dismay.

He pulled away. His arm loosened its grip and my weak knees threatened to leave me puddled on the floor. And I'm not the kind to puddle.

Boy had some mad skills.

I rubbed my hand over my arm to smooth away the goose bumps and tried to process whether the chill snaking down my limbs was from the kiss or from being caught.

Sister Rita looked as if her eyes might make a leap right over her reading glasses. She ran a hand over the cross hanging in the front of her blue sweater.

Cooper touched the back of his hand to his mouth. "Sorry. I was just about to go meet my father when I caught sight of my girlfriend in here." He paused to flash that crooked smile. "How embarrassing."

He was either crazy, or a genius, or both. But embarrassed? Not.

Sister Rita's eyes were nearly as big as mine as her head jerked from him to me and back to him.

"I wasn't aware that you and Miss. . . . " She trailed off as if placing us both in the same sentence was beyond her. She settled at narrowing her eyes.

He tipped his head in conspiracy. "Well, it's sort of on the down low. Seeing as we come from such . . . different . . . families and all."

He rubbed the back of his neck with his hand, dodging a quick glance in my direction. Funny that he'd get all fidgety when it came to the truth of it.

"I see." She looked over to me again. Then her eyes flicked back to Cooper. Her left eyebrow arched. "Did you say your father was waiting for you?"

Either Cooper's dad had some pull in this school or maybe she simply didn't want to deal with the two of us, scandalizing as we were. Ha.

Sister Rita sat down at her desk, her attention turning to a stack of papers. "You are dismissed," she said without looking back up.

Cooper picked up my bag and slung the strap over his shoulder. He held out his hand.

"Ready, Cass?" he asked.

Hell yes. Genius. Loved it. I took his hand and let him lead me out.

I know when I'm being used. But I never count it as being used if it's mutually beneficial in some way. An out from detention and . . . did I mention the mad skills?

The classroom door shut behind us. We couldn't even make it ten steps before releasing the laughter we were holding. When his gaze lingered on me, the laughter dried and I pulled my hand from his.

This was clearly not part of the plan. I glanced around but didn't see anyone in the hall. Another two classrooms and we'd reached our row of lockers. I worked my lock and tried to avoid eye contact as he slouched against his own locker only inches away from me.

"Thanks. I needed an alibi to explain why I was there," Cooper said.

My shoulders bounced with a shrug. "I figured it was that. That, that was the thing," I stuttered. I took a breath to school my emotions as the lock clicked open. All my friends were guys. Guys did not make me nervous. Usually.

Cooper rubbed the back of his neck again. "Yeah," he said under his breath.

I heard a noise by the stairs, but when I checked around again, no one was there. "What were you looking for?" I asked in a low voice, as I grabbed my French text off the top shelf.

"Sister Rita confiscated a girl's iPod in second period. I told her I'd try to get it back for her."

A girl. Figures. Then I reminded myself that I didn't care. "Whatevs. You got me out of detention early, so we're even."

"Yeah," he said again. His body was already half turned, but his shoulders seemed to be shifting back and forth with physical indecision about whether to stay or to bail.

I slammed the door and tucked the textbook under my arm. Mad skills or not, it was time to make the decision for him before he started getting any funny ideas about where this was headed.

"This never happened."

Chapter Two

I turned away from Cooper and made my way to the art hallway at the back of the school, my daily incognito escape route. I hurried past the pottery room, glancing over as the kiln in the back whooshed—the fire hardening the day's collection of bowls and ashtrays.

The fact that I had to shake my hands in an effort to rid my body of the rigid adrenaline pump was freaking me out. It was just a kiss. It didn't mean anything.

I pushed through the exit door at the end of the hall and closed my eyes as the cold blast of air hit my warm cheeks. There was no lingering Minnesota summer humidity this year. I was sure we'd be seeing snow by Halloween.

I stepped out onto the loading dock, glancing down at Mattie perched on the edge. His skateboard was next to him on his right, mine on his left. Even in fifty degrees he was already in a sweat, which told me that he was all tricked out waiting. His six-foot, skinny frame was folded up and even with sweaty hair his cowlick refused to lie. I combed it down with my hand.

He tapped his watch with his finger twice.

You're late.

It had been nine years since cancer surgery took Mattie's voice. But without even a glitch I continued to hear him—only inside my head instead of through my ears. After growing up with him, every quirk of a brow and shrug of a shoulder spoke to me. Since he's a guy, it's possible I get more words out of him now than I did before.

I shifted my weight. "I know I'm late. Sister Rit— "

He hopped to his feet, throwing his gorilla arms out wide. *Again?*

I shrugged. "She has it in for me."

He wiped his fingers across my forehead. *Chalk.*

"See? Medieval," I said.

I heard the door creak behind me and whipped around to see Cooper stepping through.

He glanced over at Mattie, and then back to me. All I could think was that he'd better play it cool and not even attempt to make contact with Mattie or I would need to injure his delicate parts. My cheeks were feeling that long lost August humidity.

Cooper held out my bag. "You forgot this. In detention."

Stupidly, I glanced down at myself. Of course it wasn't there. I stepped forward and grabbed it off him without looking at him. "Thanks," I said, but in a whisper because I had forgotten to breathe. I stared at my bag not daring to look at Mattie. I was suddenly pissed. I never blushed, never got breathless over a guy. And never hid something like this from Mattie. Whatever this was.

I stared at the pavement reading the label of a candy bar wrapper. Out of the corner of my eye I saw Cooper was turning back the way he came, until Mattie snapped his fingers.

Mattie wasn't working at getting my attention, he was looking at Cooper. Mattie pointed at Cooper and indicated his own face. I shot a look at Cooper and saw what Mattie was talking about. Cooper had the faint remains of chalk dust—my chalk dust—on his left cheek and forehead.

Cooper wiped it away with his sleeve. "Thanks. Sister Rita's chalk board needs some cleaning." His eyes went to mine for a second, and then he pulled the door open and went back in the school leaving Mattie and I in silence.

I counted to five then turned back to Mattie who raised his eyebrows at me.

"As if," I said, and left it at that.

Really? He asked with a tip of his head.

"It's nothing. It never even happened."

'It', what?

"Drop it. I have a skate park to thrash." I waited to see if he was going to interrogate me, but when he started kicking chips of loose cement over the edge into the parking lot, I figured he must be over it . . . or not interested . . . or biding his time to use it against me.

I took the steps down to the uneven blacktop, then moved behind dumpsters along the brick wall. I heard Mattie's shoes smack as he jumped down instead of using the stairs. I tried to ignore the smells of rotting carpet and glue coming from the dumpsters, as I pulled out the change of clothes from my bag.

"Sister Rita does have it in for me, though." I said, pulling the pants up over my tights.

I peeked around to see Mattie feigning a yawn.

"It's true." Pants buttoned, I unhooked the skirt. "You'd think slouching was a capital offense. What?"

His shoulders were doing their bounce of silent laughter. He shook his head at me.

You did not.

"No, I did not get detention for slouching. I'm just saying. I don't know what I did wrong. Move and breathe? I swear the woman hates everything about me." I started to unbutton my shirt.

Oh, Cass, you roll me.

He was the first to call me Cass. Not "Cassie" like my parents, or "Cassandra" like Grandma Rossi or Sister Rita. Just Cass.

When I got to the final button I realized his shoulders had stilled and his eyes were fixed.

"Mattie you have two seconds to turn your fat face before I break it."

He turned, but there went the shoulders again.

I changed my shirt, zipped on my hoodie, and tied my hair in a knot. It wasn't that he'd never seen me in a sports bra. He'd no doubt seen me in less over the years of friendship that had somehow sprouted in toddlerhood. But it was only recently that there was anything there to see. I'm what you'd call a late bloomer.

"Go ahead and laugh, but let me remind you, I did not even let out a single giggle when you started shaving—and yes I noticed—or when I found those dirty mags in your— "

He clamped a hand over my mouth and rested his forehead against my temple.

I'm sorry.

And I knew he was. Mattie never lied to me. But I never claimed to be as good as him.

He pulled away and stomped the tail of my board, catching it mid-air, before handing it over.

Two more taps on his watch. *We're late.*

You've just read an excerpt from When You Leave.

ABOUT THE AUTHOR

Monica Ropal lives in friendly St. Paul, Minnesota with her husband and three children—whom she lovingly refers to as her three-ring circus. In addition to writing and playing ringmaster, Monica also works as a hospice nurse.

Imprint: Running Press Teens

Print ISBN: 9780762454556

Print price: $9.95

eBook ISBN: 9780762456307

eBook price: $9.95

Publication date: 4/7/15

Publicity contact: Valerie Howlett,
valerie.howlett@perseusbooks.com

Rights contact: Sarah Sheppard,
sarah.sheppard@perseusbooks.com

Editor: Marlo Scrimizzi

Agent: Barbara Poelle

Agency: Irene Goodman Literary Agency

Promotional information:

- National print and online reviews
- Author blog tour
- Library outreach
- Social media marketing campaign targeting teen readers
- Local St. Paul events and media
- Mid Winter ALA featured title

CARRIE RYAN

NEW YORK TIMES BESTSELLING AUTHOR

Daughter
OF
Deep
Silence

SUMMARY

In the wake of the complete destruction of the luxury yacht Persephone, three people are left alive who know the truth about what happened—and two of them are lying. Only Frances Mace, rescued from the ocean after seven days adrift with her friend Libby (who died of thirst just before rescue), knows that the Persephone wasn't sunk by a rogue wave as survivors Senator Wells and his son Greyson are claiming—it was attacked. In order to insure her safety from the obviously dangerous and very powerful Wells family, Libby's father helps Frances assume Libby's identity. Frances has spent years in hiding, transforming herself into Libby, and she can no longer allow the people who murdered her entire family and Libby to get away with it—even if she had been in love with Greyson Wells. After years of careful plotting, she's ready to set her revenge plans into motion. The game has just begun, and Frances is not only playing dirty, she's playing to win.

EXCERPT

Chapter One

When they pull me onto the yacht I can't even stand, I've been adrift in the ocean so long. A young crewman sits me on a teak bench while he calls out for someone to bring him blankets and water. He asks me my name, but my tongue is too thick and my throat too raw from screaming and salt water to answer.

I'm alive, I think to myself. The words run on an endless loop through my head as though with repetition I'll somehow believe it. *I'm alive I'm alive I'm alive.*

And Libby isn't.

I should be feeling something more. But it's all too much, too fast. Inside I'm awash with numbness. It cocoons a brightly burning knot of rage and despair that throbs and squirms. Protecting me. For now.

A pair of crewmen pulls Libby's body from the life raft, rolling her onto her back on the yacht's gleaming deck. I think about how birds have hollow bones and how easy it must be to break them.

That's how she looks right now: hollow. Her cheeks sunken, her wrists twigs wrapped in tight skin that's turned to leather from relentless heat and exposure.

A crewman presses his fingers against her neck, a palm in the center of her chest. His expression slides from desperate hope into a mask of efficient resignation. He looks up to where an older man with a ring of white hair around his otherwise bald head hovers, waiting. The crewman shakes his head.

The older man lets out a cry, his face crumpling as he falls to his knees by Libby's side. He only says one word over and over again as he pushes a tangle of wet hair out of her face: *"No."* His voice cracks and his shoulders slump, shaking as he sobs.

If I had any tears in me I'd be crying, too, but I'm so dehydrated that all I can do is shake, my lungs spasming with hiccups. I try to talk, my mouth forming a *"Wh-"* sound over and over again.

"Shhh." The crewman who'd rescued me drapes a blanket around my shoulders. "It's okay, you're safe now."

I want to believe him. But all I can do is stare at Libby's body. An hour earlier, and they'd have found her alive. She might have survived. Seven days adrift in the middle of the ocean, and she'd lost it in the last hour.

It doesn't seem fair. We were supposed to make it together. We'd promised.

Her body is so light and brittle it takes only one person to carry her inside the ship. The older man does it, clutching her against his chest, his eyes red and lips pressed tight together.

"My baby," he whispers against her temple. Understanding hits with a physical force: This is Libby's father. He glances at me as he passes, his expression bewildered, and I know he's wondering the same thing I've already been thinking: Why am I the one who survived? Why couldn't it have been her pulled alive from the raft?

I want to apologize, but seeing him with Libby—a father cradling his broken daughter—I can't. The unfairness of it is monstrous. I would give anything to have my father here now, to feel him holding me and protecting me the way Libby's father does.

And he would give anything for his daughter to still be alive.

I close my eyes, unable to stand it. Because in this moment I truly understand just how alone I am. How no one will ever again hold me and care about me the way Libby's father does her. My parents are dead. Libby is dead. I have no relatives—no other family waiting for me.

I am alone. Utterly and irrevocably alone.

Memories storm through me, fast and sharp in an unrelenting strobe light of sensations—sounds, smells, fragments of sentences. I feel my mother's hand against my forehead, checking for a fever some night years ago. I hear the way she sneezes, big and loud, and my father laughing in response the way he always, always does.

There's the smell of the car on the winter morning we go to pick out a Christmas tree, my father singing along to the carols on the radio with his voice always just slightly out of tune. I taste French fries, my fingers slick with fast-food grease, my mom's treat to me as she drives me home from summer camp.

I lick my lips and gag at the taste of salt. The memories come faster, running over one another, drowning me. Panic claws its way through me, crushing my chest. My nails are soft and cracked from so long in the water, and they split past the quick as I try to dig them into the skin along my thighs, wishing I could gouge it all out of me: the memories, the loss, the pain. The refrain that's been unspooling in my head for days: *gone, gone, they're all gone, your life is gone.*

And inevitably, images from the attack come next: The gun pressed to my father's head. The blood drenching my mother's shirt. She'd begged, but it hadn't mattered. It didn't matter for anyone on that cruise ship. They'd all been massacred.

Three hundred twenty-seven. That was the total number of passengers and crew on the *Persephone*. It was one of the things we'd learned during the safety drill before leaving port. In the end, it never mattered how many people a life raft could hold. It never mattered where each cabin's muster station was.

Nothing we learned during the safety drill mattered.

The attack had come swift and hard in the middle of the night. One minute life on the ship was normal, the next the ship was rocked with explosions.

They blocked the exits while armed men went room to room, systematic in their assault. Faces passive, expressions detached from their actions, they'd pulled triggers and reloaded bullets with sickening efficiency.

Killing them all.

The bodies. Oh God, the bodies. And the blood and the screams and the smell of it all like overripe peaches stuffed with pennies.

I gasp and shudder. It was only luck that allowed Libby and me to escape. We'd talked about it relentlessly during those next seven days adrift: the impossibility that we'd somehow survived.

All of that and she'd ended up dead anyway. It's so brutally unfair.

The young crewman pushes a plastic bottle of water into my hand, forcing me back into the present. My throat clenches. The bottle's cold—freezing against my palm—and there's condensation dripping along the outside. I fumble to open it, my fingers useless, my muscles too weak to even lift it. Finally he takes mercy and twists the cap free.

"Drink slowly," he says, but in my world there's no such thing, and I press that bottle hard to my lips. If I'd died the instant that water rushed across my tongue, I wouldn't have cared. I'm sharply aware of each drop as it cascades down my throat and into my hollow belly. Nothing exists then but that taste—that sensation.

"Easy now," the man says, gently prying the bottle from my lips. "You don't want to make yourself sick." He's too late; already my stomach revolts in painful cramps. I turn and vomit.

The man rubs my back as I heave, telling me again that I'll be okay. That I'm safe. "What's your name?" he asks when I've recovered enough to sit up again.

I press the back of my hand to my mouth. My skin tastes like salt, making me retch again. "Frances." I try to tell him, the sound nothing more than a tattered thread.

The storm that had been threatening at the edge of the sky all day finally breaks, sending fat drops of water crashing to the deck. "Let's get you inside," the crewman says as he slides his arms gently around my shoulders, lifting me as easily as Libby's father lifted her. As he carries me, I tilt my head back, letting the rain wash across my sun-cured skin.

If it had come a few hours sooner, this rain would have saved her.

I barely pay attention as the man maneuvers me through a large salon, down a flight of stairs, and along a hallway to a stateroom. He sets me carefully on the bed.

"I'm a trained medic," he explains. He pulls over a large red bag emblazoned with a white cross and slides on gloves. "Is it okay if I examine you?"

I nod and he's ginger as he probes at the sores covering my legs and back, unable to hide his horror at what's become of my body. "You'll be okay," he tells me again, but I get the impression it's more to convince himself than me. He unzips his bag, begins pulling out various medical supplies.

"You're severely dehydrated," he explains as he runs an alcohol soaked swab across my inner arm and presses a needle against the flesh. "So the first priority is to start getting fluids in you." It takes him several tries, his forehead creased in frustrated concentration as he searches for a vein. I feel none of it.

Eventually he's satisfied and drapes an IV bag from a hook on the wall. "For now, just rest." He starts for the door, but I force the sound up my throat.

"How many survived the attack?"

He looks at me as though he doesn't understand the question. "Attack?"

"The attack on the *Persephone*," I croak in a salt-crusted voice. "How many others survived?"

Frowning, he opens his mouth, reconsiders, and closes it. Finally he says, "Two others: Senator Wells and his son."

I don't even dare to breathe. *"Grey?"* I whisper.

He nods, and I slump back into the nest of pillows, pressing the heels of my hands against my eyes. Grey's alive. *Grey's alive!* It seems so impossible that after losing everything else, this one small part survived. Like suddenly there's a bright spark of hope in the cavernous blackness my life has become.

"Hey, I'm Grey," he says, standing next to my deck chair, casting me in shadow. I have to squint when I look up at him, and though I've been ogling him all afternoon I still can't stop my eyes from dropping to his chest, skimming down to the strip of bare skin just above the waistband of his swim trunks.

They skim low on his hips, almost like a promise. I'm fairly certain he notices and my cheeks heat. But I know the reason he's here—what he's really after. He's made that abundantly clear.

"Her name's Libby," I tell him, gesturing to where Libby's standing over by the towel stand. She has her elbows propped on the counter and is leaning forward slightly, hoping to catch the hot attendant's attention. "I'd move quick if I were you," I add.

"Oh, um," he shifts from one foot to the other, and I assume he's nervous because he can't figure out how to politely ditch me to go after my friend. But I'm already expecting it—I've noticed him looking our way for a while now.

"Do you mind if I join you?" He points at Libby's empty chaise next to mine. It's so unexpected, I stare at him perhaps a beat too long. Finally I realize he's waiting for my response and I shrug.

He's barely settled before I ask, "So, what do you want to know about her?"

He smiles and ducks his head. "Actually," he says, "I was hoping to learn more about you."

While on the raft, I'd daydreamed of Grey rescuing me, even though I knew it was impossible—that he must have been killed with everyone else onboard. Over and over as we drifted toward death on the empty ocean, I'd imagined him coming for me.

It didn't matter than I'd known him less than a week; it had been long enough to fall for him with an intensity I'd never experienced before.

He was my first love. And he'd told me I was his.

He's alive.

In the black horror of what my life has become, that single point of light now shines. I've lost my parents. I've lost Libby. Nothing in my life will ever be the same again. I have no other family, no long lost relatives to take me in. There is nothing left.

But Grey. I still have Grey.

I cling to the thought as though it is a life raft, knowing that if I hold on tight enough and don't give up, I'll somehow be able to survive.

I drift asleep imagining our reunion. Already feeling his arms around my shoulders, his hands pressing against my back, holding me tight against him. He'll brush his lips against my temple and whisper over and over that it's okay, he'll keep me safe and I'll believe him.

Because he also saw the horror. He also survived it. He also *understands*. In the protection of his arms finally, *finally*, the tears will come again.

The same four words cycle endlessly through me, giving me comfort for the first time since that first shot was fired on the *Persephone*: *I am not alone. I am not alone. I am not alone.*

Chapter Two

I wake in darkness, raw and confused. There's this moment of lightness, where I move to stretch, feeling the soft bed beneath me and the sheets sliding along my skin. For a fraction of a heartbeat it feels right.

And then I remember. It comes as a physical sensation first, a crushing on my chest as my mind struggles to bend and stretch to take it all in.

The gun pressed so hard against Dad's head that it caused the skin around the barrel to wrinkle and pucker. All down the hallway shots firing, one after another after another. Systematic. My dad's bottom teeth scraping against his top lip, starting to say my name.

Gasping, I bolt upright, scraping my fingernails over my ears as though that can somehow stop me from hearing. But of course it doesn't.

The gunshot, shattering bone.

It never will.

Beneath me, the yacht rocks softly, the thrum of its engine a low vibration through my bones. The stateroom is empty, the windows dark. It's too quiet. I'm too alone. Memories of the attack circle around like hungry sharks, and I reach for the television remote, hoping that sound and distraction will keep them at bay.

When it flickers on, the TV hanging on the far wall is glaringly bright and colorful, stinging my eyes. But it's something other than silence and that's what I crave. I flip through channels absently until a familiar name stops me. *Persephone.*

My hand falls limp to the bed. Heart pounding, I watch as a news anchor shuffles papers while an image of the cruise ship floats behind her. "Breaking news on the *Persephone* disaster from last week," she announces. "Sources are confirming that another survivor from the ship may have been located. As of now, authorities haven't released any information about the potential survivor or survivors. While we wait for more information to trickle in, let's take a look at the dramatic footage of Senator Wells and his son taken shortly after their rescue."

The scene on the TV shifts to a sprawling marina bustling with activity. The camera zooms in on the gangplank of a large Coast Guard ship, focusing on a small group making its way toward the pier.

Senator Wells leads the pack. Even with a sunburned face he manages to appear debonair in an almost dangerous way, the salt and pepper scruff of his unshaven face emphasizing the sharpness of his cheekbones. The camera pans past him and my breath catches. It's Grey. Alive.

It's one thing to be told he survived and yet another to see it as truth. That same surge of relief washes through me, the sudden realization that I'm not alone. Someone else out there understands.

I devour his appearance. Grey looks much worse than his father. He clutches a thick blanket around his shoulders, his steps slow as he trails after the group. His hair sticks up from his head at odd angles, and his eyes look bruised above the shadowy scraps of stubble strewn across his cheeks and chin.

Reporters rush the two en masse, shouting questions, and Grey rears back, almost alarmed by the sudden onslaught. I press my fingers against my lips, feel them trembling. One of the Coast Guard men tries to push the camera away, but the senator stops him. "We'll answer," he says. Grey winces and his eyes squeeze shut.

"The world deserves to know the truth of what happened to the *Persephone*," the senator continues, pulling Grey toward the reporter's microphone. "It happened fast," the senator begins. I find myself nodding even though at the time it seemed like hours. Days of gunfire. Years of blood.

"It was late and I was out on deck with my son, helping him look for his phone he'd forgotten by the pool that afternoon. There was a terrible storm, and we were just about to give up and go inside." He pauses, shakes his head. "The wave came out of nowhere. I've never seen anything like it. It just . . . took the whole ship out."

Wave? I find that I can't breathe, his words grinding my thoughts to a halt. That's not what happened. There was no wave. Numbness begins to eat its way though me as I listen to their story.

Senator Wells steps aside, leaving his son facing the microphone. Every heartbeat echoes through my water slogged veins, causing my entire body to throb and rock as I wait to hear what he has to say. Grey blanches, but doesn't retreat. The familiarity of his gestures is jarring. The way he holds himself with his weight slightly on his right leg, the furrow between his eyebrows as he sorts through his thoughts before speaking.

The way he unconsciously rubs his skull, just behind his ear, whenever he's about to lie.

It's amazing the little things you can pick up about someone in such a short amount of time when you're falling in love. Every nuance, every sound and movement a code to understanding them.

"Like Dad said, it happened fast," he starts, and then he clears his throat, choked up. In my head I see it all. I *hear* it all and taste it all. Again.

Grey pulls me against him and threads a strand of hair behind my ear. When he brings his mouth closer, I stop caring about the rain. All I care about is devouring this moment as though I could imprint it into my memory forever.

Rivulets of water wash down his face, dripping from his chin and coursing along his neck. The way his shirt plasters to his chest allows me to see the outline of every muscle. I press my fingers against them, tracing the edges.

I laugh, a bubble of euphoria too large to keep contained. He kisses me right then, as though he could take my laughter into himself and make it a part of him. And still, all around us the rain crashes, but we don't care.

The reporters huddling around Grey barely breathe as they wait for him to continue. "The rain was awful and as Dad mentioned, we were . . . uh . . . out on deck." He glances toward his father before continuing. "It was unlike . . . anything. It came out of nowhere—this massive wave. And it just was there—a wall of water. It rose higher than even the top of the ship—much higher." He pauses as if reliving the moment, eyes haunted.

I'm trembling now. I don't understand. Why isn't he talking about the attack? Why isn't he mentioning the guns?

Grey inhales slowly, his shirt lifting just enough to lay bare the strip of pale skin along the edge of his shorts. He begins to rub that spot behind his ear again. "And then . . ." His voice breaks.

And then the guns. Men slamming through the corridors, cutting off the emergency exits and locking the ship down. Panicked passengers in robes and nightgowns run, screaming. Making it no more than a few steps before bullets tear them apart.

Water drips down my back, my hair still wet from kissing Grey in the rain. I press myself against the cold metal wall of the dumbwaiter, watching through the mirrored window as a tall, narrow man kicks a broken body aside. Forces his way into a room. Raises his gun. It takes seconds before he is in the hallway again, moving on to the next.

Moving on to my family's room.

A high-pitched whine climbs its way up the back of my throat, coated in acid. I clamp my hands over my mouth, knowing without question that if they hear me, I am dead.

I'm dead either way.

As Grey speaks, the reporters hang on his every nuance and gesture.

They're enraptured by him. I wait for him to mention the armed men. The gunshots. The murder.

But he never does. "It's like what Dad said. The wave just swallowed her whole. Like a toy in a tub. And then . . . the *Persephone* was gone." He shakes his head, as though he himself can't believe it. "Just *gone*."

In the silence that follows, the Senator squeezes his son's shoulder. One of the reporters shouts, "How were you able to survive?"

Grey's eyes widen, his expression one of bewilderment. The senator steps in. "Had to be luck, plain and simple. It was late and because of the rain everyone else was inside, probably asleep in their cabins. I was so angry at Grey for losing his phone, but if he hadn't . . ." He inhales sharply. Grey stares at his feet. "We wouldn't have been up on deck and thrown free when the wave hit."

"No!" I shout, the sound raw in my throat. "That's not how it happened!"

"Once we got to the surface and saw the wreckage . . ." here the senator pauses and takes a water bottle one of the rescuers holds out to him. "We tried to find other survivors, but . . ." he shakes his head, and a shudder passes through Grey. "The only choice we had was to try to stay alive. We found a life raft that must have broken free somehow and just prayed that someone would find us."

I'm gasping for air. "But . . ." I close my eyes remembering. Libby and I dragging our arms through the water, trying to put distance between us and the burning *Persephone*. Flames choking out her windows, undaunted by the rain. It wasn't until dawn that we saw the extent of it: nothing.

Not a scrap of the ship remained. No hint of other survivors. No other life rafts anywhere in sight. *How had Grey and his father survived without us seeing them?*

On TV the tenor of the reporters changes as the camera pans and zooms in on a middle-aged woman running down the pier, her perfectly coiffed blonde hair loosening in the breeze. She's wearing a skirt that hits just above her knees, and she pauses briefly to kick off her heels so that she can run faster. "Harrison! Grey!" She cries, the sound primal.

The cameraman knows how to do his job, and he instantly focuses in on Grey's face, capturing the moment it crumples and he mouths the word, *"Mom?"* And then they're hugging, sobbing, reunited. His father's arms around them both.

The video pauses on this perfect image. The intimate snapshot of an all-American family newly reunited, their heavy grief finally lifted. A miracle. The senator with his sunburned face and lightly tousled hair. His wife barefoot, tendrils of hair pulled loose around her tear-stained face. And their beloved only son between them.

My chest tightens as though it's collapsing in on itself. Father. Mother. Child. All together. All safe.

It becomes impossible to breathe.

I'll never hug my parents again. My mother will never come running toward me. My father will never place his hand on my head and tell me he loves me. I'll never feel safe ever again.

I've lost everything and somehow, Grey hasn't.

The anchorwoman's voice cuts into the empty room, and I listen with a mounting sense of incredulity as she continues. "News of another survivor certainly comes as a surprise. As you may recall, the Coast Guard called off the search for survivors last week after interviewing Senator Wells and his son and concluding that a rogue wave capsized the *Persephone*, sinking her before those belowdecks could escape."

The camera switches angles and the anchor swivels, continuing. "Though they're considered a rare occurrence, this isn't the first time a rogue wave has been suspected in the disappearance of a ship. In fact, it's widely believed that it was a rogue wave that took the SS *Edmund Fitzgerald* in 1975 and, just as with the *Persephone*, there was no wreckage found in that case either."

It takes a moment for this information to take shape in my mind. For the implications of it to settle in. The Coast Guard called off the search days ago. When Libby and I were still out there. When we both still had a chance to be rescued alive.

All because of Senator Wells and Grey. Because they lied.

I don't even realize that I'm screaming until firm hands pull me from the TV. My fists flail at it and smears of red mar the screen, blood from where I've ripped out my IV in my scramble from the bed.

"They're lying!" I shout, still flailing. "It was attacked! There was no wave! It was men with guns—they killed everyone!"

A crewman holds me steady as the medic slips a needle into my arm. "Shhh," he murmurs. "It's okay."

"No," I whimper, shaking my head. But everything feels so much heavier now. My protests fuzzy and indistinct. "You don't understand." He carries me to the bed and when he tries to leave I fumble for his wrist, holding him. "You have to believe me. They're lying. Please." A tear leaks from my eye, the first since I've been rescued.

He gently frees himself. "It's okay," he says softly, pulling another blanket over me. "You're safe now."

But I know that's not true. May never be true again. *"They killed them all and sank the ship,"* I whisper, my voice weakening. *"The killed my parents."* It comes out slurred. *"Please believe me."*

You've just read an excerpt from Daughter of Deep Silence.

ABOUT THE AUTHOR

Carrie Ryan is the *New York Times* bestselling author of multiple books for both middle-grade and young adult readers, including the *Forest of Hands and Teeth* trilogy, *Infinity Ring* series, and *The Map to Everywhere*. Born and raised in Greenville, South Carolina, Carrie is a graduate of Williams College and Duke University School of Law. A former litigator, she now writes full time. She lives with her writer/lawyer husband, two fat cats and one large rescue mutt in Charlotte, North Carolina. They are not at all prepared for the zombie apocalypse. You can find her online at www.carrieryan.com or @CarrieRyan.

Imprint: Dutton Juvenile
Print ISBN: 9780525426509
Print price: $17.99

eBook ISBN: 9780698145566

eBook price: $10.99

Publication date: 6/2/15

Publicity contact: Jessica Shoffel,
jshoffel@penguinrandomhouse.com

Editor: Julie Strauss-Gabel

Agent: Merrilee Heifetz

Agency: Writers House

Promotional information:
- 9-copy floor display
- National author tour
- Extensive blogger outreach
- Consumer advertising campaign including print and online
- Promotion at Romantic Times (May 2015)
- National media campaign including print, online, television, and radio
- Promotion and galley distribution at all national school and library conferences

FUZZY MUD

LOUIS SACHAR

SUMMARY

From the author of the acclaimed bestseller *Holes*, winner of the Newbery Award and the National Book Award, comes a new middle-grade novel with universal appeal. Combining horror-movie suspense with the issues of friendship, bullying, and the possibility of ecological disaster, this novel will intrigue, surprise, and inspire readers and compel them to think twice about how they treat others as well as their environment.

Be careful. Your next step may be your last.

Fifth grader Tamaya Dhilwaddi and seventh grader Marshall Walsh have been walking to and from Woodridge Academy together since elementary school. But their routine is disrupted when bully Chad Wilson challenges Marshall to a fight. To avoid the conflict, Marshall takes a shortcut home through the off-limits woods. Tamaya reluctantly follows. They soon get lost, and they find trouble. Bigger trouble than anyone could ever have imagined.

In the days and weeks that follow, the authorities and the U.S. Senate become involved, and what they uncover might affect the future of the world.

EXCERPT

Chapter One

Tuesday, November 2 11:55 a.m.

Woodridge Academy, a private school in Heath Cliff, Pennsylvania, had once been the home of William Heath, after whom the town had been named. Nearly three hundred students now attended school in the four-story, black-and- brown stone building where William Heath had lived from 1891 to 1917, with only his wife and three daughters.

Tamaya Dhilwaddi's fifth-grade classroom on the fourth floor had been the youngest daughter's bedroom. The kindergarten area had once been the stables.

The lunchroom used to be a grand ballroom, where elegantly dressed couples had sipped champagne and danced to a live orchestra. Crystal chandeliers still hung from the ceiling, but these days the room permanently smelled of stale macaroni and cheese. Two hundred and eighty-nine kids, ages five to fourteen, crammed their mouths with Cheetos, made jokes about boogers, spilled milk, and shrieked for no apparent reason.

Tamaya didn't shriek, but she did gasp very quietly as she covered her mouth with her hand.

"He's got this superlong beard," a boy was saying, "splotched all over with blood."

"And no teeth," another boy added.

They were boys from the upper grades. Tamaya felt excited just talking to them, although, so far, she had been too nervous to actually say anything. She was sitting in the middle of a long table, eating lunch with her friends Monica, Hope, and Summer. One of the older boys' legs was only inches away from hers.

"The guy can't chew his own food," said the first boy. "So his dogs have to chew it up for him. Then they spit it out, and then he eats it."

"That is so disgusting!" exclaimed Monica, but from the way her eyes shone when she said it, Tamaya could tell that her best friend was just as excited as she was to have the attention of the older boys.

The boys had been telling the girls about a deranged hermit who lived in the woods. Tamaya didn't believe half of what they said. She knew boys liked to show off. Still, it was fun to let herself get caught up in it.

"Except they're not really dogs," said the boy sitting next to Tamaya. "They're more like wolves! Big and black, with giant fangs and glowing red eyes."

Tamaya shuddered.

Woodridge Academy was surrounded by miles of woods and rocky hills. Tamaya walked to school every morning with Marshall Walsh, a seventh-grade boy who lived three houses down from her and on the other side of their treelined street. Their walk was almost two miles long, but it would have been a lot shorter if they hadn't had to circle around the woods.

"So what does he eat?" asked Summer.

The boy next to Tamaya shrugged. "Whatever his wolves bring him," he said. "Squirrels, rats, people. He doesn't care, just so long as it's food!"

The boy took a big bite of his tuna fish sandwich, then imitated the hermit by curling his lips so that it looked like he didn't have any teeth. He opened and closed his mouth in an exaggerated manner, showing Tamaya his partially chewed food.

"You are so gross!" exclaimed Summer from the other side of Tamaya.

All the boys laughed.

Summer was the prettiest of Tamaya's friends, with straw- colored hair and sky-blue eyes. Tamaya figured that was probably the reason the boys were talking to them in the first place. Boys were always acting silly around Summer.

Tamaya had dark eyes and dark hair that hung only halfway down her neck. It used to be a lot longer, but three days before school started, while she was still in Philadelphia with her dad, she made the drastic decision to chop it off. Her dad took her to a very posh hair salon that he probably couldn't afford. As soon as she got it cut, she was filled with regret, but when she got back to Heath Cliff, her friends all told her how mature and sophisticated she looked.

Her parents were divorced. She spent most of the summer with her dad, and one weekend each month during the school year. Philadelphia was on the opposite end of the state, three hundred miles away. When she returned home to Heath Cliff, she always had the feeling that she'd missed something important while she'd been gone. It might have been nothing more than an inside joke that her friends all laughed at, but she always felt a little left out, and it took her a while to get back into the groove.

"He came *this close* to eating me," said one of the boys, a tough-looking kid with short black hair and a square face. "A wolf snapped at my leg just as I was climbing back over the fence."

The boy stood on top of the bench and showed the girls his pant leg for proof. It was covered in dirt, and Tamaya could see a small hole just above his sneaker, but that could have come from anything. Besides, she thought, if he'd been running *away* from the wolf, then the hole would have been in the back of his pants, not the front. The boy stared down at her. He had blue, steel-like eyes, and Tamaya got the feeling that he could read her mind and was daring her to say something.

She swallowed, then said, "You're not really allowed in the woods."

The boy laughed, and then the other boys laughed too.

"What are you going to do?" he challenged. "Tell Mrs. Thaxton? "

She felt her face redden. "No."

"Don't listen to her," said Hope. "Tamaya's a real Goody Two-shoes."

The words stung. Just a few seconds earlier, she had been feeling so cool, talking with the older boys. Now they were all looking at her as if she were some kind of freak.

She tried making a joke out of it. "I guess I'll only wear one shoe from now on."

Nobody laughed. "You are kind of a goody-goody," said Monica. Tamaya bit her lip. She didn't get why what she had said had been so wrong. After all, Monica and Summer had just called the boys *disgusting* and *gross*, but somehow that was okay. If anything, the boys seemed proud that the girls thought they were disgusting and gross.

When did the rules change? she wondered. *When did it become bad to be good?*

•••

Across the lunchroom, Marshall Walsh sat amid a bunch of kids, all laughing and talking loudly. On one side of Marshall sat one group. On his other side sat a different group. Between these two groups, Marshall silently ate alone.

Chapter Two

SunRay Farm

In a secluded valley thirty-three miles northwest of Woodridge Academy was SunRay Farm. You wouldn't know it was a farm if you saw it. There were no animals, no green pastures, and no crops—at least, none that grew big enough for anyone to see with the naked eye.

Instead, what you would see—if you made it past the armed guards, past the electric fence topped with barbed wire, past the alarms and security cameras—would be rows and rows of giant storage tanks. You also wouldn't be able to see the network of tunnels and underground pipes connecting the storage tanks to the main laboratory, also underground.

Hardly anyone in Heath Cliff knew about SunRay Farm, and certainly not Tamaya or her friends. Those who had heard of it had only vague ideas about what was going on there. They might have heard of Biolene but probably didn't know exactly what it was.

A little more than a year before—that is, about a year before Tamaya Dhilwaddi cut her hair and started the fifth grade—the United States Senate Committee on Energy and the Environment held a series of secret hearings regarding SunRay Farm and Biolene.

The following testimony is excerpted from that inquiry:

> **Senator Wright:** You worked at SunRay Farm for two years before being fired, is that correct?
>
> **Dr. Marc Humbard:** No, that is not correct. They never fired me. Senator Wright: I'm sorry. I'd been informed—
>
> **Dr. Marc Humbard:** Well, they may have tried to fire me, but I'd already quit. I just hadn't told anyone yet.
>
> **Senator Wright:** I see.
>
> **Senator Foote:** But you no longer work there?
>
> **Dr. Marc Humbard:** I couldn't be in the same room with

Fitzy a minute longer! The man's crazy. And when I say crazy, I mean one hundred percent bananas.

Senator Wright: Are you referring to Jonathan Fitzman, the inventor of Biolene?

Dr. Marc Humbard: Everyone thinks he's some kind of genius, but who did all the work? Me, that's who! Or at least, I would have, if he had let me. He'd pace around the lab, muttering to himself, his arms flailing. It was impossible for the rest of us to concentrate. He'd sing songs! And if you asked him to stop, he'd look at you like you were the one who was crazy! He wouldn't even know he was singing. And then, out of the blue, he'd slap the side of his head and shout, "No, no, no!" And suddenly I'd have to stop everything I'd been working on and start all over again.

Senator Wright: Yes, we've heard that Mr. Fitzman can be a bit . . . eccentric.

Senator Foote: Which is one reason why we are concerned about Biolene. Is it truly a viable alternative to gasoline?

Senator Wright: This country needs clean energy, but is it safe?

Dr. Marc Humbard: Clean energy? Is that what they're calling it? There's nothing clean about it. It's an abomination of nature! You want to know what they're doing at SunRay Farm? You really want to know? Because I know. I know!

Senator Foote: Yes, we want to know. That's why you've been called before this committee, Mr. Humbard.

Dr. Marc Humbard: Doctor. Senator Foote: Excuse me?

Dr. Marc Humbard: It's "Dr. Humbard," not "Mr. Humbard." I have a PhD in microbiology.

Senator Wright: Our apologies. Tell us, please, Dr. Humbard, what are they doing at SunRay Farm that you find so abominable?

Dr. Marc Humbard: They have created a new form of life, never seen before.

Senator Wright: A kind of high-energy bacteria, as I understand it. To be used as fuel.

Dr. Marc Humbard: Not bacteria. Slime mold. People always confuse the two. Both are microscopic, but they are really quite different. We began with simple slime mold, but Fitzy altered its DNA to create something new: a single-celled living creature that is totally unnatural to this planet. SunRay Farm is now growing these man-made microorganisms—these tiny Frankensteins—so that they can burn them alive inside automobile engines.

Senator Foote: Burn them alive? Don't you think that's a bit strong, Dr. Humbard? We're talking about microbes here. After all, every time I wash my hands or brush my teeth, I kill hundreds of thousands of bacteria.

Dr. Marc Humbard: Just because they're small doesn't mean their lives aren't worthwhile. SunRay Farm is creating life for the sole purpose of destroying it.

Senator Wright: But isn't that what all farmers do?

Chapter Three

Tuesday, November 2 2:55 p.m.

After school, Tamaya waited by the bike racks for Marshall. The racks were empty. Most of the students at Woodridge Academy lived too far away to ride their bikes, and there were no school buses for the private school. A line of cars extended from the circular driveway up Woodridge Lane toward Richmond Road.

As Tamaya watched the other kids climb into cars and drive off, she wished she had a ride too. She was already dreading the long walk home. It would feel even longer with a backpack full of books.

Her face still burned with shame every time she thought about what had happened in the lunchroom. She was mad at Hope for saying what she'd said, and even madder at Monica, who was supposed to be her best friend and who should have stuck up for her.

So she was a good girl? *So what?* What was wrong with that?

Being good was partly what Woodridge Academy was all about. The students all wore school uniforms: khaki pants and blue sweaters for boys, plaid skirts and maroon sweaters for girls. Embroidered on each sweater, right under the name of the school, were the words *Virtue and Valor*.

Besides learning about history and math and all that, the students at Woodridge Academy were also learning to be *virtuous*. The school was supposed to teach them how to be good people. When Tamaya was in the second grade, she had to memorize a list of ten virtues: charity, cleanliness, courage, empathy, grace, humility, integrity, patience, prudence, and temperance. This year, she was learning their synonyms and antonyms.

But if you actually tried to be good, Tamaya thought bitterly, everyone acted like you were some kind of freak!

Marshall came out of the building. His hair was a mess, and his sweater, stretched out of shape, seemed to hang crookedly.

She didn't wave. He came toward her, then trudged on past with hardly a glance.

Marshall had a rule. They weren't supposed to act like friends around school. They were just two kids who walked to school together because *they had to*. They definitely were not boyfriend and girlfriend, and Marshall didn't want anyone thinking they were.

Tamaya was surprised, however, because he wasn't going the usual way. Normally they headed up Woodridge Lane and then turned right on Richmond Road. Instead, Marshall was heading toward the side of the school.

She adjusted her backpack, then caught up to him. "Where are you going?"
"Home," he said, as if she'd just asked a really stupid question. "But—"

"I'm taking a shortcut," he snapped.

That didn't make any sense. They'd walked the same way every single day for the last three years. How could he suddenly know a shortcut?

He continued around the side of the school toward the back. He was taller than her, and was walking quickly. Tamaya struggled to keep up. "How do you suddenly know a shortcut?" she asked.

He stopped and turned on her. "I don't *suddenly* know about it," he told her. "I've known about it my whole life."

That didn't make any sense either.

"If you want to take the slow way home, that's up to you," Marshall said. "No one's making you come with me."

That wasn't really true, and he knew it. Her mother didn't allow her to walk home alone.

"I'm going with you, aren't I?" Tamaya said.

"Well, then quit being a baby about it," said Marshall.

She stayed with him as he crossed the blacktop, then went out onto the soccer field. All she'd done was ask how he knew a shortcut, she thought. How was that "being a baby"?

Marshall kept glancing behind him. Every time he looked back, Tamaya instinctively did too, but she didn't see anything or anybody.

Tamaya still remembered her first day at Woodridge. She'd been in the second grade, and Marshall had been in the fourth. He had helped her find her classroom, pointed out where the girls' bathroom was, and personally introduced her to Mrs. Thaxton, the headmaster. The new school had seemed like a big, scary place to her, and Marshall had been her guide and protector.

She'd had a secret crush on him all through second, third, and fourth grades. Maybe it still lingered a little bit inside her, but lately he'd been acting like such a jerk, she wasn't sure she even liked him anymore.

Beyond the soccer field, the ground sloped down unevenly toward the chain-link fence that separated the schoolyard from the woods. As they moved closer to the fence, Tamaya could feel her heartbeat quicken. The air was cool and damp, but her throat felt dry and tight.

Just a few weeks before, the woods had sparkled with bright fall colors. Looking out the window from her classroom on the fourth floor, she'd been able to see every shade of red, orange, and yellow, so bright some days that it had looked as though the hillside were on fire. But now the colors had faded and the trees looked dark and gloomy.

She wished she could be as brave as Marshall. It wasn't just the woods that scared her—and what might or might not have been lurking within. Even more than that, Tamaya was scared to death of getting in trouble. Just the thought of a teacher yelling at her filled her heart with fear.

She knew that other kids broke the rules all the time, and nothing bad ever happened to them. Kids in her class would do something wrong, and then her teacher, Ms. Filbert, would tell them not to do it, and then they'd do it again the very next day and still not get in trouble.

Still, she was sure that if she went into the woods, something horrible would happen to her. Mrs. Thaxton might find out. She could get expelled.

A dip in the rocky ground created a gap big enough to crawl through under a section of the fence. Tamaya watched Marshall take off his back-pack, then push it through the gap.

She took off her backpack too. Ms. Filbert had once said that courage just meant pretending to be brave. "After all, if you're not scared, then there's nothing to be brave about, is there?"

Pretending to be brave, Tamaya shoved her backpack through the gap. There was no turning back.

Now who's the goody-goody? she thought.

She wiggled under the fence, careful not to snag her sweater.

You've just read an excerpt from Fuzzy Mud.

ABOUT THE AUTHOR

Louis Sachar is the author of the #1 *New York Times* bestseller *Holes*, which won the Newbery Medal, the National Book Award, and the Christopher Award; *Stanley Yelnats' Survival Guide to Camp Green Lake*; *Small Steps*, winner of the Schneider Family Book Award; and *The Cardturner*, a *Publishers Weekly* Best Book, a Parents' Choice Gold Award recipient, and an ALA-YALSA Best Fiction for Young Adults Book. His books for younger readers include *There's a Boy in the Girls' Bathroom*, *The Boy Who Lost His Face*, *Dogs Don't Tell Jokes*, and the *Marvin Redpost* series, among many others.

Imprint: Delacorte Press
Print ISBN: 9780385743785
Print price: $16.99
eBook ISBN: 9780385370219
eBook price: $10.99
Publication date: 8/4/15
Publicity contact: Casey Lloyd, clloyd@penguinrandomhouse.com
Editor: Beverly Horowitz
Agent: Ellen Levine
Agency: Trident Media Group, LLC
Promotional information:

- Major "the mud is coming..." pre-publication media, consumer, trade, and educator buzz campaign
- National media campaign
- National author appearances at book festivals and stores at on-sale
- National consumer and library print and online advertising
- "Summer of Sachar" reading promotion and *Fuzzy Mud* teaser campaign
- Major promotion at all national school and library conferences and regional trade shows
- Classmates marketing promotion targeting teachers and students
- Louis Sachar author study kit, including an educators guide and poster
- Extensive "the mud is coming..." pre-publication social media campaign

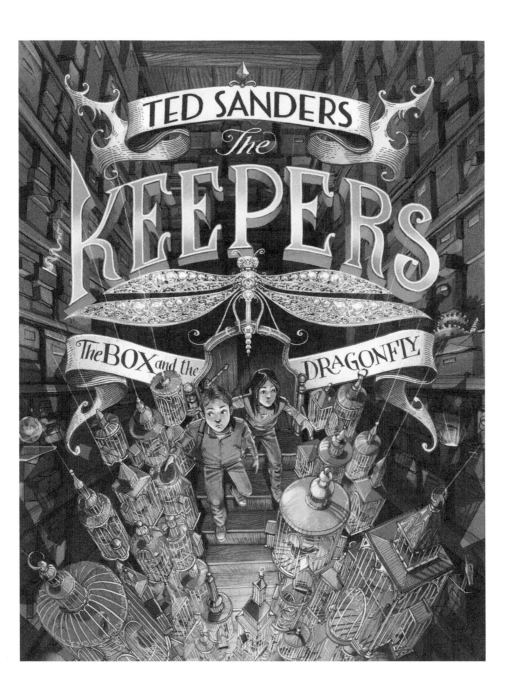

SUMMARY

Book one in a four book middle grade fantasy series about Horace F. Andrews, a quiet boy who discovers he possesses a power that can change worlds, with his friend Chloe, who can walk through walls with the help of a dragonfly pendant. The duo becomes entangled in a secret and ancient war with life as they know it at stake.

EXCERPT

The Sign

When Horace F. Andrews spotted the Horace F. Andrews sign through the cloudy windows of the 77 eastbound bus, he blinked. Just a blink, nothing more. He was surprised to see his own name on a sign, of course—and his sizable curiosity was definitely roused—but still, he took the sighting in stride. He had always been a firm believer in coincidences. Given enough time, and enough stuff, it was only natural that the universe would churn out some odd happenings. In fact, the way Horace saw it, a universe in which strange coincidences did *not* occur would be a pretty suspicious place.

The Horace F. Andrews sign was tall and narrow, hanging from the side of a building back in an alleyway off Wexler Street. It featured a long column of faded yellow words on a weather-worn blue background, but it was his name, written large at the bottom, that jumped out at him first, clear and unmistakable:

Horace F. Andrews

The bus rolled on. Just before the sign slipped out of sight, he caught a few of the yellow words in the long list above his name: ARTIFACTS. MISERIES. MYSTERIES.

Sparks of curiosity flared up inside Horace. He blinked—just once—and thought the situation through, tending those sparks like a brand-new fire. What were the odds of his seeing a sign with his exact name on it? Not terrible, he decided. Horace wasn't a very common name, but Andrews definitely was. And it was probably fairly common to have F as a middle initial—certainly better than one chance in twenty-six.

Of course, it was pure chance that he was even here in the first place. The 77 was his usual bus home from school, but this was not its usual route; normally the bus went straight down Belmont Avenue, but construction had forced the bus to detour down Wexler Street instead of driving right by. It was also pure chance that Horace had been looking out the windows at all. Ordinarily, he would have been sitting in the very back row, reading or working on a science problem for Mr. Ludwig's class, building a bubble of concentration against the noise and confusion of the bus. But today the bus was extra crowded, packed with rowdy kids from school in the back and stone-faced adults in the front. Horace had to stand in the middle, at the top of the steps near the rear door, feeling large and awkward and hating his heavy backpack, and wondering just how much he, Horace Andrews, belonged here. All he could do was look out the window and hope the ride would be short.

But then the sign slid by, and a block or two later the bus slowed and jerked to a stop. The rear door opened, and a plump old lady in a purple dress began easing down the steps, clinging to the rail with both hands. Horace looked through the back windows, but the sign was out of sight. Was it for a store? Or maybe someone's office—presumably the office of Horace F. Andrews. The sign had looked very old; maybe the place didn't even exist anymore. But then there were those words—"Artifacts," "Mysteries." And what possible reason could any business have for putting "Miseries" on its sign?

Horace watched the old lady stretch out one chubby leg, reaching for the curb below. The other passengers rustled impatiently. A scrawny red-faced kid Horace recognized from social studies leaned over the stairwell and started chanting at the old lady: *"Go! Go! Go!"*

And then Horace stepped around the woman and jumped out of the bus. He landed heavily on the sidewalk. The old lady squawked at him and yanked her foot back. "'Scuse me," Horace mumbled.

He trotted away, feeling as startled as the old lady looked. He was not ordinarily impulsive, not the kind of person who simply did things without thinking them through ahead of time. But sometimes his inquisitiveness pulled him places he wouldn't ordinarily go. And that sign . . . those words and his name together like that. . . .

The May air was cool but held a hint of thickness that spoke of summer—of freedom, and possibilities. Horace's internal clock, always accurate, told him it was 3:16. This time of day, the 77 eastbound ran every fourteen minutes. He could investigate the sign and then catch the next bus, still getting home before his mother. He hurried on down the sidewalk, searching.

Just as he thought he was drawing nearer to the alleyway, an enormous shape swept across his path, colliding with him hard and knocking the breath from his chest. Horace staggered back, almost tumbling into the gutter.

"Goodness," said a musical voice from high above.

Horace looked up—and up—into the face of the tallest man he'd ever seen. The man was so tall that he hardly looked like a man at all . . . ten feet tall or more. And thin, almost as impossibly thin as he was impossibly tall, with spidery limbs and a torso that seemed too narrow to hold organs. He had hands the size of rakes, with long, skinny fingers. He stank of something chemical and foul. Horace drew back as the man leaned over him.

"Are we all right?" the man asked, not unkindly. Again that singsongy voice. The man—if it even was a man—wore a black suit and dark, round sunglasses. A thick shock of black hair topped his head, out of place on his pale, skeletal body.

Horace tried to catch his breath. "I'm fine," he wheezed. "Sorry."

"Perfectly understandable. I believe you were distracted."

"I'm sorry, really. Just . . . looking for something."

"Ah. Do you know what it is you're looking for?" The man's teeth were slightly bared, as if he were trying to give a friendly grin but didn't know how.

"It's nothing, really," Horace said, faint threads of alarm tingling in his bones.

"Oh, come now. Tell me what you're looking for. You can't know how intrigued I am."

"I'm just looking around. Thanks, though." Horace began backing away.

"Perhaps I can be of some assistance. You *do* need assistance." He said it like a command.

"No, that's okay. I'm okay." Horace skirted wide around the strange man and hustled off, trying to hunker his big frame down beneath his backpack. He was all too aware that the man's eyes were still on him, but when he looked back, he was relieved to find that the thin man was not following. In fact, he had disappeared. Completely. How could someone so large simply drop out of sight? And how could someone be so large in the first place?

But it wasn't just the man who'd disappeared. The sign, too, was nowhere to be found. Horace went almost three full blocks without spotting it. He turned and began to methodically retrace his steps. The Horace F. Andrews sign was nowhere.

Abruptly, a looming shape stepped out of the shadows in front of him. Horace stumbled to a stop. The thin man gazed down at him, still trying that gruesome smile.

"Didn't find what you're looking for?" the man sang sadly.

Panic blooming, Horace tried to catch the eyes of people passing by, hoping to draw their attention. No one even slowed. Several people sat at tables outside a deli nearby, but no one so much as glanced at the thin man. Couldn't they see him? Horace was tall for his age, and he barely came up to the man's waist. Why was no one staring?

"I did, actually," Horace said at last, desperate, with no idea what he was going to say next. But then the words came to him. "That deli right there. My parents are inside, waiting for me."

The man's awful grin cracked open wide. "Of course they are," he said, gazing at the deli. "And I wouldn't think of keeping you from them. But first, a bit of advice." The man bent over, folding like a giant crane. He held a gaunt hand right in front of Horace's face, lifting a single long finger. The smell that came off him was burning and sour and rotten. And the man's finger was *wrong*. It was almost as if . . . did he have an extra knuckle? Horace's own terrified face curved back at him in the man's glasses.

"Watch where you roam, Tinker," the man sneered. "Curiosity is a walk fraught with peril." And with that he shot up, straightening to his full, unreasonable height. He snapped his head to the right, as if hearing some far-off sound, and then he left as swiftly as he had come, stepping out into the street. Six great strides took him across all four busy lanes, and then he effortlessly hurdled the hood of a parked car onto the opposite sidewalk. He sped down Wexler and a moment later vanished around a corner.

Horace stood there for another ten seconds and then, his limbs coming back to life, broke into a run. Whoever—whatever—this man was, Horace wanted to get far away. He made it exactly twenty-seven steps before he was halted in his tracks again. He stood in front of an alleyway, mouth gaping open. He'd passed this alley already and seen nothing—he was sure there had been nothing *to* see—but now here it was, plain as his own hands.

The Horace F. Andrews sign.

Or rather, not exactly.

Horace stared. He forgot all about catching the bus. He even forgot about the thin man. He read the sign from top to bottom again and again.

Oddments

Heirlooms

Fortunes

Misfortunes

Artifacts

Arcana

Curiosities

Miseries

Mysteries

and more at the

HOUSE OF ANSWERS

The House of Answers

HOUSE OF ANSWERS. That's what he had seen, not HORACE F. ANDREWS. Similar-looking words seen from the dirty windows of a bus. "Mistaken identity," Horace said aloud, his words echoing down the alley. The discovery disappointed him at first, but he quickly decided that the sign in reality was more intriguing than the sign he'd imagined. "House of Answers" was a name just begging to be investigated, wasn't it? And Horace—being Horace—definitely had questions.

There were tall buildings on either side of the alley: an electronics store on the right and a Laundromat on the left that looked closed for good. The floors above both obviously held apartments. The alley itself appeared to dead-end at another tall building about fifty feet back.

"I don't see any answers," Horace mumbled. He headed down the alley. It got darker and gloomier the deeper he went, and the sounds of the street faded away. He was just beginning to think he should turn around—he wasn't crazy about how narrow and high the alley was getting—when he was struck with a sense of vertigo. The back wall suddenly, dizzyingly, looked much farther away than it had. Then the alleyway seemed to open up at his feet, and Horace almost pitched down a steep flight of crumbling brick steps that he hadn't seen until he was on top of them. He caught himself, blinking. At the bottom of the staircase, barely visible in the shadows of the three buildings towering overhead, was an arched blue door. On the door was a round sign encircled with yellow lettering, too small to read—but the colors were exactly the same as the House of Answers sign.

"Holy jeez," Horace said.

He glanced around. No one was in sight. Slowly he eased himself down the dilapidated steps. The air grew cool. He reached the small wooden door and read the little round sign.

There were no other signs. No OPEN sign, no PUSH or PULL, no HOURS OF OPERATION. No windows. But this had to be the place. He tugged on the rusty handle. The door held fast.

State your name. "Horace?" he said aloud, feeling foolish. Nothing happened. "Horace F. Andrews," he tried again. Still nothing.

Horace looked again at the circle of words. "Wait. State your name or . . . name your state?" But that was ridiculous. Why would anyone want him to name his state? The door was here in Chicago, and Chicago was obviously in Illinois. "Illinois," he blurted out anyway, just to see. He tried the door again—nothing, of course. "State your name your state your name your state," Horace whispered, until the words started to make no sense to him whatsoever. And then he remembered the thin man's parting words: "*Curiosity is a walk fraught with peril.*"

"My state. My state is . . . curious. That's the state I'm in." Horace reached out for the handle again, pulling harder. "Curious and confused and a little bit p—" With a jarring *squawk*, the door flew open. Horace stumbled, his backpack dragging him to the ground.

A rich cloud of smells bloomed out of the opening—dust and wood and cloth and animal—old, thick, damp smells. And another thing, too: a wavering, high river of sound, almost like music. But the passageway was dark and cramped. Horace got to his feet warily. Tunnels were not something he handled well. He had a deep fear of small spaces—claustrophobia, technically, though he didn't like the word. He leaned cautiously in through the doorway.

"Hello?" he called. The strange chattering music seemed to swell briefly. Horace hefted his backpack onto his shoulders and stepped into the passageway.

The door swung closed behind him. His chest went tight as the unforgiving weight of the darkness crushed in from all sides. A panicky voice ribboned up in his thoughts, telling him to go back, to get out, get clear.

But his curiosity wouldn't let him turn back. He swallowed and closed his eyes, and forced himself forward. Ten feet, twenty. He pushed on until he sensed a faint golden glow against his eyelids and, opening them, found himself at the top of another dark stairway. The strange music drifted up from below. Small, busy shadows flickered in a dim amber light. His curiosity doubled, and his heart grew calmer. He descended the stairs, and as the rich sound swelled around him, he realized what it was.

Birdsong.

At the bottom of the stairs, the tunnel widened and the light grew brighter, and he began to catch flitters of movement all around. He realized the walls were filled with birdcages—no, *made of* birdcages, all kinds, wire and wicker, boxes and domes, from tiny cubes to grand bird palaces. Inside them, there were too many tiny darting shapes to count. The walls and ceiling flickered as the birds pattered about, all of them singing, so that the whole mass was in constant motion.

Horace walked through, wonderingly, and emerged from the tunnel of birds into a long and high stone room, hazy and golden. The birdsong faded. The room stretched back into darkness along a line of stone columns that rose high into wooden rafters. The golden haze came from curious amber lamps affixed to the columns, small stone containers from which drifting swirls of glittering light lazily rose. A long row of tables ran down the center of the room, and wooden shelves stretched along the walls. Shelves and tables both were piled high and crammed with bins and boxes and containers of all shapes and sizes and colors. The room was deserted.

Horace slid out from under his backpack and let it drop. He walked over to a table, his shoes scuffing loudly on the stones. He eyed the first bin he came to, trying to identify some of the strange objects it contained. A three-barbed hook hung over the side—a kind of fishing hook, but this one was two feet wide, with barbs as long as his hand. Beside it, the tip of a miniature scarlet pyramid poked into the air, and an accordion arm with a large spiky wheel on the end dangled limply. A rabbit head peeked out of the next bin over, motionless; a unicorn horn sprouted between its ears. If this was a store, it was like none he'd ever seen.

The containers themselves were neatly labeled, but the labels were bizarre. WHATSITS, one read, and another: WORTHY OF CONSIDERATION. Horace read quickly down the bins he could see.

Lost Bits

Mostly Incomplete

For the Weary

For the Wee

Truculent

Horace had no idea what truculent meant. He resisted peeking inside and kept reading.

Invisible (Defective)

Odd-Shaped

Even-Shaped

Ship-Shaped

Miscellaneous

Foul-Smelling

Unremarkable

Unsellable

Unaffordable

Unbinnable

Horace frowned at that one, a tall, blue metal container. A bin marked UNBINNABLE would have to be empty, wouldn't it? He hooked his finger over the edge of the bin, tugging.

A voice rang out: "Sign in, please."

Horace yanked his hand away. A woman's voice, husky and sharp, coming from deep in the room. Horace squinted, but saw no one. "I . . . I'm sorry?" he called out.

"No need for apologies," the voice said briskly. "Sign in please. At the podium."

Horace looked around the room. Back near the tunnel of birds, he spotted a short wooden podium, atop which lay open a large and elegant-looking guest book. He moved in for a closer look.

The guest book looked new; no one else had signed it yet. It had the usual columns for name and address, but there were a few more columns as well: AGE, REASON FOR VISIT, and finally . . . QUESTION. Horace had no idea what that meant.

Next to the book, there was a long, gleaming white quill, and beside it a green bottle of dark ink. Horace had never before written using a quill, much less an inkwell. He turned to peer once again into the depths of the store, but before he could even open his mouth—

"Sign in please."

The quill was almost as long as Horace's forearm, and surprisingly heavy. Gingerly, he dipped the sharp tip into the dark pool of ink.

Writing with the quill turned out to be more like scratching than writing. The quill rasped harshly across the paper, sending little chills up and down his arm. The ink surprised him, too—not black but a deep, glittering blue. He had to dip the quill repeatedly, but little by little, he filled out the top row:

Name   Horace F. Andrews
Address   3318 N. Bromley Street, Chicago, IL 60634

The next two required a little more thought, but he filled them out as well:

Age   12.2 years
Reason for Visit   mistake

He wrote "mistake" because he felt a little silly for having misread the House of Answers sign. But maybe "mistake" sounded a bit rude.

Reason for Visit   mistake first, curiosity second

Now he came to the final column, QUESTION. He considered that, and then wrote:

Question   Where am I?

"Right here, of course," said a voice at his ear.

Horace spun around, dropping the quill. A woman stood there—small, but with stout shoulders and a thick, severe face. She wore an old-fashioned black dress that covered everything but her head and her hands. Her dark brown hair was drawn back tightly into a bun.

The woman bent and picked up the quill, examining it intently. She ran her fingers down it smoothly, straightening the barbs of the feather. She peered at the guest book and let out a long, low hum.

"Horace F. Andrews," she said, not really asking.

"Yes."

She squared up to him and sank her fists into her hips. Her hazel eyes were as firm as packed dirt. She nodded solemnly. "You are in the right place."

Horace couldn't pull his eyes away from hers. "I . . . I am?"

"Indeed you are, but you won't believe it until tomorrow."

"Tomorrow."

"That's what I said. Tomorrow, when you return."

Horace felt dizzy. "Oh."

She frowned. "Shouldn't you be in school?"

"School's over. I'm out for the day."

"Not a truant, then. What's your best subject?"

"I don't know . . . science, I guess?" Horace said cautiously. Science was absolutely his best subject—and Mr. Ludwig his favorite teacher—but not everybody was impressed by Horace's enthusiasm for it. He didn't mind that being into science made him seem nerdy to some people, but he resented having to defend something that so clearly shouldn't need defending.

"Science," the woman said, her tone unreadable. "How practical." She clapped her hands together. "Very well. Closing time. You'll come back tomorrow." She began moving toward him, her arms spread like she meant to herd him to the exit.

Reluctantly, Horace began to back away. "But I haven't even looked around yet. What time do you close?"

"I tell you we're closing *now*, and you ask what time we close. Maybe you're just asking me what time it is?"

"I know what time it is. You close at three forty-three?"

She glanced at an enormous watch on her wrist and raised an eyebrow. "Goodness!" she said, sounding startled. "Closing is neither here nor there. Tomorrow we'll be open all day, and you'll come back. You'll look around all you like."

"But what is this place? Who are—"

Suddenly the woman lunged forward, grasping Horace's shoulders hard. She leaned closer and sniffed deeply—once, twice, three times. Her frown deepened. She stared at him hard. "You are Horace F. Andrews of Chicago. Twelve years old, here by virtue of accident and intrigue." Her breath was planty, herbal. Horace wondered if she would ever blink. "I am Mrs. Hapsteade, Keeper of the Vora." She poured that earthy gaze into him for another long, heavy moment and then released him. "Now we've been introduced. Are you comforted?"

Horace could not answer. He rubbed his shoulder. He tried not to let his face reveal the sea of uncertainty and frustration and queasy wonder that stormed inside him now. Keeper of the what?

The woman—Mrs. Hapsteade—sighed. "I see. So it is. But your comfort isn't my concern. Here, take this." She took Horace's wrist and dropped something into his hand—a large black marble. It was warm from her touch. "Keep this leestone with you at all times. And if you see the man who smells like brimstone again, walk away at once—but do not run."

Horace's skin went cold. "What did you say?"

"Do not look at the man, nor allow yourself to be seen. Do not listen to the man, nor allow yourself to be heard. Above all, if the man should come to your house, do not allow him to be invited inside. Keep the leestone with you. Return here tomorrow. All will be well. Do you understand these things I've said?"

Brimstone. The thin man. "Who is he?"

"He's a hunter."

"Is he hunting me?"

"In a way. He hunts an object you don't yet possess."

"How can that be? What object?"

"I don't know. You must return tomorrow. No doubt you're frightened and confused, but I don't apologize for that. The leestone will keep you safe. Tell no one. Go now—we are closed."

Horace backed away, gripping the leestone so hard his fingers ached. He gave Mrs. Hapsteade one last look, and then he turned and hurried toward the tunnel of birds, scooping up his backpack on the way. The birds rustled and fussed as he passed, breaking into little flurries of voice. He was almost to the steps leading back to the blue door when Mrs. Hapsteade called out. Her words reached through the birdsong like an outstretched hand, gentle and warm.

"Remember, Horace F. Andrews, fear is the stone we push. May yours be light."

You've just read an excerpt from The Keepers: The Box and The Dragonfly.

ABOUT THE AUTHOR

Ted Sanders is the author of the short story collection *No Animals We Could Name* (Graywolf Press, 2012), winner of the 2011 Bakeless Prize for Fiction. His stories and essays have appeared in many publications, including the *Southern Review, Confrontation, Georgia Review, Gettysburg Review*, and *The O. Henry Prize Stories* anthology. A recipient of a 2012 National Endowment for the Arts literature fellowship, he lives with his family in Urbana, Illinois, and teaches at the University of Illinois, Urbana-Champaign. This is his first book for younger readers. You can visit him online at www.tedsanders.net.

Imprint: HarperCollins
Print ISBN: 9780062275820

Print price: $16.99

eBook ISBN: 9780062275844

eBook price: $13.99

Publication date: 3/1/15

Publicity contact: Gina Rizzo gina.rizzo@harpercollins.com

Editor: Tony Markiet

Agent: Miriam Altshuler

Agency: Miriam Altshuler Literary Agency

Promotional information:

- Printed sell sheet to launch series
- Custom ARE packaging featuring "the box" and "the dragonfly"
- Edelweiss e-galley promotion
- Goodreads ARE giveaway promotion
- ARE school sampling
- Downloadable series resource and excerpt
- Teacher-targeted advertising
- Promotion at classactsbooks.com
- Promotional buttons
- Video trailer to launch series
- Downloadable retailer kit
- New York Comic Con featured promotion

BOOKSELLER BLURBS:

"When I read the first paragraph of *The Keepers* I was suddenly transported back to the first time I read *Harry Potter and the Sorcerer's Stone*. To say I enjoyed this book would be an enormous understatement. My only problem is that it doesn't come out soon enough for me to get my own copy and get copies of it in the hands of as many people as I can."—Katherine Megna, Books Inc. Laurel Village

"I absolutely love this fantasy. It was thrilling and scary but not too grotesque—a fine line these days. Really, this just has everything, and I think it's going to do very well indeed."—Michele Bellah, Copperfield's Books

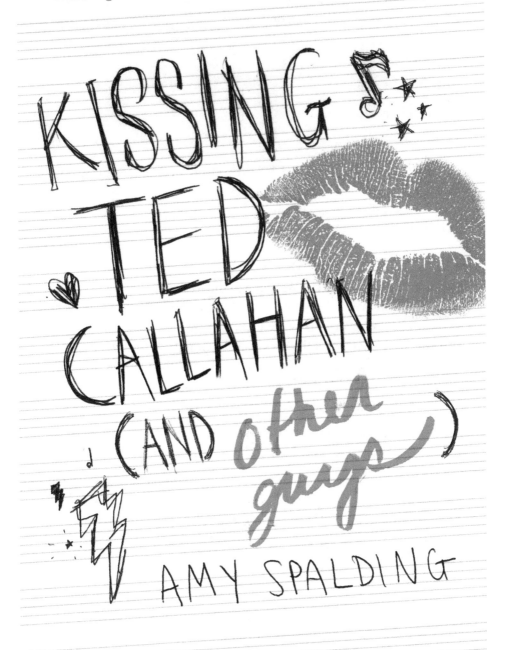

KISSING TED CALLAHAN (AND *other guys*)

AMY SPALDING

SUMMARY

With a voice similar to MTV's breakout hit "Awkward" and a set-up reminiscent of E. Lockhart's *The Boyfriend List, Kissing Ted Callahan (and Other Guys)* is an addictive YA read about the soaring highs and embarrassing lows of dating in high school.

EXCERPT

Two Months Ago

"This summer is a failure."

"Reid, get a grip," I say.

"It's emblematic," he says, and I don't roll my eyes because Reid says things like *emblematic* all the time. He's a writer, but also he's just Like That. "This is the summer before our junior year, and it isn't going how I wanted."

"It's one sold-out show," I say.

We didn't buy tickets to see Welcome to the Marina in advance because even our bandmates, Lucy and Nathan, said their record wasn't very good, and *Pitchfork* said they were even worse live. But as soon as we drove up to the Center for the Arts Eagle Rock and saw the line wrapping around the entrance and stairs, we realized we should have just ponied up the extra money for the Ticketmaster fees and bought tickets in advance. "What should we do now? Pastrami and shakes at the Oinkster?"

"I'm too disappointed for a pastrami sandwich," Reid says. "Let's just go back to the garage and see if Lucy and Nathan want to practice more."

This seems like a good solution, even though I'd really been hoping for one of the Oinkster's ube shakes. Today's had been one of those band practices where, if not for Reid and I having plans, we could have played all night.

I love being in a band with people who care about it as much as I do.

We shout-sing along with Andrew Mothereffing Jackson's latest album on the drive back and pull up to Lucy's house less than an hour after we left it. Nathan's car is still there, so we made the right call.

"You guys were wrong," I say as Reid opens the door to the garage. "That show is completely sold out."

A Crocodiles song is blaring from the stereo, but somehow the room still seems completely silent because no one is talking. I see it like a horror movie, all quick flashes of skin and slo-mo devastation. Nathan is on Lucy, or maybe Lucy is on Nathan, but regardless of who is on whom, it's Lucy and Nathan. Lucyandnathan.

Now everything's in fast-forward instead. Lucy and Nathan are fully dressed and talking at exactly the same time, but Reid and I might as well be turned into stone.

"We wanted to tell you guys," I hear Nathan say.

"We were *going* to tell you," I hear Lucy say.

"Nothing changes about the band."

"*Yes.* Everything will be exactly the same."

Reid and I manage to break our stone spell at the same moment. I know if I wanted to, I could speak again. But all we do is back out of the garage together and get into Reid's car without another word.

Chapter One

> We, the undersigned, agree to document our journeys in search of true love and/or sex. No detail is too small, too humiliating, too stupid.
>
> We will also provide one another with advice on how to capture the attention of the opposite gender. No line items should be taken as criticism, merely assistance and guidance to complete our ultimate goal.
>
> Signed:
Riley Jean Crowe-Ellerman
Reid Daniel Goodwin

Chapter Two

Ted Callahan is walking to my car.

I am trying to act normal. Like a normal person. Pick up one foot, put it down, repeat with the other foot. Do not look like a robot while doing so. Do not tip over. Do not, under any circumstances, let out any joyous squeals. Do not grab Ted's face and scream, "Dear god, you are here and you are real and you are beautiful and you are about to get into my car."

"Thanks," Ted says.

I've been in love with him for at least five months, but he doesn't talk to me often. His words are blue sky, cutting through the clouds of our previously uncommunicative ways.

"It's no problem. I drive this way anyway." It's scary how fast this flies out of me. Stop talking, Riley. "And I never mind driving. I *love* driving. Ever since I got my license, it's all, if I can get in the car and go, I totally will."

Why did I say that? It isn't even true! I neither love nor hate driving.

Ted nods politely as I unlock the doors to my car. It's as he's about to sit down that I realize something horrifying—way worse than my stream-of-consciousness ode to the open road—is about to occur. When I dropped off Ashley at school this morning, she left behind her copy of...*Gill Talk*.

On the front passenger seat.

Faceup.

The cover features a pale mermaid with flowing blond locks. Instead of the traditional shell bra, she's wearing a gold shirt that looks like it was purchased at Forever 21, and instead of scales, she appears to possess sequins.

"That isn't mine." I chuck it into the backseat. "I wouldn't read that. It's awful, right? Oh my god, it's so awful."

Ted smiles, but it's like when you're in a terrible situation, such as getting your legs blown off in the war, and you have to pretend for the sake of the children or the elderly that things are actually totally fine, except your crappy fake smile is fooling no one, Ted. Ted! Don't think I'm a weirdo who reads books about teenage mermaids making out with each other.

"I didn't even notice," he says.

"It's so embarrassing." My mouth now works independently of my brain. Or I have some new, secondary brain whose only function is to make boys think I'm stupid. Apparently, this new brain was raised on a diet of bad teen movies and CW dramas. Brain Number Two, I hate you. "One time my sister left that book in this deli, and she didn't realize until later, so I had to go back and ask this old man who runs it if I could have it back. And he doesn't know it's my sister's! So now he thinks I read books that have sparkly people with fins for feet making out on the cover."

Ted fidgets with the zipper on his bag. "Probably he didn't notice."

Then he changes the subject. "What kind of car is this?"

I'm not sure what to make of the question. I do not drive a cool car, and I do not drive a crappy car. I drive Mom's hand-me-down, very normal and nondescript. It's a little dark outside, but he could have it figured out just by walking up to it and getting inside.

Oh! Maybe he's trying to make conversation with me?

"A white 2009 Toyota Corolla." Years pass before the way-too-many words leave my mouth. And why did I say that it was white? The one thing about the car that doesn't need any clarifying is its color.

Ted nods, and I am sure this thing where we exchange words that I can't quite—even being generous—call a conversation is ending. I'm also already turning into the parking lot next to his mom's office building. After Yearbook, when I made this magic happen by offering him a ride, I'd asked him where he was heading. But supertruthfully? I already knew. I spotted him walking here last week.

"Thanks for the ride." He gets out of the car. Swiftly. Too swiftly? Is he afraid I'll lob more word fits at him? Ted, come back! Ted, I'll learn to be normal! Ted, it isn't fair we sat two feet apart and I didn't get to touch your hair!

"Anytime," I say. "Seriously, I don't mind."

"Cool." He picks up his messenger bag and slides it over his shoulder. I admire boys who basically carry purses. They aren't afraid of what the world thinks. "See you, Riley."

"See you."

He walks off toward the building. I wait for it, a glance back. A glance back would hold so much meaning and potential and material for analysis. But Ted walks toward the big glass doors, tries one, and when it's clearly the wrong side, opens the other and disappears inside.

I plug in my earphones and reach for my phone. I saw Reid when school let out at three, but so much has changed since then.

"The plan is doomed." I know it sounds overdramatic, but I also know it isn't. Not at all. "Ted was in my car."

"Ted? Ted Callahan?" His voice washes over with realization. "Ted Callahan is the Crush?"

"*TED CALLAHAN IS THE CRUSH.*" I sound insane. Brain Number Two seems to be planning an overthrow.

"We'll meet up." Reid is all business. Often, it's what I like most about him. "The usual? Now?"

"Now."

Chapter Three

Reid's Goals (in Order):

    1. Flirting

    2. Chemistry

    3. Hanging out

    4. Dates

    5. Making out

    6. Love

    7. Commitment

    8. Sex

Riley's Goals (in Order):

1. Witty/sexy banter

2. Listening to music/going to shows together

3. Doing it!!

Chapter Four

There used to be four. Lucy and Reid and Nathan and me. Against the world. Well, not the world. Not really against anything.

Lucy and I have been best friends since we were five and stood next to each other in Beginners Tap. Reid went to our school and had since kindergarten. He'd seemed like kind of a dork for a long time, but he sat behind us in freshman English, and he made great jokes about the ancient stuff we were forced to read. More importantly, his taste in music was excellent, though sometimes he could make even *that* dorky, like by geeking out over original vinyl pressings. Still, once we found out the battered Moleskine notebooks he was never seen without were filled with lyrics—and really smart and funny and heartbreaky lyrics at that—I knew for sure I wanted him around.

Back then Nathan rolled with a preppier and more athletically inclined crowd, but some mutual acquaintance told him we should talk about music, since we often ended up at school wearing the same band T-shirts. And then everything started happening.

The four of us listened to music, and then played music, and then wrote music. About a year and a half ago, we started calling ourselves a band— the Gold Diggers—and then Nathan's cousin booked us to be the opener at his wedding. (Yes, apparently some weddings have multiple bands play—especially if one of those bands is made up of a cousin you feel bad for and his friends.)

It was actually as easy and awesome as it sounds.

Last summer, Lucy's dad let us convert their garage into rehearsal space, I saved enough Christmas and birthday money to upgrade my drum kit, Reid let Lucy and me take him shopping so he'd stop dressing like his mom picked out his clothes (she did), and Nathan designed a band logo and found us two more gigs. Things were Happening. I walked around in the kind of mood where I wanted to high-five people and shout about how great life was.

But then the Incident happened.

Reid and I have talked about it a lot since. Not, like, in graphic detail. But things have shifted. We don't know what our group is anymore, even though Nathan and Lucy say "It's just the same!" while holding hands and whispering into each other's ears and sliding into the booth side of our usual table at Palermo Pizza while Reid and I get stuck in the rickety chairs facing them.

And permanent relocation to rickety chairs is definitely *not just the same.*

* * *

"Yo." Reid slides in across from me in our new usual spot at Fred 62, which has become our place. It's a diner with old-fashioned orange-and-brown booths and a menu that stretches on for years. It's open twenty-four hours, so it's just as good after concerts as it is after school or band practice.

Maybe I'm just suspicious, but Reid looks smirky. Self-satisfied. Knowledgeable of Things.

His silence is too much. I must make him talk. "Just say it, Reid."

"Ted Callahan?" Reid asks.

I leap forward and shove my hands over his mouth, which is dumb considering he's already said it, and what I'm doing is way more attention-drawing.

"Ow!"

"You're a wimp."

"I know I'm a wimp." He leans forward to grab my bag. I don't argue because we've determined it's the safest place for the Passenger Manifest. One of Reid's notebooks seemed like the perfect place to start logging our plans and thoughts on helping each other in our quest to find love. Well, Reid wants to find love, and I want to do more than awkwardly kiss a boy outside a ninth-grade dance I didn't even technically go to. Reid named it the Passenger Manifest because it's some reference from that old TV show *Lost*, and that guy loves hanging on to random factoids.

Anyway, if I trust Reid with all of my boy thoughts, what do I care if he sees my lip gloss or tampons?

"Don't put his name in that," I say. "Or his initials. Everyone will know who I mean by his initials."

"I'm putting his initials," Reid says. "I wrote down *names*. No one but us will see this. And if they do, by his initials people could think it's Tyler Cole or Titus Culliver—"

"Gross," I say. "Who would have a crush on Titus Culliver? Sometimes he leaves his prescription goggles on after gym class—"

"Or Tito Cortez," Reid says.

"I had no idea you had some kind of superpower with initials," I say.

"Yeah, it's amazing I don't have a girlfriend, right?" He isn't joking. I have no idea what will happen if everything we've planned works. Reid's identity seems forged around his lack of a lady friend. It's stupid because Reid is good at lots of things that matter: music, school, crossword puzzles. And, apparently, initials. "Oh, this was the thing in your list in the Passenger Manifest: 'Join a club he's in. Give him a ride,'" he says, pointing to the notebook.

"Yearbook," I say. "Last week I noticed he always walks down Sunset to some office building after our meeting, so I offered to drive him."

Reid props his elbows on the table and puts his hands together like he's an evil dictator taking stock of his newly invaded countries. "Not a bad plan."

"I know it's dumb I like him." I lace my fingers and hold my hands over my face like a mask. "You can say it."

Reid laughs. "Well."

I wait for the list of reasons why it's dumb. I'm not breathtakingly pretty, Ted barely knows who I am, I have no boyfriend experience, and I'm aiming too high right out of the gate.

"He's kind of short," Reid says. "And he makes *me* look cool. You know I'm not cool, Ri, no matter what you and Luce say." Reid makes a couple of strange arm movements, and I realize he's imitating the way Ted moves his hands when he's talking.

I feel like yelling at him, but the resemblance is more than uncanny. I am speechless at how it is the exact opposite of canny.

"He's so awkward."

"What?" A protective sensation rises up within me. I had no idea I'd have to defend Ted, ever. "But he's *gorgeous*. And a genius! He runs the freaking *Fencing Club*, you know." The *Fencing Club* is not, as it sounds, a club for fencing, but an underground blog that used to be an underground newspaper that dates back to 1964, the year our school was founded.

"I know he does," Reid says slowly. "Do you think that makes him cool?"

"Yes?" I stare at Reid. "Do you mean Ted isn't cool?"

"Ted Callahan—"

"*STOP USING HIS FULL NAME!*" I kick Reid in the knee. My legs aren't freakishly strong, like my arms are from drumming, but it's easy to hurt someone's kneecaps. "He could have some relative here. Or a friend we don't know. *BE CAREFUL.*"

Reid's clearly trying to act as if he isn't wounded from my powerful knee kick. "I'm just saying."

"I'm just saying," I say in my mocking-Reid voice. It sounds like a cartoon chipmunk, so I don't know why it's my go-to for making fun of him. Reid has never sounded like a cartoon chipmunk. "So you're saying Ted is *not* out of my league?"

"I'll be diplomatic," he says, "and leave it at that. Yes."

"You're serious?"

"Riley, you're in a band," he says. "You are a Rock Star. I don't even know if Ted listens to music."

"No, I'm sure Ted listens to music." But the authority I would have made that pronouncement with earlier is gone. "So he isn't cool?"

Reid shakes his head. "He is definitely not cool."

My worldview has shifted. Is it possible I might totally and completely be capable of Getting Ted Callahan?

You've just read an excerpt from Kissing Ted Callahan (And Other Guys).

ABOUT THE AUTHOR

Amy Spalding grew up in St. Louis, but now lives in the better weather of Los Angeles. She received a B.A. in Advertising & Marketing Communications from Webster University, and currently works as the Digital Media Planner for an independent film advertising agency. Amy studied longform improv at the Upright Citizens Brigade Theatre, and can be seen performing at indie theaters around L.A. Visit her online at theamyspalding.com.

Imprint: Poppy
Print ISBN: 9780316371520
Print price: $18.00
eBook ISBN: 9780316371513
eBook price: $9.99
Publication date: 4/14/15
Publicity contact: Melanie DeNardo;
melanie.denardo@hbgusa.com
Rights contact: Kristin Dulaney; kristin.dulaney@hbgusa.com
Editor: Pam Gruber
Agent: Kate Testerman
Agency: KT Literacy LLC

Territories sold:
World

Promotional information:
- National print and online advertising
- National review coverage
- Local author appearances
- Digital promotion

GOODBYE STRANGER

REBECCA STEAD

SUMMARY

Bridge and her friends live on the Upper West Side of Manhattan. When Bridge was in third grade, she survived being hit by a car, and ever since she's wondered: why am I here on earth? There must be a reason. Bridge and her best friends Tab and Emily start 7th grade, and dramas unfold: Emily suddenly has "a body" and is getting lots of attention, including texts from a popular older boy who sends revealing photos of himself, wanting Em's photos back. Tab immerses herself in the human rights club and feminism. Bridge becomes good friends with Sherm, a boy who makes her question a lot of things, such as: did Apollo 11 really land on the moon? And she wonders: what's the difference between liking someone, and love?

EXCERPT

Dollar-Eight

The waitress at the Dollar-Eight Diner seemed genuinely happy to see Bridge. "Hey there, Cinnamon Toast. Little while no see!" She grabbed two menus from a stack and handed them to Sherm, winking at him. "Sit anywhere, guys. I'll be right with you."

Sherm was impressed. "You weren't kidding—she really does call you Cinnamon Toast."

Bridge smiled and slid into a booth. "Are you opposed to splitting a vanilla shake?"

Sherm said he wasn't at all opposed to a vanilla shake.

"Good. Because a vanilla shake goes really well with cinnamon toast."

Sherm grinned.

She kept waiting for the strangeness to arrive—being at the diner with Sherm Russo. This is strange, she told herself. They'd met in front of school and walked here together, pretending it was perfectly normal, which it wasn't. Only it didn't exactly feel strange, either.

Bridge had once read a story about a girl who goes on a date to a restaurant where she's too shy to order anything but the cheapest thing on the menu, which is a cream cheese and olive sandwich.

"Have you ever had a cream cheese and olive sandwich?" she asked Sherm. Not that this was a date.

"No," Sherm said. "Have you?"

"No." They looked at their menus. "You can order anything you want," Bridge said. "I have money."

"Thanks. But we came for cinnamon toast, right?"

The waitress came back with two glasses of water. "You guys know what you want?"

"Two orders of cinnamon toast, please," Bridge said. "And a vanilla shake in two glasses."

The waitress smiled. "You sure you need two glasses? I could bring one glass and two straws." She winked again.

"Two glasses," Bridge said. "Please."

Suddenly she worried that when the waitress walked away and she and Sherm were sitting across the table from each other with no menus between them, they would have nothing to say to each other. There would be what her brother Jamie called awkward silence.

That was what Jamie said whenever the conversation died down at dinner: "Awkward silence." And when their mother said, "It's *comfortable* silence, Jamie. There's nothing awkward about it," Jamie would wait a beat and then say, very doubtfully, "If you say so." Once, this routine had made Bridge's friend Emily laugh so hard she practically snorted her dinner through her nose and had to leave the table to pull herself together in the bathroom.

"You know that riddle?" Bridge said to Sherm. "With the two brothers guarding the two doors, and one door leads to heaven and the other one leads to hell?"

Sherm shook his head. "Never heard of it."

"Really?" Bridge leaned forward. "So there are two brothers. One brother always lies, and one brother always tells the truth. You want the door to heaven, obviously, but you're only allowed to ask one question."

"One question each?"

"No. One question."

"Do I know which brother is which?"

Bridge thought. "No. You don't know which is which."

The waitress brought their food, and Sherm picked up two toast halves together, like a sandwich.

"Stop!" Bridge said. "What are you doing?"

Sherm's hand froze. "Eating my cinnamon toast?"

"You can't eat it like that! You have to eat one piece at a time, faceup, so that the cinnamon and the sugar hit the roof of your mouth."

Separating the two sides of his toast, Sherm muttered, "You're lucky I'm used to living with bossy women."

"Very funny." Bridge felt herself go red. "I'm just trying to give you the real experience here."

Sherm took a bite of the cinnamon toast.

"Well?" Bridge said.

"It's delicious," Sherm said. He bowed his head. "Thank you for showing me your planet."

"You're hilarious."

"I especially enjoy the way the cinnamon and sugar feel against the roof of my mouth."

"Double hilarious. Just go ahead and pretend this isn't the best thing ever."

"It is, actually," Sherm said, looking her straight in the eyes, the way he had during the intruder drill. "Best thing ever."

Bridge pushed his glass toward him. "And you haven't even tried it with the shake!"

There were no awkward silences. When the check came, they each paid four dollars. Bridge never left less than a twenty percent tip. Her mom said that was the definition of a good New Yorker.

"Nice wallet," Bridge told Sherm. "Looks about a hundred years old!" She grabbed it. "Check out all the secret pockets!" She turned it upside down, and something fell to the table.

It was a worn square of paper with a date written on it in big letters.

"What's February fourteenth?" Bridge asked, reading upside down. She felt bad all of a sudden, about grabbing the wallet and shaking it like that. She closed it and held it out to Sherm.

He took the wallet and then picked up the slip of paper from the table.

"It's Valentine's Day, dummy."

"And you just like to carry that piece of information around so you don't forget?"

"Actually, this was my grandfather's wallet. And this"—he held up the paper—"is his birthday."

"Oh God, sorry," Bridge said. "I didn't—"

"He's not dead," Sherm said quickly. "He moved out over the summer. My grandparents always lived with us, but now it's just my grandmother. He left her, after fifty years."

"Oh. Wow. Where did he go?"

Sherm made a face. "He moved to New Jersey."

Watching Sherm tuck the slip of paper into his wallet so carefully, Bridge felt even worse. "I'm sorry," she said. "That really sucks."

"I write to him sometimes," Sherm said. "Letters. Do you think that's weird?"

"It's not weird. It's nice. Does he write you back?"

Sherm looked up. "I haven't actually mailed any of them."

"Why not?"

He shrugged. "He doesn't deserve letters. He just left. My dad says he's moving in with some woman he met. Which feels kind of crazy, to tell you the truth, because he's a great person. I mean, he was. We don't really talk about it much. That's another crazy thing, not talking about it. But my parents are really busy and my grandmother only likes to talk about happy things. Happy things, or books."

Bridge nodded. "I get that."

Sherm rubbed the worn leather of the wallet with his thumbs. "I remember when you got hit by that car," he said.

There was a funny feeling that traveled down Bridge's legs sometimes—a zinging rush to her feet. "You do?"

"Yeah. It was right at the end of my block."

"Your block? That's so random. I didn't realize you even knew about that." She laughed. "Even I forget about it sometimes."

"Everybody knows about it." Sherm raised his head and the light hit his eyes. Now they looked greenish-blue mixed with light brown. Bridge thought they looked like tiny planet Earths. "What was it like?" he asked.

"The accident? I don't remember it. All I remember is the hospital—the nurses, and stupid stuff like these paper menus they had with pictures of animals all over them that you were supposed to color in with these broken crayons. I remember that."

"You almost died, my dad said."

"Yeah, everyone says that. But I don't remember it."

Now Sherm stacked sugar packets on the tabletop, carefully shaking each one first to make it lie flat. "My grandparents went to the hospital," he said. "That first night. They sat in the lobby."

"Really?" That was strange to think about.

Sherm looked at her. "A bunch of people were there, my dad said."

"Who?"

"Just people. From the neighborhood, I guess. The next day my grandmother wanted me to pray with her, but I ran out of her room." His eyes flicked to Bridge's, then back to his sugar tower. "I feel weirdly bad about that."

"That's okay." Bridge got an achy feeling at the bottom of her throat and took a sip of her water. "You were just a little kid. It wouldn't have made a difference. I mean, I'm fine!" She reached her arms up over her head and wiggled her fingers as if this were universal proof of being fine.

Sherm smiled. "Yeah."

"Actually," she said, "I lied before. I don't ever forget about the accident."

He nodded, unsurprised.

Bridge hesitated. "After the accident, this nurse at the hospital told me that I'm here for a reason."

"Here?"

Bridge nodded. "She said that's why I didn't die. It kind of weirds me out, actually."

He was the first person she'd ever told. She hadn't planned to tell him— she hardly knew him. It had something to do with how he had tucked that little piece of paper back into that cruddy wallet. The way he seemed to meet her thoughts wherever they went. The look on his face.

Sherm said, "My grandfather used to say that everyone alive has already beaten the craziest odds, just being born. Like one in a trillion. Your parents could have had a million different kids, but they had you. And before that could happen, your parents had to be born themselves, and *their* parents had to be born." He picked up his shake and used the straw to vacuum the bottom of the glass. "I mean, think about it. It goes all the way back."

Bridge laughed. "I don't know if that makes me feel better or worse."

"Maybe it should just make you feel lucky. Yeah, you were really lucky you didn't die after the accident. But you were a lot luckier to be born in the first place. So if you're here for a reason, maybe we all are."

"I guess. Yeah."

"You never told me the answer to that riddle."

"Oh," Bridge said. Then she laughed again. "You know what? I can't remember."

Sherm

October 24

Dear Nonno Gio,

Nonna made lasagna and you're pretty sad you missed it, even if you don't know it.

I tried cinnamon toast today and it was great. Do you think people are born for a special purpose? I don't. I think it's just something that happens.

Sherm

P.S. Three months, twenty-one days until your birthday.

Valentine's Day

You have to tell your mom you aren't in a ditch. That's kind of weighing on you. There's a copy shop on Broadway, near the university, where you think you can get online. You'll send her an email.

You turn north, pull your hood up again, and play hot lava all the way there.

The copy place is busy: there are college kids sitting at computer terminals, two men with a stroller at the counter, and people waiting for the copiers. You get in line behind the couple with the baby and watch a woman struggle with a color copier. She keeps hitting the big green button, but nothing is happening. A man in a down jacket is using the paper cutter near the door, trimming a stack of pale blue cards. Invitations, you think. He pauses. Walks over to the woman at the copier. "Not working?" he says.

She gives him a frustrated smile.

After the apocalypse, they'll have three kids, you decide. The middle kid will turn out to be some kind of genius. The younger one will be an artist. The older one might marry the baby in the stroller, who's trying to jam his straw into his juice box. He's having problems. Don't worry, you think at him. After the apocalypse, there will be no more juice boxes.

Gina invented the apocalypse game. The game sounds creepy but it isn't. Not super-creepy, anyway.

"What if there was a nuclear bomb, and only the people in this room survived?" Gina asked one day last fall. You remember that she was wearing a sweatshirt with a picture of Smurfette on it. You were at Dollar-Eight, feeling relaxed and goofy. No Vinny.

"Nuclear bomb, nice thought," you said.

"Yeah, but who do you think you'd end up with? I mean, we'd all have to pair up and have babies, right? To repopulate the planet." Gina scanned the diner. "Oh, I think I want him."

From her lap, she mini-pointed to a kid sitting alone near the window, reading a paperback.

You'd laughed. "So everyone we know is dead and your first thought is dating?"

Gina looked fake-hurt. "For the sake of the human race."

"Okay. I'll take the one at the counter. We both like French fries."

She leaned, looked. "I approve. So what about everyone else?"

And the two of you sat, arranging families and assigning jobs.

"Those two are made for each other!"

"He looks like a doctor, doesn't he?"

"That woman is definitely the president of something—look at those killer shoes. She can be in charge."

"Okay. But she still needs a love life. . . ."

That was the game.

"We'll stay best friends, of course," Gina said that day. "Those girls in that booth over there look nice too. They can hang with us."

Best friends. You remember the happiness of that.

At the copy shop, you play the game by yourself, feeling in your pocket again and again for your phone. It's beyond weird to be without it.

Every time the door swings open, your fragile world gets a little more broken. First, the color-copier lady leaves without even saying goodbye to the blue-invitations man, and their three kids evaporate like mist. Then the woman in the funky glasses walks away from her true love in the suede shirt at computer terminal #3. He doesn't care, just stares at the document on his screen as if nothing has happened. It's sad. Everything they would have come to feel for each other—gone.

You reach *again* for your phone without meaning to. Stupid neighbor.

Or Is She a Woman?

Bridge loved Tab's living room. Her dad's plants on the windowsills, the black-and-white photographs on the walls, and jars of nail polish scattered across the coffee table like pretty rocks. There were sheer ivory curtains under embroidered turquoise ones and small brass sculptures on the bookshelves. Bridge couldn't remember if they were from France, where Tab's parents lived before they had kids, or from India, where they were born. She loved the way her feet sank into the carpet, the bowls of salty soy nuts, the way their cat snuggled with them on the couch. Jamie was allergic to cats.

"What do you think goes through her mind when she looks in the mirror?" Bridge said. She and Tab were on a homework break, huddled in front of a laptop on the couch, looking at a picture of Julie Hopper, the eighth grader from Em's soccer team who'd had her legs across Em's lap during the clubs fair. "Does she see what we see? Like how other people see her? I mean, *boom,* she's beautiful. You know?"

"Well, *I* see her as kind of naked," Tab said, clicking the picture to make it bigger. "Like a naked person with a towel over her shoulders."

"She's wearing a bathing suit. Everyone looks half naked in a bathing suit."

Celeste, Tab's sister, walked in and said, "Who's naked? That's *my* laptop, Tab, bought with *my* babysitting money. You're supposed to ask first, remember?" She dropped down on the couch next to them. "Hold the phone. That's Julie Hopper? When did she get so gorgeous? Wait—she put that up on her own page? It kind of looks like she's not wearing pants."

"It's a bathing suit," Bridge said.

"Oh. Maybe the angle is weird. Looks like she forgot to put on pants."

"See?" Tab said. "Told you."

"You know Julie Hopper?" Bridge asked Celeste.

Celeste looked at her. "I actually went to your middle school, remember? Last year? I was the one with the gorgeous bod and the perfect makeup?"

Bridge smiled. "I remember. I just didn't know you knew Julie."

"She's only a year behind me. Last spring, some poor kid wrote her a letter about how much he liked her and she read it to her homeroom. She was famous for at least a week after that."

"Wow—that's mean," Bridge said.

"He probably deserved it," Tab said.

"Eighty-eight comments!" Celeste said, squinting at the screen. "Bridge, scroll down."

Bridge scrolled down, reading the comments on Julie's page, mostly things like "Gorgeous!" and "So hot!"

Em had written: *OMG. I wish I was you. Serious.*

And Julie had written back: *Aw thanks! ILY.*

And Em had written back: *ILYSM.*

"Don't worry," Celeste said, looking at Tab and Bridge. "You guys just haven't, you know, grown those parts yet. Julie's a year older than you guys. You'll look just like that! More or less."

"Do I look worried? I'm not worried," Tab said.

Tab would probably look like Celeste, Bridge thought. Celeste had the kind of body Bridge would want, if she could choose: not too much, not too little.

"I'm just saying it seems like a big deal, but it isn't." Celeste threw her shoulders back and took a deep breath, which pushed her chest out and made Bridge think that Celeste actually did think it was kind of a big deal.

"Again," Tab said, "not worried."

"Do you guys ever watch *The Twilight Zone*?" Bridge asked.

"The vampire books?" Celeste asked vaguely. She had taken control of the laptop and was scrolling through Julie Hopper's photos.

"No, *The Twilight Zone*. It was this old show on TV. These different stories."

"Sounds cute."

"They're kind of creepy, actually. There's this one about a woman in a hospital bed and her whole head is wrapped up in gauze. Just her head. And the nurses—but you can only see their hands, not their faces—are starting to unwrap her. And the doctor, but you can't see him either, you can only hear his voice, is telling her she shouldn't get her hopes up, because the surgery might not have been successful."

"Notice how the nurses are women and the doctor is a man?" Tab said, nodding.

"I didn't say the nurses were women," Bridge said.

"Oh. Were they?"

"Yes," Bridge admitted.

"Ha!" Tab said.

"Shush. So finally the bandages fall away and she's *perfect*. She's, like, ridiculously beautiful. The room goes silent, someone passes her a mirror, and then she starts screaming her head off. She's *horrified* by what she sees in the mirror."

"I don't get it," Tab said.

"You're not supposed to yet. *Then* the camera pulls back and for the first time you see the faces of the doctors and nurses in the room, and they all look like *pigs*! They have these *snouts*!"

"What?" Celeste looked up, suddenly interested.

"Snouts! Like *pigs*! It's this other reality, where she looks like a supermodel but *she's* the ugly one. Get it?"

"I wouldn't want to live on a planet where everyone looks like a pig." Celeste fake-shuddered.

"You're missing the point," Bridge said.

"Maybe you had to be there." Celeste closed her laptop and looked at Bridge. "Your hair is getting so long. Have you ever tried a messy bun?"

"Messy bun?" Tab said. "Is that to eat? Mmm, messy bun. Sounds delicious."

"Don't be mental."

"Mental," Tab told Bridge, as if Celeste weren't sitting right there. "She gets that from these hair videos she watches on YouTube. A lot of the girls are British. Now she runs around saying everything is either 'brilliant' or 'mental.'"

"I do not. But, Bridge, did you know there are like a hundred thousand videos on the Internet about how to put your hair up or do your makeup? It's this whole *world* of information."

"Yeah, I'm pretty sure that's why they invented the Internet," Tab said.

"You know what, Tab? You don't have to make a statement every five seconds." Celeste looked at Bridge thoughtfully. "Or maybe a sock bun."

"What's a sock bun?" Bridge asked.

"Mmm, sock bun," Tab said. "Sounds delicious."

"It's a bun rolled up around a sock," Celeste told Bridge. "Looks prettier than it sounds. And your hair is so dark and heavy . . . it'll be beautiful. Even with the cat ears." She paused, leaned back. "You know, I think I like the ears. They give you some nice height."

Tab burst out laughing. "Tell me you didn't just say that."

"Ignore her," Celeste instructed Bridge. "Want to try it? The sock bun?"

"Uh. Maybe," Bridge said.

"I'll go get the stuff!" Celeste jumped up, glanced at herself in the mirror hanging over the couch, and did a double take.

"No. No! It's still there. It's—*bigger!*"

"What is?" Bridge asked.

"She can't pass a mirror without looking at herself," Tab said.

"This zit!" Celeste turned, her finger aimed at a place to the left of her chin. "I paid, like, twenty-eight dollars for this stupid cream that was supposed to boost my radiance. What did I get for it? A four-dimensional zit!"

"It's tiny," Bridge said. "I didn't even see it until you pointed."

Tab rolled her eyes. "Four dimensions? Does it smell or something?"

"Ew, no. The fourth dimension is *time.* This thing has been here for two weeks!"

Tab said, "Stop laughing, Bridge. You're encouraging her."

Celeste glared at the spot in the mirror. "Leave, thing! *Leave!*"

"I can't help it," Bridge said. "She's funny!"

"You realize our fifteen-minute break was over half an hour ago, right?" Tab pointed to their books on the coffee table.

Celeste spun away from the mirror and squinted at the computer. "Is it four-thirty? I'm so sorry, Bridge, I have to pick up Evan from computer club. I'll show you the sock bun later, okay? Promise."

"Anyway, we're supposed to be doing French," Tab told Bridge. "Remember? Did you look at the flash cards I made you?"

"Sort of." Bridge rooted around in her backpack for her flash cards. "There's this new girl at the Bean Bar. She says French is the language of love. And that's why she refuses to speak it."

Tab made a face. "That's stupid. How can there be a language of love? And Bridge, is she really a 'girl'? Or is she a woman?"

You've just read an excerpt from Goodbye Stranger.

ABOUT THE AUTHOR

Rebecca Stead is the author of *First Light*, the Newbery Medal winner *When You Reach Me*, and the five-starred, award-winning *Liar & Spy*. She lives in Manhattan with her husband and two children.

Imprint: Wendy Lamb Books
Print ISBN: 9780385743174
Print price: $16.99
eBook ISBN: 9780307980854
eBook price: $10.99
Publication date: 8/4/15
Publicity contact: Casey Lloyd, clloyd@penguinrandomhouse.com
Editor: Wendy Lamb
Agent: Faye Bender
Agency: Faye Bender Literary Agency

Promotional information:
- Extensive pre-publication media, consumer, trade, and educator buzz campaign
- National media campaign
- National author tour (6—8 cities)
- Book festival author appearances
- National consumer and library print and online advertising
- Feature at Book Expo America

- Parent/child discussion guide
- Major promotion all national school and library conferences and regional trade shows
- Rebecca Stead author study kit, including an educators guide, poster and classroom giveaway
- Classmates marketing promotion targeting teachers and students
- Classroomcast video
- Social media campaign across all platforms

PEOPLE CALL ME BIGGIE.
NOT ALL PEOPLE.
MOM AND SOME TEACHERS
CALL ME HENRY,
BUT FOR THE MOST PART, I'M

BIGGIE

DEREK E. SULLIVAN

SUMMARY

Henry "Biggie" Abbott is the son of a baseball legend from Finch, Iowa. But at an obese 300+ lbs Biggie himself prefers classroom success to sports. As a perfectionist, he doesn't understand why someone would be happy getting two hits in five trips to the plate. "Forty percent—that's an F in any class," he would say. As Biggie's junior year begins, the girl of his dreams, Annabelle Rivers, actually talks to him. Hundreds of people have told him to follow in his dad's footsteps and play ball, but Annabelle might be the one to actually inspire him to try. What happens when Biggie steps out of the shadows of being invisible into the harsh glare of the high school spotlight?

EXCERPT

Chapter One

Getting Tagged

People call me Biggie. Not all people. Mom and some teachers call me Henry, but for the most part, I'm Biggie.

Do I like the nickname? No. Of course, I don't. Nor do I care much for Brian Burke, who, nine years ago, thought up the moniker when we were playing tag during second-grade recess. I should have just told him to shut up or said something mean in verbal retaliation, but I didn't. I just stood there, head hung, shoulders fallen, hands swaying in the icy wind of early December.

It would have been so easy to fight back. He was tiny, wore the same ratty, torn Notre Dame T-shirt every day, and loved—and I mean loved—investigating the inside of his nose with his long fingernails.

That day, instead of getting caught up in the cherished elementary school game of I can be meaner than you, my lips locked. I stood there like some sap with my eyes focused on trampled snow, which was filled with small shoe prints from seven-year-olds avoiding the flailing arms of the kid who last heard, "You're it."

Even today, I can still remember that day nine years ago when everyone was laughing and snickering the first time Brian said my nickname out loud. Over time, the memory is more the background laughter of my classmates than Brian's repetitive teasing of "You're so big and fat, we should call you Biggie." I learned that Friday that you didn't need to be touched to get tagged.

***

Do I deserve my nickname? Sure, I'm not going to lie or sugarcoat the situation. I stand six-foot-two and weigh north of three hundred pounds.

Last year, my mom had to start ordering T-shirts online. I'll keep my size to myself, but let's just say there're enough Xs in it to make a porn-store owner blush. For at least a little while longer, I can still get my shorts and jeans at John's Big and Tall, which is located an hour from my hometown of Finch, Iowa (population: a handful). Lately, my jeans, new and old, feel like tourniquets wrapped tightly around my thighs.

***

How did I get this way? Or a better question: Why have I let myself grow to over three hundred pounds? Simply put: now, I'm invisible. Funny, isn't it? The more I weigh, the less people ride me about it. By living up to my nickname, I have accomplished an amazing feat. I'm the only high school student in the world who doesn't get made fun of on a daily basis.

It doesn't stop there. I'm also the only teenager in America whose parents leave him alone. Millions of people in the world give up the foods they love or drop billions of strands of sweat to avoid being called fat. I have managed to avoid the taunts, glares, and verbal abuse without giving up anything or wasting most of my life on a treadmill. I pull this off by shutting my mouth, staying in my bedroom at home, and sitting in the back of the room at school.

Standing in the shadows of my high school, I have noticed one undeniable fact: high school kids are cruel, mean sons-of-bitches, and not just toward fat people. Nobody is immune to the constant ripping. I can't take a step without hearing some kid make fun of another kid. Every second, students are laughing at someone else's dumb outfit, clumsy behavior, or poorly chosen words. It's not a battle, but a never-ending verbal war. In this conflict, I choose to be a pacifist. To avoid being hit by spoken bullets, I have decided to never point that gun at anyone else. I keep my mouth shut at all costs.

At my desk, I disappear from everyone: the jocks that rip on kids who don't have God-given talent; the do-it-alls, who come to class every day, try out for the spring play, run for student council, and so on; and the sleepers, who rest their heads on desks and could care less about school.

Sure I feel the urge to say something now and then, raise my hand to answer some teacher's question, or say hello to one of the few kids I don't despise at this small-town hellhole, but it's not worth the risk. When you're fat, insults hurt and come in droves, like ammunition from a machine gun. I hate being made fun of for my weight and will do anything—I mean anything—to avoid it, even if that means adding weight.

A funny thing happened a year ago when my weight neared three hundred pounds. People stopped looking at me, staring in disgust, or delicately shaking their heads at the sight of me. In the past year, I have learned that being slightly overweight is a lot more annoying than being obese.

For example, the summer before the start of high school when I weighed around 220 pounds, the football coach called our house every week and told me that if I played for his team and, more importantly, if I committed myself to the weight room, I could play college football as an offensive guard or nose tackle. But sports aren't for me, and I definitely don't need athletics to get into college.

Since my school started giving out As, Bs, Cs, Ds, and Fs in third grade, I've missed out on getting an A once. At the end of my seventh-grade year, my physical education teacher wrote that I didn't participate effectively and gave me an A-minus. Participate effectively? What does that mean? The way I see it, if a kid stands there and keeps his mouth shut, he deserves an A.

Want another example? Having a thirteen-year-old weighing well over two hundred pounds bugged my mom, so she got me up early and forced me to walk on a treadmill. When I came home from school, she, as if she were on CSI, searched my backpack and pockets for junk food wrappers. She worked so hard to keep me from eating junk food that hiding the wrappers from candy bars, hamburgers, and Twinkies took up most of my time. Would it have been easier to just not eat my favorite foods? Probably. But they're my favorite foods. I'm a fat kid who has to stay quiet all the time to avoid constant ridicule. Eating Snickers now and then is the only way I don't go completely insane.

So it didn't surprise me at all when no matter how hard Mom worked, my weight kept rising and rising. Soon, the doctor's office staff weighed me out at 270 pounds. Mom said little the next few days. Then one morning she said she was done begging me to work out and pleading with me to eat healthy. The words were music to my ears. Now, other than making healthy meals, she has stopped being my athletic trainer. No more early-morning door poundings, no more rummaging around in my stuff, no more getting on my case about my weight. I am free to be me.

If I had followed my mom's orders and stopped with the junk food and embraced the exercise plans, I would still be working out in the mornings, living off vegetables, and being all-around miserable, twenty-four hours a day, seven days a week, 365 days a year. Plus, if I look even the slightest bit fit, coaches at sports-obsessed Finch High School would never leave me alone.

Some days, I feel like I'm the only person in Finch who doesn't share a passion for sports. What I don't understand is why someone would want to fail so much for just a small taste of success. For example, Matt "Jet" Wayne, the baseball team's best hitter, batted only .418 this summer. So 58.2 percent of the time he failed, and he's an all-state award winner on the diamond. Wouldn't all of the failure make someone hate sports?

Another thing about me: I'm a perfectionist. Not only have I mastered my school's curriculum and perfected a way to avoid insults, I have also never missed a day of school in ten years. Not one. I have never been sick a single day in my life. If junk food is so horrible for your health, how do I stay so healthy? I'm sure the anti-junk-food crowd has no answer for that.

Anyway, a real perfectionist could never enjoy sports. Sports are for guys like Brian Burke, who unfortunately stopped picking his nose. As I got bigger and bigger, adding more and more credence to his nickname for me, he got stronger and faster. Ever since sixth grade, he has been the school's top athlete. He's the quarterback, power forward, and starting pitcher. By junior high, Brian wasn't the only one calling me Biggie. Everyone did. Everyone worshipped him—so much that he got to pick his own nickname, a rarity at any high school.

The story goes that his father used to wear a homemade T-shirt to baseball games that had a big yellow jacket—the school's mascot—on it, along with the words Brian Burke, Finch's Killer Bee. Brian loved it so much that one day he told everyone to call him Killer, and to this day they still do. Thanks to Brian, he's Killer and I'm Biggie.

Chapter Two

Kit Kats

School isn't the only place I remain silent. Four nights a week, I work at Bob's Fuel and Food. Outside the small convenience store sit two gas pumps and inside is just one register. The owner hates spending money, so he schedules only one person at a time. Most workers would complain about having to run the register, cook the food, load the empty shelves, and mop the footprint-filled floors by themselves, but I appreciate my boss's frugality.

I can sit up there and read novels, comic books, and textbooks and rarely be bothered. These days, most people pay at the pump, so all I have to do is call the cops when they drive off without paying, which happens more than people think. Outsiders driving through Finch on their way to Dubuque or Chicago think we don't have policemen in this small town, so they pump and dash. They are all idiots because I write down their license plate numbers before turning on the machines. I doubt they get very far out of town before a state trooper pulls them over.

Every now and then, someone will come in for a twenty-ounce pop, twelve-pack of beer, or a candy bar. Last year, when I was a dumb convenience-store rookie, I would mutter the total bill through the same forced smile I use on school picture day. Then one day I retired the crooked grin and waited for customers to toss a buck or a ten- or twenty-dollar bill on the counter. I just calmly glance at the charge on top of the register. Once they see the total, they get out their cash or debit cards. No small talk needed, wanted, or expected, and no one ever says I'm rude. Here's a secret to all future convenience-store workers: no one wants to talk to you, no matter what the bosses or company motto says.

I love making the food. I cook greasy snacks like chicken fingers and egg rolls. It isn't that much work; I just toss the snacks into a heater below the counter and then place them into small paper carriers or into my belly.

I'll admit it; I'm addicted to chicken fingers and egg rolls. One night, I bought thirty of them, but most nights I eat between twelve and fifteen. I used to eat them with blue cheese dip, but lately I've been soaking them in the hot cheese we normally sell with soft pretzels.

While cooking is my favorite job, the highlight of my night is watching Annabelle Rivers shoplift.

Three times a week, Annabelle, a classmate since kindergarten, comes into the store before her shift at Molly's Drive-In. She buys a Monster Lo-Carb energy drink and also drops two Kit Kats in her garbage-bag-size purse. Last year, she used to steal M&M's, and before that, Twix bars, but right now she's swiping Kit Kats.

Annabelle thinks she's so sly. She looks at the candy bar with one eye and me with other. She notices me going to add some egg rolls to the heater and drops the dollar treat into her purse. She then grabs a Lo-Carb and pays for it. I would let her steal that too, but I always go mute when she's around. Someday I'll tell her how I feel.

She does her routine every time she walks into the store, even if there are other customers. I just love to watch the precision she takes in swiping the candy bars. As a perfectionist myself, I appreciate her attention to detail. She comes in and always walks down the first aisle, the one closest to the windows, which are covered with red and blue advertisements for pop, cigarettes, oil, and Little Debbie snacks. She's five-foot-six, so her dark hair with red highlights pokes over the top of the shelf.

Her pace can only be explained as quick walking. She doesn't skip, jog, or run, but she's in a hurry, as if she's trying to move just fast enough that I can't focus on her. She then stares through the glass cooler doors at the pop, single-serving milk containers, and energy drinks before turning ninety degrees to slide like a ninja into the candy aisle.

At this point, no matter what I'm doing, I turn away and pretend to be too busy to watch her every move. Then I hear the cooler door open again. She grabs the Monster drink. How do I know she steals Kit Kats? Well, her precision to detail ends when she pulls the Kit Kat out of her purse when she starts her car.

She comes in every Monday, Tuesday, and Thursday around six fifty. Tonight's Friday so I'm surprised to see her show up. She walks in, sees me texting, and smiles. She doesn't normally even make eye contact with me, so a big smile makes me blush and I stand at attention. Then Mike Robinson, a senior whose only real skill is owning a motorcycle, follows her into the store.

"Please don't be together," I whisper.

Mike and Annabelle giggle together as she hands him two Monster drinks: Lo-Carb and Mean Bean coffee. She stands back as Mike walks up to my counter. He tosses down six bucks in extra-crisp dollar bills. The drinks cost $2.79 apiece and six bucks easily covers them, but there are the two Kit Kats and one Snickers in Annabelle's purse that I have to deal with before letting them get back on his motorcycle.

Annabelle and I have an unspoken cat-and-mouse game that lights up my boring nights behind the counter. But tonight, with him, she's paying. They don't get to laugh about stealing from me, not on his motorcycle.

"Biggie, I need my change," Mike says while my eyes are on Annabelle's purse. I can tell he has never shoplifted before, which surprises me. "My change, forty cents or something."

I ring up the drinks and candy bars. "Nine ninety-eight," I answer.

"For two energy drinks?" he snaps back.

I hold on to the counter to keep from fainting. It's tough for me to admit, but I'm kind of a pushover. I normally don't want a confrontation or to get in the middle of a shouting match, but Annabelle gets free food, not Mike "Never Read a Book Without Pictures in My Life" Robinson.

"The candy bars," I say.

"Biggie!" Annabelle shouts.

"There are no candy bars. You hear me?" Mike says.

Like I do with everyone who doesn't have enough money to pay, I grab the energy drinks off the counter and place them on a small table by the gas reader. My hands shake so much that I half expect the drinks to explode out the pop-top. Turning away from them allows me to get some air. The choppy breaths form a small circle of condensation on the window, which looks out to the parking lot. Watching cars fly by on the highway calms my nerves.

"Forget it, Anna. This fat fuck thinks he's a gas-station god," Mike says.

"Mike, get me the drinks," she commands. "Just pay for the Kit Kats and let's go."

"Look at me!" He picks up the money off the counter.

I slowly twist my neck and see him squeezing the now-crinkled dollar bills like a tube of toothpaste.

"New plan," he continues. "I'm not paying for anything, and if you say something or call the Harpers, I'll tell them I caught you jerking off to those magazines back there."

"Cameras," I whisper with my fingernails pressing into the edge of the countertop.

"What?"

"There're cameras always on the front counter. I'm not allowed to look at them."

"The cameras?" Mike asks.

"No," Annabelle jumps in. "You're both idiots. He means his boss knows if he looks at porn and there are cameras recording us right now, so just pay him."

"I only have six bucks after buying you dinner," he whispers.

"Whatever," she says and tosses a ten on the counter.

My blue eyes connect with her green ones, just like when she walked in few minutes ago. Annabelle has been in this store a hundred times, but tonight is the first time I've really looked at her up close. Although we live in the same town, go to the same school, and sit in the same classes, everything about Annabelle seems to take place at a distance. She always seems far away. But right now, we are eye to eye, inches from each other, and I can't look away. I'm looking at her bangs, pink freckles, and naked red lips.

"My change," she blurts out.

"You don't have to pay," Mike says. "Let's get Dilly Bars instead."

"Give me my Monster, Biggie." She ignores Mike's plan. "I liked you a lot better when you kept your mouth shut. C'mon, baby."

As Annabelle walks out, Mike turns with a little unsolicited advice, "Being an asshole will never get you the girl."

As the door closes, I mutter to myself, "Works for you."

You've just read an excerpt from Biggie.

ABOUT THE AUTHOR

Derek E. Sullivan is an award-winning reporter at the *Rochester Post-Bulletin* in Minnesota. He has written more than 1,000 stories about the lives of teenagers, which he attributes to helping him find his YA voice. He has an MFA from Hamline University and lives in Minnesota with his wife and three sons. This is his first novel.

Imprint: Albert Whitman Teen

Print ISBN: 9780807507278

Print price: $16.99

eBook ISBN: 9781504000789

eBook price: $9.99

Publication date: 3/1/15

Publicity contact: Annette Hobbs Magier: marketing@albertwhitman.com

Rights contact: John Quattrocchi: JohnQ@albertwhitman.com

Editor: Kelly Barrales-Saylor

Agent: Sara Megibow

Agency: Nelson Literary Agency

Promotional information:
- Trade, library, and consumer print and online advertising
- ARC distribution at ALA Midwinter and via Netgalley
- Prepublication buzz campaign
- Social media campaign across all Albert Whitman & Company profiles
- Giveaways via Twitter
- Select author appearances
- Inclusion in ABA Children's White Box mailing.

AN
EMBER
IN THE
ASHES

A NOVEL BY

SABAA
TAHIR

SUMMARY

Laia is a Scholar living under the brutal rule of the Martial Empire. When her brother is arrested for treason, Laia goes undercover as a slave at the empire's greatest military academy in exchange for assistance from other Scholars who claim that they will help to save her brother from execution. At the academy, Laia meets Elias, the academy's finest soldier—and secretly, its most unwilling. Elias is considering deserting the military, but before he can, he's ordered to participate in the Trials, a ruthless contest to choose the next Martial emperor. It is not long before the far-reaching arm of Trials snatches not just Elias but Laia as well; and soon the two will find that their destinies are more intertwined than either could have imagined and that their choices will change the future of the empire itself.

EXCERPT

I. LAIA

My big brother reaches home in the dark hours before dawn, when even ghosts take their rest. He smells of steel and coal and forge. He smells of the enemy.

He folds his scarecrow body through the window, bare feet silent on the rushes. A hot desert wind blows in after him, rustling the limp curtains. His sketchbook falls to the floor, and he nudges it under his bunk with a quick foot, as if it's a snake.

Where have you been, Darin? In my head, I have the courage to ask the question, and Darin trusts me enough to answer. *Why do you keep disappearing? Why, when Pop and Nan need you? When I need you?*

Every night for almost two years, I've wanted to ask. Every night, I've lacked the courage. I have one sibling left. I don't want him to shut me out like he has everyone else.

But tonight's different. I know what's in his sketchbook. I know what it means.

"You shouldn't be awake." Darin's whisper jolts me from my thoughts. He has a cat's sense for traps—he got it from our mother. I sit up on the bunk as he lights the lamp. No use pretending to be asleep.

"It's past curfew, and three patrols have gone by. I was worried."

"I can avoid the soldiers, Laia. Lots of practice." He rests his chin on my bunk and smiles Mother's sweet, crooked smile. A familiar look—the one he gives me if I wake from a nightmare or we run out of grain. *Everything will be fine*, the look says.

He picks up the book on my bed. *"Gather in the Night,"* he reads the title. "Spooky. What's it about?"

"I just started it. It's about a jinn—" I stop. Clever. Very clever. He likes hearing stories as much as I like telling them. "Forget that. Where were you? Pop had a dozen patients this morning."

And I filled in for you because he can't do so much alone. Which left Nan to bottle the trader's jams by herself. Except she didn't finish. Now the trader won't pay us, and we'll starve this winter, and why in the skies don't you care?

I say these things in my head. The smile's already dropped off Darin's face.

"I'm not cut out for healing," he says. "Pop knows that."

I want to back down, but I think of Pop's slumped shoulders this morning. I think of the sketchbook.

"Pop and Nan depend on you. At least talk to them. It's been months."

I wait for him to tell me that I don't understand. That I should leave him be. But he just shakes his head, drops down into his bunk, and closes his eyes like he can't be bothered to reply.

"I saw your drawings." The words tumble out in a rush, and Darin's up in an instant, his face stony. "I wasn't spying," I say. "One of the pages was loose. I found it when I changed the rushes this morning."

"Did you tell Nan and Pop? Did they see?"

"No, but—"

"Laia, listen." Ten hells, I don't want to hear this. I don't want to hear his excuses. "What you saw is dangerous," he says. "You can't tell anyone about it. Not ever. It's not just my life at risk. There are others—"

"Are you working for the Empire, Darin? Are you working for the Martials?"

He is silent. I think I see the answer in his eyes, and I feel ill. My brother is a traitor to his own people? My brother is siding with the Empire?

If he hoarded grain, or sold books, or taught children to read, I'd understand. I'd be proud of him for doing the things I'm not brave enough to do. The Empire raids, jails, and kills for such "crimes," but teaching a six-year-old her letters isn't evil—not in the minds of my people, the Scholar people.

But what Darin has done is sick. It's a betrayal.

"The Empire killed our parents," I whisper. "Our sister."

I want to shout at him, but I choke on the words. The Martials conquered Scholar lands five hundred years ago, and since then, they've done nothing but oppress and enslave us. Once, the Scholar Empire was home to the finest universities and libraries in the world. Now, most of our people can't tell a school from an armory.

"How could you side with the Martials? How, Darin?"

"It's not what you think, Laia. I'll explain everything, but—"

He pauses suddenly, his hand jerking up to silence me when I ask for the promised explanation. He cocks his head toward the window.

Through the thin walls, I hear Pop's snores, Nan shifting in her sleep, a mourning dove's croon. Familiar sounds. Home sounds.

Darin hears something else. The blood drains from his face, and dread flashes in his eyes. "Laia," he says. "Raid."

"But if you work for the Empire—" *Then why are the soldiers raiding us?*

"I'm not working for them." He sounds calm. Calmer than I feel. "Hide the sketchbook. That's what they want. That's what they're here for."

Then he's out the door, and I'm alone. My bare legs move like cold molasses, my hands like wooden blocks. *Hurry, Laia!*

Usually, the Empire raids in the heat of the day. The soldiers want Scholar mothers and children to watch. They want fathers and brothers to see another man's family enslaved. As bad as those raids are, the night raids are worse. The night raids are for when the Empire doesn't want witnesses.

I wonder if this is real. If it's a nightmare. *It's real, Laia. Move.*

I drop the sketchbook out the window into a hedge. It's a poor hiding place, but I have no time. Nan hobbles into my room. Her hands, so steady when she stirs vats of jam or braids my hair, flutter like frantic birds, desperate for me to move faster.

She pulls me into the hallway. Darin stands with Pop at the back door. My grandfather's white hair is scattered as a haystack and his clothes are wrinkled, but there's no sleep in the deep grooves of his face. He murmurs something to my brother, then hands him Nan's largest kitchen knife. I don't know why he bothers. Against the Serric steel of a Martial blade, the knife will only shatter.

"You and Darin leave through the backyard," Nan says, her eyes darting from window to window. "They haven't surrounded the house yet."

No. No. No. "Nan," I breathe her name, stumbling when she pushes me toward Pop.

"Hide in the east end of the Quarter—" Her sentence ends in a choke, her eyes on the front window. Through the ragged curtains, I catch a flash of a liquid silver face. My stomach clenches.

"A Mask," Nan says. "They've brought a Mask. Go, Laia. Before he gets inside."

"What about you? What about Pop?"

"We'll hold them off." Pop shoves me gently out the door. "Keep your secrets close, love. Listen to Darin. He'll take care of you. Go."

Darin's lean shadow falls over me, and he grabs my hand as the door closes behind us. He slouches to blend into the warm night, moving silently across the loose sand of the backyard with a confidence I wish I felt. Although I am seventeen and old enough to control my fear, I grip his hand like it's the only solid thing in this world.

I'm not working for them, Darin said. Then whom is he working for? Somehow, he got close enough to the forges of Serra to draw, in detail, the creation process of the Empire's most precious asset: the unbreakable, curved scims that can cut through three men at once.

Half a millennium ago, the Scholars crumbled beneath the Martial invasion because our blades broke against their superior steel. Since then, we have learned nothing of steelcraft. The Martials hoard their secrets the way a miser hoards gold. Anyone caught near our city's forges without good reason—Scholar or Martial—risks execution.

If Darin isn't with the Empire, how did he get near Serra's forges? How did the Martials find out about his sketchbook?

On the other side of the house, a fist pounds on the front door. Boots shuffle, steel clinks. I look around wildly, expecting to see the silver armor and red capes of Empire legionnaires, but the backyard is still. The fresh night air does nothing to stop the sweat rolling down my neck. Distantly, I hear the thud of drums from Blackcliff, the Mask training school. The sound sharpens my fear into a hard point stabbing at my center. The Empire doesn't send those silver-faced monsters on just any raid.

The pounding on the door sounds again.

"In the name of the Empire," an irritated voice says, "I demand you open this door."

As one, Darin and I freeze.

"Doesn't sound like a Mask," Darin whispers. Masks speak softly with words that cut through you like a scim. In the time it would take a legionnaire to knock and issue an order, a Mask would already be in the house, weapons slicing through anyone in his way.

Darin meets my eyes, and I know we're both thinking the same thing. If the Mask isn't with the rest of the soldiers at the front door, then where is he?

"Don't be afraid, Laia," Darin says. "I won't let anything happen to you."

I want to believe him, but my fear is a tide tugging at my ankles, pulling me under. I think of the couple that lived next door: raided, imprisoned, and sold into slavery three weeks ago. *Book smugglers*, the Martials said. Five days after that, one of Pop's oldest patients, a ninety-three-year-old man who could barely walk, was executed in his own home, his throat slit from ear to ear. *Resistance collaborator.*

What will the soldiers do to Nan and Pop? Jail them? Enslave them?

Kill them?

We reach the back gate. Darin stands on his toes to unhook the latch when a scrape in the alley beyond stops him short. A breeze sighs past, sending a cloud of dust into the air.

Darin pushes me behind him. His knuckles are white around the knife handle as the gate swings open with a moan. A finger of terror draws a trail up my spine. I peer over my brother's shoulder into the alley.

There is nothing out there but the quiet shifting of sand. Nothing but the occasional gust of wind and the shuttered windows of our sleeping neighbors.

I sigh in relief and step around Darin.

That's when the Mask emerges from the darkness and walks through the gate.

II. ELIAS

The deserter will be dead before dawn.

His tracks zigzag like a struck deer's in the dust of Serra's catacombs. The tunnels have done him in. The hot air is too heavy down here, the smells of death and rot too close.

The tracks are more than an hour old by the time I see them. The guards have his scent now, poor bastard. If he's lucky, he'll die in the chase. If not. . .

Don't think about it. Hide the backpack. Get out of here.

Skulls crunch as I shove a pack loaded with food and water into a wall crypt. Helene would give me hell if she could see how I'm treating the dead. But then, if Helene finds out why I'm down here in the first place, desecration will be the least of her complaints.

She won't find out. Not until it's too late. Guilt pricks at me, but I shove it away. Helene's the strongest person I know. She'll be fine without me.

For what feels like the hundredth time, I look over my shoulder. The tunnel is quiet. The deserter led the soldiers in the opposite direction. But safety's an illusion I know never to trust. I work quickly, piling bones back in front of the crypt to cover my trail, my senses primed for anything out of the ordinary.

One more day of this. One more day of paranoia and hiding and lying. One day until graduation. Then I'll be free.

As I rearrange the crypt's skulls, the hot air shifts like a bear waking from hibernation. The smells of grass and snow cut through the fetid breath of the tunnel. Two seconds is all I have to step away from the crypt and kneel, examining the ground as if there might be tracks here. Then she is at my back.

"Elias? What are you doing down here?"

"Didn't you hear? There's a deserter loose." I keep my attention fixed on the dusty floor. Beneath the silver mask that covers me from forehead to jaw, my face should be unreadable. But Helene Aquilla and I have been together nearly every day of the fourteen years we've been training at Blackcliff Military Academy; she can probably hear me thinking.

She comes around me silently, and I look up into her eyes, as blue and pale as the warm waters of the southern islands. My mask sits atop my face, separate and foreign, hiding my features as well as my emotions. But Hel's mask clings to her like a silvery second skin, and I can see the slight furrow in her brow as she looks down at me. *Relax, Elias,* I tell myself. *You're just looking for a deserter.*

"He didn't come this way," Hel says. She runs a hand over her hair, braided, as always, into a tight, silver-blonde crown. "Dex took an auxiliary company off the north watchtower and into the East Branch tunnel. You think they'll catch him?"

Aux soldiers, though not as highly trained as legionnaires and nothing compared to Masks, are still merciless hunters. "Of course they'll catch him." I fail to keep the bitterness out of my voice, and Helene gives me a hard look. "The cowardly scum," I add. "Anyway, why are you awake? You weren't on watch this morning." *I made sure of it.*

"Those bleeding drums." Helene looks around the tunnel. "Woke everyone up."

The drums. Of course. *Deserter,* they'd thundered in the middle of the graveyard watch. *All active units to the walls.* Helene must have decided to join the hunt. Dex, my lieutenant, would have told her which direction I'd gone. He'd have thought nothing of it.

"I thought the deserter might have come this way." I turn from my hidden pack to look down another tunnel. "Guess I was wrong. I should catch up to Dex."

"Much as I hate to admit it, you're not usually wrong." Helene cocks her head and smiles at me. I feel that guilt again, wrenching as a fist to the gut. She'll be furious when she learns what I've done. She'll never forgive me. *Doesn't matter. You've decided. Can't turn back now.*

Hel traces the dust on the ground with a fair, practiced hand. "I've never even seen this tunnel before."

A drop of sweat crawls down my neck. I ignore it.

"It's hot, and it reeks," I say. "Like everything else down here." Come on, I want to add. But doing so would be like tattooing "I am up to no good" on my forehead. I keep quiet and lean against the catacomb wall, arms crossed.

The field of battle is my temple. I mentally chant a saying my grandfather taught me the day he met me, when I was six. He insists it sharpens the mind the way a whetstone sharpens a blade. *The swordpoint is my priest. The dance of death is my prayer. The killing blow is my release.*

Helene peers at my blurred tracks, following them, somehow, to the crypt where I stowed my pack, to the skulls piled there. She's suspicious, and the air between us is suddenly tense.

Damn it.

I need to distract her. As she looks between me and the crypt, I run my gaze lazily down her body. She stands two inches shy of six feet—a half-foot shorter than me. She's the only female student at Blackcliff; in the black, close-fitting fatigues all students wear, her strong, slender form has always drawn admiring glances. Just not mine. We've been friends too long for that.

Come on, notice. Notice me leering and get mad about it.

When I meet her eyes, brazen as a sailor fresh into port, she opens her mouth, as if to rip into me. Then she looks back at the crypt.

If she sees the pack and guesses what I'm up to, I'm done for. She might hate doing it, but Empire law would demand she report me, and Helene's never broken a law in her life.

"Elias—"

I prepare my lie. *Just wanted to get away for a couple of days, Hel. Needed some time to think. Didn't want to worry you.*

BOOM-BOOM-boom-BOOM.

The drums.

Without thought, I translate the disparate beats into the message they are meant to convey. *Deserter caught. All students report to central courtyard immediately.*

My stomach sinks. Some naïve part of me hoped the deserter would at least make it out of the city. "That didn't take long," I say. "We should go."

I make for the main tunnel. Helene follows, as I knew she would. She would stab herself in the eye before she disobeyed a direct order. Helene is a true Martial, more loyal to the Empire than to her own mother. Like any good Mask-in-training, she takes Blackcliff's motto to heart: *Duty first, unto death.*

I wonder what she would say if she knew what I'd really been doing in the tunnels.

I wonder how she'd feel about my hatred for the Empire.

I wonder what she would do if she found out her best friend is planning to desert.

III. LAIA

The Mask saunters through the gate, big hands loose at his sides. The strange metal of his namesake clings to him from forehead to jaw like silver paint, revealing every feature of his face, from the thin eyebrows to the hard angles of his cheekbones. His copper-plated armor molds to his muscles, emphasizing the power in his body.

A passing wind billows his black cape, and he looks around the backyard like he's arrived at a garden party. His pale eyes find me, slide up my form, and settle on my face with a reptile's flat regard.

"Aren't you a pretty one," he says.

I yank at the ragged hem of my shift, wishing desperately for the shapeless, ankle-length skirt I wear during the day. The Mask doesn't even twitch. Nothing in his face tells me what he's thinking. But I can guess.

Darin steps in front of me and glances at the fence, as if gauging the time it will take to reach it.

"I'm alone, boy." The Mask addresses Darin with all the emotion of a corpse. "The rest of the men are in your house. You can run if you like." He moves away from the gate. "But I insist you leave the girl."

Darin raises the knife.

"Chivalrous of you," the Mask says.

Then he strikes, a flash of copper and silver lightning out of an empty sky. In the time it takes me to gasp, the Mask has shoved my brother's face into the sandy ground and pinned his writhing body with a knee. Nan's knife falls to the dirt.

A scream erupts from me, lonely in the still summer night. Seconds later, a scimpoint pricks my throat. I didn't even see the Mask draw the weapon.

"Quiet," he says. "Arms up. Now get inside."

The Mask uses one hand to yank Darin up by the neck and the other to prod me on with his scim. My brother limps, face bloodied, eyes dazed. When he struggles, a fish on a hook, the Mask tightens his grip.

The back door of the house opens, and a red-caped legionnaire comes out.

"The house is secure, Commander."

The Mask shoves Darin at the soldier. "Bind him up. He's strong."

Then he grabs me by the hair, twisting until I cry out.

"Mmm." He bends his head to my ear, and I cringe, my terror caught in my throat. "I've always loved dark-haired girls."

I wonder if he has a sister, a wife, a woman. But it wouldn't matter if he did. To him, I'm not someone's family. I'm just a thing to be subdued, used, and discarded. The Mask drags me down the hallway to the front room as casually as a hunter drags his kill. *Fight*, I tell myself. *Fight*. But as if he senses my pathetic attempts at bravery, his hand squeezes, and pain lances through my skull. I sag and let him pull me along.

Legionnaires stand shoulder-to-shoulder in the front room amid up-turned furniture and broken bottles of jam. *Trader won't get anything now*. So many days spent over steaming kettles, my hair and skin smelling of apricot and cinnamon. So many jars, steamed and dried, filled and sealed. Useless. All useless.

The lamps are lit, and Nan and Pop kneel in the middle of the floor, their hands bound behind their backs. The soldier holding Darin shoves him to the ground beside them.

"Shall I tie up the girl, sir?" Another soldier fingers the rope at his belt, but the Mask leaves me between two burly legionnaires.

"She's not going to cause any trouble." He stabs at me with those eyes. "Are you?" I shake my head and shrink back, hating myself for being such a coward. I reach for my mother's tarnished armlet, wrapped around my bicep, and touch the familiar pattern for strength. I find none. Mother would have fought. She'd have died rather than face this humiliation. But I can't make myself move. My fear has ensnared me.

A legionnaire enters the room, his face more than a little nervous. "It's not here, Commander."

The Mask looks down at my brother. "Where's the sketchbook?"

Darin stares straight ahead, silent. His breath is low and steady, and he doesn't seem dazed anymore. In fact, he's almost composed.

The Mask gestures, a small movement. One of the legionnaires lifts Nan by her neck and slams her frail body against a wall. Nan bites her lip, her eyes sparking blue. Darin tries to rise, but another soldier forces him down.

The Mask scoops up a shard of glass from one of the broken jars. His tongue flickers out like a snake's as he tastes the jam.

"Shame it's all gone to waste." He caresses Nan's face with the edge of the shard. "You must have been beautiful once. Such eyes." He turns to Darin. "Shall I carve them out of her?"

"It's outside the small bedroom window. In the hedge." I can't manage more than a whisper, but the soldiers hear. The Mask nods, and one of the legionnaires disappears into the hallway. Darin doesn't look at me, but I feel his dismay. *Why did you tell me to hide it*, I want to cry out. *Why did you bring the cursed thing home?*

The legionnaire returns with the book. For unending seconds, the only sound in the room is the rustling of pages as the Mask flips through the sketches. If the rest of the book is anything like the page I found, I know what the Mask will see: Martial knives, swords, scabbards, forges, formulas, instructions—things no Scholar should know of, let alone re-create on paper.

"How did you get into the Weapons Quarter, boy?" The Mask looks up from the book. "Has the Resistance been bribing some Plebeian drudge to sneak you in?"

I stifle a sob. Half of me is relieved Darin's no traitor. The other half wants to rage at him for being such a fool. Association with the Scholars' Resistance carries a death sentence.

"I got myself in," my brother says. "The Resistance had nothing to do with it."

"You were seen entering the catacombs last night after curfew"—the Mask almost sounds bored—"in the company of known Scholar rebels."

"Last night, he was home well before curfew," Pop speaks up, and it is strange to hear my grandfather lie. But it makes no difference. The Mask's eyes are for my brother alone. The man doesn't blink as he reads Darin's face the way I'd read a book.

"Those rebels were taken into custody today," the Mask says. "One of them gave up your name before he died. What were you doing with them?"

"They followed me." Darin sounds so calm. Like he's done this before. Like he's not afraid at all. "I'd never met them before."

"And yet they knew of your book here. Told me all about it. How did they learn of it? What did they want from you?"

"I don't know."

The Mask presses the shard of glass deep into the soft skin below Nan's eye, and her nostrils flare. A trickle of blood traces a wrinkle down her face.

Darin draws a sharp breath, the only sign of strain. "They asked for my sketchbook," he says. "I said no. I swear it."

"And their hideout?"

"I didn't see. They blindfolded me. We were in the catacombs."

"*Where* in the catacombs?"

"I didn't see. They blindfolded me."

The Mask eyes my brother for a long moment. I don't know how Darin can remain unruffled beneath that gaze.

"You're prepared for this." The smallest bit of surprise creeps into the Mask's voice. "Straight back. Deep breathing. Same answers to different questions. Who trained you, boy?"

When Darin doesn't answer, the Mask shrugs. "A few weeks in prison will loosen your tongue." Nan and I exchange a frightened glance. If Darin ends up in a Martial prison, we'll never see him again. He'll spend weeks in interrogation, and after that they'll either sell him as a slave or kill him.

"He's just a boy," Pop speaks slowly, as if to an angry patient. "Please—"

Steel flashes, and Pop drops like a stone. The Mask moves so swiftly that I don't understand what he has done. Not until Nan rushes forward. Not until she lets out a shrill keen, a shaft of pure pain that brings me to my knees.

Pop. Skies, not Pop. A dozen vows sear themselves into my mind. *I'll never disobey again, I'll never do anything wrong, I'll never complain about my work, if only Pop lives.*

But Nan tears her hair and screams, and if Pop was alive, he'd never let her go on like that. He wouldn't have been able to bear it. Darin's calm is sheared away as if by a scythe, his face blanched with a horror I feel down to my bones.

Nan stumbles to her feet and takes one tottering step toward the Mask. He reaches out to her, as if to put his hand on her shoulder. The last thing I see in my grandmother's eyes is terror. Then the Mask's gauntleted wrist flashes once, leaving a thin red line across Nan's throat, a line that grows wider and redder as she falls.

Her body hits the floor with a thud, her eyes still open and shining with tears as blood pours from her neck and into the rug we knotted together last winter.

"Sir," one of the legionnaires says. "An hour until dawn."

"Get the boy out of here." The Mask doesn't give Nan a second glance. "And burn this place down."

He turns to me then, and I wish I could fade like a shadow into the wall behind me. I wish for it harder than I've ever wished for anything, knowing all the while how foolish it is. The soldiers flanking me grin at each other as the Mask takes a slow step in my direction. He holds my gaze as if he can smell my fear, a cobra enthralling its prey.

No, please, no. Disappear, I want to disappear.

The Mask blinks, some foreign emotion flickering across his eyes—surprise or shock, I can't tell. It doesn't matter. Because in that moment, Darin leaps up from the floor. While I cowered, he loosened his bindings. His hands stretch out like claws as he lunges for the Mask's throat. His rage lends him a lion's strength, and for a second he is every inch our mother, honey hair glowing, eyes blazing, mouth twisted in a feral snarl.

The Mask backs into the blood pooled near Nan's head, and Darin is on him, knocking him to the ground, raining down blows. The legionnaires stand frozen in disbelief and then come to their senses, surging forward, shouting and swearing. Darin pulls a dagger free from the Mask's belt before the legionnaires tackle him.

"Laia!" my brother shouts. "Run—"

Don't run, Laia. Help him. Fight.

But I think of the Mask's cold regard, of the violence in his eyes. *I've always loved dark-haired girls.* He will rape me. Then he will kill me.

I shudder and back into the hallway. No one stops me. No one notices.

"Laia!" Darin cries out, sounding like I've never heard him. Frantic. Trapped. He told me to run, but if I screamed like that, he would come. He would never leave me. I stop.

Help him, Laia, a voice orders in my head. *Move.*

And another voice, more insistent, more powerful.

You can't save him. Do what he says. Run.

Flame flickers at the edge of my vision, and I smell smoke. One of the legionnaires has started torching the house. In minutes, fire will consume it.

"Bind him properly this time and get him into an interrogation cell." The Mask removes himself from the fray, rubbing his jaw. When he sees me backing down the hallway, he goes strangely still. Reluctantly, I meet his eyes, and he tilts his head.

"Run, little girl," he says.

My brother is still fighting, and his screams slice right through me. I know then that I will hear them over and over again, echoing in every hour of every day until I am dead or I make it right. I know it.

And still, I run.

***

The cramped streets and dusty markets of the Scholars' Quarter blur past me like the landscape of a nightmare. With each step, part of my brain shouts at me to turn around, to go back, to help Darin. With each step, it becomes less likely, until it isn't a possibility at all, until the only word I can think is *run*.

The soldiers come after me, but I've grown up among the squat, mud-brick houses of the Quarter, and I lose my pursuers quickly.

Dawn breaks, and my panicked run turns to a stumble as I wander from alley to alley. Where do I go? What do I do? I need a plan, but I don't know where to start. Who can offer me help or comfort? My neighbors will turn me away, fearing for their own lives. My family is dead or imprisoned. My best friend, Zara, disappeared in a raid last year, and my other friends have their own troubles.

I'm alone.

As the sun rises, I find myself in an empty building deep in the oldest part of the Quarter. The gutted structure crouches like a wounded animal amid a labyrinth of crumbling dwellings. The stench of refuse taints the air.

I huddle in the corner of the room. My hair has slipped free of its braid and lays in hopeless tangles. The red stitches along the hem of my shift are ripped, the bright yarn limp. Nan sewed those hems for my seventeenth year-fall, to brighten up my otherwise drab clothing. It was one of the few gifts she could afford.

Now she's dead. Like Pop. Like my parents and sister, long ago.

And Darin. Taken. Dragged to an interrogation cell where the Martials will do who-knows-what to him.

Life is made of so many moments that mean nothing. Then one day, a single moment comes along to define every second that comes after. The moment Darin called out—that was such a moment. It was a test of courage, of strength. And I failed it.

Laia! Run!

Why did I listen to him? I should have stayed. I should have done something. I moan and grasp my head. I keep hearing him. Where is he now? Have they begun the interrogation? He'll wonder what happened to me. He'll wonder how his sister could have left him.

A flicker of furtive movement in the shadows catches my attention, and the hair on my nape rises. A rat? A crow? The shadows shift, and within them, two malevolent eyes flash. More sets of eyes join the first, baleful and slitted.

Hallucinations, I hear Pop in my head, making a diagnosis. *A symptom of shock.*

Hallucinations or not, the shadows look real. Their eyes glow with the fire of miniature suns, and they circle me like hyenas, growing bolder with each pass.

"We saw," they hiss. "*We know your weakness. He'll die because of you.*"

"No," I whisper. But they are right, these shadows. I left Darin. I abandoned him. The fact that he told me to go doesn't matter. How could I have been so cowardly?

I grasp my mother's armlet, but touching it makes me feel worse. Mother would have outfoxed the Mask. Somehow, she'd have saved Darin and Nan and Pop.

Even Nan was braver than me. Nan, with her frail body and burning eyes. Her backbone of steel. Mother inherited Nan's fire, and after her, Darin.

But not me.

Run, little girl.

The shadows inch closer, and I close my eyes against them, hoping they'll disappear. I grasp at the thoughts ricocheting through my mind, trying to corral them.

Distantly, I hear shouts and the thud of boots. If the soldiers are still looking for me, I'm not safe here.

Maybe I should let them find me and do what they will. I abandoned my blood. I deserve punishment.

But the same instinct that urged me to escape the Mask in the first place drives me to my feet. I head into the streets, losing myself in the thickening morning crowds. A few of my fellow Scholars look twice at me, some with wariness, others with sympathy. But most don't look at all. It makes me wonder how many times I walked right past someone in these streets who was running, someone who had just had their whole world ripped from them.

I stop to rest in an alley slick with sewage. Thick black smoke curls up from the other side of the Quarter, paling as it rises into the hot sky. My home, burning. Nan's jams, Pop's medicines, Darin's drawings, my books, gone. Everything I am. Gone.

Not everything, Laia. Not Darin.

A grate squats in the center of the alley, just a few feet away from me. Like all grates in the Quarter, it leads down into the Serra's catacombs: home to skeletons, ghosts, rats, thieves . . . and possibly the Scholars' Resistance.

Had Darin been spying for them? Had the Resistance gotten him into the Weapons Quarter? Despite what my brother told the Mask, it's the only answer that makes sense. Rumor has it that the Resistance fighters have been getting bolder, recruiting not just Scholars, but Mariners, from the free country of Marinn, to the north, and Tribesmen, whose desert-territory is an Empire protectorate.

Pop and Nan never spoke of the Resistance in front of me. But late at night, I heard them murmuring of how the rebels freed Scholar prisoners while striking out at the Martials. Of how fighters raided the caravans of the Martial merchant class, the Mercators, and assassinated members of their upper class, the Illustrians. Only the rebels stand up to the Martials.

Elusive as they are, they are the only weapon the Scholars have. If anyone can get near the forges, it's them.

The Resistance, I realize, might help me. My home was raided and burned to the ground, my family killed because two of the rebels gave Darin's name to the Empire. If I can find the Resistance and explain what happened, maybe they can help me break Darin free from prison—not just because they owe me, but because they live by *Izzat*, a code of honor as old as the Scholar people. The rebel leaders are the best of the Scholars, the bravest. My parents taught me that before the Empire killed them. If I ask for aid, the Resistance won't turn me away.

I step toward the grate.

I've never been in Serra's catacombs. They snake beneath the entire city, hundreds of miles of tunnels and caverns, some packed with centuries' worth of bones. No one uses the crypts for burial anymore, and even the Empire hasn't mapped out the catacombs entirely. If the Empire, with all its might, can't hunt out the rebels, then how will I find them?

You won't stop until you do. I lift the grate and stare into the black hole below. I have to go down there. I have to find the Resistance. Because if I don't, my brother doesn't stand a chance. If I don't find the fighters and get them to help, I'll never see Darin again.

You've just read an excerpt from An Ember in the Ashes.

ABOUT THE AUTHOR

Sabaa Tahir was born in London but grew up in California's Mojave Desert at her family's 18-room motel. After graduating from UCLA, Sabaa became an editor on the foreign desk at *The Post*. Three summers later, she came up with the concept for her debut novel, *An Ember in the Ashes*. Sabaa currently lives in the San Francisco Bay Area with her family. For more information, please visit SabaaTahir.com or on Twitter @SabaaTahir.

Imprint: Razorbill
Print ISBN: 9781595148032
Print price: $19.95

eBook ISBN: 9780698176461

eBook price: $10.99

Publication date: 4/28/15

Editor: Gillian Levinson

Agent: Alexandra Machinist

Agency: ICM

Promotional information:
- 9-copy floor display
- National author tour
- Massive deluxe galley distribution
- Extensive early consumer and trade buzz campaign
- Major national media campaign focusing on commercial, literary, and fantasy media Major national consumer advertising including print, television, radio, movie theater, and online
- Extensive online promotion Integrated social media outreach
- Launch consumer website
- Extensive promotion at consumer book festivals
- Major promotion and deluxe galley distribution at all national school and library conferences

ASK
THE
DARK

Henry Turner

SUMMARY

Billy Zeets has a story to tell. About being a vandal and petty thief. About missing boys and an elusive killer. And about what happens if a boy who breaks all the rules is the only person who can piece together the truth. Gripping and powerful, this masterful debut novel comes to vivid life through the unique voice of a hero as unlikely as he is unforgettable.

EXCERPT

Chapter One

I feel better now. I can move my arm some, and walk around a bit. Ache in my belly's still there, but the doctor says it'll go too. Says there's almost nothing that can hurt a fifteen-year-old boy forever, and I'll grow out of that pain like I grow out of a pair of old shoes.

Loads of people have asked me 'bout what happened. Police and doctors and just about everybody in the neighborhood. I never had so many visitors. Tell the truth, I'm tired of getting asked. I feel like just getting on with what's happening now, and not thinking of what's gone by. I want to answer everybody all at once and get it all the hell over with.

But there's one big thing — where to begin.

Because you don't know me.

Maybe you seen me on the streets walking around, or riding Old Man Pedersen's bike if you was ever up at night. I mean that girls' bike with the tassels on it. Or maybe you just seen me hanging round Shatze's Pharmacy.

But really knowing me, few people do.

Sam Tate does. He's a boy my age, and he said something true. He come up here to my room the other day and we talked, not just 'bout what happened, but 'bout other things too, things we did together before all this big mess. He was sitting near my bed, right there on the windowsill, looking out the window at the trees. Then he looked at me and said, *The real thing is, you'd never have done it, never even found out about it, if you hadn't done all the things people hated you for. It turns out those were the right things to do, Billy. Isn't that funny? All that stealing and never going to school. It's what made it so you were outside a lot, seeing things nobody else saw. Hidden and secret things.*

He was dead-on right with what he said. I laughed. I saved three boys, so they tell me. Got beat and shot doin' it. And Sam says I'd never of done it, 'cept I was always stealing and busting things, and creeping around people's yards at night. That is funny.

But I s'pose it's true.

I don't ride that girls' bike no more. Got a new one. There it is, leaning against the wall over there, bright and shiny. Got twenty-one gears, so I'm told. I'll have to figure that out. How to use'm. Man that brought it was Jimmy Brest's father, the Colonel, USMC. He wheeled it in, laughing and smiling. My daddy was with him a minute, then left and it was just the Colonel and me. And you know what he did? He come over to the bed and took my hand, and he called me the bravest boy he'd ever known, for what I done to save his son. He said I was a hero, and he was quiet a minute, and was almost gonna cry.

But that's like everybody. It seems no matter who gets wind of what I done, from my sister or Sam Tate or one of them news shows on TV, they all start bawling their heads off. So I figure I best tell it myself and get things straight.

'Cause I don't want to make nobody cry. 'Specially colonels, USMC.

The fact is, I ain't no hero, and I aim to prove it. What I done, if I done anything, was get my daddy a fruit stand. See, my daddy was feeling bad and needed money and couldn't do for hisself, so I done it. And to tell this right you gotta know about that, and other things too, like about us losing the house and what my sister done to get herself to be having a baby. You gotta know all that, 'cause if you do, everything else I say will make sense. Sort'f add up, know what I mean?

I ain't hardly left my bed in four weeks, just hanging around my room. I couldn't stand lookin' out the window no more and seeing the days and nights come and go, I was goin' crazy. So I got one of them video games. Hand-held. Sam Tate brought it. What you do with it is move this little monkey through a maze and traps. Monkey's gotta jump and roll and bounce, and if he don't make it he falls through a gap and you gotta start over. You use these little buttons to make him jump. Thing makes beeping noises. Plays a little tune if you do it right.

Can you imagine being that little monkey? Jumping and rolling all day? I kept thinking I was him, and I got so bothered by it, what with whipping my fingers all over it and my eyes jiggling, that I threw the damn thing out the window and heard it bust on the ground.

So now I'm in trouble again 'cause I got no idea what I'm gonna tell Sam Tate.

Since I busted that monkey game I got me a little TV, my daddy brung it up here to me. I started watching that all the time, and just this morning I saw something that explains pretty good why I decided to go 'head and tell all this. There was this talk show on, one with the big fat lady who always got guests on with problems like Welfare and drinking and drugs and whatnot, usually yelling and screaming and hitting each other right there on the show till cops come out and arrest'm, which I can't say is real or not, or if they just getting paid money to say all them things. But this morning she had on a lady who went through cancer and divorce and all sorts of troubles, only to get rich decoratin' folks' houses, famous folks, after she was on her feet again. Anyway, this lady said that even on her darkest day, she always had her dream that kept her going when nothing else did.

Now that's just like me. Just like me'n the fruit stand. 'Cause when all this was going on and I was trying to make all that money to save the house, I don't think a day went by that I didn't say to myself, *I gotta get that fruit stand! Gotta get my daddy that damn fruit stand.*

Scuze my language.

After the lady told 'bout her dream, she said one more thing. I liked it.

She said, *If I did it, you can too!*

That's just how I feel. And that's why I ain't no hero. If I did it, you can too. 'Cause I ain't better'n nobody.

So here goes.

Chapter Two

The first boy got took last September, just a week after school began. I knew him, boy named Tommy Evans, he was fourteen then, same as me. We didn't get along too good. I 'member once he caught up with me in an alley over behind them shops on Fister Street and he started whaling away on me, mostly chest and back, yelling some shit 'bout how I stole his bookbag and threw it in a dumpster and someone saw me do it. But that someone was lying his ass off, 'cause I never stole it. Stole Evans's jacket one day, off a bench at a park over near Dayton Avenue. That I done 'cause I heard he was sayin' nasty things 'bout me, but he never knew 'cause I tossed it down and he found it, so he was hitting me for nothing.

Anyway, after I run I went by his house, running kind of weak 'cause my chest and back was full of bruises, and I hove a brick at his house. Not just brick, cinder block. Damned thing weighed so much it fell out my hands and hit my foot. Didn't break nothing, 'cept the pain made me so mad I got it up and hove it again. But that didn't mean much, 'cause that cinder block was heavier than a motherfucker and I only threw it 'bout three/four foot.

Scuze my language.

'Cept for stuff like that I never knew him much. Ain't like we went to the same school'r nothing, or hung round any the same places. I mean, a couple boys round my way really can't stand me and spend a lot of time just thinking up fresh ways to kick my ass. But this Tommy Evans, he weren't that sort, and prob'ly didn't like me 'cause'f how I'm in trouble all the time, and his parents prob'ly told'm I ain't the right sort of boy for him to know.

Anyway, he got took they say when he was walking home from school. Different people say they seen him last. There was Mrs. Steinwitz, who runs the grocery. Said she seen him, sold him a candy bar or something. Then a lady named Jenkins, whose son he knew, was out scrubbing her porch rail spars and she said she seen him too, and also seen the car that picked him up. But on her life she couldn't remember that car, or truck, or van, 'cause each time the cops asked her she seemed to think it was something different.

Anyway, that's how it began. At the time I was in seventh grade the second time, like I still gonna be, and I spent most of my time downtown at school and didn't get much news 'bout what happens up our way, 'cause my teachers down there're just a bunch'f nuns and they ain't never had much to tell me, 'cept to say I got stains onmy soul.

But Evans getting snatched made news all over. So on weekends I was going out with Marvin and hanging posters now instead of the sales flyers from Shatze's, Shatze's Pharmacy where I go sometimes for work. Usually with Marvin I just drive beside him in the delivery van 'cause his leg is bad, I mean his foot with the big shoe on it, and he don't like getting out of the van. So I do it. When we make deliveries he gives me half the tip and when we dump flyers he pays me a buck'n hour, which ain't good but I like talking with'm, so it's fair. He an old black man, Marvin is, and got his bad foot in a war somewhere, and when the time's right I'll let you know more 'bout him.

Them weekends, first ones after Tommy Evans got took, we hung posters. I mean posters of Tommy Evans, and I know you seen'm. They the ones with missing printedunder that school picture of Tommy's face and the date and some details. Just like on milk cartons and them flyers you get in the mail and throw away. But they never found him. Posters didn't help, and when the snows come with winter they got all mulched and soaked away to bits with just the tape left on phone poles and walls where I used to hang'm.

Next boy got took was Tuckie Brenner, twelve years old. Him I didn't know. First thing I thought driving around with Marvin was how funny his name was on the posters. I mean, who the hell names their boy Tuckie Brenner? Course, that ain't the worst I ever heard. Worst was this boy Billy Hill, he was in school with me. When the nun called out his name she done it last name first, so it come out *Hill, Billy*. Can you imagine that? Hillbilly. Shit. We all laughed, it was morning and we was at assembly in the gym, whole school was there, and even though on the next mornings every day the nun said different and called his name *Hill, William,* it didn't matter and the boys called out, *Hillbilly!* 'cause who could ever forget that? So old Billy Hill, he didn't last long in that school of mine.

Anyhow, this Tuckie Brenner, he got took four/five months after Tommy Evans. They say he was playing in a field round the time of sundown when it happened, wintertime. Other boys he was with left him to go home and so he was alone, and that's the last anybody seen him, 'cept they found a scarf he was wearing lying on the ground later. Marvin and me, we hung posters again but 'cause nobody ever found Tommy Evans it felt like a waste of time.

After Tuckie got took the whole neighborhood went a little crazy. Everybody was scared and putting up fences and new locks on their doors and some boys said their daddies bought guns and such. And no boy my age or older, up to eighteen, was allowed out after dark. Curfew, they called it. And even though there weren't no curfew in the daytime there was a lot more police cars in the neighborhood, and we was s'posed to walk round only in groups of three or more if we could manage it.

Round the time all that started I was still staying up nights. Couldn't sleep since my mother'd died, about two years back. Most nights I'd be up till morning, 'cause my thoughts bothered me, and I couldn't make'm stop.

But just lying in bed made me antsy. So I started going out. I'd see them little branch shadows waving on the sheet hung over my window, sort of calling me away. Then I'd get up. Floors might creak, so I can't walk the halls — I climb out the window. I hold tight to the shutters and crawl around. I pass my daddy's window and there he is under the covers, a lump in the dark.

House used to be apartments, so there's a fire escape out back, made'f wood. Wouldn't do any good in a fire, burn right up, but it's great for climbing. Down at bottom I'd run crost the yard to the alley and in a minute I'm free.

I'd keep real quiet and hear the wind whistle through the trees, and cars swish by out front, and sometimes even the ring of a train far away. I never had to worry 'bout getting seen, 'cause at three or four in the morning ain't nobody out but me.

Most nights I just stayed in the neighborhood. Nothing was going on. Just houses dark and yards empty. Course it was scary at first. I even creeped around the woods in places so dark I felt maybe I should run on home. But it weren't too long afore I was used to it, and would go anywhere no matter how scared I got.

Like I said, I started doing this after my mother died, two years back in springtime, and at first I stayed close to home. But when summer came I got all bold and sometimes snagged my neighbor's bike to ride downtown, going through side streets and alleys so cops won't see me and ask me why I'm out so late. I loved it down there, with the buildings quiet and hardly a car going by anywhere, but all the streetlights still on and me riding through the cool wind. City was all my own. And thinking didn't hurt so much like when I was lying in bed.

You can imagine how it got in my way when the curfew come a couple years later. But I still snuck out some nights. And it was funner than ever before. Because now the curfew was up it felt different at night, more dangerous for sure, but real wild too, know what I mean? 'Cause since them boys got took I knew something bad was out there in the dark. And that gave me a feeling. Sort'f like a tingly feeling I get when I know something's up for sure.

A few months after Tuckie got took I went out early while it was still dark and ran down to the woods. I was headed to this man's house I know, man who leaves his lawn mower out in his yard all night. He don't never use it, so I figured I'd take it away, maybe make a go-kart out of't, real electric go-kart like some boys have, with a wood frame and metal sidings.

Coming 'long the trail, branches batted my face, and soon my feet was sloshin' in my shoes all wet from the grass. I went down crost the stream and then uphill to where the houses was, huge houses all lost in the trees, behind a big stone wall higher'n my head. Moss on them stones was slippery from dew, and I smacked myself good on the elbow climbing over, and then tossed down to the other side where I crouched low lookin' round the dark.

I didn't see the mower. So I went over to the toolshed and looked in the window that had glass with chicken wire in it that don't break, reinforced glass. There it was, right inside. Mower, I mean. I could just barely see it in the little red light glowing off some tool chargers.

I tried the door but the old man had locked it good, and that made the whole walk through them woods worth nothing at all, 'cept for scaring the shit outta me. I was wet, besides, 'cause the dew had soaked my pants and shoes, and my face was all scratched up and bleeding from cutting through brambles in the dark.

So I went back. It was getting light, and I was coming through the woods toward the stream. I was right below where the wood-chip trail cuts over the field up from where the stream gully is, and there're some big houses farther up, behind big trees.

Then I stopped.

A boy lay on the bank of the stream. He was naked, that boy, 'cept one shoe, with his body on the sand and rocks but his head partways in the water, the hair waving like weeds in the stream. He lay on his chest but his head was turned to the side and I saw his face good, all covered in cuts and blood.

I looked a long while, but I didn't say a word, or yell out.

It was Tommy Evans.

I seen a piece of paper sticking all red and bright to his dead, naked ass. I walked over real lightly, stone to stone and not leaving no marks in the sand. I figured if it was me lying there I wouldn't want no trash sticking to my ass for any and all to see. So I bent down and snatched it up. I knew I couldn't just throw it down once I touched it, so I put it in my pocket. Paper stuck to my fingers a second when I did that, 'cause glue was on it. Then I crost the stream and climbed a tree real high, till nobody could see me, but I could see everything, peeking down through the leaves and branches.

I figure it was 'bout six when a jogger ran by huffin' and puffin', steam comin' out his mouth. But he didn't see nothing. A little after that came one of them goody-two-shoes families, out to pick up litter so's to keep the woods neat. They dawdled on the wood-chip trail, picking here and picking there, stuffin' what they got in trash bags. The kids was dressed for camp in little uniforms, and their daddy wore a gray suit and everything else for work, 'cept his feet and pants legs was stuffed in galoshes. They didn't come near the stream, though. When they was gone I had to take a leak and did it down through the branches, making no noise at all.

Then a lady came out from a house I could just see through the trees, and she came down to the water. When she saw, she screamed her head off, running back up to her house.

I climbed down and ran. No one saw me. I knew it wouldn't be five minutes 'fore the police was there, swarmin' all round, and damned if I'll be stuck up in a tree all day.

I took a trail that headed for a street. Walking along I swat branches, and let'm swat back at my face just for fun, and it hurt a little. I stuffed my hand in my pocket and felt that piece of paper. *Well, at least I got the trash off'm*, I thought, and I made to toss it away, but that didn't seem right. So I hung on to it, squeezing it twixt my fingers.

I was thinking back on how Tommy Evans used to call me nasty names, bad ones. Shit. I wouldn't care now what all names he'd call me, if he could get up and walk around again. But cut up like he was, I knew that couldn't happen.

I come out the woods at them two towers where the college students live behind their school, dormitories. I had to ford the stream, climb a hill, and climb a wire fence, right up over the barbed wire. Then I let down and crost the parking lots, slinking 'tween the cars and looking inside. But I didn't see nothing I wanted and didn't even try the doors, which all was locked anyways, prob'ly. So I went crost the lots and up the street, into where's all the houses is in the neighborhood all lost in trees.

Chapter Three

This the same day the letter came, but I weren't home then. I was feeling too riled to go home 'cause I seen Tommy Evans, found him, I mean, though I never told it till now, 'cause wouldn't you'f wondered why I was in them woods so early in the first place? That's why I never told it.

I wanted to see what I might hear 'bout it before going home, who they think might'f done it and so on. One place to do that was Shatze's, so I figured I'd head up'ere, running through backyards and alleys. But afore I got there I seen Richie Harrigan goin' by in that old pickup he drives. He yells, Hey, Monkey Boy, come ride with me! And I figure I might learn more drivin' round with him than hanging round Shatze's with Marvin, so's I went over and got on in.

We drove around back alleys looking for what we could salvage in yards, and asking neighbors what they had in their garages we could maybe take away. Some of them alleys are real narrow, and driving through'm in Richie's pickup the branches was smacking on the windshield like to break it, and the tires was bumpin' over the broken ground, so we inside was bouncin' crazy on our asses, damn near smacking our heads on the window frames.

But we didn't find nothing.

Finally Richie had this idea to go check out the big fields behind his old high school 'cause there'd be cans there to bag up and recycle, maybe make a buck off that. I knew that was time to quit. I knew 'cause I'd done it before with'm, and once he started picking up cans and bottles he'd go on to other junk like old tires and empty boxes and anything he could get his hands on, thinking maybe he could sell it for scrap, but really thinking it was his turn to go pickin' up the whole damn neighborhood, like it's some sacred duty he got to get it all clean.

So I went home.

First he drove me not too far from his house, which ain't nowhere near my house, me in the truck bed now 'cause he wants me to hold down this mess of loose posters he found on the street. We did hear about Tommy from some people we saw, parents on lawns, mainly, who we was asking for junk. They said he was found and he was dead, and it was sad to hear it. More'n sad, really. Horrible. But there weren't no word on who done it.

So there I was up Richie's way and I gotta walk home. That Richie, he got money — I mean his daddy has it — but me, I live on this one skinny little street about a mile from him, where people who ain't got so much live. I was walking feeling that piece of paper in my pocket, same one I got off Tommy Evans, because I tell you my mind was sort of stuck on him, and wondering who the hell might'f killed him. Because I didn't really tell you how he looked. His face, I mean. And I ain't gonna tell you. But it weren't something a person does, I mean no regular sane person.

Second day of summer vacation. Hot. Bright. Me, I'm walking through the neighborhood with a nice breeze blowin' in the trees, and sunlight shining off the house fronts as I go passin' by. Tell the truth, when my mind got off Tommy, I was feeling pretty good, especially since I'd dodged Richie, who by now was prob'ly up to his waist in weeds digging up trash like a crazy man, for no special reason at all.

Then I passed the house, and that should'f clued me. Should'f let me know what might be up at home.

See, about a year ago — no, more'n that, two years ago, now that fall's come round again — was just when my daddy was painting that house.

I stopped and come up to it, it all quiet and neat and now painted perfect, where before it had looked haunted with rusty window screens and tar-paper peeling off the roof and dead leaves everywhere. Perfect it was, and I looked at it, the sun shining down and the cool breeze on me. I looked at the eave, the top one there, up by them box-windows three in a row.

I'm talking now about the time just after my mother died, when all them bills was coming. Doctor bills. First there was just what they call "deductible," then the whole thing went crazy because the insurance company stopped paying at all. Make ends meet my daddy took on more work. He was working too much, sometimes going at two jobs a day, say eight hours on a house job, then maybe four after dark and by lamplight, going over a fence or shoring up a pipe or you name it.

That eave up there, that's where it happened. My daddy was out painting one night, there where that little piece of roof give just enough inches for a foothold. He took a step back, and *pow!* Tripped on a power cord, all snagged up. Fell off that roof. Hit bushes down at bottom. Messed up his back good — fractured the spine.

After that he's in the hospital. Can't pay. So next up came the mortgage. Second mortgage. My daddy owned the house. Paid for it by workin' all his life. But a man came to him and told'm it's worth a damn sight more'n what he paid, and with a second mortgage he could make hospital payments.

I'd like to shoot that man.

Anyway, he did that, my daddy, to pay up best he could. But it weren't enough. And while all this was happening and my mother's funeral expenses come and Daddy can't work at all no more, we start going out to Social Services.

Welfare. Medical. You name it. Little offices where all you do is wait forever and when somebody do come out to see you, they never give you what you want and look at you like you ain't washed your clothes.

So I just stood there. Lookin' at that house. I thought maybe there was some kind of secret there. Some kind of answer. The eaves and the drainpipes and the gutters looked all complicated like a riddle.

But there weren't no answer. Just wood and tarpaper.

I walked on. Didn't think about it. Just kept going. Walked along the sidewalks and half hour later I come up the stairs to our place and went inside.

Straight back's the kitchen, that's where Daddy was sitting. Sittin' still, squat, and gray, not moving, letter on the table. I come in, amble past, and get a drink of water at the sink. He don't move at all. It's dark in there 'cause the window curtains is drawn, but he don't open'm, I do.

I say, How're you, Daddy?

He don't answer for a while. I'm leaning on the sink, drinking my water, and he says, They're taking the house.

How so?

He ain't looking at me, just staring down at the letter. He got his glasses on, ones that bug his eyes. I can't pay, he says. Missed too many payments. Now they want it all. Foreclosure. We have three months. Pay or quit.

Uh-huh, I say.

I stare at him a minute. Then I go upstairs and lie on my bed.

Ten minutes later my sister, Leezie, come in. I didn't look up. I was staring at a little patch of wall, just staring at it, place where the plaster's all flaky.

She says, Billy, we gotta help Daddy.

I know, I said.

We can't lose the house, Billy.

Um-hmm.

I felt her come closer, lean over me. Though I didn't look up and she didn't make no noise.

Can you do it, Billy?

I gave a little laugh. I said, Leezie, you sixteen and can get a job. Why put it all on me?

I couldn't never make so much alone, she said. Anyhow, Billy, you got ways. She talked real quiet.

I stared at that flaky place. Didn't want to answer. *I got ways?* I wondered if she knew what she was askin' me.

Then I said, I'll try.

You promise?

I felt her standing there, waiting.

It took me a minute, but I said yeah. Then I looked up at her.

Will you do something for me? I said. Go down ask'm what he owes?

She murmured yes and walked away. I could barely hear her. Footsteps soft as breath.

Room was empty now. Everything felt still.

Minute later she came back.

Forty-eight, she said.

I rolled over on my back.

Thousand?

Yes, Leezie said, swallowing a catch in her voice.

Don't cry, I said.

I won't, she said.

She bent down and kissed me. Then I heard the door close.

I lay there. Looking at the ceiling.

Forty-eight thousand.

God fuckin' damn.

Scuze my language.

You've just read an excerpt from Ask the Dark.

ABOUT THE AUTHOR

Originally from Baltimore, the award-winning independent filmmaker and journalist Henry Turner now lives in Southern California. *Ask the Dark* is his first novel.

Imprint: Clarion Books
Print ISBN: 9780544308275
Print price: $17.99
eBook ISBN: 9780544313453
eBook price: $17.99
Publication date: 4/7/15
Publicity contact: Hayley Gonnason hayley.gonnason@hmhco.com
Rights contact: Candace Finn candace.finn@hmhco.com
Editor: Anne Hoppe
Agent: Daniel Lazar
Agency: Writers House

Promotional information:
- Prepublication buzz campaign targeting key media, booksellers, librarians, educators, industry bigmouths and teens
- Author events
- National media outreach focusing on commercial, literary, young adult, thriller outlets

- National advertising campaign, featuring print and online outreach to teens, trade, and institutional
- Integrated social media outreach (Twitter, Tumblr, Instagram, Facebook) #askthedark
- Book trailer
- Conference promotions
- Dedicated website: hmhbooks.com/askthedark
- Promotion on SingularReads.com

BOOKSELLER BLURBS:

"*Ask the Dark* is like no YA novel I have ever read before. I love Billy's singular voice, his eye for justice, his ability to observe all that is going on around him, and I love his heart. We all know kids like him, the ones everyone discounts, believing they will never do anything with their lives. But these kids can surprise us with their courage and hidden smarts. They can be unexpected heroes to our communities, to their own families, and most of all, to themselves." —Becky Anderson, Anderson's Bookshops

"A gripping page-turner. Being in Billy's head reminds readers to keep a measure of compassion when dealing with difficult kids. Highly recommended."—Valerie Lewis, Hicklebee's

"Who could be a more convincing and compelling detective than a rough and roughly-used boy who can't afford illusions? *Ask the Dark* takes hold of the reader with remarkable vigor. Its narrative extends into the reader's inner landscape and stirs up a nest of sleeping assumptions. How narrow is the distance between what we regard as moral and its behavioral opposites? If character is revealed only under pressure, is safety a dangerous luxury? Ask the dark."—Kenny Brechner, DDG

COPYRIGHT